DEDICATION

For Brian, who may never know how much he inspires me…

ACKNOWLEDGMENTS

As is the case with any great endeavor, I owe many thanks to all of the wonderful people who helped make this dream come true. First, to my dear Mumsy; my first sounding board, my biggest cheerleader and critic, and the one who taught me to love language. Thanks to my baby sister, Gianna (I look up to you more than you can imagine), for her honest opinions and willingness to jump in and help at every point along the way. Next, I want to thank the members of my book club, and all those who read my early drafts and provided clarity, advice, inspiration, and support. Thank you to Tyler, who was the expert in all things technical and photographic. Finally thank you, dear readers for taking a chance on a newbie, and for your comments and praise. For you I am eternally humbled and grateful.

PROLOGUE

Tia Hastings stared blankly at the sea of faces that swam in and out of focus before her. The vast majority were familiar, but the expressions they wore twisted and contorted their faces into alien landscapes that made her want to turn away and avoid all contact. They wanted to comfort her, she knew, but there was nothing they could possibly do or say that would bring her the slightest bit of relief from the hell into which she'd been thrust.

On her right stood her parents, doing their best to hold everyone together and keep the parade of people moving. They forced tight smiles for each mourner, and responded to their condolences when it was all Tia could do to nod her head in acknowledgement. Her mom reassured her every few minutes with a slight touch, a soft pat on the back, or a supportive hand under her elbow. At her left, Paddy and Siobhan, whom she'd called Mom and Dad for the past five years, tried bravely to maintain a stoic dignity. Directly in front of her, on the couch that sagged sadly from the constant weight of despair, sat Lexi Summers. She'd been Tia's constant best friend since their awkward teen years, and had been the glue for Tia this past week—it was Lexi who'd stayed at her house and gotten her out of bed each morning, forcing coffee and cereal into her and making her get dressed as if she were a normal person. It was Lexi who'd run Tia a bath this morning, and who'd brushed out her tangled mass of dark hair while she sat unknowing, uncaring. Tia would have been more than willing to pull the shades on the world and never leave her bed, but Lexi forced her to go through the motions. She now sat with a box of tissues, dabbing often at her own eyes, but also making sure that the five of them had a constant fresh supply. She forced bottles of water on them as well, and made sure they were at least choking down enough food to sustain them.

But as much as Tia didn't want to confront the looks of pity and well-intentioned but empty words of sympathy, she couldn't turn around. Behind her, her future lay crushed—literally and figuratively—in a mahogany box. And as bad as it was to stand there and hear the same monotonous whispers of "I'm so sorry" from person after person, she knew that the coming weeks and months would be even worse. Everyone here would go back to their lives; this day a momentary sad distraction for most; and she would be expected to go on as well. However, seeing that her life would be under six feet of earth and concrete by this time tomorrow, she didn't see a way that she could. All of her plans for the future involved Nick, and never once, in the past five years, did she even entertain the idea of a life without him. Now, either fate or coincidence had taken that from her. She couldn't even begin to imagine getting out of bed tomorrow, much less moving forward with a life that no longer had meaning.

As had happened several times already, the finality of it all—the *weight* of it all—pushed down on her like a physical entity. Tia's knees buckled and she felt herself begin to sink. Her mom and Siobhan were beside her instantly, and Lexi leaped up to guide her out of the room and into a quiet alcove where they sank into an oversized sofa as Lexi wrapped her arms tightly around Tia.

"I can't do it Lex, I just can't," Tia croaked as a fresh river of tears cascaded down her face. "I don't know how I can go on without him."

Chapter 1

"*Last Stop*? You're kidding, right? That's where you decided to go? There have to be at least a dozen places you could go in this city—why in God's name would you pick that dump?"

"Why not? It's as good a place as any," Tia answered, trying her best to sound casual and confident. Going out for a couple beers on a Friday night wouldn't normally be a big deal, but for Tia, on this night, it was big. It was huge. And although she'd already committed her mind, her body was having second thoughts—a flock of butterflies had settled in the pit of her stomach, and their numbers seemed to be growing exponentially as the clock ticked away the minutes. She flopped onto the couch and plucked a cracker from her plate, added a hunk of cheese, and took a bite. There was no way she could force a meal into the fluttering mass that was her stomach, but she knew that she had to eat something. "Besides," she continued, "I can be anonymous there. I don't think there's any chance of running into anyone I know."

"Oh Tia," Lexi moaned. "You really shouldn't be alone tonight. I should just come with you." She paused for a heartbeat before her voice came back strong. "I'm coming with you. I'm still at work, but give me an hour and I'll…"

"That's sweet, Lex, really," Tia interrupted, "but you have that fancy lawyer dinner tonight…"

"I could cancel," she interjected. "You might need me more than Ryan does tonight."

"I appreciate that, but tonight's way too important to Ryan. If he wants to make partner, he has to go to these functions—you've said that at least a hundred times. And if you're going to be the supportive wife, you need to go too. Plus, it's about time the two of you get to be a couple without me hanging around."

"We love having you around, hon, you know that." Lexi's voice softened. "You know I love you, Tia, and I'd cancel in a second if you needed me. Believe me, there'll be plenty more of these dinners in my future—Ryan would understand if I missed one. I just don't want to think about you being all alone, especially in that place…oh, it gives me goose bumps!" Her voice dropped to a near whisper. "Why don't you just go to the memorial instead? At least if you were going to *Paddy's* I'd know you were with other people who loved you. You know I'm going to worry about you all night if you're going to insist on going to the armpit of the city."

Tia grabbed another cracker. Regardless of how she was feeling about tonight, she was determined to put up a strong front for her best friend. "Aren't you being a little overdramatic?" she asked through a mouthful of crumbs. "The armpit?"

"Yuh huh," Lexi continued. "Have you ever even been by the place? All the guys there have dirt under their fingernails and probably ninety percent of them have shotguns in the back windows of their pickup trucks." Her voice leveled, got serious. "Listen, Tia. The guys there—the *people* there—are on a different rung of the social ladder than you and me. They're also on a different rung of the class ladder, the educational ladder, the *economic* ladder..."

"That's hardly the point, Lex...*I'm* on a different rung of your economic ladder too, remember? That doesn't mean anything to me and you know it. Actually, that's what makes it an easier place to go—I don't have to pretend to be anything or anyone—I can just sit back and observe. Plus, seeing as I'm not planning on holding any hands or getting into any pickup trucks, I think I'll be pretty safe. It's a public place."

Lexi grunted. "Public place doesn't necessarily mean safe place, Tia," she said. "That kind of joint can get pretty rough sometimes. It's a whole other world, sister, and some of the guys that hang out at places like that can be shady characters. When I think about you going there alone—let's just say that scenes from bad horror movies keep flashing through my head, and I can't get them out. Plus, you've been off the market for a long time now," she added. "It's been a long time since you've had any...male attention. It might be hard to..." her voice trailed off.

Tia sighed. "Give me a little credit, Lex. It's not like I'm going to throw myself at the first piece of meat I see just because I've been lacking in the sex department."

"It's not about giving you credit—I know you have impeccable taste in men and good sense. It's just that the libido is a carnal instinct, not a case of mind over matter. Your depression turned off your natural instincts, and now that you've decided to start living again, it's going to start rearing its head, maybe at the most unlikely times." Tia tried to interrupt, but she continued. "I'm not saying you're going to jump in bed with the first guy you see—of course not. I'm just saying that you might not have as much control over it as you think you do."

"Oh God, that's the last thing on my mind, believe me. I'll say it again—I'm not looking to meet someone—quite the opposite, actually. I'm not even planning on talking to anyone. I'll probably be in and out. An hour or two, a beer or two, a little people watching, then I can call it a successful night and head home." She drew in a deep breath and let out another long sigh. "And to answer your other question...no. I really don't think I can do the memorial. As much as I love Paddy and Siobhan, and Sean and the rest of them—I just don't know if I can do it. This past year has been a long, hard road, and I'm finally at the point where I think I can get on my own two feet again. Being there—I don't know," she whined, trying to put her feelings into words. "I'm just afraid that it's going to bring all the old sad memories rushing back and that I'm going to lose the positivity I've worked so hard for. I have to move forward."

"Positivity? Is that even a word?"

"Oh, I don't know," she said defensively. "That's hardly the point."

"Then what is the point, Tia? I'm still not sure I really get why you feel like you have to 'put yourself out there.' You have lots of friends who love and support you, who will help you 'find yourself' again if you need them to—and for the record—I don't think you're as lost as you think you are. You're just too damned stubborn and analytical to believe that things'll just work themselves out in time. I know it's been a year, but there isn't a magical formula for grief, you know. There isn't a timetable that you can follow—you just have to take it day by day."

"I do know that Lex, but three hundred sixty five days have already passed me by, and I've neglected most of my friends the entire time. Shit, if it wasn't for you and Mom, I probably wouldn't have even left the house except to go to work. And if I've learned anything during my year of seclusion, it's that life is short and I've wasted too much of it already. I can almost hear Nick screaming at me to suck it up and get over myself, you know?"

Lexi's voice went soft around the edges. "Yeah, honey, I know. But that doesn't mean that you have to go out to strange places all alone to do it. Besides, we're going to the concert tomorrow—there'll be thousands of strangers there. Can't you wait one more night and find yourself then?"

Despite her strong emotions, Tia laughed. "An InHap concert is completely different than what I'm doing tonight. Tomorrow is going to have its own set of difficulties and I just can't do it twice."

"Meaning?"

"Well, obviously the music is going to bring back a lot of memories, and I won't be able to stop thinking about Nick. That's part of the reason I'm skipping the memorial. I can't imagine two nights in a row of being bombarded with reminders of everything I've lost."

Lexi sounded worried. "I'm telling you right now, you are NOT bailing on me for that concert, young lady, even if I have to drag you bodily—and don't test me, 'cause you know I will."

"I don't doubt that for a second," Tia smiled, "and you know I wouldn't want you any other way. It'll be a great show, as always, and I'm determined to enjoy every minute of it—I *will* enjoy every minute of it. But for tonight I need noise, and people, and anonymity."

Lexi groaned into the phone. "There'll be noise and people at *Paddy's*. People who know you and love you, Tia, not like in a smoky barroom full of strangers."

"I understand why you're worried; I do. But really—all I plan to do is find a little spot in the corner of the bar and do some people watching. I just need to be part of a crowd and soak up some of the energy. It's been so long since I've been a single girl in a bar—a single girl anywhere—and I don't even know what they do anymore. It's hard to imagine it right now, but I'm going to need those skills eventually, and it's been six freaking years since I've needed them. Tonight's going to be a little training course, that's all. So you and Ryan go to your fancy dinner, enjoy a night together as a couple, and have a great time without your constant third wheel tagging along."

"You're never a third wheel, Tia. Don't ever think that. Ryan loves you too, you know."

"I do know, and you know that I love you both back. You've been my rocks this past year, and I could never thank you enough."

"Jace has been there a lot too, you know."

Tia snickered. "Yeah, like he's not sick and tired of having to babysit me."

"I really don't think it's much of an imposition for him at all. I think he likes you."

Tia laughed and let the comment roll off her back. "Not likely. He just feels sorry for me, like everyone else at the Club does. I can feel their pitiful eyes on me all the time and it's getting really old." She curled her legs under her and massaged her temples. "Look. For the past year I've done nothing for myself except to drown in self-pity, and it's way past time to knock it the hell off. I have to discover who I am now; just me."

"Oh, all right," Lexi conceded. "I can see I'm not going to talk you out of this. But I want you to call me the minute you get home, understand? I don't care what time it is, you *call* me. I'm going to be worrying about you all night."

"No need to worry," Tia said confidently, but inside, her nerves were starting to gnaw at her.

"And no picking up any guys unless you carefully inspect their fingernails. And their wallets. Understood? Actually," she added, "no picking up guys at all. I like that idea better."

"Yes mother," Tia groaned sarcastically.

"Hey," she said. "Not funny. You know I could call your mother and tell her what you're up to tonight. You know she'd be just as thrilled about it as I am." It was an empty threat, Tia knew, and when she didn't respond Lexi said again, "Just promise you'll call me."

"I will."

"And consider going to the memorial. It would mean a lot to Paddy and Siobhan, and I really think you'll regret it later if you don't go."

"I'll think about it, but no guarantees."

"Fair enough. And be careful."

"I will. Love you, Lex."

"Right back at you, girlfriend."

Tia tapped the end call button and walked to the sliding glass door that led out to her little deck. Spring had slipped in, and new life was blossoming everywhere. Green once again tinted the stark branches of trees, daffodils and bluebells sprung from the ground, and the birds were starting to sing again. The robins and the hummingbirds were back; and the world around her was being reborn. It was about time that she started living again, too.

She took a deep breath, held it for a moment, then went into her room and sat on the bed, contemplating the significance of the evening. Letting go of the past, starting a new chapter in her life, discovering her own identity—it was a lot to ask from one night at a little hole-in-the-wall pub, but she had to start somewhere. It had been a year since she'd been out in a crowd of strangers and Lexi was right—*Last Stop* wasn't her kind of place, but then again, that was the reason she chose it. If she made a fool of herself, or started crying in her beer, she could write it off with her standard vacation mantra that she'd never see these people again, so what did it matter? There was almost no chance she'd run into anyone she knew—and that was the way she wanted it—she just wanted to be a fly on the wall, an anonymous spectator rather than a participant.

She'd be lying to herself if she didn't admit that a big part of her was terrified at the idea of joining the world again. She readily admitted that getting involved in another relationship at any time in the near future was more than daunting, it was downright frightening. The thought of starting over with someone new, going through the motions of first kisses, first dates, uncomfortable silences—she shuddered to think about it. Right now there was still a lot of pain associated with Nick, but she was learning to push it back and get on with her life. He would have wanted that for her, she was sure of it.

So get on with it, she thought, getting up to stare into her closet. She pulled out a pair of weathered jeans and a blousy top. Not too form fitting, not too low cut, not too flashy. She grabbed a pair of simple tan pumps with a low heel, and considered her outfit complete.

Sitting down at her vanity, she contemplated her image in the round mirror. It had taken many months, but the dark circles had finally disappeared from her below her eyes. She didn't cry nearly so much anymore and actually had some good days once in a while. There was her work...God she loved her work...her ten year old students never failed to make her feel loved and she knew she made a real difference in their lives. She had her friends—and good ones at that, especially Lexi, and she was fairly confident that once she got back in touch with the rest of them; the next part of her plan to take back her life; they would forgive her blatant avoidances of the past year. Her parents, although they could sometimes be major pains in the ass, were always there for her and had really helped her through.

What she didn't have was Nick, and a sense of individual identity. After being one half of their couple for so many years, she just didn't know how to *be* without him. That was what she needed to get back, and her most prominent reason for venturing out tonight. She was still young, after all, and couldn't spend the rest of her life longing for something that would never be, could never be. She had to find out who Tia Hastings really was.

It wasn't going to happen tonight, but at least it was a start. Getting back in touch with the world, especially the single world, was going to take a concerted effort on her part. She didn't know if she remembered how to flirt, how to flash a smile that sent a message in the level of the eyes, the toss of the hair, or the tilt of the head. She didn't know if the old pick-up lines were replaced by new ones, or even if it was still acceptable to refuse a kiss on the first date. What she needed was to get out there and relearn what it was like to be young, single, and ready for whatever the future held.

    She applied some clear gloss to her lips, a brush of gold shadow over her green eyes, and pulled her long dark hair back into a simple knot. The clock read 7:00 and she grabbed her small bag, keys, and cell phone from the table by the door. "Time to start living again," she said aloud as she stepped out into the unseasonably warm May evening and headed for *Last Stop*; the first stop on her journey into her own future.

Chapter 2

It was early when she arrived, but she still had to park more than a block away. She had hoped to slip in when the place wasn't too busy and grab a seat in the corner somewhere, but obviously the clientele here was already celebrating the start of Memorial Day weekend, a three-dayer, and the official start of summer in the Midwest. Inside, gratefully, the place was dark enough that she slipped in unnoticed, and the bar area was nearly empty. Most of the patrons were playing pool or darts, or were sitting at round tables in groups. Tia ordered a Sam Adams, the only beer on the menu that didn't have some form of 'Light' in its name, and settled in to observe.

The bar was a horseshoe shape, and she perched on a stool closest to the door. Shania Twain crooned from the fuzzy-sounding speakers of the jukebox, and a trio of tattooed girls in skin tight jeans and tank tops stuffed bills into the machine and argued over their next selections. There were three pool tables, and each hosted a testosterone-filled good-natured match. Most of the men wore baseball caps, faded jeans, and t-shirts advertising sports teams and various brands of mostly cheap beer. One proudly labeled its wearer as a member of the FBI—Female Body Inspector. There were a couple of cowboy hats and plenty of flannel shirts, and, as Lexi had predicted, most of the guys looked as though they'd put in a hard day's work. They were rough around the edges without a doubt, and certainly not the sort that hung out at the country club. That was the point, though, and she sipped her Sammy and watched as a group of girls sauntered over to the pool tables to flirt with the men. Feeling a bit voyeuristic, she settled in to watch the interaction, which quickly turned to giggling, hugging, and one girl plucking the eight ball off the table just as a pretty decent looking blonde struck the cue ball.

She let her gaze wander around the room as Keith Urban's *Some Days You Gotta Dance* came blasting out of the jukebox. What could only be described as a whoop and a holler rose up out of the crowd as most of the women and a few of the men flocked to the empty spot of worn wood that doubled as the dance floor, formed a line and started to dance. Although she wasn't really a fan of country music and had never done so much as the Electric Slide, she found herself caught up in the sounds and the way the bodies moved to the beat. There was a comfort level, a camaraderie between the dancers as they switched partners, swung and twirled, and their boots stomped a rhythmic beat into the floor. She found herself tapping her leg with her fingers to match the rhythm. When one of the pool players wandered over and asked her to dance, she smiled, thanked him, and politely declined.

Suddenly, the hair on the back of her neck prickled and she felt eyes on her—the sense that someone was staring. She swept her gaze across the bar, and then she saw him. He was sitting alone on the other side of the bar sipping what could only be a martini. The fancy glass with the floating olive was definitely out of place amongst the Miller Lite mirrors and sports paraphernalia adorning the dark walls. He held her glance for just a moment and then quickly turned his gaze away. A flicker of recognition passed over her, and she tried to place the face—hoping it wasn't someone she knew from school. She looked over again to find him turned away from her, watching the dance floor behind him. Her quick glance was enough to see that he was good looking, but he desperately needed a new hair style and a shave. He had a dark brown mullet, circa Billy Ray Cyrus—did people actually still wear their hair like that? She thought that fad died when Bono finally cut his off back in the 80's. But when he turned his head, something else caught her eye, and she noticed a much lighter tuft of hair waving out just over his ear. He was wearing a wig; she realized—is that what you called it on a guy? She found herself intrigued. Why in the world would any man, who obviously had at least some blonde hair, choose to: A) wear a wig and B) make it a mullet? And why was there something so familiar about his face? Well, she decided, she was here to observe, after all, and he was as good a candidate as any. She watched without being too obvious as he studied the dance floor.

As she focused in on her target, Tia wove ridiculous stories in her mind. Maybe he was an undercover FBI agent on a surveillance mission just waiting for his mark to slip up. She glanced around the room at the pool players, dart throwers, dancers and drinkers. Could one of them be a fugitive from the law? Or maybe the guy was just going horribly bald, and was trying to delay the inevitable, or to look younger for the ladies. *Yeah, right*, she thought, smiling to herself—as if any self-respecting woman in this day and age would be seen with a guy sporting a mullet! She settled back into her stool and sipped her beer. Suddenly, this observing was getting a bit more interesting. But then, Lexi's warnings started creeping into her mind and her thoughts grew darker. Maybe he was in disguise because *he* was a fugitive. He could be a serial killer stalking his next victim, hoping that the nationwide manhunt would be focused on a guy with a really bad hairdo—he'd commit the crime, and then dump the wig and be walking around with a luxurious head of long blonde hair...she shivered then at the idea that he had been watching her.

Getting a grip on her own mind she laughed at herself and her sudden bout of paranoia. What were the chances, really? But then she thought about her car, parked over a block away on a dark and deserted street lined with closed businesses and crisscrossed with unmarked alleyways. A tingle ran up her spine, and she suddenly realized how alone she was here amongst all these total strangers. She decided then that she wouldn't leave the bar alone; she'd ask the bartender to recommend someone who could walk her to car or, if she chickened out on that and she needed to, she could always call someone to come and meet her. It would be one more thing Lexi would hold over her head and gloat about forever, but Tia knew Lexi would come if she asked. In the meantime, mysterious mullet man was a curiosity, and if someone did come up missing tomorrow, she could at least give a good description of him—and foil his mullet ploy.

She started taking notice of the details, glad to have something on which to focus. His shirt, she noticed, although just a standard button down in a solid color, seemed a little too fitted and nice for this place—*duh*, she thought, it was about the only one in the place that wasn't flannel. And as he rested his elbow on the bar and leaned his head into his hand (was he trying to hide his face?), there was no tell-tale sign of dirt under his fingernails. He looked too clean—too put together—for *Last Stop*. He was drinking a martini, obviously out of place in a joint like this, and he wasn't interacting with anyone. No game of pool, no dancing, no hitting up girls; he was just sitting alone, like she was, at the opposite corner of the bar. Another observer, perhaps? Another lost soul looking for something in anonymity? Then, as she watched, he reached around for his martini glass and she saw the tattoo on his hand.

The Chinese symbol for younger sister looks something like a one hundred degree angle intersected perpendicularly with a wishbone, followed by a sweeping vertical line with a sort of skirt near the bottom and two more perpendicular lines crossing the top. An unusual choice for a tattoo, but one that obviously held some sort of sentimental meaning to the bearer. She realized suddenly that she'd seen that tattoo before, in an issue of Rock's Finest magazine. A name popped into her head instantly—Dylan Miller—mega-star, two time Grammy winner, actor, Sexiest Man on Earth as chosen by the readers of *Person to Person* magazine, rock's hottest bachelor according to *Rock's Finest*. She had tickets to see his band; Incidental Happenstance or InHap, to fans; play tomorrow night, and it was the summer's hottest show—both the Saturday and Sunday shows had sold out in less than an hour. It was likely that he was already in town, and he was known to make random appearances around the city when he was. *No way*, she thought—it was impossible that one of the most popular performers in the world was sitting across from her at a cheesy country bar out of town...*wearing a mullet which was sure to have girls avoiding him and men ignoring him...*

"Whoa," she whispered to herself, her heart suddenly pattering a little irregularly in her chest. She shook her head slightly and tried to get a better look at him. She was sure the mullet wasn't his real hair, and she was pretty sure about the tattoo as well, the one Dylan Miller had done after his younger sister died of leukemia. She thought that the symbol was right, and it was certainly not the typical place to put a tattoo; on the back of the hand, just below where the thumb and index finger meet. But he had turned away again, and she couldn't get a good look at his face. The lighting wasn't good here, either, and the shadows hid his features rather effectively.

Finally, the song on the jukebox ended and Carrie Underwood's mellow voice flowed in, slowing the crowd. Much of the group left the dance floor and only a few couples remained, wrapped up in each other and swaying to the seductive rhythm. Finally, the man turned back to the bar.

She tried to watch him from the corner of her eye, looking at him without actually looking at him. If it wasn't Dylan Miller, she definitely didn't want him to think she was checking him out. And if it was, then what? He was obviously hoping not to be recognized, wanting to blend in with the crowd, not unlike herself. She couldn't even imagine what it must be like to never be able to go out for a simple drink without being mobbed by fans. If she called attention to him everyone in the bar would surround him, wanting autographs, pictures or begging him to perform. That wouldn't be fair to him, and, on a more selfish note, her quiet night of people watching would be over as well.

She watched with sideways glances as the song on the jukebox ended, and the notes of the next selection drifted from the speakers. It was *Untangled*, an InHap song with just enough southern influence to have spent some time on the country charts. The man's head rose alertly and he stiffened for a moment, his eyes quickly spanning the room. A small smile lifted the corners of his mouth, and he relaxed again, watching the exchanges on the dance floor as more and more couples slid in to sway with the melody. Tia watched his interest with her own, and as he lifted his glass again and drank she looked intently at the tattoo. Despite the shadows, she felt more confident that it was the right symbol. Just then, the bartender leaned in and said something to him and he smiled—and then she knew.

She had never been star struck—rarely watched the tabloid TV shows or read the magazines, except for an occasional issue of *Person to Person* when she went on a trip and needed something mindless to read in the airport. But here she was, ninety eight percent certain that she was sitting across from one of the biggest stars of the day—a singer/songwriter/actor whom she'd admired since her college days. She'd seen dozens of his concerts—Incidental Happenstance had been a part of much of her adult life. His band was one of Nick's favorites too; in fact it was at an InHap show that they first met, introduced by her old college roommate. She and Nick knew all their songs—Nick had played guitar and sung every one of them. She sang harmony, sometimes just the two of them, and occasionally at the pub. It was to one of InHap's songs that they would have had their first dance as husband and wife.

Memories of Nick flooded her suddenly, and she was quickly overwhelmed. How many nights had he played his own guitar and sung Dylan Miller's songs? She saw Nick's face for an instant, and knew that he would be furious with her if she passed up an opportunity to tell Dylan Miller just how much his music had impacted her life—their lives. But should she? What would she say? How could she do it without blowing his cover? And why was she having such a hard time catching her breath? She glanced over again and saw that his martini was nearly empty. Emboldened by the story she would whisper to Nick later that night and boast to everyone else in the morning, she hailed the bartender with her index finger and ordered another martini for the stranger across the bar. As he mixed it, she made her way nervously around to where he sat. Her heart pounded in her chest—she couldn't believe that she was so nervous.

She slid into the bar stool next to him just as the bartender delivered the martini. "A drink from the lady," he said, tipping his head toward the stool Tia had just occupied. Then he quickly turned away to take another order.

Dylan Miller looked at her. Before he could speak, she whispered, "Listen, I know who you are. I'm not going to blow your disguise or anything, you're obviously here incognito and I respect that. I just couldn't pass up the chance to say thank you. Your music has been a huge part of my life and I'm a big fan. Your songs..."

"Sorry, Miss," he interrupted, looking down at the bar and avoiding eye contact. "I don't know who you think I am, but I'm afraid you're mistaken." He glanced up at her briefly before quickly averting his eyes again, plucking a pair of glasses from the bar and sliding them on. *Nice try*, Tia thought, *but I'm not fooled*. She'd caught the quick flash of surprise in his eyes when they met hers; he was obviously flustered at being recognized. Plus, she heard the touch of his blended Australian/British accent, which she thought sounded more British, and that made her ninety eight percent jump up to ninety nine point five, at least.

"Oh, I'm not mistaken," she said confidently. "But I can easily see that you're looking for privacy tonight, and I'm sorry to interrupt that. I'm not going to try to hang out with you, or ask for an autograph or anything. I just couldn't pass up the opportunity..."

He looked down at the fresh drink. "Yeah, well, thanks for the drink; it really wasn't necessary. I'm sorry to disappoint you, but I'm not anybody, and I did come here for some alone time tonight, so if you'll excuse me..."

"Yes, of course. I didn't mean to intrude, really. I'm not a crazed fan or anything; I just ... anyway, thanks for the music. It's kind of been the soundtrack of my life, and I think you're incredibly talented. Thanks for sharing your gift with the world—it's meant a lot to a lot of people, and I'm one of them." She slipped off the stool and turned to go. "I'll leave you alone now."

He nodded and murmured something unintelligible, turning back to his drink.

She started to walk away and then turned back. "Oh, one more thing."

Here we go, Dylan thought. He looked irritated, but glanced patiently in her direction, lifting his eyebrows in question. "Yes?"

"You really need to fix your wig," she whispered. "There's kind of a big hunk of your real hair sticking out on the right side. Other than that, pretty good disguise, by the way." With that, she walked away and returned to her own seat. She looked over once to see him tucking the stray locks back into the wig, then purposefully turned her attention back to the pool players once more.

It was all she could do not to look at him again as her heart settled back into a normal rhythm. Wait until she told Lexi about this encounter! She would never believe that Tia had (sort of) met Dylan Miller, and at *Last Stop* of all places! They'd actually (kind of) had a conversation! Lexi would absolutely freak out, and Tia looked very forward to telling her that her choice of venue tonight had been exactly right.

But she of all people knew what it was like to have unwanted eyes on you constantly, and she'd respect his need for privacy. For her, it had been the looks of pity she got after she lost Nick—she couldn't even imagine being a superstar and never being able to go out in public without being accosted. She didn't want him to feel that some fan was staring him down, and she thought he might leave if he felt uncomfortable. It was stupid, she knew, but she felt a certain sense of excitement just knowing that he was sipping the drink she'd bought for him, even if they weren't drinking together. She ordered another Sammy and tried to focus on the interactions between the sexes, but her concentration was gone. Unconsciously, she glanced at him again and he tipped his glass toward her. It wasn't an invitation, but at least it was an acknowledgement. She tipped her bottle in return and smiled. He smiled back, wryly, and turned away.

Shit, Dylan thought. He didn't think there was any way anyone would recognize him in a place like this, a dive bar far enough out of the city to be a local hangout and dark enough to conceal identities. All he'd wanted was a simple drink, some noise, and some people—to be one person in a crowd and not some rock star seeking attention. He thought the mullet would be the perfect disguise—he looked like some 80's throwback and knew he wouldn't be attractive to women, and figured the men would just ignore him. It had worked until the woman across the bar somehow recognized him.

He took a sip of his martini and glanced over curiously at the woman again. The cheap gin burned his throat and reminded him of the old days, when a bottle of Boodles was a prized possession. She was pretty, the woman. She had dark hair that was pulled into a casual twist, and he'd just caught a glimpse of the green of her eyes. Nice eyes, he thought. She was natural, good looking even without a lot of makeup, which was pretty much the polar opposite of the rest of the women in the place. Although it seemed that she tried to blend in to the crowd, it was obvious that she was an outsider here too. He wondered what it was that made her seek refuge in this little dump of a bar, alone, and obviously not looking to meet anyone. He'd noticed a couple of the boys from the pool tables checking her out, and one had even approached her and asked for a dance. She had politely but firmly declined.

He reached for his martini again and felt a pang of guilt. He'd been pretty rude to her, he thought. He was the one who made millions of dollars, and here was a girl, all alone, buying him a drink, thanking him for "sharing his gift with the world," and he'd asked her to leave? She'd caught him completely off guard and he hadn't even asked her name or thanked her for the compliment. That wasn't the kind of person he was at the core, and he felt badly about it. But hey, he deserved to be able to sit at a bar and have a drink alone, didn't he? And he'd learned from far too many past experiences that you couldn't trust women. They all wanted something from him—the spotlight, a record contract, their faces on TV and in those damned tabloids...plus, opportunities for him to be anonymous didn't come along very often, so he had to take advantage of them when he could.

But, he thought, almost sadly, if he wasn't recognized and hassled by fans everywhere he went, if he was ever allowed to just be himself, she was the kind of girl for whom he might buy a drink. Oh hell, should he buy her a drink? It would be the gentlemanly thing to do; he could at least reciprocate the kindness and not leave her thinking that he was some kind of rich asshole megastar who couldn't be bothered with 'regular' people. But that would mean opening up conversation, and that wasn't what he wanted to do tonight. He looked her way again. She was trying very hard to concentrate on the pool players without looking obvious.

What was her deal, anyway? Part of him had difficulty believing that she was going to accept their meeting as a random event and walk away without so much as a request for an autograph or a picture. That alone puzzled—and surprisingly—intrigued him.

He wondered if maybe he should go—find a different place to be anonymous—but he hadn't thought to bring any of his other disguises along and the ridiculous mullet wouldn't fit in anywhere else but a place like this one. He glanced at her again and smiled at how intently she was trying to avoid looking at him. It really didn't look like the mystery woman was going to blow his cover, or bother him again. In fact, it looked as if she were working awfully hard to look everywhere else but at him. As a man with manners, however, he couldn't just let things go as rudely as he'd left them. He focused his gaze on her until she looked over and caught his eye and he tipped his glass in her direction, smiled, and looked away. It would have to be enough.

Chapter 3

Behind her, the door crashed open. Tia jumped in her stool and turned to see over six feet of cowboy lurch into the bar in faded jeans and a dirty work shirt. Her first thought was that this was exactly the guy that Lexi had in her mind when she joked about checking under fingernails. He was obviously a regular, and just as obviously had already started partying before stumbling into *Last Stop*.

"Happy Friday Everyone! Three day weekend, so let's get the party started!" he bellowed. Every head turned in his direction—he had just successfully become the center of attention. His loud announcement was met with a few cheers and the raising of more than a few bottles and glasses in his direction. He raised his arms, anointing them as his subjects, and approached the bar.

"Hey barkeep! Let's go Lester; I've been standing here for over ten seconds now! Don't keep a thirsty man waiting for his first brew on a Friday night!"

"Gotcha, Bud," the bartender replied, already twisting the cap off a Miller Lite. "Glad to see you haven't lost the virtue of patience—you have heard of the virtue of patience, haven't you?"

"Hell, my daddy taught me to grab life when I wanted it, and right now I want that beer!" He swept the frosty bottle from Lester's hands, turned, and looked straight at Tia.

"Well, now," he smiled, flashing crooked, yellow teeth. "Speaking of grabbing life when you want it…isn't this here a pleasant surprise—somebody new in my bar tonight—and a pretty somebody new at that. Must be my lucky night. How're ya doin', sugar?" He moved in closer to Tia and held out his hand, pressing his large body against the back of her bar stool.

Tia was frozen in her place. She could still smell the day's work on him; grease and gasoline, mixed with a splash of whiskey that seemed be emanating from his pores. She was caught off guard, and didn't know how to react. In all the time she'd spent pondering this night; taking the first step in reclaiming her life; this was a scenario she hadn't considered, and she wasn't prepared. Her first thought was to quietly make her exit, but he stood firmly between her and the door and directly behind her chair, preventing her from sliding it back away from the bar. She was essentially pinned, and a slight panic rose in her. Quickly, she tried to calm herself. After all, if she was going to get back into the world again, she would have to deal with people like this guy Bud. His kind was found in every bar and at every party in the world.

"Name's Bud," he said with a crooked and tobacco stained smile. "And you are...?"

She ignored his hand, but not before noticing a healthy dose of dirt under his fingernails. Lexi's words rolled in her mind; *public place doesn't mean safe place...shady characters*...She replied coolly, "Just about to leave. If you'll excuse me..." She pushed back on the stool, but it didn't budge.

Instead of making way, he moved in even closer, and she got the distinct feeling that taking no for an answer was not something he considered an option. "Now come on, don't be that way, honey. Night's young, weekend's long, and you certainly can't leave just yet... not before we've even been properly introduced."

"I'm afraid I really have to be leaving." Tia kept her voice calm, but his intrusion into her personal space—not to mention her anonymous evening—was making her uncomfortable. She made another attempt to push back the bar stool, but he stood firmly behind it. Tia shivered in spite of herself, and Bud was close enough to feel it—use it to his advantage.

"Now don't be scared, sweetheart. I'm just your good old-fashioned southern gentleman." He raised his voice to address the patrons. "Friends, tell this lady here that I am a perfect gentleman, will you?" he prodded.

Most of the guys raised their bottles in Bud's direction, but said nothing. Several of the girls, Tia noticed, looked away.

"See?" Bud continued. "No need to worry. Let's just have a beer and get to know each other a little bit. But first, be nice and tell me your name why don't you?"

His voice dripped honey and sugar and he made a pathetic attempt at a puppy face, but his glassy eyes were anything but friendly. He lifted his hand and in one quick swoop tugged Tia's hair out of its knot with his filthy fingers, brushing the fallen strands behind her ear and smiling down at her. Repulsed, she slapped his hand away, and he laughed. He felt in perfect control of this situation, that much was obvious. This man was used to getting what he wanted, Tia thought, and right now, it seemed that he wanted her. She was physically trapped by his huge body; she needed to use her brain to get herself out of this. Her serial murderer scenario flashed through her mind again, and suddenly she was no longer interested in finding herself. All she wanted to do was to get out of here, chalk it up as a hard lesson learned, get in her car, and go home to the safety of her own little house.

"Leave her alone, Bud, the lady obviously ain't interested," Lester said weakly from behind the bar.

Thank you, Tia's mind whispered, but Bud just scowled at him. "Mind your own goddamn business, Lester," he barked in reply. "I'm just tryin' to buy the lady here a drink, is all. I ain't hurtin' nobody."

To Tia's dismay, Lester turned away and busied himself washing glasses at the small sink under the bar, obviously not willing to go any further with the big man.

She took a slow breath and hoped that she radiated a calm she most certainly didn't feel. "That's a very kind offer, Bud, but I just stopped in for a quick beer, and I have somewhere else I need to be, so I really need to be going now. If you'll excuse me, *please*."

Now he was really irritated. "Listen to that fancy talk, *'I have somewhere else I need to be, please excuse me'*" he mocked. "Geez, honey. All's I wanted to do is to buy you..." he picked up her bottle and spun it in his hand. "...one of your fancy beers here and make some general conversation. No need to be a bitch." He put his hand on Tia's arm, and she could feel the pressure of his fingers digging into her flesh. Shit, she was in a little trouble here, and she wasn't quite sure how to get herself out of it. Dealing with unwanted attention from men was just one more thing with which she hadn't had any recent experience. She looked around the room to see if anyone was going to step up and help her out, but they all seemed suddenly very focused on everything but what was going on in her little corner of the room.

Bloody hell, Dylan thought, taking in the scene across the bar. The obnoxious cowboy had the poor girl trapped, and he was looking at her as if she were a goddamn ice cream cone that was begging to be licked. Not good. He looked around the room, hoping that someone would come to her rescue. Most of the guys had gone back to their pool games or their conversations, and the girls were trying unsuccessfully to avoid the scene unfolding; watching out of the corners of their eyes or stealing short glimpses from the dance floor. It seemed everyone in the place was concentrating very hard on not seeing what was going on. He turned back and saw the girl's wide eyes scanning the room, looking for a savior. She was trying to look calm, but he could almost feel her discomfort from where he was sitting.

Shit. It was pretty obvious that no one else in this dump was going to go to her rescue, and he'd been raised to be a gentleman. He couldn't stand guys like Bud who thought they could treat women like objects, and couldn't stand to see her so obviously uncomfortable. Besides, she was a fan, had already recognized him, and furthermore she'd bought him a drink. His response to that kindness had been to be rude and ask to be left alone. Damn it, he had no choice really; he was going to have to go to her rescue. But how to do it? He could whip off his disguise—it was horribly itchy anyway—get the attention of the whole place, and create a diversion so she could escape. Once he was recognized, though, he'd never get out of here, so he put that aside as a last option. But then he reconsidered. The absolute last option was to confront the guy and possibly start a bar brawl. He had a show tomorrow night, and the next, and frankly, the dude looked like he did heavy lifting for a living—confrontation was out of the question.

An idea occurred to him then, and as her eyes swept in his direction, he caught her glance. He put a finger over his lips to indicate secrecy, then walked his fingers through the air with his right hand while pointing to himself with his left, mouthing, 'follow me,' to her. He didn't know if she understood, but she seemed to calm a bit; her eyes at least lost that deer in the headlights look. He made his way around the bar and stood behind Bud.

He cleared his throat loudly, then belted out, "Excuse me...Bud is it?"

Bud turned and faced Dylan. "What do you want, partner?" There was no friendship in his tone.

He cleared his throat again and ignoring Bud's question said, "Come on Francine, let's get out of here."

Tia couldn't see him behind the behemoth of a man, and the slight southern accent wasn't his own, but she'd know that voice anywhere.

"I said, COME ON, Francine," he repeated, more urgently. "You were right, as usual, and I'm sorry for what I done. Can we just go home now?" She twisted her upper body in the stool so she could see past Bud and saw Dylan standing there with his hand extended toward her. She wanted to grab at it like a life raft, but it was still out of reach. Bud saw it as well, and turned his head toward Dylan, keeping his large body firmly planted behind Tia's stool.

"What are you DOING, stranger?" he sneered.

"That's *my* woman there, Bud. My Francine."

"Oh, is that so?" There was something that sounded like a dare in his voice. "She looks pretty alone to me right now."

"Yeah, well we had a bit of a falling out earlier. We been staring at each other across the bar, trying to patch things up."

Bud fired a look at Lester, who was quick to confirm. He nodded, and said, "Yup, they was talkin' earlier—she bought him a drink. Looked like they was tryin' to patch things up, alright."

"Really. Well maybe Francine doesn't want to patch things up. Maybe she's ready to move on to bigger and better things. Maybe what she needs is a real man; not some moron with a goddamn mullet who leaves a pretty lady like her sittin' all alone in a bar full of willing men." He took a step back to face Dylan, leaving Tia with just enough room to scoot the stool away from the bar and slip off.

Tia had already caught on to Dylan's act, interpreting his 'follow me,' and joined in immediately, grabbing at the opportunity to escape. Ignoring Bud's comment, she focused all of her attention on Dylan Miller. "Do you mean it, Chester? I'm still your girl?" She tried to sound surprised, simple, natural.

"Hell, Francine, we been together too long to call it quits now. I'm sorry for what I done. Can you forgive me?"

Tia dashed around Bud and threw her arms around Dylan enthusiastically, hoping she was playing the right part. "Oh Chester," she said, swooning. "You know I just hate it when we fight."

Dylan smoothed her hair, releasing the strands Bud had touched. "I know baby, I know. We won't fight anymore, I promise. Now can we please just get out of here and go make up proper?"

"You must be reading my mind!" Tia said as he nudged her toward the door and she gladly let him lead her.

"Yeah, whatever," Bud relayed loudly from behind them. "I'm here every Friday night, Francine, if you decide you want to try a real cowboy." He dismissed them, and loudly ordered another beer as they reached the exit.

Tia didn't acknowledge the comment, and pushed through the door with her arm around Dylan Miller. They walked away from the bar, and once they'd passed a couple buildings, they simultaneously burst into laughter. Tia bent over and put her hands on her knees, catching her breath and exhaling a huge sigh. She was shaky, but she felt relieved, thankful, and safe, and she burst into more nervous giggles. "Holy crap, you just saved my life!" She stood up and looked at the man who'd saved her. Dylan Miller.

"I wouldn't go that far," he said modestly. "But that guy was a real asshole, and he wasn't going to give up until he got what he wanted. I just couldn't stand to see the look on your face for another minute."

She leaned against the side of the building for support, still not sure of her own legs. She was still trembling a little bit, but could definitely see the humor in the situation, now that she was safely away from it. "Yeah, but the look on his face when we were walking out the door was better—am I right?"

Dylan smiled, and Tia felt her heart skip a beat. "I must admit, his was pretty good too. It was awfully close, though, I wouldn't want to have to take bets."

She slapped him lightly on the shoulder. "Wait though," she giggled. "Francine? When you had to make up a name, that's the one that popped into your head?" she joked, still breathing heavily but at least able to stand on her own two legs again.

"Well, I didn't get your name, so I had to come up with something quick."

"Yeah, I get that, but why not 'Sue,' or 'Mary'—something more common?" She put her hands on her hips and glared at him. "And please don't tell me that I look like a Francine," she joked, "I don't think I could take it."

Dylan smiled with one half of his mouth, a look that made him appear mischievous and sexy at the same time and one that had often appeared on the covers of magazines. "I'll have you know," he smirked, "that Francine just happened to be the prettiest girl from the wrong side of the tracks when I was growing up. I had it something bad for her when I was fourteen. No offense, but you seemed like you were sitting on the wrong side of the tracks tonight." He shook his head and smirked again. "Besides, it's better than Chester! Where did that come from? You knew my real name."

"Did I?" Tia asked slyly. "I thought you said I was mistaken."

Dylan half-smiled again and looked at her from dropped lids. "I didn't think you believed it."

"I didn't. Not for a second. And, just to clear the air, I never had it bad for a guy named Chester. He was the janitor at my elementary school. The smell of that guy Bud made me think of him—he was all grease, gas, and moonshine."

"Your elementary school janitor smelled like moonshine?" he joked.

"Only on Tuesdays and Fridays," she joked back.

They were almost a block away from the bar now, nearly to where she'd parked her car, and they stopped on the sidewalk.

"Listen," she said, her voice getting serious. "I really can't thank you enough. I was way out of my league in there, and I was more than a little freaked out."

"I could tell," he said. "What in the world were you doing in a place like that, anyway? There are some rough characters in those kinds of places, and you don't exactly look rough around the edges."

"Thanks, I think," she said shyly. "You're right though, that is definitely not my usual kind of hangout. I was just looking for some solitude, some noise, some...well, anyway," she said, sure he wasn't interested in her life story, "now you have personally had an impact on my life, aside from your music." She put her left hand over her heart, bowing her head slightly, and held out her right. He reached out and shook it. "I appreciate it so much. Thank you again."

"Don't mention it. It's the least I could do. You're a fan, after all. Plus, you bought me a drink, and I was feeling bad about the way I treated you."

"Oh," she added sadly, "but now I feel bad that I ruined your evening. You were obviously looking for some solitude yourself, and now you can't go back in there."

"No, I'm definitely not going back in there," he chuckled.

"It's still pretty early for a Friday night though," she said glancing at her watch, "and I imagine you don't get too many chances to be alone, and I just would feel horrible if I ruined your night out. So, if you're still looking to have some fun—well, I wouldn't have called that place fun, but whatever—if you go down this road about five miles to Central Avenue," she pointed, "and hang a right, there're a few places there where you could disappear into a crowd, especially this time on a long weekend. There's a *Dick's Sports Page*, a karaoke bar—called, of all things, *Sing-Along-Cassidy's*—a kind of a biker bar called *Crowbar*, and a very nice Irish Pub called *Paddy's*."

"OK, well thanks," he said, bowing his head appreciatively. "It is early yet. Maybe I'll try that—Central Avenue, you said?"

"Yep. Turn right. The bars start about a mile and a half down the road, and they're all kind of bunched together so you can't miss them."

"Appreciate the advice," he said with another polite bow.

"It's definitely the least *I* can do," she gushed. "I'm so sorry I messed up your evening, but I'm also so glad you were there. You're my hero, Chester." She grinned at him then and shook her head. "Damn, no one'll ever believe this story! I don't know if I even believe it!" Although she thought it would be really amazing to stand around and have a conversation with Dylan Miller, she didn't want to push her luck hanging around *Last Stop* and didn't want to sound like a blathering idiot. She was painfully out of practice when it came to talking to men, and this was not the kind of guy you practiced on. She felt a blush rise in her face, and decided it was time to go and let him have his peace. He'd already done more than he needed to do, and she of all people understood the need for solitude. "Listen, it was...really amazing to meet you. And I meant what I said inside—your music has done more for me than you can ever know. Thanks for that, too. Now I've taken up entirely too much of your time and I should..." She turned and motioned toward the other side of the street.

He reached out impulsively and put his hand on her arm. She felt her pulse quicken just at the light touch. This was Dylan Miller! He'd just saved her from who knows what, and they were standing out here on a deserted street having a real conversation—Lexi would freak! She'd have to call her as soon as she put this awful place behind her—she'd been so adamant that Tia avoid *Last Stop*, but once she heard about this chance encounter, she was going to be positively green with envy. Right now though, she should really just get out of here and let him be. He was probably sick of people constantly wanting to be around him, hence the disguise.

"At least let me walk you to your car. I wouldn't want Bud to pop his head out to see if you're still around."

"Actually, it's right there," she said, motioning across the street to her Mini, "so you already have." She made it to the curb and then turned back. "Hey—thanks again, I'm sorry again, and I'll see you tomorrow!"

Dylan stopped. "What's that?"

"I said, 'I'll see you tomorrow.'" Dylan looked confused, so Tia continued. "At your concert? I've had my ticket for weeks. I'm really looking forward to it. You guys always put on an excellent show—I go see you every time you're in town."

He smiled. "Really? Well, I appreciate that too."

"I'll wave to you," she laughed.

This woman had personality, he thought, taking the bait. "And where will you be," he asked, "so I can be sure to wave back?"

"Second pavilion, section 209, row 14."

"Pretty crappy seats."

Tia put her hands on her hips and nodded. "I thought so too. I would have thought that being a member of the fan club would warrant me better. I've been a member since it started, and have never once gotten any really good seats. You should really look into that—the lottery system sucks."

He did this thing where he raised just one eyebrow—it made him look inquisitive and incredibly sexy at the same time and it drove the girls wild. "I'll have to look into that. You're right, loyal fans like you should do much better."

"How about this, if I could be so bold?" she suggested. "Maybe, say at the beginning of the third song, you could give me some kind of signal, like a peace sign, or two fingers pointed in my direction, and I'll know it's for me."

"A peace sign?" he smirked, that one eyebrow rising again. "I think maybe I can do a little better than that. How about I dedicate the third song to you? Then everyone'll know it's for you. I'll play it for Francine."

"I like that even better. It'll certainly make my story about tonight a little more believable, although I'm still not sure I even believe it. What a crazy night! It couldn't be more different than I expected."

She skipped across the street, opened her car door and turned back. "Listen, Dylan Miller, I can never thank you enough for what you did for me tonight, but I'll never have another chance so I'm going to say it one more time. Thanks." She put her hands together below her chin as if in prayer and bowed slightly. "And have a good rest of the evening. Try to keep that tattoo covered so you don't get mugged by girls at the next bar."

Dylan watched as the light from the car illuminated her. She really was a pretty girl. Away from the shadows of the bar he could see her high cheekbones, her creamy skin, her pouty lips. As she slipped into the car he stood there for a moment, amazed and confused. After the crazy experience they'd just shared, she'd really just been thankful. She didn't ask for an autograph, or a picture, and didn't whip out a cell phone to get a picture of the two of them together. She didn't ask to join him, and didn't ask for front row seats or backstage passes for her and her friends. It was kind of unheard of in his world, and it caught him off guard. It always seemed like everyone wanted something from him; it was the nature of the beast. He stood there, surprised as she closed her car door and started the engine. She really was going to just drive away. Suddenly, impulsively, he didn't want that to happen. He didn't meet real people very often, and the bizarre conversation he'd just had with her was the most normal one he'd had with a stranger in a very long time.

He sprinted across the street and knocked on her window just as she was pulling away. She jumped in her seat and put her hand to her chest; not an unexpected reaction after the chaos in the bar. She hit the brake, threw the car in park, and rolled down the window, a question on her face.

He leaned casually against the roof of the car and slouched in front of the window. "Hey. I still didn't get your name."

She looked up from her seat at his carelessly easy pose. He emanated manliness, she thought, and her stomach turned a little flip. She smiled up at him. "Tia," she said. She stuck her hand out the window and he shook it again.

"Nice to meet you, Tia."

"Really nice to meet you too, Dylan," her smile literally seemed to brighten. "Really nice."

He held on to her hand, and hesitated only for a second before extending the invitation. "So, I was thinking. No sense both of us having our evenings cut short or being alone on such a beautiful night. What do you say we continue the evening, together but anonymous, at a different location?"

She hesitated for a second, and he saw the brief flash of doubt in her eyes. Again, she surprised him—he couldn't remember the last time he'd had a woman not instantly jump at the chance to be with him, and he was sure that a good number of them only wanted to be able to tell their friends that they had been with Dylan Miller. Instead of irritating him, however, her indecision intrigued him more.

"Wow," she breathed. "Wow." She'd never have a chance like this again, she thought, spending time with a guy like Dylan Miller. But more than that, she thought, how many chances would she have to just talk with a man who probably wouldn't remember her after tonight, even if she made a total mess of things with her complete lack of practice in dealing with the opposite sex? God knew she needed the practice, but certainly an international superstar was not what she expected to use to brush up on her flirting skills. Still, how could she pass up a chance like this? She was petrified and excited at the same time and once again, thoughts of Nick flashed in her mind. She could almost physically feel him pushing her, and knew that he'd be absolutely furious with her if she passed up the chance to spend time with one of their shared idols.

She hesitated before she spoke, and her words faltered. "There's a big part of me that wants to take you up on your offer, and another part that says that I've already had more than my share of excitement for the evening."

Her answer knocked him back, made him more determined. "But the part that wants to come out with me is bigger, right?" He smiled the smile that made him famous, another one that graced the covers of many a magazine. It lit up his entire face and made his blue eyes flash like deep water.

She smiled back and lowered her eyes. "Yeah, that part's bigger," she admitted shyly.

Dylan's mind reeled. He couldn't believe he'd have to convince her, and he kind of liked doing it. In his world, he never knew if people were being straight with him. Most people just tended to agree with every word he said so as not to fall out of his good graces, and it drove him absolutely mad. He welcomed the opportunity to have a real conversation with a good-looking woman who didn't seem to want anything from him except his company—and only part of her even wanted that. His manhood had been challenged for the first time in a long time, and he rose to meet it.

"What could happen?" he shrugged. "I'm your fearless protector, remember? And since I've already saved you from one evil cowboy tonight, you should feel completely safe. Besides, I owe you a drink, and I couldn't live with myself if I didn't pay my debts. Especially to damsels in distress."

"Believe me," she said, "it's not about feeling safe. I'd feel perfectly safe with you." She pondered for just a moment longer. What the hell? How could she pass up this opportunity? "And I guess I can't be responsible for giving you a guilt trip." She smiled up at him and nodded her head. "OK, let's go. Hop in."

"Great!"

He grinned at her again, and she could see the superstar in his smile. Even with the horrible hair, he was an incredible looking man—tall, sexy, confident—and the hint of British accent in his smoky voice was smooth enough to spread on bread. She smiled to herself as he ran around the front of the car and jumped into the passenger seat.

He climbed in and wondered in the back of his mind if she'd eventually get around to asking him for front row seats. In the front of his mind, he hoped she wouldn't.

Chapter 4

Penelope Valentine stood and examined her naked body in front of the long mirror. Not perfect yet, but another couple months with Jean Phillipe and she'd be back in movie shape. It had been a long hard six months—her latest film a flop at the box office, bad press, that bastard Jason Whitten dumping her for that wanna-be Italian supermodel, more bad press—then a few months of seclusion where she refused to take any calls and ate whatever she wanted. Oh, and she drank way too much. It was going to take another minor procedure to get rid of the little red veins that streaked across her cheeks.

But she was on a comeback, and her luck had finally turned. It was time to get back on the fast-track again; time to make her grand entrance back into the Hollywood limelight. She was lucky to nab the starring role as Anastasia in *Ambient Rain*—she knew two other actresses had passed on the role because of prior commitments—but she didn't let that bother her. Well, maybe a little. She hadn't read the book or the script, but knew that it had spent quite a few months on the New York Times Bestseller List. Plus, when she found out who her co-star was, she knew it was the perfect role for her comeback. Dylan Miller wasn't the biggest actor in Hollywood, and spent much of his time touring with his band, but he was good, and his last two movies had gotten rave reviews, as had he. He was just what she needed to get back on her feet—successful, adored, and incredibly good looking. He was on the cover of the Sexiest People on Earth issue of *Person to Person* last year—she was also in the issue, although a little further back. Dylan was much better looking than that rat bastard Jason, as a matter of fact, and with a little work on her part, they could be the perfect Hollywood couple.

It didn't hurt, either, that they'd be filming in New Zealand with a little hop over to Bora Bora. They couldn't be further from Hollywood there, and Bora Bora, in her opinion, was the most romantic place on the planet. After a few months together, they could be the next hot thing—Dylanope, or some stupid mix of their names that the tabloids could put on their covers, and she'd be back on top of her game.

She ran her hands over her nearly flat stomach. Jean Phillipe was a miracle worker, that was certain, but it hadn't been easy. A private chef, daily workouts, stress management—it was all part of the plan. She'd follow it to the letter, though, because it was her ticket back to the fame and adoration that she couldn't live without.

Her mind ran back to Dylan Miller. Sexiest Man on Earth, she thought, and if her memory served her, he was on tour right now with his band. She slid into a silk kimono and sat down at her desk. In the deep side drawer, she kept her extensive collection of magazines in which she'd appeared so she could pull them out and look at them anytime she wanted. She pulled out the "Sexiest Stars" issue with Dylan on the cover, and another magazine graced by her own face. It was a picture taken on Oscar night, three years ago, and if she did say so herself, she was stunning. Her dress was a DeHoya, made exclusively for her, and it perfectly accentuated her figure and the new breasts she'd splurged on six months earlier. The neckline plunged daringly, and she dripped in borrowed diamonds. They'd given her 'best dressed' honors that night and although she hadn't won the Oscar, she'd been the darling of the after parties. She held the two covers next to each other to see how they'd look as a couple. He oozed masculinity--the faint scruff on his chin and cheeks, the longish, wavy, carelessly unkempt blonde hair, the incredible blue and expressiveness of his eyes rimmed in long dark lashes, a firm jaw line. He wore what could almost be called a pout and his lips looked made for kissing. They would look good together, and as a couple they would knock Jason and that Italian slut off the covers of the magazines. She flipped through the issue until she came to Dylan's photo spread. Great smile too, she thought, and the picture of him singing on stage clearly showed the passion he had for music. She held up several combinations of the two of them together, and liked what she saw. Suddenly, she couldn't wait to get started on reclaiming her place at the top.

She booted up her computer and checked out his web site, scrolling through more photos and reading his bio. She had to do her homework, know a little about him, so that when they met they'd be able to slide effortlessly into a relationship. *That's how things work in Hollywood* she thought, relationships were more about appearances than they were about love. Love was overrated, anyway—it was all just an act, really, and she knew how to act. A guy like Dylan Miller would be easy enough to wake up to every morning, and everyone seemed to love him. He never got bad press, and being attached to someone like him would soften the hard edges she'd acquired over the years. Her excitement mounted as she read—they even had a few things in common besides acting.

She checked their tour schedule, and figured, why wait? Let's get this party started as soon as possible. One call to her assistant Angela and the arrangements were already being made. Chicago wasn't too bad at this time of year. Not warm yet, but a few sessions in the tanning booth and she'd have a healthy glow that would look great against the fish-belly-white Chicagoans who'd been covered up all winter.

She'd just show up at the concert and surprise him with the news that she'd be his costar. The studio wasn't planning to make the announcement until the following week, so he'd hear it first from her, and it would be a valid excuse to show up at his concert unannounced. Obviously he'd show her the professional courtesy of meeting her, and then the romance could begin.

She drew herself a bath, pinned her long blonde hair on top of her head, and slipped into the luxurious salts harvested straight from the Dead Sea that Jean Phillipe had insisted she buy. *Good for the skin*, he'd said in his obnoxious French accent. *Rid your body of impurities*. Hell, she'd just rid her life of impurities, and she was ready for a fresh start. Just a few days to primp, and then it was off to the Windy City, and her new lease on life.

Chapter 5

"So, where are we going?" Tia asked.

"Are you up for some adventure and a little fun?" Dylan answered with his slightly crooked smirk and slightly cocky accent.

"After what just happened in *Last Stop*? I don't know if I need any more adventure, but the fun part sounds good. What'd you have in mind?"

"I thought we'd hit *Sing-Along Cassidy's*."

She looked him up and down and laughed. "Yeah, your mullet'll probably fit in there. Actually, though, I do have somewhat of a reputation to uphold in this town. Any chance you have another disguise in your pocket? One a little less...obnoxious?"

"Nah," he smiled. "I'm sportin' this look tonight. Deal with it, sister."

She'd deal with it. Absolutely she'd deal with it. She was surprised that he seemed like such a nice, normal guy, and she was completely taken aback that she felt so comfortable with him right off the bat. That was part of being famous, she guessed. Everyone thought they knew you. "Oh, alright," she said with mock disappointment in her voice. "Let's do it then," she laughed, and threw the car in gear.

"So, if you're a fan, you know some of my music, right?" Dylan asked as they were seated in a corner booth a good distance from the main stage.

"Only all of it," Tia replied. "I've been a fan for a lot of years."

"Then tell me this, Tia—are you a sing-along kind of girl?"

"Well actually," she paused, not knowing how much she wanted or needed to give away at this point. She certainly didn't want any sympathy about Nick—the whole purpose of this night was to get away from the sympathy and just be a normal person. *Someone who didn't lose the love of her life a year ago to the day,* she thought. "A few of my friends play guitar, and know a lot of your songs. Sometimes they play at this pub I hang out at a lot, and once in a while I'd do harmony if they needed someone." She realized that she'd spoken the last part of the sentence in past tense. It had been a long time since she'd sung at the pub; sometimes it seemed like a lifetime ago. Dylan didn't seem to notice.

A huge smile crossed his face. "Seriously? Well that's just perfect! Do you know harmony for *"Lost in You?"*

"That's one of my favorites, actually, but..."

"Hold that thought." Dylan slid out of the booth. "I'll be right back."

"Dylan, wait!" she called as he walked toward the reception table pulling his wallet from his back pocket. He wasn't seriously signing them up to sing karaoke, was he? She was at once mortified and thrilled. She'd sung in front of crowds before; that wasn't a big deal. And like *Last Stop*, she didn't think anyone who ran in her social or professional circles was big into karaoke, so she wasn't too concerned about making an ass of herself. But having the chance to sing, on a stage (albeit at a strange venue) with Dylan Miller? Especially to sing one of the songs she and Nick had loved so much? She knew he would want her to do it—if he were here, he'd push her onto the stage if he had to. And yes, Dylan was returning with a song sheet in his hand—not that either of them would need it.

"We're all set. I entered us in the duet contest. Looks like we have some stiff competition, too. See that couple over there?" He tipped his head toward a table aside the stage where an older couple dressed in full country-western compliment were pouring over a song sheet and squeezing lemon into their water glasses. "They're doing Dolly Parton and Kenny Rogers."

"Oh God. Not *"Islands in the Stream."*

"The very one. And, Candy at the reception table tells me that they're regulars. They're big winners—kind of an institution around this place. She wasn't going to let me enter so late in the game, but apparently not too many people are willing to cough up the entry fee when they have to go against the local champs. They might be tough."

"Dylan, it's been a while since I've sung in public. I know all the notes, but..."

"Well, you said you liked fun and adventure. What could be more adventurous than karaoke?" He lifted her face with his finger, taking in the look of indecision on her face. He forced her to meet his eyes. "Hey," he said. "It's just for fun; I'm not going to judge you or anything. But if you're not comfortable, we can back out if you really don't want to do it; no big deal."

The serious look on his face, and his touch under her chin boosted her confidence. She'd still been singing at home. She could do this. Actually, she thought, how could she not do this?

"Oh no," she smiled, hoping she conveyed more confidence than the butterflies that had suddenly taken flight in her stomach allowed her to feel, "I was just thinking how those country bumpkins are goin' down!"

"Thata girl!" Dylan smiled that incredible smile, and she knew she would sing her heart out. For Dylan, and for Nick.

The country bumpkins turned out to be Frank and Joy Walker, and they were actually really good. Her voice was clear and bright, and his was deep and rolling. They complimented each other nicely, and got a rousing applause from the audience. It was cute how they dressed for the part, too. She was wearing a flouncy skirt, circa 1970's line dancing competition, and he was pure cowboy, complete with boots, hat and bolero tie. When their song ended, they drifted into each other's arms and kissed before taking a bow. Dylan and Tia shared a look that said, 'tough competition, indeed' as they clapped and cheered along with the rest of the crowd.

Two more couples performed, one newlywed and one a pair of girls. Both were painful to listen to. Then the mc stood up and called for Chester and Francine to take the stage. Tia's heart began to flutter as her butterflies suddenly turned into bats—nervously, she looked up to her singing partner, who was smiling down at her. This couldn't really be happening! If this was a dream, she definitely didn't want to wake up from it. Dylan gallantly extended his hand and she took it gracefully, rising from her seat and walking to the stage. It was all a show now, so they set up the song by staring deep into each other's eyes as they took their places in front of their mikes. It was a love song, after all.

As soon as the music started, Tia lost herself in the ebb and flow of the notes and the rhythm of her heart changed to match the music—slow and easy. Dylan's voice glided in with the gravelly, honest sound that had won the hearts of millions. When Tia chimed in with the harmony, their voices blended beautifully, rising and falling in piano and crescendo. Their eyes locked, and the passion of the music played out in their faces. Around the room, conversations halted and glasses stopped in mid-rise. Neither of them noticed, but Frank and Joy exchanged first a pained look, then a hug, as they conceded to the young couple on the stage who were so obviously in tune with one another.

When they sang the last line, *"Please don't try to find me, I just wanna stay lost in you,"* Dylan tipped his head so that their foreheads were touching and their eyes were locked on each other. The room was silent for a moment, and then it erupted in a fury of applause, catcalls, and whistles. Tia felt humbled and proud, and wondered if Dylan still felt like this after every performance. She couldn't imagine this kind of adulation ever getting old. Dylan took her face in his hands, kissed her on the forehead where his own had just been resting, then turned her to take a bow. As they made their way back to their booth, there were handshakes, pats on the back, and congratulations from many of the patrons. They were barely in their seats when drinks arrived at their table.

"Compliments of Frank and Joy," the waitress smiled. Then she leaned in conspiratorially and whispered, "You guys were great! I just know you got this!"

"Thanks a lot," Dylan smiled back. They both raised their glasses to Frank and Joy who had switched from water to champagne, and who held up their own glasses for a long-distance toast.

"That was so amazing!" Tia breathed, grinning widely. "How do you even live with yourself when you have thousands of people worshiping you every night?"

"All in a day's work," he joked. "But it is a pretty awesome feeling, isn't it? It really never gets old."

She respected him for that. It was obvious from a fan's standpoint that Dylan gave his best at every show, and it appeared that he truly loved performing for his audience. But he was an actor, too, so she was genuinely glad to see that he was so real.

Two more couples followed, but the buzz around the bar was that there was a new power couple at *Sing-Along Cassidy's*. After a very short judges' deliberation, the mc stood up to announce the winners. When Chester and Francine were named couples' champs, the roar of appreciation once again rose from the crowd. Dylan and Tia rose and accepted their small plastic microphone trophy and took a final bow, but when the judges handed them an oversized check for $250, Dylan's eyes shadowed. They took one more bow, and returned to their booth.

"I didn't know there was prize money involved," Dylan said. "I had no idea." His eyes were troubled. "I sing for a living. I have no business taking money for this."

Tia understood. "I feel bad stealing the thunder from Frank and Joy too," she said. "Look how cute they are!" They both looked over at the older couple who were once again raising their glasses toward them, Frank's arm resting comfortably around Joy's shoulders. "I have no problem telling them that they deserve it more than us—the fun and adventure of this experience was more than enough for me."

"Really?" Once again, this woman surprised him. He was about to say more, but suddenly, Frank and Joy were at their table.

Frank spoke first. "You got some set of pipes on you, little missy," he grinned. "I was so wrapped up in them that I almost forgot I was listening to some rock and roll song."

Her pipes? She'd just sung with one of the world's most popular singers, and he was talking about *her* pipes? Tia shook her head in amazement, and then smiled warmly at him. "Thank you very much," she said humbly.

Joy chimed in, "You sound beautiful together! It brought tears to my eyes to see the love you had for the music—and for each other." She winked at Tia, who glanced over at Dylan as he was trying to stifle a mischievous smile. "And you, young man!" she exclaimed, batting her false eyelashes at Dylan, "you should think about singing professionally—I've never heard a more unique voice—it's like smoke, honey and sandpaper—very sexy!" She blew Dylan an air kiss. "Have you two been singing together long?"

"Not nearly as long as the two of you, from what I understand," he replied, taking Joy's hand and kissing the back of it. "You two are wonderful together." She giggled girlishly at the compliment and the kiss, and waved her hand in a humble dismissal.

"We'd better be," Frank broke in. Thirty-seven years today we've been at it. It's our anniversary. If you can't harmonize, you dematerialize, that's what I always say."

"That's so wonderful!" Tia said. "Happy Anniversary!" She glanced over at Dylan, who nodded for her to continue. "We just loved your performance too, and we both agree that you deserve the prize more than we do. You're practically icons at this place—everyone knows you."

"Consider it an anniversary present," Dylan added. "We really want you to have it."

"Oh now honey that's so sweet of you, but we don't need the money!" Joy bubbled. "We got all we need. Frank worked hard so we could have a good life, and we couldn't ask for more. You keep it. You deserve it! After all, you won fair and square."

No we didn't, Dylan thought, feeling even worse. "No, really, we insist," he said firmly.

Frank waved them off with a shake of his hand. "We wouldn't consider it for even a minute. Joy and I do this for fun, not for money.

You young people enjoy it. Have some fun; go out for a nice dinner or something."

The waitress snaked around the older couple with another round of drinks from admirers. As she reached in to place them on the table, Frank and Joy hastily shook their hands and made a quick exit.

"You folks have a really good night, now, you hear? Congratulations!" Frank called over his shoulder.

"It was so nice to meet such a lovely young couple—keep singing!" Joy chimed in as they slipped out the door.

"Well, that went well," Dylan said sarcastically. "They really are a sweet couple, though." He looked out the window and waved once more to them. "Considering they're climbing into a very flashy Mercedes right now, they probably don't need the money. But still, I can't take it. It wouldn't feel right."

Tia looked out the window and watched Frank open the door and help Joy inside before going around to the driver's seat. "Oh," she said. "That is a sweet ride. They're just adorable, aren't they?" she smiled wistfully.

"You keep the money, Tia," Dylan said. "They were right, you know. You really were brilliant up there. I'm incredibly impressed." He meant every word.

Tia blushed crimson and held her hands to her cheeks to cool her face. "Really?" she grinned, unable to believe that she'd just received a compliment on her voice from one of her favorite singers of all time. She was losing the battle with the blush, and couldn't seem to erase the smile from her face. Dylan smiled back. "Really," he said sincerely, taking her hand from her face and kissing it much as he had Joy's. Their eyes locked, and Tia felt the room start to spin in slow circles.

Just then, the mc stepped up to their table and slid into the booth beside Tia. "Hi there folks," he said in a sing-song voice. "Name's Corbin," he said, shaking their hands in turn. "Sure was a fine job you did out there tonight. It was almost like being at a real live concert or something. I tell ya, it's refreshing to actually hear some great singing. Some of the acts we get in here... well, let's just say I wish I had earplugs!"

"I can imagine," Dylan answered, smiling politely.

"So, I take care of the business end of things here, and I need to know if you want two separate checks to split the amount, or just one. And I need your last names, too. There's a little bit of paperwork to sign..."

"I don't..." Dylan began.

"Actually," Tia broke in. "We've decided that we'd like to donate the money to charity. Would you be able to make the check out directly to them?"

Corbin looked taken aback, but quickly regained his composure. "Well now, that's real generous of you. Real generous! A first, I can tell you that. Of course I can make it out to anyone you want." He tilted his head and looked at them with mock innocence. "I can tell you how to spell my name, if you want. I could use some charity!" He winked a smile in Tia's direction. "Kidding, kidding," he said, laughing at his own joke. "I'd be proud to do it." He pulled his pen from his shirt pocket and opened his small notebook. "Just spell it out for me, so's I can be sure I get it right."

"It's called Diligence, but not the way it sounds. D-Y-L-A-G-E-N-T-S," she spelled.

Dylan looked at her across the table, eyes wide, and an awestruck look on his face.

"I ain't heard of that one," Corbin said. "What do they do?"

"It's a children's charity," Tia answered. "They do kind of a 'making dreams come true' thing for kids with leukemia."

"Well, that sounds like a fine organization. I'll go take care of that in the back, and be right back with your check." He slid out of the booth and through a door that led to the back of the club.

"You..." Dylan began, but for the first time in a very long time, he was unable to find his voice.

"What?" Tia smiled. "I told you I was a fan. I've supported your charity too. You do good work, and you get personally involved—I like that. I've seen pictures of you visiting some of those kids in the hospital. You make a difference in their lives and I really respect that. A lot." She lowered her voice, and impulsively took his right hand in hers, tracing the outline of the tattoo with her finger. "You know this was what gave you away in the end, right? I was pretty sure, but not positive it was you until I saw it. It's the Chinese symbol for younger sister, and I know your sister lost her battle with leukemia, and that the tattoo and the charity are for her." She dropped her voice to a whisper. "I'm really sorry."

He wrapped his fingers around hers and squeezed. "Oh my God. Are you real?"

Tia smiled. "I've been asking myself the same thing about you all night. Me, I'm about as real as they come. But tonight, with you—I hope you're not offended, but you seem pretty real too. Way more real than I would have imagined an international superstar and," she added a British accent to her voice, "'Sexiest Man on Earth as voted by *Person to Person* readers' to be."

"Oh, that," he smiled, taking back his hand, waving it in exaggerated dismissal and finally finding his voice again. Who is this woman, he thought, and where has she been all my life? She knew who he was, knew about his charity, his life—because she'd read about him. And still she'd been treating him like a normal guy. Suddenly he wanted to know a lot more about her.

"Yeah, well, it was kind of hard to miss. That cover was staring me in the face every time I went to the grocery store, the book store, even the hardware store."

"And did you buy the issue?" he asked secretively, tilting his head to the side and looking up at her coyly.

"I confess," she raised her hands in the air in surrender. "I did. I almost never buy those things, actually—they're so full of crap most of the time. Sometimes I pick one up when I need some frivolous reading, like when I'm going on a flight or something—it helps to absorb the mind-numbing boredom of sitting in an airport." She dropped her eyes and the corners of her lips turned up ever so slightly. "But I bought that one, yes." Dylan couldn't hide his sly smile.

Corbin returned to their table with a check, and slid once more into their booth, much to Dylan's dismay. This woman was fascinating him, and he wanted to get to know her without the constant interruptions.

"Now missy, check to see that I spelled the name of that place right, will you? And you need to sign here that you received it, and you'll get a copy, but you won't have to pay taxes on it or anything, since you're giving it all to charity." Tia took the check, and Dylan signed the paper. "I sincerely hope we'll see the two of you out here again. You could be quite a draw for our little hole-in-the-wall!"

"Thanks Corbin," Dylan said cordially, shaking his hand. "It was a pleasure to meet you and to perform here. If we're in the area again, we'll be sure to stop in."

Corbin looked pleased, and smiled large, showing a couple gaps where teeth used to be. "Well I'd like that! Can I persuade you to maybe do an encore? I'm sure the crowd would appreciate it."

"We'd like to, but I'm afraid we have to be going. Rain check?"

"You bet! Anytime. Y'all take care now." Corbin took his leave, asking for one more round of applause for the winners, and announcing that they'd donated their winnings to a charity that "helps sick kids."

The applause grew even louder, forcing the pair to stand for yet another bow.

"Ready to get out of here?" Dylan asked.

Tia's heart dropped a couple inches in her chest. Her original plan for the evening had been to stay out for a couple hours and she'd already well exceeded that, but she hadn't even imagined that she could actually have fun tonight, or that she'd meet someone like Dylan. She liked him—he was an incredibly nice guy. Part of her was amazed that he was so down-to-earth; he wasn't snobby or pretentious like she'd imagined a celebrity to be. Most of all, she was amazed that she was having such a good time. She liked the feeling; had missed it terribly. She felt comfortable with Dylan, and their conversation was going better than she'd expected. To say she was disappointed that her time with him was coming to an end already would be a huge understatement, but it was his call. "Sure," she replied softly.

They made their way to the door and stepped out into the cool May night. "Let's walk," Dylan suggested.

He took her hand casually, intertwining their fingers, and Tia's breath caught in her chest. Incredible how it felt, just that, the feeling of someone's hand wrapped up around her own, and it made her stomach roll in delicious little swirls. He had big hands, with calloused fingers from so many years of playing guitar. The rough pads of his fingertips caressed the back of her hand as they made their way down the street.

"So tell me," Dylan asked, "what is it you do, Tia, when you aren't getting moonshine cowboys all hot and bothered in dive bars?"

Tia had to laugh. "Well, that is my primary occupation," she teased back, "but my hobby is teaching—I teach fifth grade."

"Really?" he said. "A very noble profession. Do you like it?"

"I love it," she answered sincerely. "The kids are great, and I love the people I work with." She smiled to herself, thinking of Lilly. "There's a girl I work with, Lilly, who's our secretary. I just love her to death—she's the best person—and she is so in love with you." Dylan looked at her with one eyebrow raised. "She calls you her 'real husband.'"

"Does she now?" he asked, obviously amused.

"She'll be at Sunday's show, I think," she said. "We'll be comparing notes on Tuesday."

"That's right, Memorial Day weekend, huh?"

"Yeah, my job has some perks too. Summers off, breaks during the year...it's not a bad gig."

Dylan stroked the soft hand that he cradled in his own. It had just felt natural to reach for her, and he was completely comfortable walking with her hand in hand. In his mind, however, he fought to keep his thoughts focused. It wasn't an easy task. She was pretty amazing, this woman. He'd just met her, but already he was feeling things he hadn't felt in a long time. He'd dated Hollywood A-listers, top models, sports stars; and none of them had ever had the effect on him that this woman was having in just a few short hours. Maybe that was it. Although he found it hard to believe that his famous girlfriends, the ones who had it all, wanted more from him than this woman he'd picked up in a crappy bar, he thought that it just might be true. He'd been used and abused by celebrities, and he was long past being naïve about the dangers of entering into any sort of relationship. But Tia was so real, and natural, and fun; and she honestly seemed to like him for who he was, not *who he was*. It elated him and scared the hell out of him at the same time.

Chapter 6

Tia stiffened when she realized they were approaching the pub. She'd been so wrapped up in Dylan—literally and figuratively—as they talked that she'd paid no attention to where they were going. Once she saw where they were headed she hoped to guide him right past the door, and hoped that no one she knew would come out while she was strolling past. The memorial would be in full swing by now, and she didn't know how she'd explain her reluctance to join the gathering to either Dylan or her old friends. She tried to keep the conversation light, and to keep him walking, but to her horror, Dylan started heading for the entrance. "Let's check this place out, then. This is the place you said was pretty decent, right? *Paddy's*?"

Tia's knees suddenly went weak and she felt her stomach sink like a rock. She opened her mouth to speak, but found she'd suddenly lost the power of speech. She was powerless as he put a hand on her lower back and eased her toward the entrance. As he opened the door, she croaked out an inaudible "I don't know..." but by then it was already too late, and she'd have no choice but to face the music. Who was she kidding, anyway? She wasn't some Hollywood diva who dated guys like Dylan Miller. This was her reality and she couldn't hide from it; not for long. One night out with a celebrity didn't change who she was or what she'd been through. Dylan would find out more than he ever wanted to know about her now, and no doubt he'd go running for the hills once he found out the real reason they ran into each other tonight. Who wanted to deal with that kind of baggage? She certainly didn't want to deal with it, and it was her cross to bear. Her heart started pounding as she stepped into the pub and the familiar sounds and smells of the place wafted over her. *Paddy's* had pretty much been her second home for five years, but it had been twelve full months since she'd stepped through its huge wooden doors, and part of her feared that she'd no longer be welcome.

"Dylan, I..." she began, feeling slightly woozy.

He turned to look at her and saw that the color had drained out of her face. "Are you OK?" he asked, his voice filled with concern.

"It's just that...I know a lot of people here. Probably all of them."

"Is that a problem?"

"Well...I really should explain..."

But that wasn't going to happen. They hadn't taken two steps into the pub before Siobhan saw her and came running to her side.

"Oh Tia! I just knew you would come. I'm so glad you came!" The large red haired woman pulled her into a bear hug and swayed with her slowly back and forth. Tia's heart lifted immediately in the warm embrace and she sighed into the woman, returning the affection and breaking into a relieved smile. She could actually feel the blood rushing back to her face. The woman pulled back and held her at arm's length, looking her up and down. "You look good, sweetheart," she said, planting a kiss on Tia's cheek. "Everyone's been asking about you. I told them that you would make it if you felt you could, but in my heart, I knew you wouldn't miss it. Oh, do come and say hello to Paddy; he'll be so glad to see you! He's tending, of course—you think the man would let anyone else work tonight?" she said sarcastically. Her voice dropped to a whisper and she leaned against Tia. "Nick is here with us tonight too sweetheart, I can feel him everywhere. He's at peace, you know, and you should be too."

Dylan watched the exchange with curiosity. As he followed the women toward the bar, he quickly observed that this was no ordinary evening at the pub. The entryway was set up like a shrine; a small table was set up and it was covered with flowers, full bottles of beer, guitar picks and handwritten notes, most of which read, "RIP" or "We miss you, Nick." There were pictures hanging on the walls around the table of a young man who had apparently passed away—this was obviously a memorial of some sort for him. When he took a few steps into the pub, he noticed some of the patrons wore t-shirts with the man's photo emblazoned on the front with RIP printed beneath the likeness. He suddenly felt like an intruder; he knew he didn't belong here, but it sure looked like Tia did. He watched as the bartender, a friendly-looking and obviously Irish man came from behind the bar to envelope her in a familiar hug. She must have known this Nick. Was that the reason she was looking for solitude tonight? It would certainly explain why she looked like she was about to faint when they first walked in here.

He glanced around the homey little pub and watched as the patrons rushed over to greet Tia with obvious affection. There were lots of hugs, and soon it seemed that everyone in the place had left their tables or their pool games to come over and welcome her warmly. In his mind, subtle clues started connecting. Was this the pub where she performed his songs? Was Nick the guitar player she mentioned? And had it been his imagination, or had one of her references to singing been made in the past tense? Could that be the reason she hadn't sung in front of a crowd in a long time?

He wondered if he should just sneak out right now, and leave Tia to her friends. She was at home here, in the hands of people who obviously loved her. He was pretty confident that there weren't any Buds in this place tonight, and that she'd get home safely. She didn't need him tagging along at an event that was obviously very personal to her, although he wondered why she hadn't been here in the first place and had all but passed out when he suggested they come in. *She's a mystery wrapped in an enigma*, he thought, and his curiosity piqued even more.

But, if he left now, he'd likely never see her again. He didn't know her last name, her phone number, and if he just slipped out, the only connection he'd have with her would be a song dedication at tomorrow night's concert. Most of the time they'd spent together so far had been chaotic, and they hadn't really had much of an opportunity to get to know each other on a personal level. He realized he wanted to know more—their conversation thus far had been so easy and natural, and they'd already shared a couple of very unique experiences—the kinds of experiences that bonded people. They hadn't had many chances to just talk—their first initial encounter had been intense, and the karaoke bar was loud and not conducive to conversation. They were involved in the competition, of course, and it seemed like someone was stopping by their table every couple minutes. Easily, he decided that wasn't enough—he was enjoying her company more than he thought possible, and wanted more of it.

Maybe he'd go hang around outside, give her a chance to catch up with the friends who were still queuing up to grab some of her attention, and then come back in to have a moment with her before making his exit. He could get her number and call her tomorrow, he thought. He was turning to do just that when a big meaty hand landed firmly on his shoulder. When he turned, he looked into the open and friendly face of the man who'd been behind the bar.

"Welcome, stranger! Name's Paddy, Paddy Shaugnessy," he said enthusiastically, gripping Dylan's hand in a firm and friendly handshake.

"I'm Dylan. It's a pleasure."

"Listen, I'm sorry for stealin' Tia away from ya like that when ya just walked in and all, but she's like part of the family and we haven't seen her in a while, ya know?" His voice contained just enough Irish lilt to let you know he was from the old country.

"That's OK. I can see that she's got a lot of friends here."

"Ah, that she does, that she does. She doesn't always know it, but we love her like one of our own."

"I'm...uh...sorry about Nick."

Paddy looked down and shook his head slowly. "He was such a good lad. A huge loss—to all of us." He dropped his shoulders as his mind wandered for just a moment. "I can't believe he's been gone a year. Sometimes it seems like just yesterday he was sittin' right here on this stage, and sometimes I can't seem to pull up his face from my memory. But," he said with a thoughtful smile, patting Dylan on the back as if they were long-time friends, "tonight is not about mournin'. Tonight is a celebration of his life, and I'm so glad you could join us for it."

"Actually," Dylan said, "I was thinking that maybe I shouldn't stay. I'm sure Tia doesn't need me hanging around such a..."

Just then, a good-looking guy with jet black hair and light eyes jumped onto the bar and called the place to attention in a raucous voice. "HERE HERE!!" he cried, to which the crowd replied "WHERE'S HERE?" They raised their glasses in unison, and waited for the toast.

"We are now as complete as we can be," he said happily, "because we have our family together. Tia, I'm so glad to see you back among the living!" Again, cheers from the crowd. "We've missed you something awful, and let me just say, right off, that we forgive you for all the things going through your little head that you think we're mad about. You will always be part of us—time and distance won't do anything to change that! TO TIA!"

"TO TIA!"

Watching the exchange and the glow that had returned to Tia's face, Dylan barely noticed that Paddy had left his side. The man was quick, Dylan thought, because before the glasses were raised and the final toast to Tia called, Paddy had pressed a perfectly poured; ice cold Guinness into his hands. He raised the glass with the rest of them, and felt even more intrigued by this mysterious woman, who was obviously loved by all these people.

"Now about your leavin'," Paddy said, his arm around Dylan's shoulder, "I won't hear of it. Any friend of Tia's is a friend of ours. And I owe you, my new friend Dylan. I didn't think she'd show tonight, and I was afraid she'd be sorry later if she didn't. I want to thank you for bringing her here, for looking after her, and for bringing the happy back into her face. She looks real good, doesn't she?"

Dylan looked over at Tia and saw her laughing with a group of girls. "She certainly does," he answered without taking his eyes off her.

Tia's eyes spanned the room and she noticed Dylan standing with Paddy and broke away from the group. As she made her way to him, she felt lighter and happier than she had in a long time. She was already glad that she came. Instead of the sad memorial atmosphere she expected, it was a happy feeling, an air of peace and acceptance. These people wouldn't show her pity, she should have known that from the start. They were mourning just as much as she was; or nearly as much at least, and despite the fact that she'd virtually ignored them all for the past year, they welcomed her back into the fold with open arms. This was shaping up to be an incredible evening—much more than she could ever have dared to hope for. Even Dylan looked at ease, sipping a Guinness with Paddy and smiling at her as she made her way toward him. She figured she'd explain the situation, and let him make up his own mind about leaving or hanging around. She felt as if she was ready to talk about it here, now, with all the support of her friends behind her, and she owed him at least that much. He had to be a little freaked out right now, she figured.

"I see you've met the crazy Irishman," she giggled.

"Crazy, yes," Paddy agreed. "That's why I got to make sure ta take me medicine," he replied with a healthy dose of brogue, lifting his mug into the air to toast again with Dylan. "I've met your young man here, too. He seems like a passable fellow," he winked in Dylan's direction. "I'll have to see how he holds his liquor before I pass final judgment, however! Join me, Master Dylan, won't you, for a wee shot of the nectar of the gods?"

Dylan looked over his shoulder as Paddy led him to the bar, and shrugged at Tia. "Aren't you joining us?"

She smiled, and it lit up her entire face. At that moment, he saw something in her eyes that he wanted to see again and again, because it was so pure and honest. "Wouldn't miss it," she answered happily, stepping between the boys and linking her arms through theirs. "Are you pulling out the good stuff? None of that watered down crap you usually serve up."

"Now, now, I won't be takin' any of your lip, lassy," he teased as he bent down and planted a big kiss on her cheek. "But I am downright beside myself to see that you've got it back!"

He reached into a lower cabinet and pulled out a bottle of Tullamore Dew. "He brought that one back with him from his last trip to

Ireland," she whispered to Dylan. "You must have made quite an impression; he doesn't pull that out for just anyone."

"You're the one who made the impression," he whispered back, "I'm just along for the ride."

He smiled again, and accepted the drink in a pewter shot glass. They raised their shots in the air and Paddy gave the toast, "May you have warm words on a cold evening, a full moon on a dark night, and a smooth road all the way to your door. Slainte!" They downed their drinks in traditional Irish style, in one quick swallow, and slammed the glasses down on the bar top. "Now you're official, young man. Welcome to *Paddy's*!" He gave Dylan a serious slap on the back, and shook his hand enthusiastically.

"Wow, that's good!" Dylan enthused, picking up the shot glass again and tipping it over his mouth in case a few drops had collected at the bottom of the glass.

"It's me all-time favorite, and our traditional Irish friendship drink here at *Paddy's*," he said, pouring him a second shot. "Better sip that one though," he warned, "it's powerful stuff!"

Dylan heeded his advice, and took the second one slowly, knowing that it was the man's special bottle, and suspecting that he'd gladly continue to share as long as Dylan continued to drink. He seemed like an honestly good guy, Dylan thought, and probably generous to a fault. Maybe he'd pick him up a fresh bottle when he was in Ireland this summer, he pondered, and then stopped himself. What was he thinking? He felt welcome here; no doubt about it; but it wasn't like he was ever going to be a regular. Still, they were obviously good people. He could always get the address of the place and send him a bottle or two, just to say thanks for making him feel welcome.

Just as he registered the thought, Tia's friends started wandering over in groups and Dylan was engulfed in a dizzying sea of names and faces as she made introductions. There were warm open smiles, handshakes and hugs, and many offers to buy him a pint. It seemed they all wanted him and Tia to join them at their tables and by the time he'd gotten through meeting them all, he felt like a welcome part of the group. This was turning out to be a pretty damn fine night, and he was really glad that Paddy had asked him to stay. Everyone had kind words to say to and about Tia, and they were all thanking him for bringing her tonight. Although it had been a complete accident on his part, he was still glad he had a hand in it. Her face had gone from pretty to beautiful the moment they'd walked in, and he was pleased to have played a small part in making it happen.

Dylan asked Paddy over the bar, "Do you have more of that Dew stuff? The regular kind?"

"Well of course I do, it's an Irish pub, isn't it?"

"And you said that it was the traditional Irish friendship drink here, right?"

"Indeed it is," he agreed, "but for new friends such as yourself, I'm proud to share a wee bit more of me special blend!"

Dylan put his palm over his shot glass before Paddy could pour more into it. "I appreciate that, Paddy, and appreciate the welcome I've gotten here even more. I'm obviously an outsider; I didn't know Nick; but this is a great bunch of people here, and I'm so glad Tia has people like you in her life. I'd like to buy a round for the house." He watched Paddy open his mouth and look around the room. There had to be sixty or more people drifting about, and it was an expensive proposition.

"Well, that's a mighty generous offer, Dylan," he said, "but that's a lot of shots we're talkin' about here. You go offerin' that up, and I don't see anyone who's going to take a pass."

"I hope they don't," Dylan replied. "Do you have enough? What do you think we'd need, five or six bottles?"

"Again," he said with a sly smile, "I'd like to point out to ye that it's an Irish pub. We always have plenty of whiskey on hand. But are you sure you want to do that?"

"Positive," he said, adding, "but it's just between you and me who's buying, OK? Just pass them out and make a toast—say they're on the house."

He nodded, smiling, and headed for the back room of the pub. Dylan had barely turned back to the bar when Paddy leaped onto the stage and spoke into the mike.

"My dear friends!" he exclaimed, the crowd quieting immediately and turning toward him. "It's not often that a person with any smarts offers to help ye along the way to your drinkin', but I just know this guy's got smarts, cause he came here with Tia! And her new friend—*our* new friend Master Dylan, is buying a round of Tully for the house!"

Oh shit, Dylan thought, but then everyone rose to their feet and held up glasses in his direction and yelled, "Slainte!" to which he had no choice but to smile and raise his own glass.

Siobhan immediately started pouring into a line of shot glasses set up along the length of the bar and Paddy returned with more bottles, efficiently placing the shots on large trays that were quickly distributed. Once everyone had a drink in their hands, they looked to Dylan to make the toast. Hesitantly, he stepped up to the mike, while Tia smiled encouragingly. Dylan was making one hell of an impression and she couldn't be happier—she was again amazed at what a great guy he was.

"I, ah, know I just met you all tonight, but even though I'm an intruder on your private celebration, you've made me feel incredibly welcome and for that, I thank you. But this night is for Nick, and although I never knew him, I know he must have been a hellova guy to have all of you for friends. So, here's to Nick."

"TO NICK!" the group answered back before tossing their shots and slamming their glasses onto their tables in unison.

Tia was visibly moved as she made her way over to Dylan. "That was an incredibly nice thing you just did," she choked.

"Well, it wasn't exactly the way I planned it—I told Paddy to say they were on the house; I just wanted to buy a drink for your friends. They seem really cool."

"They are." She dropped her eyes, and pulled Dylan off to the side to get a little bit of privacy. "Listen, Dylan," she said. "I know this is not at all what you had in mind when you said you wanted a little anonymity."

"Definitely not what I expected, that's for sure," he agreed.

She sighed. "There's so much I could explain to you, but I don't even know if I should. I've got a long sad story, and you didn't sign up for any of this." Dylan looked at her, confused, but he let her continue. "If you want to leave before you get tangled in a crazy web, I would understand."

"Do you want me to leave?" he asked, letting the decision be hers.

"No. I *definitely* don't want you to leave. But..."

"Then I'm staying," he said. "This is the most fun I've had in a long time, and I still don't know anything about you. I'd like to hear your story."

Tia smiled thinly. "You might be sorry you asked after you've heard it, but maybe we could find a quiet table and..."

They were interrupted by a line of people coming up to shake Dylan's hand and thank him for the drinks. She made introductions again, and Dylan was again dizzied by the array of names and faces passing before him. Finally, the guy who'd made the first toast to Tia made his way over and wrapped her in a protective embrace.

"I'm so glad you're here, sweetheart," he said to her. "Are you going to introduce me to your guest?" Tia smiled and squeezed him back.

"Sean, this is Dylan. Dylan, Sean. Typical obnoxious Irishman, but generally a great guy."

The two men shook hands. "Nice to meet you," Dylan said.

"That was a straight up thing you did there. A round for the house! Very cool. Thanks, man."

"My pleasure," Dylan said, "Although I didn't want Paddy to make a federal case of it. I just wanted him to pass them around."

Sean smiled, "Yeah, well that's Uncle Paddy for you. Even if the shots had been on him, he'd try to give someone else the credit. The man's just way too humble, if you ask me."

"Paddy's your uncle?" Dylan asked.

"Yeah, and Nick was my cousin."

Dylan held his hand out again to shake Sean's. "Wow, I'm really sorry about your loss," he said sincerely.

"We all are," he said, looking at Tia. "Thanks. But hey, we're not here to feel sorry for ourselves tonight—he'd hate it if we did that."

Dylan nodded. "I understand."

"Hey, you throw darts at all?" Sean continued. "A couple of us are getting up a game, and I could use a partner. You in? The next drink's on me."

He threw a look at Tia who shrugged and tossed one back that said, *"You're on your own."* Dylan contemplated the offer for just a moment, his lips turning down and his head nodding slightly. This was turning into an even better night than he thought it could be. All of a sudden he was just one of the guys, and he relished the thought of just blending in. "How could I say no to that?" he replied, and smiled at her. "We'll have that talk a little later?" he said as he walked off to join the guys gathered around the dartboard, dropping quarters onto the top of the machine. Tia nodded, thrilled that there was going to be a 'later,' and went and joined a table full of girls, where she was quickly handed another Guinness.

The other two dart players greeted him like an old friend, and extended their enthusiastic thanks for his round as well. It wasn't what he intended, but now each of them was pledging to buy his next drink. He met Dave and Tim, and they settled up into two teams and started a game of 501. Dylan was nervous—not about playing darts; when you spent a good chunk of your life on the road, you found ways to entertain yourself. They had a little electronic dart board they always kept on the bus, and he could throw with the best of them. He worried about where the conversation with the guys would lead. He figured they'd be curious about him, and was working on a story that wouldn't be a lie, but wouldn't be the whole truth, either. For Tia's sake, he didn't want to say they'd just met a few hours ago at little dump, or that she was only here accidentally because of him and had had no intention of coming here tonight. It was obvious that they were glad she showed up, and even more obvious that she was where she needed to be. Selfishly, he was hoping to learn a little bit more about her from her friends, but he didn't want it to look like he didn't know anything, which was pretty close to the truth.

Aside from that, it felt weird being so comfortable in the company of others. He looked across the room and saw Tia sitting with a group of girls. She looked so comfortable and happy here. He was glad they came.

"So, Dylan, I haven't seen you around before. Do you live around here?" Sean asked casually.

Here we go, Dylan thought. *Showtime.* "I'm actually here on business," he said. "My main base is in Colorado, but I come to Chicago as often as I can. I love this city."

"Colorado, huh? What part?"

"I'm about an hour and a half outside of Denver."

"I love Colorado," Sean said. "I get out there at least once a year, to ski or hike. It's a gorgeous place."

"I agree. You ever ski Copper Mountain?"

"Oh man, that's my favorite place to go! Vail is so overrated," Sean said.

"And overpriced," Dylan agreed.

"You ski there a lot?" Sean asked.

"Every chance I get."

"Maybe I've seen you there before or something—you look kind of familiar to me."

"That's a possibility," Dylan said, adding, "I thought the same thing about you." He pushed the glasses up and tipped his head down to get more shadow on his face. Being recognized would put an unwanted twist on the evening; that was certain. He raised his glass and drank, to further hide his features. Thankfully, Sean seemed to accept a possible chance encounter on the mountain, and moved on.

"So how often do you get out to Chicago?"

"Never often enough, that's for sure."

"I hear that, brother." Sean had to get up to take his turn, and Dylan breathed a small sigh of relief. So far so good, but this could get tough. He and Tia obviously hadn't come up with any matching stories ahead of time, and he was confident that she wasn't going to give away his identity, so he had to stick as closely as he could to the truth so she wouldn't unknowingly dispute anything he'd said. He'd try to turn the conversation in a different direction, and hopefully learn something about Tia in the process.

Sean returned after hitting a trip twenty and two eighteens.

"Nice shot," Dylan said admiringly.

"Thanks man. So, what do you do?"

Dylan tried to sound casual, and to be vague. "I work in the entertainment industry mostly, on the business end." He was on the business end of the industry alright.

"Yeah? That sounds interesting, what kind of entertainment?"

"Different stuff, you know, music, film, awards shows; things like that." He hoped Sean wouldn't ask for specifics.

"That sounds pretty cool. Do you like it?"

"Mostly, I love it, but I have to travel a lot, so I don't get to be home much. That part sucks."

"I can imagine," Sean replied.

Thankfully, it was Dylan's turn to throw. He stood and took aim, and hit the bull on his first shot. "Yeah, that's what I'm talking about!" Sean exclaimed, high-fiving him. His next shot hit double seventeen, and then he nailed another bull.

"Damn, I picked the right man for my team!" he said, taunting Dave and Tim, who were now more than a little behind.

"Always glad to help out," he said modestly, but with a sheepish grin on his face. Sean turned to him again.

"Listen, you seem like a stand-up guy..."

Oh crap, Dylan thought, *here it comes.*

"I just want to get this out there right away. Nothing personal or anything."

"Shoot," Dylan replied, casually taking a sip of his beer.

"Tia's like a little sister to me," he began.

Dylan exhaled a breath he didn't know he'd been holding. He was afraid that Sean was going to tell him that he and Tia were an item, or had been, and tell him to keep his distance.

Dave added, "She's like a sister to all of us." Tim nodded his agreement as well.

"We just really care about her and all. I just want you to know we've always got her back."

"I can see that. She's lucky to have you."

"We're lucky to have her. She's pretty amazing."

Dylan nodded. "I agree."

"I don't know what's going on between the two of you—if you're just friends or more than that—and it's none of my business," he said, holding up his hands in surrender. "I'm just saying that I couldn't stand to see her hurt again, and I hope that you'll keep her best interests at heart."

Hurt again? Dylan thought. He felt bad knowing she'd been hurt, and the way Sean said it, it sounded like it was a guy who'd hurt her. But since he didn't know anything about her personal life, he couldn't really ask for more details. "You got no worries there," he answered honestly. They didn't know each other well enough to cause the other pain.

"Glad to hear it," he answered sincerely, patting Dylan on the back. "But if you don't mind my asking—and you can tell me shut the hell up if you want to—how do you feel about Tia?"

Dylan looked across the room and saw her sitting with a group of girls at a round table. As if she knew he was looking at her, she turned and met his eyes and sent him a smile that set his heart to beating a strange rhythm. Returning the smile and without taking his eyes off her he said the first thing that came to his mind and no one was more surprised than he when the words rolled out. "I think I could get lost in her, man."

Sean slapped him on the back. "She has that effect on people, doesn't she?"

"She certainly does on me." The simple truth of the statement was like a smack on the head.

Dylan closed out the game with a trip 20 and an 11, much to Sean's delight. In that short time, it was like Dylan had made three new friends. They laughed and joked around, and the talk didn't come back around to him and why he was here or what he did for a living. He didn't get any information about Tia, though, either, so when they asked him for another game; he politely bowed out, saying that he wanted to spend some time with her. They let him off the hook easily, but not before they extended him an invitation to their weekly Tuesday night poker game. "We play every Tuesday, and switch off houses. The host buys the beers and everyone brings junk food. You're welcome anytime—even this Tuesday, if you want," Sean added.

"I'd love to, absolutely, but I'll have to take a rain check," he said. "I'm going to be out of town on Tuesday." *Playing a concert in Cleveland.* "I'll definitely keep it in mind, though. I'd love to get in on that."

"Rain check, absolutely. Tia can always find out who's hosting." He jumped up from the table. "Well, ladies, I'd love to stay and shoot the shit, but I think it's almost time for me to take the stage. Gotta set up some of the equipment."

"Are you playing tonight?"

"Yeah. Some of Nick's favorites and some of the stuff we used to play together."

"Tia was telling me she sang with you sometimes." Finally he could make a comment that eluded to him knowing her more than a few hours.

"Yeah. She's got some pretty tight vocals. I would have asked her sing with me tonight, but I really didn't think she was coming. I got Danny on backup." He nodded over his shoulder to a dark-haired guy messing with some wires on the stage; hooking up amps. "Anyway, the offer for the poker game stands. Hope to see you there sometime."

They shook hands again. "Thanks for making me feel so welcome."

Sean shrugged it off. "If Tia likes you, you must be a good guy." He headed for the stage, and Dylan set off to collect Tia, and to hear her story.

Chapter 7

They finally made their way to a corner table, and everyone seemed to respect that they wanted to be alone. Dylan pulled her chair out for her before sitting down across the small table.

"Finally," he said. "I was wondering when I was going to get to talk to you again." He smiled at her warmly. "You seem so happy here. These are really nice people, and they obviously all love you. They've been vying for your attention all night."

"Well you've certainly made a good impression on them. You wouldn't believe the comments from the girls. They all give their approval, by the way, but they insist I get you to cut your hair," she smirked.

"Well, mullet or not, I'll have you know that I have a standing invitation to the Tuesday night poker game," he said slyly.

"You mean the Tuesday night drinking fest?" she said sarcastically. "I don't think any of them even owns a deck of cards."

"Yeah, but I'm still invited. Too bad—it would probably be fun. You know, it's been pretty awesome just being one of the guys tonight. I can't even remember the last time I felt like I fit in at a place like this." A shadow covered his eyes, and he looked at her intently. "But you didn't want to come in here at first—actually you looked like you were going to pass out when we walked in the door. What was it, Tia?"

She looked down at the table and started wringing her hands nervously. "I really do owe you an explanation, Dylan. It's just that tonight, with you...it wasn't supposed to happen..."

"I don't know what you mean."

"God," she sighed. "You've been so incredibly nice to me tonight. You've given me exactly what I needed to get through what I thought it would take months to accomplish. Once again, you've come to my rescue; this time just by being yourself."

He shrugged. "Now you've really lost me."

She took a long deep breath. "Just give me a minute to explain, then if you want to run away and pretend like this night never happened, I'll understand completely and try not to hold it against you."

He opened his mouth to protest, but she held up her hand, and continued.

"Nick—he wasn't just some guy...he was my fiancé. We were supposed to be married last June."

"Holy shit." The pieces of the puzzle started falling into place, and Dylan could finally start to see the big picture.

"We dated for over five years," she continued. "Nick was an engineer." She drew a long breath and her eyes wandered over his shoulder for a moment before she continued. "He was supervising at a job site, and there was this crane hoisting some big heavy beam, and the cable snapped...he was killed instantly."

"Oh, Tia," he said softly.

"Tonight is the one year anniversary of his death."

"I'm so sorry..." He reached across the table and cradled her hand in his.

"Thanks," she choked for a moment, but quickly regained her composure. This night had been spectacular, and she was glad that she'd come and laid the last of her fears about Nick to rest. She could honestly envision being able to go on with her life now, keeping him close as a warm and beautiful memory.

"But it's OK, see?" she continued. "That's what tonight was about for me. I spent the past year completely shutting myself off from the world—I spent the entire summer—I have summers off, remember—hardly ever leaving the house.

Fuck, he thought, doing the math. *He died a month before their wedding*. He squeezed her hand tighter, and found her eyes. She smiled thinly, and continued.

"When fall came, I got up and went to work; forced myself through the motions. My best friend Lexi pulled me out to the country club—tried to get me back among the living. She included me in everything, and I felt like the eternal third wheel between her and her boyfriend. Again, I went through the motions, but I was always pretending to have fun, so she wouldn't worry so much about me. But when I was alone, which I tried to be as much as possible, it was your music that slowly brought me back. I'd listen to you constantly, loving the soothing sound of your voice and the way your words told me exactly what I needed to hear.

"In the beginning, it was mostly the sad ones, and the ones that Nick and I listened to together. And of course the ones he played on the guitar and sang with me. But in the past few months, it was especially your song, *I'll Pull You Up*. I know the old cliché; that it was like you were singing right to me, but that's exactly what it was like. I *felt* your words, and Nick was there pulling me up; or trying to, anyway. Those lyrics were always just what I needed to face the next task, to put on a normal face and deal with the outside world. *'When the skies are gray and stormy, I'll pull you through the clouds, so you can see the sun's still shining, above the earth's dark shroud...'* I can't tell you how many times those words got me out of bed in the mornings. And the last line—*'I can't take this journey, and that we've always known, but in my heart I know you have the strength to get there on your own?* That was the one that finally got me living again."

He pressed her fingers to his lips and felt his heart go out to her. He knew the feeling of hopelessness when someone you loved was taken from you; knew the grief and how long and hard it was to heal; to wonder why you still deserved to be living when someone you loved couldn't. He tried to convey that with his eyes, his touch; because he knew it was hard for her to continue. She took a few deep breaths before going on.

"So tonight was about me joining the world again," she continued. "I had done my mourning; probably way more than I should have, and I knew Nick would be really pissed that I'd taken so much time. He would have wanted me to go on, and to be happy. I chose this night as my 'getting back into the world' night. I thought I needed to do it on my own, and I didn't know where to start." She looked straight into his eyes. "I'm a complete mess, Dylan. I don't know how to date anymore, or how to flirt, and I feel so far removed from the single life—I don't know what people do anymore. So I wanted to be a fly on the wall, to watch people, to see how they reacted to each other. I wanted to be far from my usual hang-outs so I wouldn't run into anyone I knew—I didn't want to be social, I just wanted to be *part* of something social, do you know what I mean?"

Dylan nodded and squeezed her hand to show he understood, his eyes never leaving hers. He knew exactly what she meant—it was precisely what he himself had been after tonight.

"I was afraid to come here—to be with all the other people who loved Nick. I was afraid it would make me feel sad again, make me feel the hole where he used to be, and make me forget to move on. I wouldn't have come if it weren't for you, and I would have regretted it so much tomorrow if I had missed it; if I'd let these people down. So, once again, you saved me. That makes three times now."

"You saved yourself, Tia. It was always you. You are strong; I can see that in you. And I do know what you're going through. You lose a part of yourself when you lose someone you love. It must have been horrible for you, this past year."

"So many parts of it seem like they never even happened. I spent a lot of time in a fog, feeling sorry for myself, feeling guilty for still being here when he wasn't. We were a couple for so long; it was Tia and Nick, Nick and Tia, and my identity was so wrapped up in *us*, that I sort of forgot who *I* was. It took me a long time to find myself again. I actually don't think I've fully figured it out yet. Tonight was the first step on a long road.

"But coming here? It hasn't made me sad at all. I know now that I can celebrate his life without mourning his death, and I wouldn't have figured that out tonight if I hadn't come here. He helped make me the person I am today, and my life was so much better for having him in it. I can finally admit that, and I think that this was the final hurdle to really starting my life—my alone life. It's time. These people have been there for me all along, and I've spent so much energy shutting them out. Paddy and Siobhan are two of the kindest, most supportive people I've ever met, and I didn't even return their calls when they left me messages, even when they called to invite me here tonight. And still they welcomed me with open arms."

"And me. All night everyone's been telling me how happy they are that I'm here with you to help you through this, but I didn't understand, I didn't know. I wish I had, I could have done more..."

She shook her head slowly and smiled thinly. "Oh Dylan, you'll never know how much you've helped me—you couldn't have possibly done more," she said, meeting his eyes. "It's funny you know, you're supposed to be a dream, a fantasy, a voice on my iPod. And here you are, the famous Dylan Miller, helping me through yet another difficult time in my life." Dylan smiled warmly and laced his fingers through hers. Tia continued, "When I look at you, though, that's not what I see. I don't know if it's the bizarre circumstances under which we met, or maybe the mullet,"—he flashed a smile—"but when I look at you, I just see a really awesome guy who saved a damsel in distress and turned what she thought was going to be a painful and short evening into the best night she's had in a very, very long time. I don't know how I can ever thank you for that, but you can bet I'll remember this night for the rest of my life."

"I don't think I'll ever forget it either," he said, meaning every word.

"So this is the part where you tell me if you want to get the hell out of here—forget you ever met me and my problems."

He brought her hand once more to his lips and rested them there while holding her gaze. "I'm not going anywhere."

"I'm glad," she smiled.

He started to say more, but before he could begin, applause and whoops of appreciation went out toward the stage. She turned toward the sound of the mike being tapped and whispered, "Uh-oh, it's time for the Sean show."

But he couldn't take his eyes off her as she turned her head toward the stage. He wanted to tell her—would tell her—that this night meant as much to him as it did to her. He had wanted a quiet night, too, an anonymous evening among everyday people. He was also uncomfortable being social, because it always meant he had to lie about what he did or worry about being recognized. She made him feel normal, just one of the guys, and he really liked the feeling. Still, after all this time, she hadn't asked anything from him except his company, and he was more than happy to give it. She was witty, smart, funny, and getting more beautiful by the minute. She wasn't trying to impress, not trying to be a Hollywood starlet, not wearing designer anything, and she was making more of an impression on him than anyone he'd met in a very long time. He slid his chair closer to hers and draped his arm around her shoulder, glad when she leaned into him and sighed softly in the back of her throat.

Sean began to speak. "Hey, y'all. I want to thank you all for coming out tonight, and for making this party exactly what Nick would want it to be—a raucous bunch of Irishmen and wanna-be Irishmen toasting to all the good things his life brought to us! We were all privileged to know him, and we're so lucky to have each other to lean on whenever things go wrong. I've said it before and I'll say it again—that Nick was a son-of-a-bitch!" The crowd voiced their agreement. "But he was OUR son-of-a-bitch, and we loved him!" Once more, the crowd agreed wholeheartedly.

"I want to thank you all for myself, and on behalf of Paddy and Siobhan, for being here for us this past year. We all knew that we could always find comfort and love here, and that together, we'd find a way to heal." Sean turned toward the bar and pressed his hands together under his chin, bowing in thanks toward their direction. Tia felt a small pang of guilt that she hadn't sought refuge here over the past year; that she had doubted that these wonderful people would have helped her through.

Sean continued enthusiastically. "Nick would have been so happy to see all the love and support in this room. We're all better people because of that crazy Irish bastard, so I'd like you now to lift your pints to one of the best sons of bitches to ever have walked this planet. To Nick!" He raised his glass in salute.

Almost a hundred glasses raised and clinked in unison. "To Nick!"

"Now, as you know, music was a big part of Nick's life. And Tia's life too—so glad you're here tonight by the way," he added, raising his glass in her direction. "And I know I've never been as good as Nick was, but the guitar has kind of been my life raft this past year, and I've actually gotten kind of decent." A few chuckles and catcalls came up from the crowd, and he waved them away with a laugh. "OK, you can be the judges. But we all know who Nick's musical hero was, right?" Again, a murmur of agreement from the group rose up. "So I want to play for you one of his favorite songs; one that really helped me—and Tia as well—through a lot this year. It's called, *I'll Pull You Up*.

Tia looked at Dylan with her palms upturned and shrugged. "I should have known," she smiled. "Well, I can't promise anything, but I hope he at least does it justice. Unless you want to take the stage?"

He took her upturned hand in his and turned it over, kissed it. "Actually, I'd rather have the dance. May I?"

She could say nothing against the lump in her throat, but nodded, rose and stepped into his arms. He circled her waist and pulled her closer. It had been so long since she had had a man's arms around her, and she realized how much she'd missed it, how much she needed it. He was tall enough that her head rested on his chest and she heard his heart beating and felt his warmth against her cheek; breathed in the masculine scent of him. The guitar sounded sweet and sad as it wound around the intro. She waited for Sean to sing the words that had meant so much to her, but instead, Dylan lowered his head to her ear and began softly singing to her. All the times she'd imagined him singing those words just to her—and here he was, swaying gently on a makeshift dance floor, holding her up as she nearly collapsed from the intimacy of it all, singing just for her, his voice soft against her ear, his breath on her face. And when he sang that final line, *I can't take you on this journey, and that we've always known, but in my heart I know you have the strength to get there on your own...*, a tear fell from her eye, and in that tear was the last sorrow for Nick, knowing that he was smiling down on her, and the first joy she'd felt in a long time, for finally finding some peace in her own heart.

Dylan held Tia against him and he was suddenly flooded with emotion. This was the second time tonight she'd thrown him completely off balance; although, if he wanted to really admit it, he'd been off balance since this mysterious woman had slipped into his life. God, was it really only six hours ago? He knew the demons she'd fought this past year—losing someone you loved was a real bitch to get over—but she'd fought back in a lot less time than it had taken him. He might not even be to the point she was yet, and it had been a lot of years since Shelby had been taken from him.

He hadn't sung Shelby's song for anyone since he recorded it, and even that had been really tough. Every time he heard the opening notes his mind brought back her tortured face as she fought against the pain of her losing battle. "It's time for me to go, Dylan," she'd whispered with a voice as light as air. "Write me a song that says goodbye." He wrestled for days, trying to come up with just the right words. Part of him thought that if he put it off, didn't finish it, she wouldn't go—wouldn't leave him without hearing her song. But as the days went by, she got weaker and weaker, and he knew that he couldn't let her go without giving her that one wish—that one song that he could sing just for her that would give her what she needed to say goodbye. When he finally got it right, finally got the best lyrics and music that his seventeen year old mind could create—words that would give her the strength to go and him the strength to go on, he sat next to her bed and played for her and in a shaky voice said goodbye. How strange, then, that as he held this woman in his arms, this woman who'd gone through the same kind of pain and somehow found a way to push through, he could feel his little sister now, encouraging him to sing it again, to let her go and leave the pain behind. Knowing that he was also helping Tia put the pain behind her gave him the courage he needed just then. He took a deep breath and sang the first words, the first notes that helped him to let go, and to his surprise, it wasn't painful at all.

It helped that the moment she'd moved into his arms and he'd encircled her, he felt something he could only describe as electricity pulsing through his entire being. It felt so comfortable, and her hair smelled so amazing, like some sort of summer day, and when she rested her head against his chest he couldn't help but pull her in closer. Tia demanded nothing from him, and yet he wanted to give her what she needed, and when he felt her relax against him, he felt a sense of accomplishment that he'd helped to make it happen.

He heard her sigh, and readjusted himself to pull her even closer. Just that, that pulling close, created more electricity that zinged through his entire body. It was as if he could feel every cell that was touching one of hers. He rested his lips on top of her head and made a decision that he knew he might regret later. Take it as it comes, it was all he could do. Might as well enjoy each other's company while they could, because he still wanted more of hers.

The song ended, and Sean broke into one of InHap's more energetic numbers. Dylan held Tia for a moment longer, and then they broke apart. He instantly felt the heat of her body leaving him, and wished for it back.

Tia looked at him and smiled, wiping a couple stray tears from her cheeks. "You sang for me," she said softly, "just for me."

"Yes," he said, reaching over and wiping away another rogue tear with the pad of his thumb, "just for you."

"But you never sing that song. Never." Her eyes were wide—she knew what the song meant to him, which made it mean that much more to her.

"It was long overdue," he said simply, taking her hands in his, "and I couldn't think of a better person to sing it for." The look on her face was so open, so honest, and so grateful, that he feared being overwhelmed himself. They stared into each other's eyes for what seemed a long time, speaking volumes without saying a word while they swayed absently to Sean's voice. Heat rose in Dylan's body, and he found he needed a minute to cool down and collect his thoughts.

He pulled out her chair for her and excused himself. "I...have to go for a minute—I'll be right back. I need to check in at the office, so to speak," he said. "My assistant has probably already filed a missing person's report; I don't usually stay out so late alone without checking in, especially the night before a show." He kissed her hands and stood up. "I'll be right back."

What the hell am I doing? he thought once the cool May air hit his burning skin. More importantly, what the hell was he feeling? He liked her, he had to admit it. In fact, if their circumstances were different, he would have already asked for another date.

But what of it? He was in town for two shows this weekend, and then they had one more week in North America before they headed out for the summer tour in Europe. After that, he was scheduled to film a movie in New Zealand—could he be any more on the other side of the world?—in September. Chances were that he wouldn't see her again for a long time, if at all, after this weekend. And where would their lives be a year from now, by the time he was finished with all that? And why the hell was he even thinking these things about a girl he just met a few hours ago?

He leaned up against the cool stone of the wall and tried to wrap his head around the situation. Take it slow, he thought, start at the beginning. It had started as an innocent night on the town, a little seclusion to get him away from the tour, and the bus, and the guys—they all needed their alone time, or they started getting on each other's nerves. He'd picked a disguise that would practically guarantee he'd be left alone, and went to a little hole-in-the-wall where he was sure no one would interest him. He was going to have one more drink and call it a night, and then Tia exploded into his world. Not at first, though, he thought, at first she'd just come to thank him, to buy him a drink and tell him how much his music meant to her. She'd left, gone back to her own little corner of the bar and tried hard to ignore his presence, presumably to give him the solitude he had come for. He knew now that she understood his need because of her own, and she was just going to let their encounter go.

But then Bud entered the picture, and he'd had to go to her rescue. She'd understood his coded message, and jumped headfirst into his game. Even then, though, he'd had the opportunity to let her go—chalk it up as an interesting experience, a great story to tell the guys, and walk away. Only he was too intrigued that she was so willing to walk away too—it bothered him, on some strange level that he couldn't quite put a finger on. He had to try and find what made her tick. But now? Now he knew without a doubt that he wanted to see her again; he wanted to make a date with her and spend more time getting to know her, even though he knew it wasn't fair to either of them.

Sean had said he didn't want to see her hurt again, that he had her back, and Dylan had assured him that he wouldn't hurt her. Seeing her again could be a huge mistake. What if they really decided they liked each other? What if he had to leave with unresolved feelings on one or both sides of the equation? He knew it would be better for both of them if they just walked away after tonight, but he still pulled out his phone and made the call that could open a door better left closed.

Tia was still trying to calm her heart when Sean slid up and plopped into Dylan's empty seat.

"So, how'd I do? Did I at least do him justice?"

"Better than that—you were great! He would have been so proud Sean, really."

"He'd be proud of you too, Tia, you know that, don't you?" he looked toward the door Dylan had exited and tipped his head. "He's a nice guy. I like him."

"Yeah, he's pretty great."

"So, is it serious?" He waggled his eyebrows at her and smiled.

Tia smiled back sadly. "He lives out of state, Sean, and he travels a lot for work, so, I don't put a lot of hope in it going anywhere," she sighed. "But, I'm really glad he was with me tonight; he really helped me through a lot."

Sean smiled mischievously. "Yeah, I saw how he did that. That was a pretty intense dance there. You were the only two people in the room, and it was getting pretty steamy."

She reached over and slapped him playfully on the arm. "Knock it off, Sean." He winced dramatically and grabbed his arm in mock pain. "I'm not there yet—I can't even imagine being there yet." But in the back of her mind, she could imagine it going somewhere with Dylan if their circumstances were different. "He's a great guy, and I'll leave it at that."

"As long as he's good to you; that's all that matters," he said seriously. "You deserve to be happy, and Nick would want that for you too."

"I know," she said, giving him a hug, "and I'm getting there. I'm finally ready to move on, and it feels pretty good."

"I invited Dylan for poker night," he said.

"He told me. That was nice of you."

"I meant it," he replied. "Make sure he knows the offer is real, and not one of those things people say in bars when they've had too much Guinness and Tully."

"I will." She looked over and saw Dylan stepping back in.

Sean jumped up and turned to Dylan as he approached the table. "Just checking in with my biggest critic," he said smiling. "I used to jam here a lot with Nick, and we'd always try to get Tia on stage with us."

"I've heard her sing—she's amazing," he agreed, glad to have another comment that made it sound if they knew each other better than they did. "Hey—really impressive set, man," Dylan said. "Great song choice, too."

"Yeah? Thanks a lot. You a fan of Incidental Happenstance?"

"I've followed them since the very beginning," he replied with a wink at Tia.

"Well, no one can quite match Miller, but I do what I can." He started away and turned back. "I meant it about poker night, bro. Any time."

"Thanks," Dylan answered. "I'll do what I can."

They stayed until Paddy closed the bar at two am. Dylan was thrilled just to sit and talk with her, and was amazed that their conversation was so comfortable. He learned that she hated horror movies and most chick flicks but would definitely go see his on opening night, that she absolutely loved dogs, that she loved her job, was an only child, and a hundred more trivial things that he liked about her immediately. He was disappointed when Paddy announced last call, but he was more determined than ever that he wanted to see her again.

Outside the door there were more rounds of hugs and promises to call, and more invitations extended to Dylan for poker night. When they stepped out into the street, Tia shivered, and not just because of the chilly spring air. She couldn't believe this night—couldn't have dared to hope for something more perfect, and now it was over. Dylan would be just a vivid memory that she would see in her dreams, both sleeping and waking, and she would go on, try to start over, and find herself again. In just one night, she already felt more for him than she ever thought she could feel again, and now, because of the life he led, he would be gone. Why couldn't he just be a car salesman or something? Why did the guy she'd already come to like so much have to be a star so far out of her league that they weren't even in the same universe? She tried to compose herself, control all the emotions that threatened to betray her calm, and turned to him as her friends jumped into their cars and drove off into the deserted neighborhood. She and Dylan started walking back toward her car, and to her delight, he draped his arm around her shoulders.

"Wow," she breathed. "I don't even know how to describe what I'm feeling, or how to say what I want to say. There aren't words invented yet for me to tell you how much this night has meant to me Dylan—how much you've meant to me." She hesitated, tried to stop herself, but the words came tumbling out anyway. "Damn it, why can't you just be a normal guy?"

"I am a normal guy, Tia," he said, pulling her closer. "I'm just not in a normal situation."

"But it's over too soon. Tomorrow you'll be gone forever—a little ant on a big stage far, far away...it'll be like I never even knew you, like a wonderful dream I'll never dream again..." she couldn't help herself and started to giggle, dropping her head. "I'm sorry. I swore to myself I wouldn't do this."

"Do what? Show some emotion? Bloody hell, Tia. You've been through hell the past year. I know. And look how strong you are. Look what you faced tonight! You amaze me."

"*I* amaze *you*? I don't even know what to say to that." She looked down at the ground. "I certainly don't do anything amazing..."

"You don't?" he asked incredulously. "Really? You have no idea, do you? And that's what's driving me so crazy!"

"I'm sorry...?"

He tightened his grip on her shoulder and pulled her into an alleyway between two buildings. He held her arms, and looked straight into her eyes. "You want to know what you did, Tia? Let me tell you what you did. First, you keep saying how I saved you, but you really have no idea what you did for me, do you? You treated me like a real person, and I haven't had that happen in a very long time. Then, you shared your friends with me. You never called me out, and never even hinted that I was anyone who might be different from the crowd. Do you have any idea how long it's been since I played darts in a bar with a bunch of strangers? I couldn't even tell you. And because you treated me like a normal person, so did they. And I had a great time!"

"I'm so glad, Dylan, really," she said, looking at the ground humbly. "But I didn't make that happen—you just are..."

He put his finger under her chin and raised her head to meet his gaze. "Wait, I'm not done yet." He looked at her with an intensity that made her feel dizzy. "You trusted me with your story, and helped me see that I haven't moved on from Shelby's death the way I should. But, the kicker is, you never asked me for anything. Never once did you take a picture of me, ask for an autograph, nothing. You just took me as I am and let things roll. All night you've been telling me how I saved you. But don't you see, Tia? You saved me too. There are perks to being famous, and I'll be the first to admit it, but there are sacrifices, too, and one of the biggest ones is that you lose your sense of self—you forget who you really are. Tonight you helped me find myself too, Tia, and I can't thank you enough."

She couldn't believe her ears. She'd helped him? It was crazy, she thought. But as she opened her mouth to speak, he silenced her by placing his index and middle fingers over her lips.

"Please, let me finish." His eyes darted around as if he were contemplating something serious and the agitated look returned, twisting his features into confusion. "I've already gone this far, and it's probably a big mistake on my part, because the last thing I ever want to do is to hurt you...but damn it, Tia, you've made this such an incredible night for me, and..." he paused, and focused his gaze on hers. "...you have no idea how badly I want to kiss you right now." He reached up and took her face in his hands and looked deeply into her eyes, her soul. "Please say I can kiss you right now."

The question was so unexpected, so unbelievable, that it took a moment for her process it. But once she did, there was no question in her mind. She looked into the burning embers that were his eyes, flecks of gold blazing in sapphire blue, and didn't hesitate before she whispered, "Please, yes."

He cupped her face in his hands and stared into her—through her—before bringing his face down to meet hers. Their lips met, gently at first, and he whispered against her mouth, "Tia, Tia, I can't believe that I found you tonight," and then the kiss deepened, slowly rising to match the intensity she saw in his eyes. Her arms slid up around his neck and his moved down around her waist and he pulled her to him. She could feel his heart beating against her own, and when his tongue brushed her lips she accepted it gladly, rushing out to meet it, giving herself completely to the hypnotic rhythm until they were both breathless. She felt a bloom of heat start to simmer in her heart, and as the temperature of the kiss increased—when it became hot and hungry and full of need—it flared into an inferno that took her over. When the kiss ended, he held her still, running his hands swiftly and sensually along her back, through her hair, along her cheek, and she nearly exploded with the beauty of it, the incredible feeling of being so close and open with another human being. Lexi was right again—shut out from life for so long, she felt herself opening into his arms, felt his breath in rugged gasps against her ear and she raised to kiss him again, to belong to someone, if only for a moment, and to give herself to the feeling. She was still here—she could still feel joy, and she could definitely still feel passion. Parts of her that were closed for so long were bursting open, and she was almost embarrassed at the way she was kissing him back—had to pull back to maintain some dignity. He returned his burning gaze to hers.

"It doesn't have to be over Tia," he whispered. "I really want to see you again."

She looked at him wide-eyed and started to speak, but he silenced her with a kiss before he continued. It was hard to say it, but it had to be said.

"But we have to be honest with each other here. I'm here for a couple days; that's it. It's not a matter of choice. Then I have a European tour this summer, and I start filming a movie after that. In New Zealand."

"I know. I read the book," she offered weakly.

"I just can't make any promises to you Tia. And I don't know if it would be worse to spend more time together and stir things up even more."

"Worse than saying goodbye right now and never seeing you again?"

"Worse than hurting you more in the long run," he said sadly. "The last thing I want to do is hurt you. You've been through so much pain already." A tear slipped down her cheek, and he caught it with his fingertip. "But I do want to see you again. If you want to."

"I want to," she managed to whisper, trying to hold on to her emotions. "I definitely want to."

"That phone call I made when I left? I arranged things. I was hoping you'd say yes."

"Oh, Dylan," she breathed. "Did you doubt it for a minute?"

"One thing I've learned in life is that you can never tell what a woman's thinking." She smiled at him. "But I was hoping." He saw the look on her face change to disbelief and smiled back and nodded. "I was pretty sure."

He was hoping? Her heart leaped in her chest and she leaned into him. "Just tell me when and where. I'll be there."

"Well, unfortunately, I don't have a free day tomorrow. It's our first show here with some new mixing equipment, and I have to do some sound checks, a couple phone interviews, and one personal one, but I was hoping maybe you'd come and hang out backstage with me tomorrow, kind of spend the day together. You could maybe help me sound check the mikes for the backup vocals...hardly a quality first date, but I'll pretty much be stuck at the arena..."

"It sounds great!" Her mood immediately lightened. He wanted to see her again! "I've never been back stage before. Do I get a laminated pass and all that?"

"Absolutely. They don't let just anyone run around back there, you know. Special invitation only."

"And I can just spend the day with you, hanging out?" His heart lifted at her words. She wanted to spend time with him—the real Dylan Miller. "It sounds like a perfect date to me."

"After the show, if you're up for it, we're going out to celebrate Bo's birthday. It would be a celebrity outing, though—no disguises, and the possibility of paparazzi…"

"I think I can handle that!" Her face changed as her mood brightened even more. "Oooh…"

"What?"

"I just realized that tomorrow when I see you, you won't be wearing the mullet. You'll have your real hair. And you'll be Dylan Miller, international superstar with fans falling at your feet and girls throwing bras at you…"

He smirked at her from the side of his mouth. "Are you worried you won't like me without the mullet? Because I can keep it on—if you want."

"No, no," she laughed. "Let's not do anything drastic. It's just that…all night, even though I knew who you were, I wasn't looking at you that way. It'll be different, that's all."

"Listen, Tia. I'm the same guy, no matter what my hair looks like. You got to know me for me, and that's more than most people can say. And I love that you're not star struck by me. That's what I hate the most about being around people. It's why I wear the disguises."

"I know, and I'll get over it. Just don't freak out if I freak out a little when I first see you, OK?"

"Fair enough. Can I ask, though, who you're bringing to the concert? It isn't a date, or anything, is it?"

She laughed. "If it were, I'd cancel it in a heartbeat! But no, I'm going with my friend Lexi." She would have to call her and cancel their plans to have dinner before the show. *Oh crap*! she thought. She never called Lexi! She'd promised to call when she left *Last Stop*, and said she'd only be gone a couple hours—she had to be worried absolutely sick! She'd have to call the minute she was free, and beg forgiveness. "I told you about her."

"That's your best friend, right?" Tia nodded. "Can you have her pick up her ticket at will-call? I'd tell you to invite her backstage, but I'm going to be selfish and keep you to myself, if that's all right with you."

"I wouldn't have it any other way!" She threw her arms around him and pulled him in for a hug. "Oh this is so exciting! I can't wait! But don't worry, Lexi already has her ticket, so she can just meet me at the seats."

Could this girl get any better? She was still going to be happy in her crappy seats and seemed excited about spending the day with him while he worked. This could get complicated, he thought. You didn't meet a girl like this every day. Some people never did.

He smiled at her and shook his head. "But, like you said earlier—and rather eloquently I might add—the lottery system sucks. I've upgraded your seats for you, so she'll have to pick hers up at the arena."

"I've been upgraded?" she smiled. "So you won't look like a tiny ant?"

"I'll be larger than life. You'll be able to see the sweat pouring down my face, and every one of my hideous attempts at dancing. You'll probably be able to smell me—now there's a horrible thought." He shook his head to push it away. "I've got you in the front row, right where I can see you any time I want to."

She squealed and jumped up and down. "The front row!? Really? I've never been in the front row for anything before!! I can't believe it!" She stepped up on her toes and kissed his cheek.

"I'm doing tomorrow night's show for you, Tia, and I want to be able to see you when I sing to you again."

"Oh, my God, Dylan. I still can't believe that you're real. Are you sure I'm not dreaming? Maybe you should pinch me, or something."

"I like *'or something'* better," and he leaned over and took her mouth with his again.

Chapter 8

"Holy shit, Tia! Where the hell have you been? Do you know how worried I've been? I've been calling hospitals, Tia—*hospitals*! It's almost three in the morning! I thought you'd been killed and buried by some psycho!" Lexi shouted as soon as she answered the phone.

"Sorry," Tia giggled. Nothing could put a damper on the fantastic night she'd just had. Not even one of Lexi's famous tirades.

"Are you *laughing*?? You damn near gave me a heart attack tonight! What the hell happened?"

Suddenly, Tia didn't want to share it all. She thought it would be fun to watch Lexi discover for herself just who captured all her attention tonight. "I met someone," she whispered.

"Goddammit, Tia," she hissed, obviously frustrated. "I told you not to go to that place. Please tell me you left, and met him somewhere else and not at that pit."

"No, I met him at *Last Stop*."

"Oh, God help me. Did you at least inspect his fingernails, like I told you?"

"His fingernails were clean. I checked. He's in a band."

"You made off with a guy from the band playing at Last Stop? That's just as bad—maybe worse!" Her voice softened. "Oh, honey. I was just so worried. I kept calling and calling, and it just went straight to voice mail. You didn't even have your phone on. I called *Paddy's*, hoping maybe you'd decided to go to the memorial, but no one had seen you. And you *promised* to call me." She said the last words with a serious pout in her voice.

"I know. I did, and I'm sorry I didn't call sooner. But I had fun, Lex! Actual fun! I laughed, I danced, I drank... and I did go to the memorial; I just didn't get there until late."

"Oooh, I am really glad you did that. You needed to be there. I know you would have regretted it if you didn't go."

"I would've. And I'm so glad I went. It was great to see everyone, and they were all so nice..."

"Yeah, but you still didn't call me, and I am seriously pissed at you!" Tia heard a tired grumble in the background, then Lexi covered the phone and said to Ryan, "It's Tia—she's alive, but not for long once I get my hands on her—she met some guy and stayed out all night with him." Tia smiled to herself. Lexi returned to the line.

"Now wait a second, back up a little bit there. Did you bring the "someone" to the memorial with you?"

"Yeah, he went."

"Seriously? You met some guy, and then invited him to your dead fiancé's memorial service? And he went?"

"That's not exactly how it happened, but he went, and he was very gracious about it."

"And that doesn't strike you as creepy? At all?"

"He's a great guy, Lexi. I know you'll like him..."

"What do you mean, 'I'll like him?' I don't like the sound of that..."

"I have to cancel dinner tomorrow."

"I knew it!" she hissed. "You're going to see this guy again, aren't you?"

"I'm going to spend the afternoon with him. He has a gig tomorrow night in the city. We're going to meet up with him after the concert and go to a club."

"We?"

"Yes, we. It's his drummer's birthday, and we're going to celebrate." Tia smiled, imagining the look on Lexi's face.

"With a bunch of people I don't know? While you put the moves on some guy and completely ignore me? I really don't think so, Tia. You'll have to count me out on that one."

"Maybe this will change your mind," she added, hoping it sounded enticing. "He has an in with the management at the venue, and he was able to upgrade our seats to first pavilion. You can pick up your ticket at the will call booth, and I'll meet you at the seats before the show starts. Please, Lex. I just know you'd like him."

"Absolutely not, girlfriend. Now I'm sorry, but you're on your own on this one. I'm not going to be a third wheel on your first date, and I surely don't want to be a single to your couple with a bunch of guys you met at *Last Stop*. No offense, but you're setting your sights way too low if you're picking up your men at a place like that. You can do so much better."

"Well, you think about it, and you can decide later." She tried to keep the smile out of her voice. This was going to be fun.

"You're not going to convince me so don't even try—not even if he got us in the front row. I don't think you should go, either, but I'm sure I can't stop you."

"Try and be happy for me Lex, he's a really great guy."

"Oh honey, it's not that I'm not happy for you. I really want you to meet someone and be happy again, you know that. It's just that you're worth more than you think you are, and I think you can do better. Jace is a nice guy, and seriously, I do think he likes you."

"Seriously. He's been dating Ditzy Randall for almost a year now, and in all the time I've known him, he's never once asked me out or made any kind of move. Not that I'd want him to anyway—he's a nice enough guy I guess, but he's not my type. Too conceited for me."

"Yeah, OK. It would just be so perfect if the two of you were together since he and Ryan are best friends, and you and I…"

"Not gonna happen, so get it out of your mind. Besides, you wouldn't say this guy wasn't my type if you met him. Honestly. He's not at all what you're assuming he is. But if I can't change your mind, I'll go by myself. No hard feelings."

"You're sure?"

"Absolutely. But when you're begging me to go—on your knees—just remember this little conversation. Nothing is going to convince you, you're positive?" she was very glad that Lexi couldn't see her face right now—it was going to be so much fun when she found out.

"I. Am. Positive."

"OK then, now go get some sleep, and I'll see you tomorrow at the show. Don't forget—pick up your ticket at the will call booth. I'll be in touch and let you know when I'm on my way."

"K. Night."

"Night."

Tia woke early after a restless night of delicious fantasies battling with anxious concerns. At first, she was afraid to sleep, fearing that she'd wake to discover it was all just a dream. But she only needed to touch her swollen lips to know that Dylan was real, and her body was responding to the mere thought of him in the most perplexing of ways. However, she couldn't help hearing his voice as he told her that he couldn't make her any promises; they had only a couple days, at best, and then he'd be off again dating Hollywood starlets and she'd still be trying to find herself. It would be back to the old routine and hanging out at the country club as the eternal third wheel. She'd never wanted that stupid membership—wasn't a tennis or croquet player and hated how the people there were always trying to outdo each other, but it had been an engagement present from her parents and they'd insisted she keep it after Nick died. Probably to keep a better eye on her and make sure she got out once in a while.

But the Dylan thing. Oh, she liked him so much. He was so unexpected—so down to earth and easy to talk to—and she felt comfortable with him right off the bat. He was funny, adventurous, and so much more normal than she ever could have imagined someone famous could be. And sexy. God was he sexy. Just thinking about seeing him tomorrow without the god-awful hair, then all sweaty on the stage in front of thousands of adoring fans and knowing that he was dedicating the concert to her was making her tingle in places she'd long thought had gone dormant. But those two words kept rolling around in her mind--*no promises*. They were from two completely different worlds, and she didn't see any way that those two worlds could co-exist in this lifetime. Europe, then New Zealand, and he wouldn't even be back in the states for nearly a year. It was childish and ridiculous to think that a relationship of a couple days would survive a year apart, not that she could call one crazy night a relationship. Just a strong attraction and some damn hot kisses. Finally, exhaustion got the better of her, and she slipped into a fitful rest.

Chapter 9

    Penelope secretly hated Hollywood parties. Oh, she put on the right act with the rest of them, exchanging air kisses with the girls and small hugs with the men, pretending to be thrilled to share the same space with them, but it was all a competition, really, and they were all so fake. Everyone talked about themselves, where they'd traveled, who they'd worked with, which designer had agreed to make them a dress or tux for an upcoming award show, where they'd be seated at the award show—anything to make themselves look better than to whomever they were speaking. It was all a game, and she played it as well as most; better than some.
    This one, however, was going to be hell. She was still planning her comeback, and was still plagued by the bad press and her suspicious absence from the whole scene for the past few months. In her seclusion, she didn't have to answer questions about why Jason had dumped her for some Italian whore or why her latest movie had flopped. Plus, she didn't have a date, and didn't want one—if she was going to attach herself to Dylan Miller, she didn't want any rumors flying about her and someone else; so she wasn't about to start calling people, sounding desperate, asking for an escort. She'd been away from the game for too long; didn't know who was available and who wasn't; and wasn't in a position to step on any toes. Not yet.
    Skipping this one, though, wasn't an option. At least she knew that Jason wouldn't show up—the latest tabloid she'd read had him sexing it up on some beach in St. Tropez with his Italian superbitch—so she didn't need to have a real date, just an escort. She decided on Peter Michaels, an up and coming designer who was so openly gay that no one would ever tag them as a couple. He'd wanted to make something for her to wear since she was on the best dressed list at her Oscar debut, and since she'd fallen out of the good graces of the business over the past few months, she thought she'd give him a shot at creating the dress she'd wear for the premier of her new movie. She wanted something that would highlight Dylan's blonde hair and rich skin tone, maybe something the color of his eyes, which were the most alarming color of sapphire. It was months away yet, but since she'd be on the other side of the world for so long, he'd need to get some

measurements and some drawings made up for her approval before she left.

He accepted her invitation immediately, in his high-pitched and irritating voice. "Oh honey, you know I'd just love to go with you to that party! I can throw together something fabulous for you if you want to stop by!" He drew out the word love for about two seconds, and over accentuated the 'a' in fabulous. Nope, she thought, no one would ever peg them as a couple.

In the end she did let him dress her, and he didn't do a bad job. He put just the right emphasis on her cleavage and highlighted her long neck with a simple diamond teardrop. It wasn't real, of course, he didn't have that kind of pull yet in the industry, but no one else would know that. He was even more thrilled when she suggested he make her dress for the movie premier, dropping casually who'd be escorting her.

"Ah, isn't he just yummy!" he said when she mentioned Dylan's name. "It's really too bad he's straight—I could just eat him right up!" Penelope agreed wholeheartedly then he added, "Do you think he'd let me dress him too?" He started getting excited, throwing his hands in the air and rubbing them together. "I could do his tie in the same color of your dress," his eyes widened as an idea inspired him, "ooh, ooh! Something in a blue, like his eyes, now you know the man's got gorgeous eyes!" He put his hands on his hips, daring her to disagree with him, which of course, she didn't.

Oh hell, she thought, getting through a night with him was going to be trying, but it was better than not having anyone.

The party was a housewarming for newly-married Evangaline Prisco and Clayton Timms, so of course Penelope had to bring an extravagant gift. They'd never last, she figured, Hollywood power couples seldom did. He had a taste for young Asian girls, a fact that was widely known but seldom publicized, and she was the poster child for high maintenance. Penelope figured she'd been invited mostly as a curiosity—she'd worked once with Evangaline on a film, but wouldn't call her a friend. In this business, you couldn't really call anyone a friend, at least not in Penelope's experiences.

The house was gorgeous, of course, all huge and marble and dripping with original artwork and expensive furniture. The pool was filled with floating candles and a huge tent had been erected in the expansive back yard; waitresses flitted among the guests offering champagne and canapés, and a six piece band played soft background music.

Penelope greeted her hosts warmly, gushed openly at their beautiful new home, introduced Peter, and made her rounds. She deftly deflected questions about her seclusion, her box office flop, and her disaster with Jason, sipped mineral water and nibbled lightly at hors d'oeuvres. She still had six more pounds to drop before she hit her target weight, and was determined to do so before she had to start fittings with Peter.

Penelope switched tactics, and started opening conversations about the film she'd make with Dylan. The studio hadn't announced her officially as the female lead yet, but it would only be a couple more days, so what the hell? She chatted lightly about New Zealand and her new co-star.

"Have you met him yet?" Gabriella Evonovich, star of a long-running TV series, asked.

"Not yet," she said casually, "but I'm heading out to Chicago tomorrow to see a friend," she lied," and I thought I might catch one of his shows and introduce myself. I heard he was playing there this weekend."

"I hear he's an absolute doll," she whispered. "Hot as hell, too."

"He is that," Penelope agreed. "Have you met him?"

"No, but I have a couple friends who worked with him on one of his other films—*Flip Side of Tomorrow*? They were both in love with him by the second day of shooting. Both of them agreed that he's even sexier in person, and that he's one of the nicest guys you'll ever meet. One of them--you know Susannah Atwald? She actually dated him for a couple months. She still says she wishes she hadn't screwed it up. Says he was the best boyfriend she ever had."

Now Penelope was seriously interested, but she kept her face, gestures, and voice calm. "Really? What happened to mess it up?"

Gabriella waved her hand through the air. "Oh, you know...the usual. The star of her next movie was more famous than Dylan—he was still pretty green at that time as far as the film scene, anyway—the guy promised her a starring role in his next film, and she got a little careless when there were cameras around."

"Wow," Penelope whispered, hanging on every word, hoping she'd continue.

"Yeah, she still says it was the biggest mistake of her life. He's a keeper, she said. Better be careful, or he'll have you under his spell too!"

"Now wouldn't that be something," Penelope replied, her mind racing around the idea.

She found several others who either knew Dylan personally or knew someone who knew him. There weren't a lot of personal details; it seemed he kept his private side private as much as possible. He didn't live in California at all, but had a ranch somewhere in Colorado; of course, he was on the road so much, he didn't spend much time there, anyway. Everyone had only good things to say about him, and these weren't people who had good things to say about anyone. As she was working her plans in her mind, she wondered if she could really genuinely like this guy. That would make things easier, and considerably more fun.

It was only an hour before Peter abandoned her to chat up the rest of the guests in a blatant attempt to try and increase his own client base, but by that time, she was tired of the scene anyway. She'd learned what she could about Dylan and had had enough idle chatter. She was also convinced that too many people were talking about her—she noticed sideways glances and conversations that became suddenly hushed as she approached. She knew she didn't have any real friends here, but she suddenly felt uncomfortable and nabbed a glass of champagne from one of the waitresses—tiny and Asian, she noticed—and walked away from the bright lights of the party to a gazebo that sat back in the shadows of the yard. Plopping herself on a swing, she moaned as she kicked off her shoes and massaged her aching feet. It'd been a while since she'd worn stilettos, and her toes and arches were simultaneously and loudly screaming their protests.

From her vantage point she looked down at the party, couples mingling, smiling at all the right places, tossing their heads in polite laughter, talking business and making deals. As usual, she was an outsider looking in, and it just wasn't fair. She'd worked hard to get where she was, but a little bad press and she was suddenly on the outskirts.

She'd grown up with television and movies; her mother was always too busy working two jobs to support the family that her father'd abandoned for another woman, making a new life with her and their kids and ignoring the kids he'd already had. Her sister Tatiana was a natural beauty, and as a gawky teenager, Penelope was never able to measure up. She didn't get the grades, the attention, or the boys that her sister took for granted, and no matter how hard she tried, she was always in the shadows. Movies were her escape—she'd save her meager wages from allowance, birthdays, and the occasional babysitting job and hide out in the theater, spending her weekends dreaming herself into the glamorous life of a movie star or on-screen character. She finally found her niche in high school, landing the lead role in the school play. She threw everything she had into the project, and when the curtain rose, she was someone else, someone beautiful and eccentric, and she bathed in the applause and adulation. The time she spent center stage was like being on top of the world, which made falling back into her own life even harder. Rural Connecticut was no place to become an actress, however, and before the end of her senior year, one week after her eighteenth birthday, she quit school and moved to California, much to chagrin of her mother, and vowed to never look back.

    She'd had to, though. After six months she was broke and broken, and she had to go crawling back to her mother's pathetic two-bedroom ranch house to regroup. She'd failed again, in her mother's eyes, and they butted heads on everything from how she dressed to how she spent her time. Her mother was convinced that she'd ruined her life and looked at her with distaste; when she looked at her at all. Penelope hated everything about her life in Connecticut in a pathetic little town full of pathetic little people. She'd had enough of a taste of the good life in California—had seen the stars in the streets and at premiers and in the salons; had seen the beautiful homes they lived in and the cars they drove—and she was hungry for more. Tatiana was still the golden child, graduating from college with a business degree and launching a successful career. She was getting married, too, to some guy named Preston, of all things, from a well-to-do family, and Tatiana considered herself so much better than her sister that she didn't even ask her to stand up in her wedding.

    It was six months before Penelope taught her sister an important life lesson, six months before she got Preston into her bed. He wasn't that good looking and was a mediocre lover at best, but the look on her sister's face said it all when she let the indiscretion 'slip' during an argument at Thanksgiving dinner. Penelope had won; finally she'd come out on top. Her bags had been packed for days, and when she closed the door on their screaming and carrying on, she knew that no matter what happened, she'd never go back again, never be a part of their broken little family.

    It didn't take her long to land a job on her second attempt; she was no longer a skinny teenager and had figured out that she could use her body and her feminine attributes to her advantage. Men were gullible creatures, easy to manipulate, and she got enough work to keep her afloat. She hadn't slept her way all the way to the top, though; she was smart enough to know when she could take control of her career without using sex to get it, and when she landed her first decent role in a major motion picture, she sent postcards to her mother and sister that read simply, "Who's the big shot now?" and put all of her energy into her climb to the top. She'd stepped on a lot of people to get there, but it was all part of playing the game.

She drifted out of her memories and drained the last of her champagne. She wanted more, but could already feel it going to her head since she hadn't eaten more than a couple of nibbles all day. Glancing down again at the gathering by the pool, she saw the happy couple, arm in arm, smiling, him bending down to tenderly kiss her lips to the oohs and aahs of the guests, and felt a rock in the pit of her stomach. She deserved to be happy, too, didn't she? She'd had nothing but shit most of her life, and she longed to have someone to call her own, someone to love her. It had never been easy for her to give of herself or to be open or real with anyone, but it wasn't too late for her to be happy. She was only twenty eight, for chrissakes. Maybe fate had finally intervened on her behalf and she would find the love that had always been missing in her life—maybe Dylan was the key. If she played her hand right, maybe he could be more than another step on her ladder to the top. Maybe he was her future.

She shoved her feet back into her painful shoes and headed back toward the party. She'd do all the right things for another hour, feign a headache, collect Peter, and call it a night. She had a lot of planning to do.

Chapter 10

She'd just poured her second cup of strong coffee when the phone rang. She glanced at the clock, and saw that it was just past 7:00. She had hours yet before she was meeting Dylan, and she was already nervous. He'd said he was doing an interview early in the morning, and she grabbed at the phone, expecting to hear his voice—who else would be calling so early?

"Well, good morning," she said in a voice that she hoped sounded sexy and not like someone who'd just rolled out of bed.

"Is it?" replied the caller.

It was definitely not Dylan. "Who is this?"

"It's Jace. Were you expecting someone else?" Immediately Tia recognized a condescending tone in his voice.

He'd never called her before and she couldn't imagine why he'd be calling her now, especially at seven fifteen in the morning, but she tried not to sound too surprised. "Oh. Hi Jace. Well, I sure wasn't expecting you. What's up?"

"I'm sure you weren't. I missed you last night at the club. Did you have a nice evening?"

"Yes..." she answered cautiously. He sounded angry, and she couldn't imagine why. "Thanks for asking?" She purposely put a question in her voice. *What was going on?*

"Well. I'm glad." He certainly didn't sound glad, and Tia wrinkled her face in confusion.

"Jace, is something wrong?"

"I guess you could say that. I was talking to Ryan, and he mentioned a three in the morning phone call where you told Lexi that you hooked up some guy last night." He paused for a moment, and then lowered his voice menacingly. "Is it true?"

"Well, I don't see that it's any of your business, really, but yes, I met someone. Why are you so interested?"

"Why am I interested?" His tone was really unpleasant now, and Tia still couldn't figure out why. "Why? Well I guess I would have appreciated hearing it from you!"

She could feel the heat rising in her face and she sank into a chair. "What are you talking about? Since when do I consult you about anything that goes on in my life? I'm a little confused here, Jace. You want to tell me what's going on?"

He continued as if she hadn't even spoken. "It's not like we were having problems or anything. Why would you go out slumming and hook up with some random guy? What did I do? Were you going to tell me, or just dump me and not even have the courtesy to let me know?"

Tia moved the phone from her ear and stared at the receiver. Was she hearing this correctly? What was he talking about? She felt a slow boil starting in her blood, and let it bleed into her own tone.

"What is this, high school?" she said hotly. "When were we ever going out? What do you mean, 'dump you?' Are you sure you have the right number?"

"Oh, come on Tia. You haven't been seeing anyone but me for almost a year now. It isn't fair for you to deny it just to suit your situation."

"Whoa. Whoa!" Holy crap, the boy was delusional! "Listen Jace, I don't know what you're talking about, but you have things a little mixed up here. We've never even been on one date. You've never asked me out. As a matter of fact, this is the first time we've ever even had a phone conversation. You never even asked for my number! How is that a relationship? Besides, you've been dating Ditzy for months now!"

"Her name is Bitsy, and she's nothing to me. A man's got needs, and until you were ready, I had to fill them somewhere."

"Are you *serious*?? You can't really believe any of this."

"We see each other at least a couple times a week. We've had dinner together dozens of times..."

"As part of a group," she interrupted hotly. "Holy shit, and you think that makes us in a relationship? Listen, Jace, I'm sorry if you got the wrong impression, but you're Ryan's friend, and you two are always together, and since Lexi and I are always together at the club, it just ended up that way. There was no design to it—it was just convenient, that's all. I never led you on in any way, and we've never had more than a casual conversation."

"We never had a date, because I was respecting your space! I knew you were still pining over what's-his-name—"

"Nick. His name was Nick. Have some fucking respect." She had completely lost her patience now, and there was venom in her voice.

"—Nick, whatever. And I didn't want to make a move until you were ready. I *was* trying to be respectful, and look where that got me.

Obviously you were ready and I missed the memo, so you went and threw yourself at some sleazebag in cowboy boots."

OK, now she was really pissed. "I do *not* appreciate your tone, Jace, and you have no right to talk to me this way. I'm going to spell this out for you one time, and listen good." She said each word clearly, and spoke slowly for effect. "Again, I'm sorry if you feel misled in some way, but we never had a relationship. You were a friend of a friend, and we hung out together socially, occasionally, as part of a group. That's it. I consider you a friend, so don't ruin it by blowing this all out of proportion!"

"Out of proportion!? This running off with some loser from a dive bar is out of proportion? I understand you have to get back on your feet, but why not with me? I've been nothing but patient and kind while you dealt with your situation, and this is how you treat me?"

"Oh," she said coldly. "You mean my situation with what's-his-name? We never discussed it, not once, nor did we discuss dating or having a relationship! This is coming out of left field for me, and I really don't appreciate it!" She could feel her excellent mood slipping; the heat of anger burning her cheeks.

His voice sounded so angry she was almost frightened. "So I never asked you out. Fine. So then let's..."

"Jace, this conversation is over. I can't believe the way you're talking to me, and I'm actually shocked that you could be so rude. You need to calm down, and so do I. This is going nowhere."

"Wait--"

She hit the end button on the phone and sat back on the couch. She wanted to pound something and realized that that was the weakness with cordless phones—and cell phones too, for that matter—no matter how badly you wanted to slam the phone down in someone's ear, all you could do was hit a button and maybe, at best, they'd get a beep. Someone needed to come up with an ap that mimicked a real hang-up.

She sat for a moment, regulating her breathing. Where the hell did that come from? She had never considered Jace anything more than a friend, and hadn't ever gotten the impression that he felt anything for her other than friendship, either, despite what Lexi said yesterday. She certainly wouldn't date him, even if she hadn't met Dylan. Not only was he conceited and pretentious, but he wasn't at all her type. He was a nice enough guy on the surface, but Jace was number one in his own world, and everything else was second—she could never be with someone like that. The phone rang again in her hand, startling her from her thoughts.

This time she looked at the Caller ID. When she saw Jace's name, she set the phone down to let the machine pick it up.

"Look, it's me again." There was a long pause. "I'm sorry I didn't handle things well a bit ago, and I'm hoping you'll just talk to me. Please pick up." The hum of the machine's recording device was the only sound in the room. "OK," he sighed after a few moments of silence. "So you won't talk to me. I understand that you're mad. I'm sorry I was so pissed off. It's just that I thought we were starting something and…let's give it a try. Let me take you to dinner. A real date—just the two of us. We can get to know each other on a different level and see where things take us."

"Yeah, right," she said to the machine.

"Please. You won't be sorry. You pick the time. And the place. Just call me back. Please, Tia. I'm sorry." He sounded whiny now, and she frowned at the direction of his voice. *When hell freezes over*, she thought, and then the machine recorded another moment of silence before clicking off.

Chapter 11

Tia's heart was thumping in her chest as the security guard led her to the backstage entrance. She'd walked past a group of about a dozen girls hanging around the entrance hoping to catch a glimpse of one of the band members or flirt their way into getting backstage passes, and they were none too happy to see her stroll right through the little gate after a brief word with the guard on duty. She'd taken considerably more time getting ready today—she dressed in what she hoped was a much more flattering outfit, had done her hair, and had carefully applied her makeup. She felt happy today, seeing Dylan, despite the disaster earlier in the day. In the end, though, she had no trouble putting Jace's phone call out of her mind when she thought about seeing Dylan again, and she was already smiling when the guard swung open the heavy metal door.

He was standing at the top of a short staircase, leaning languidly against the wall and smiling down at her. Her heart and stomach seemed to switch places when she saw him, his dark blonde waves hanging messily around his face and bringing out the blue in his eyes. He was even sexier than she remembered, and she blushed with the sudden heat that flooded through her body.

"Hey there," he said.

"Hey yourself," she replied, and then he was down the stairs, pulling her into his arms for a slow and romantic kiss that brought even more heat.

"I was worried you wouldn't come," he admitted.

"Really," she said, matter-of-factly. "And I was afraid you'd tell them not to let me in."

He held her out at arm's length and looked her up and down. "You are really beautiful, Tia. I'm so glad you're here."

She blushed again, and felt the heat creeping through her body. "And you..."

"A little different without the mullet right?" He grinned, putting his hands on his head in an exaggerated self-conscious gesture, messing his locks. "What, you don't like it? Should I put the wig back on?" He raised one eyebrow at her, and smiled warmly.

"You'd be wonderful no matter what kind of hair you had," she whispered, and his heart nearly melted at the honesty in her eyes. He could get used to a girl like this, he thought, better be careful. "But I do like this much better," she added, running her fingers slowly through the soft curls.

He pulled her into another embrace and kissed the top of her head. "Welcome to my place of business," he said, "for today, anyway."

"I have to admit," she said, glancing around at the gray walls and concrete floors, "not as glamorous as I imagined."

"Oh, it does get better," he said. Then he leaned down and whispered in her ear, "but not much. Come on, I told the guys I'd introduce you as soon as you got here."

He led her down a maze of hallways into a large common room that was like a small cafeteria. Long tables held food, and soft drinks and beer bottles floated in large bowls of icy water. Flower arrangements were scattered about, and numerous fruit baskets and other gifts were mixed in. There was a small kitchen, and a few round tables with space for about two dozen people to be comfortable. Along the walls were a couple of faded sofas, a few reclining chairs, and a large flat screen TV.

"This is the general hang-out area," Dylan said as they walked into the room. "And these are the blokes that earn me my paychecks and make me look good." The rest of the band members got up from their seats and came over to greet her.

"So this is the little lady we've been hearing so much about today," Bo Collins said. He looked Tia up and down. "Damn, dude, you said she wasn't that good lookin'," he said with a wicked smile. "What are you blind? She's gorgeous!"

Dylan just laughed and punched him on the arm. "I said *you* weren't that good lookin'. What are you, deaf?" They both laughed at each other's jokes like two old friends who knew each other well.

"Bo Collins," he introduced himself, "and if this loser doesn't treat you right, you just let me know, and I'll steal you away from him." He smirked at Dylan, and took Tia's hand in his own and kissed the back of it.

"Back off, Bobo, before I have to shove one of your drumsticks up your ass," Dylan said with mock irritation.

Bo flashed his famous huge smile, white teeth against the creamy chocolate color of his face. "You'd have to take your head out of there first, Little Strummer Boy, but I'd love to see you try." Dylan grinned back.

The exchange was laughed off by the rest of the guys; they'd obvious seen it before; spending so much time on the road with the same people had to give you a unique relationship.

The rest of the band members were introduced in turn; Ty Waters; bass, Tommy Fletcher; keyboards, Angelo Isley; everything else—he played woodwind and brass, and filled in with extra guitar when needed. Tia shook their hands, and was once again struck by how average they seemed in their jeans and t-shirts, sitting around a casual space, bullshitting each other like any group of friends. They greeted her warmly, with handshakes and hugs, and let her know in no uncertain terms that she was all Dylan had talked about the entire day while he stood slyly by and just smiled at her. They weren't larger than life, well, except for Bo maybe, who at six-four was built like a football player; they were just a bunch of guys who genuinely liked each other and loved playing music together. Still, she was among greatness—her musical idols, and she had to let them know it.

"I have to say this, but I'll only say it once, because your heads are obviously already full of yourselves," she said with a grin. "I'm a huge fan, I love your music, and it really is an honor to be in the same room with all of you. I appreciate the welcome, and..." she noticed them all grinning at her. "I'll just shut up now, before I make an ass of myself. Thanks."

"Dylan, did you ask this girl if she has a sister? I like her already," Ty spoke up. "I'm glad to hear you're a fan, and glad that you gave our man Dylan here such a good time last night. He's been actin' like a little kid all morning, and frankly, we're all glad you're here, because we were getting pretty sick of it."

Dylan stepped over and put his arm around Tia. "I really wonder sometimes why I picked a bunch of assholes like you to travel around the world with." He turned to Tia. "Seriously, they give me shit all the time, they snore, they hog up all the good food..."

"Now you know that we have to keep you in good shape, brother," Bo chimed in. "We all know you ain't the talent in this organization, so we need to exercise a little control, that's all."

"Yeah, right. Well, as much as I'm enjoying your company," Dylan said, flipping them the bird, "I'm going to take my lady on a little tour, and have her help me with the sound checks. You think they got the amps hooked up yet?"

"I just got the call a couple minutes ago that they're ready," Angelo answered.

Dylan led Tia out of the common room. "Sorry about that," he said. "They can be a bit obnoxious at times. Most times, actually."

"Are you kidding me? They're great! You guys genuinely like each other—that says a lot after all the years you've been together."

"Yeah, they're my family, pretty much. A great bunch of guys, really. Just a pain in the ass sometimes, is all." He stopped and looked at her. "They were right about one thing, though. I have been talking about you all morning. I'm so glad you're here." He took her in his arms and pulled her close. She breathed in the scent of him, something dark and earthy and fiercely masculine. Then he dipped his head toward hers and kissed her full on the mouth with no subtlety; there was a definite hunger behind the kiss, and she returned it with equal fervor. When they broke apart, he took a huge breath and shook his head. "Damn. I have to stop doing that right now, or I'm not going to be able to focus on anything else."

She smiled up at him. "That would be OK with me," she said, "but the fans wouldn't be too happy."

"Yeah, and the fans pay the bills," he replied, leading her out onto the enormous stage.

She had never been on such a huge stage before. Looking out at the tens of thousands of seats she felt flutters in her stomach, despite the fact that they were all empty. A few workers milled about, picking up forgotten trash, sweeping aisles, and wiping down seats. The InHap crew was at work setting up lighting, speakers, the mixing booth, and the stage—a huge backdrop of monitors was being erected at the rear, static cameras were placed, the drum kit was being set up, and marks were being placed on the stage in two colors of tape so that the transition between opening band and headliner would go seamlessly.

Dylan took her hand and walked her to the X that marked where his mike would be. "Pretty awesome, huh?" he said.

"How do you do it?" she asked. "Honestly, how do you walk out here every night, knowing that tens of thousands of people are here to see you, and not die of fright?"

He tossed her that crooked smile from the corner of his mouth. "Don't you know the big secret?" he asked sarcastically. "You just picture everyone in their underwear."

She slapped him on the arm playfully. "Seriously, don't you get nervous?"

"Every single night," he admitted. "But once I get on stage and start singing, nothing else exists. It's just me, the audience, and the music. And then it doesn't matter how big or small the audience is—I want to do my best for them."

She leaned against him and he encircled her waist with his arm. "You do, Dylan. I've probably seen twenty of your concerts in the past six years, and you always put on a great show."

"You mean to tell me that I've been in the same space with you twenty times and never found you?"

"Yeah, well, the lottery system sucks, remember? I've never been close enough to the stage to even see you clearly."

He pointed down to two chairs that didn't match the rest of the seats in the stadium. They were front and center. "No? Well you have good seats tonight. Those are yours."

"Holy shit," she replied. "I actually won't have to watch the monitor to see what you look like!"

"I want to be able to see you, too. I told you, I'm dedicating this show to you, and I mean that. So you have to tell me some songs that you want me to play for you, and I'll do my best to get them on the set list."

"Oh wow, that's a tough one!" she exclaimed. "I love so many. Of course, my first choice is the one you haven't done in concert—ever."

"*Pull You Up.*"

Tia nodded. "It's always been a favorite, but after last night, when you sang it to me, it'll always be my absolute favorite song." A shadow crossed his eyes. "But I understand why you don't play it. It was for your sister, and it's too personal to play live. It's more than enough that you sang it for me last night; better even. Forget I even mentioned it."

"You know, I actually wrote it sitting next to her hospital bed when I was seventeen years old. She loved hearing me strum the guitar and of course had her favorites that she'd always beg me to play for her, but she asked me to write her a song that was just for her...and that was what she got. I only got to sing it for her once before she died. It was hard even playing it in the studio when we were recording the album."

"I completely understand..."

"Singing it to you last night was the first time I've sung it for anyone since it was recorded."

She was touched, and astounded. "Oh Dylan, I didn't realize..."

"But hey." He took both her hands in his and pulled her close. "After last night, maybe it is time. It would honor her memory, too, and make a statement about me letting go of the past."

"It's too much to ask. I shouldn't even have mentioned it. Really, forget it." She tried to switch gears. "A concert dedicated to me? Even one song dedicated to me, sung by you, is more than I ever dreamed. How about, *"Time and Again*?" That'll get the audience moving. Not that you have to do anything more than step out on the stage to make that happen," she added.

"I can definitely put that one list. And I'll think about *"Pull You Up."* No promises, but I'll think about it. I don't even know if we can pull it off live. It's been a long time, and we've never rehearsed it." His mind obviously wandered. "Maybe I could do it acoustic."

Again, he'd said "no promises." It reminded her that her time with him was short, and that she shouldn't waste a minute of it. She didn't want to think about saying goodbye to him, maybe even after this night was over, and she shook her head to blow out the sadness that was already starting to form there. "Don't even worry about it," she said. "I have plenty of other requests." She started listing her favorites, and Dylan took a notepad out of his pocket and started taking notes and nodding.

"I'll talk to the guys about the set list. We mix it up every night, so most of these shouldn't be a problem at all. We usually decide at the last minute, pretty much, depending on everyone's moods. I told them that this one was for you tonight, so I'm sure they'll agree with whatever I give them. Especially on *"Into the Blue"* and *"Seepage."* We all love playing those live. Now, let's go do a sound check, shall we?"

"Excuse me, Dylan?" a voice spoke from behind them.

Tia turned and saw a woman approaching. She was perhaps in her early thirties, but her Asian heritage kept her face flawless, making her look much younger. She was a tiny thing, perhaps just over five foot tall, with dark hair and deep-set slanted eyes.

"Ah, there you are, Jessa!" Dylan remarked. "I've been wondering when you were going to make an appearance." He turned to Tia. "Tia, I want you to meet Jessa, my personal assistant and the one who keeps me sane. Jessa, this is Tia."

She looked warmly at Tia and extended her hand. "It's a pleasure to meet you," she said formally.

"Nice to meet you, too," Tia smiled.

"So, what's up?" Dylan asked.

She pulled a Blackberry from the pocket of her ill-fitting vest. "I just wanted to let you know that dinner'll arrive around 5, and that I was able to move the interview to 8:00 am tomorrow, like you asked. And the studio called. They've arranged your flights and accommodations for shooting starting on the 15th of September, and are planning to announce your co-star publicly in the next couple days. They wouldn't even give me hint—believe me, I tried."

"You're awesome, Jessa. Thank you."

"No problem."

"And Jessa, one more thing?"

"Yes?"

"I want to make sure that Tia has full run tonight, OK? Let security know that she has full access, in case I get called away. And keep her company while we have the pre-show meeting. I don't want her to get bored and run off on me." He winked at Tia, and smiled at his assistant. "There's a lot of testosterone back there, especially right before a show. Make sure she isn't smothered."

Jessa smiled warmly at Tia. "I can do that, especially if it keeps me away from that feeding frenzy. I'll check back with you in a little while."

"Sounds good." Dylan took Tia's arm and led her to one of the X's marked on the stage with blue tape. "This is the back-up mike. I'm going to grab a guitar and play the opening for *"Lost in You."* I know you know that one." Tia nodded, fondly remembering last night's karaoke performance. "I'll start, and you chime in so we can check the sound levels, all right?"

"Got it!" she said enthusiastically. Even without a crowd, it was intimidating being on such a huge stage in front of so many seats. Dylan signaled to the sound guy in the booth set up about fifty yards from the stage. When he got the thumbs-up, he started strumming the intro. Tia joined in with the harmony, and adjustments were made to ensure even and optimal sound.

After several attempts, the sound guy gave another thumbs-up, signaling that the mikes were synced properly. He launched the song again, and this time, Bo and Ty joined them on stage, adding in the drums and bass to the mix.

"You're right, Dyl. She is pretty good!" Ty chimed in. They ran through the song a couple more times before switching over to a livelier tune. Angelo joined them, and Tia took a seat at the edge of the stage to watch the rehearsal as the rest of the sound guys wandered in to complete the warm-ups. After a few minutes, Jessa joined her.

They watched in silence for a few minutes, and then Jessa spoke up. "Aren't they just awesome?" she said absent-mindedly. The question was definitely rhetorical—her feelings were clearly conveyed in the countenance of her face and the sparkle in her eyes.

"Yeah, they sure are," Tia agreed. "So how long have you been working for Dylan?" she asked.

"Oh, just over a year now," she replied. "I started as an intern, and just loved it. He's so nice, and so talented, and so…nice. He never treats me like a peon, you know? Not like some other big stars. I have a friend who works for Bryce St. Cloud, and she's always complaining about what an asshole he is to her. Dylan's never been like that. It's a great gig."

"I just met Dylan last night," she admitted. "But still, I know what you mean. He's the real deal, isn't he? Just a good person with a big heart—almost too good to be true."

"Exactly!" she agreed. "He doesn't get into all that 'star' bullshit. He tells me like it is, and I do the same with him. I felt comfortable with him right away. With all of them, as a matter of fact. They're a great bunch of guys, and really easy to work for."

"So, do you travel with them, and all that?"

"Yeah, I go pretty much wherever Dylan goes."

Tia felt a twinge of jealousy that this woman got to spend so much time with Dylan. "Is that hard?" she asked. "Don't you have a family, a boyfriend?"

"Nah. It's just the band. And just Dylan when he's filming a movie." Tia looked at her questioningly. "But it's a choice I made. I love my work, and couldn't imagine doing anything else, really." She looked at Tia, and saw the questions in her eyes. "I know. Why would I give up my own life for someone else's, right?" Tia nodded. "Well, this *is* my life right now. I get to travel all over the world, go to all the best shows, live the good life…I don't know. I think eventually I'll meet someone and move on, and have a family…but it isn't yet. Right now, I love what I do, and I'm getting pretty good at it, so I figure, what the hell?"

"I'd drink to that, if I had a drink," Tia said. "Doesn't sound like a bad life at all." Being with Dylan all the time actually sounded really good and she felt the sadness creep in again, knowing that her time with him was so short.

"I can make that happen—be right back," Jessa said. In less than a minute, she rolled over a cooler filled with beer. "I always have these on hand," she said. "They're the band's favorites. She pulled out a couple frosty Newcastle Brown Ales. "Let's indeed drink to that," she said as she uncapped the icy bottles. She handed one to Tia, and they clinked bottles before drawing on the cold drafts. "To Incidental Happenstance," she said, and Tia joined her toast.

Chapter 12

Forty-five minutes later, with the sound check complete, Tia felt as though she'd made a new friend. Jessa was open, kind, and she confirmed what Tia already knew in her heart; that Dylan was as good as he seemed. She learned a few things from Jessa about Dylan; that he had a weakness for peanut M & M's, was a nature lover, and that he was an adventure seeker. He'd been skydiving, bungee jumping, and scuba diving, and always looked for opportunities to have unique experiences while he traveled. He called his mother in Australia twice a week, and really enjoyed his charity work. Although Tia had gotten a strong impression that Dylan had integrity, he was a professional actor after all, so she was glad to know that someone else who knew the real him had the same thoughts about the kind of person he truly was.

They had dinner in the common room with the guys from Outcast, the opening band. Tia enjoyed listening to the men tease and harass each other good-naturedly, and warmed every time Dylan caught her attention and rolled his eyes as if to excuse their rudeness, but then joined right back in with them. Throughout the meal, he rested his hand lightly on her leg or encircled the back of her chair with his arm, absent-mindedly running his fingers across her shoulder or down the side of her arm. She felt completely at ease with them all, but was happy when dinner ended and Dylan excused them to go to his dressing room and prepare for the evening. Before leaving, Dylan passed around a proposed set list, and Tia saw the guys' eyes widen slightly as they scanned the paper. There were no objections, however, and Tia and Dylan slipped down the hall into a room labeled with Bo's name.

"Isn't this the wrong room?" Tia asked. "I know you have identity issues," she teased, "but you do know your own name, right?"

"Precautionary measure," he answered, opening the door and motioning her inside. "Being the front man has some perks, but some disadvantages, too. Usually if someone—a fan, a reporter, a worker from the venue, a celebrity—manages to get backstage, they make a beeline for my dressing room. So I always have a different name on mine. Bo loves the attention, and he especially loves the looks of surprise he gets when he answers the door, so I usually swap with him."

"Does that happen a lot?" Tia asked. "The security seemed pretty tight when I came in today."

"It varies from place to place," he said. "You just never know. But I do know I especially don't want to be interrupted tonight." He sat down on the love seat that was the only significant piece of furniture in the tiny room and pulled her down onto his lap. Then he tipped her, laying her against the armrest and leaned in to kiss her. Again she felt the bloom in her center as his lips brushed hers, and she gave herself fully to the kiss, caressing his tongue with her own and running her fingers through the soft waves of his real hair. She felt herself giving in; giving herself over to all the feelings she hadn't experienced in such a long time. It was all she could do to let him lead—she wanted so much more from him.

She knew it was a combination of factors that loosened her hold on self-control—now that he'd awakened the passionate side of her that she'd held dormant for such a long time every kiss, every stroke of his hands, every intense stare brought forth a deep ache of need that flooded her entire being and shook her nearly breathless. Little zings of electricity zipped through her when he nipped playfully at her lower lip and her stomach rolled over and over in delicious waves of pleasure. The rational side of her brain shut down and she surrendered to pure bliss, feeling her limbs turn to liquid and letting a small moan escape from the back of her throat. She may regret it later—she'd never had a one-night-stand in her life, but right now, all she wanted was him, and the intimacy that she'd been craving for months. Her breathing quickened as he intensified the contact, pressing his body along the length of hers and she felt, against her thigh, the undeniable evidence that he wanted more as well. His lips were sliding their way down her neck when the beep of an incoming message from his cell phone jerked them both upright. "Ten minutes, Dyl," Bo's voice announced from the phone on the dressing table.

Dylan slid off her and slowly rose to his feet. It was impossible to miss the flames that burned in his eyes, and she wondered if her own passion was as obvious. "You have to go?" she whispered in a husky voice that she barely recognized as her own.

"I always introduce the opening band," he croaked, his voice even more gravelly than usual. "And I promised them I'd join them for the fourth song in their set." He looked at her with eyes so intense she felt they could melt all her defenses, if she had any defenses left. "I can't remember a night that I wished I didn't have to work. I could get my head all wrapped up in you, Tia." His voice was serious, and his gaze never left hers. "But I do have to work, and I need to get going, and then we have Bo's party tonight, and then..." he hesitated, shaking his head slightly and turning his gaze toward the ground. "As much as I want to, I don't know if it's a good idea, this," he gestured toward her, still lying on the sofa, needing the support of the armrest until she gained back some control of her liquefied body.

He put his hand on the doorknob, then turned back and looked deep into her. "But if it does happen," he added intently, "I don't want it to be in a tiny backstage dressing room. You're too good for that." He reached down and pulled her to her feet, and finally, his gaze slid away. "I just really can't make you any promises, Tia. I told you that. I want to, but I can't."

"I know that, Dylan, and I'm not asking for any. You've already given me more than I could have ever hoped for." Oh, but she wanted so much more.

He kissed her again, lightly. "The thing is, Tia? You keep saying that, but have you considered that you've given me more than I'd hoped for, too?" He took her hand, and they headed for the stage entrance while she pondered his words.

She had a pretty good view from backstage as Outcast took the audience by storm. Their music was raw, edgy, and had a bit of Brit punk influence that got the audience on its feet immediately. They watched the first three numbers arm in arm, swaying to the beat of the music while maintaining constant contact. Dylan gave her a quick kiss before grabbing his guitar and joining them on stage. She watched with a sense of pride and awe—she'd seen him perform dozens of times before, but it was completely different seeing him not only from the physical perspective of being backstage, but the emotional perspective of knowing him as a person, and not merely a persona. That one letter made a world of difference, she thought.

She took a moment to check out the front row. She was off to the side of the stage, but she could just make out Lexi, on her feet and, in typical Lexi style, trying to get herself noticed by the guys on stage. Tia pulled her cell phone out of her pocket and punched in Lexi's number. She watched Lexi reach into her bag to pull out her own phone.

"Hey Tia!" she yelled over the crowd noise. "Where the hell are you? Do you know where I am right now?" She didn't wait for an answer before blurting, "The front fucking row, baby!!!" she screamed into the phone.

"Seriously? That's awesome!" she replied. "I can hear the music, and I can just see you now, jumping up and down and trying to get the band's attention."

"Of course—Dylan Miller's on stage right now doing a song with Outcast and—holy shit! He just looked right at me! Hold on a minute..."

Tia watched the exchange with amusement. She hadn't mentioned to Dylan that she was planning to let Lexi discover for herself just who she'd met last night, so he assumed she knew. He went to the front of the stage and nodded at her, smiling, and motioned back stage with a toss of his head indicating that Tia was there. Lexi, of course, thought it was all for her. Tia watched Dylan move across the stage to address the rest of the audience, and Lexi was back on the line.

"Holy crap, Tia, I swear, Dylan just looked me right in the eye, smiled at me, and motioned backstage! He winked at me!" she exclaimed. "Maybe we can get back there!"

Tia stifled the laugh in her voice and tried to sound serious. "Sure he did. He was probably laughing because you were making an ass out of yourself trying to get him to notice you, as usual."

"I am completely dead serious!" she said with conviction. "These seats are so close I can see the buttons on his shirt—he looked me right in the eyes, I swear! You have to get here!"

"I'm...tied up at the moment. But don't worry; I'll be in my seat by the time InHap takes the stage."

"You're going to miss the whole opener? These guys are really great live! You need to get here—hurry! Oh my God," she gushed, "I'm going to try to get us backstage—this could be my lucky night!"

"I'll be there as soon as I can. In the meantime, don't embarrass yourself, OK?" she giggled.

"Hurry up—the weird guy in the seat next to yours keeps trying to dance with me, and it's creeping me out. I need you as a buffer."

"A buffer—yeah, thanks. I'll be down as soon as I can, but like I said, it'll probably be right before InHap hits the stage."

"Aw, Tia..." Lexi moaned.

"I can't help it. I'll explain more when I see you in just a bit. See you in the front row!"

"Just hurry!"

She broke the connection and watched Lexi toss her phone carelessly back into her bag. She had no sooner done so when the guy next to her sidled up and tried to entice her to dance. Tia laughed at the exchange, and turned her eyes back to Dylan.

He was amazing on stage. It was like he became possessed with another spirit once he was in front of an audience. He moved, he danced, his facial expressions moved the audience, and he owned the stadium. The audience responded, regardless of what he did. He was only a backup in this number, but still you could feel that he had everything under his complete control. When he finished, he took a modest bow, and stepped out of audience view, back to where Tia was standing.

"Holy crap," she said breathlessly. "That was so amazing. I just know that when I'm out there watching you...." She shook her head, unable to finish her sentence.

"And when you're out there, it's all for you," he said.

He was sweaty and breathless, and she found herself incredibly enamored by him. Again.

"Let's head back to the dressing room," he suggested. We have about a half hour before I need to meet with everyone for our pre-show meeting." They were heading in that direction when his phone beeped again.

"Hey guys? I have a Hollywood A-lister here looking for Dylan," Bo's voice boomed. "Has anyone seen him since he left the stage?"

"Maybe he headed to his dressing room," Angelo replied. "I haven't seen him."

"Fuck, not tonight," Dylan said. "Let's get moving," he put his hand on the small of her back and led her quickly down the hall.

"What's going on?" Tia asked as Dylan was hustling her back toward the dressing rooms.

"Some celebrity showed up, and thinks that I want nothing more than to meet her," he replied, shaking his head. "I swear I get so tired of this. They think that since they're actresses, they can just show up, uninvited and announced, and get an audience with whomever they like. It really pisses me off sometimes, but never as much as it's pissing me off right now. We have to head back to the dressing room and hide out."

Tia mused. "How do you know it's a her? What do you have, some sort of secret code for visiting celebrities?" she asked.

"Absolutely—we have to. Hollywood A-lister means famous actress. Hollywood hero means it's a dude. There's a whole other code for those on the B-list, one for sports stars, local politicians... Either way, it pisses me off that they can just walk back here because they're famous and think that everyone else is just going to drop whatever they're doing because they're so thrilled to see them." He led her back down the hall toward the dressing room marked with Bo's name. "It's either deal with them, or avoid them, and right now, I'm going with option two."

They hurried into the room and shut the door. Another message came over the phone. "I don't know where he is. He did the fourth song with Outcast, and disappeared. Maybe he's in his dressing room, but you know how he is—probably left his phone lying around someplace, as usual. I'll keep my eyes open."

Dylan was clearly agitated when they got back to the room, and he began pacing the tiny space. "I shouldn't have to hide out at my own show just because some Hollywood starlet thinks she should be able to meet me." He turned to Tia. "You see? That's what I like so much about you. You aren't here because I'm some celebrity or because I was voted "sexy" by some tabloid readers. I get so tired of this scene sometimes. Everyone I meet wants something from me—they don't want to get to know me, they're just interested in where I can get them—to all the right parties, premiers; or they're looking for an acting career or a record contract. That's what draws me to you so much, Tia. You honestly seem to just want to be with the real me. Not the Hollywood actor, not the singer—just me. And you have no idea how refreshing that is. It's been so long since I've met someone like you, and we have such a short time together. I don't know what to think about that."

Tia absorbed this with more than a little shock. He was excited that she wanted to know him as a person? That she wasn't looking for fame or celebrity by attaching herself to him? She never wanted fame or celebrity, in fact, wondered how any person dealt with being constantly followed, constantly watched. It was aggravating enough to her sometimes that she couldn't go to the grocery store or the mall without running into former students or their parents. She never in a million years thought that she would mean something to someone like Dylan Miller, someone who seemed to have it all, but who was still longing for a little normalcy, a little belonging. She walked over to him and took him in her arms. She felt him stiffen at first, but then he relaxed against her.

He pulled her close, burying his face in her hair. "Sometimes I just want to be a normal person in a normal place, you know?—but it hardly ever happens. Even when I go in disguise. I try to make myself repellent to girls, but then I alienate the guys too. Last night was the most normal I've felt in a very long time, and I really miss the feeling. How would the people at *Paddy's* have reacted if I'd pulled off that damn mullet? I'd have been instantly put on some sort of pedestal I don't deserve. Sean would never have been able to take the stage because they would have all been asking me to do it. And if I went out as myself, I would never have met someone like you—someone so real and honest."

"It's still kind of hard for me to understand that, but I'll take it," Tia replied, taking his hand.

They quieted as they heard voices coming down the hall. One was Bo, and the other was a woman who was clearly agitated.

"What do you mean, you can't find him?" she squeaked. "How many places could he go? It's just a backstage—he has to be somewhere!"

"Well, Miss," they heard Bo reply calmly, "we don't keep track of each other 24/7. He could have stepped out to get some fresh air, and left his phone behind..."

Their voices trailed down the hall as they passed the room where Dylan and Tia listened at the door.

Bo must have sent her on her way, because a minute later, he was back on the open line. "Airwaves clear for everyone?"

Everyone responded in turn. "She's waiting in Dylan's dressing room," Bo's voice replied. "She's a real piece of work, let me tell you."

"Who is it?" Dylan asked.

"Penelope Valentine," Bo answered. "She's pretty hot, but seems like kind of a bitch. She's demanding front row tickets, too, and says she isn't leaving until she sees you. Says there's something real important she needs to talk to you about. Her assistant is waiting in the common room, so steer clear of that, too."

Dylan got on the line. "No way. Tell her there's nothing available in the front row. There isn't, anyway, they had to add chairs to get Tia and her friend in there."

Jessa got on the line. "I got a couple in the fourth—how about those?"

"Fine," Dylan conceded. "Then we don't look like pricks and she doesn't get what she wants. Perfect." He chirped off the line.

"Bloody hell," Dylan said, mostly to himself, running his fingers through his hair in frustration and continuing to pace in the room. He turned to Tia. "Listen, I'm going to need to hide out in here, like a fucking caged animal, or go deal with some diva with a goddess complex. I hate for you to miss Outcast—they do a really good show. You can go watch if you want to, and meet me back here after their set."

The phone chirped again, and a whispered voice said, "She's ba-ack, air's not clear," then cut off.

Tia looked at Dylan. "Thanks, but I'd rather stay here," she raised her eyebrows in question, "if you don't mind."

Dylan's answer was to pull her into his arms for a smoldering kiss. When it started reaching fever pitch, he pulled back and exhaled sharply. "Whoa. I better lay off you for now or I'm not going to have any energy left for the stage!" He laughed, and sat in the chair at the dressing table. "So what the hell do we do now? Play Monopoly or something? I don't think there's even anything like that in here…"

Tia sat on the edge of couch and leaned toward him. "I have about a million questions I could ask you." He looked at her, surprised. "There's so much more I want to know about you."

"Great idea," he said. "But you know ten times more about me than I know about you, so I get to go first."

For the next half hour they talked, and it didn't take Dylan long to move from the chair to sit next to Tia on the couch and pull her against him. They talked about their childhoods, her work, his rise to stardom, hopes and dreams, travels, their families. Then Tia said, "OK, here's a question for you. I've always wondered how you came up with the name for the band—I really like the implications and double meaning. Who named it?"

"It was me who first said the words, I guess," Dylan said. "We were sitting in Ty's basement, tossing around ideas, and I didn't like any of them. But what I did like was the feeling I was getting from the guys and the music we were making. I was remembering when I first met Bo in a little club in London. I'd happened to see a flyer tacked up on the wall at this little coffee shop I hung out in that said, 'Real American Blues.' It was my favorite kind of live music when I lived in America, and there really wasn't anything quite like it on the London scene. The club was way out of town, and I hadn't planned on heading out that way, but it kept itching at the back of my mind, and at the last minute, I decided to go.

"When I saw Bo play that night, the itch came back. I don't know how else to describe it—it just felt like I had to talk to him and ask him for a jam session. I don't think any of them took me seriously at first—I was kind of in my punk phase then, and didn't exactly have any of the outward qualities you'd think of in a blues musician."

"You had a punk phase?" Tia asked. "That opens up a whole host of new questions."

"Oh, that was an interesting time," Dylan said with a smile. "Lots of good stories there."

"I can't wait to hear those too," she said with a smirk. "But finish this one first."

"OK, so Bo and I clicked right away—or right after our jam, anyway. We could both feel it. It was almost like we knew what the other would do before they did it, and we were on the same page musically, too. So when we were discussing names, months later, I said that it was by incidental happenstance that we all met—it was all coincidence, but it somehow seemed like it was meant to be. Everyone agreed, and the name just kind of stuck."

"That's a great story. And it's true—life is like that sometimes, isn't it?"

"More often than not, I think. It's kind of the way we met, too."

"How so?" Tia asked.

"Neither of us was planning on meeting anyone last night; in fact, we both started the evening determined not to. We were both in a place that neither of us had been in before, and were both out of our comfort zones. And yet, here we are. Like no matter what we did, it was meant to be, so it was going to happen. Incidental Happenstance."

"I have to say," Tia smiled, "that that's my favorite incidental happenstance."

He took her hand and looked into her eyes. "I'm really glad I met you, Tia."

"Me too," she said.

"OK, my turn," Dylan said, looking into her very soul. "Tell me about Nick."

He felt her stiffen, just for a second, and was glad when she relaxed back against him. She sighed, and told Dylan about the five years she and Nick had together. It felt so much easier to talk about him after last night—she was again so glad she'd gone to the memorial. He was a good memory now, instead of a painful hole in her heart.

"And you were going to dance to one of my songs on your wedding night?" he asked. She nodded. "Which one?"

"*Just Us*," she replied.

"But you put that one on your list for us to play tonight. Are you sure you're alright with that?"

She turned to look him in the eye. "Absolutely. It'll be coming from you."

He leaned in to kiss her, and she returned the kiss, but then pulled back, looking him in the eyes. "Now it's my turn—tell me about Shelby," she whispered.

Chapter 13

Dylan had a great childhood. His parents genuinely loved each other, and life. They both had rewarding careers; his dad owned a successful automotive repair shop and loved the challenge of making things work, and his mom was an artist. He'd always loved watching her work in her studio; the sun shining through the big windows his dad had put in so she could have natural light, listening to her hum as she painted or worked deep red clay into incredible treasures. Because she worked from home, she was always there for her family, encouraging and supporting them in all they did. When Dylan asked for a guitar for his eleventh birthday, they'd taken him into town and immediately signed him up for lessons. He practiced constantly, loving the sounds he was able to coax out of the wood and strings. Even his eight-year-old sister loved listening to him play, dancing and singing as he strummed the first simple pieces he'd learned at his lessons.

He excelled quickly, and soon got too good for his instructor. Playing felt natural to him, the instrument an extension of himself, and his mother drove him further away, into Melbourne, to pursue more advanced training. He soon grew bored of the basics, however, and found himself creating his own sounds, and then graduating to writing lyrics to go with them. Sometimes when his mother was working she'd ask him to sit in the studio with her, to play her something that fit the mood of her current project. He loved that challenge, trying to make the guitar sound soulful, happy, sad, thoughtful, playful—whatever her piece inspired in him.

He spent every dime he could get on building a music collection from all genres, and took odd jobs whenever he could to make more money. He spent his time listening to the nuances of the songs, copying them by ear, and imagining instruments that would blend harmoniously with his own uniquely developing sound. He played at church, at family parties, at nursing homes—anything to get an audience. Inspiring joy on people's faces with his music lifted him to places he didn't know existed, and he rarely left home without his guitar slung over his back. It was the Christmas he turned sixteen that he got his first Martin, a sleek and beautiful instrument that made his well-worn First Act look pale in comparison. He reveled in the sounds he could create with it, and began seeking out others to start a band. Most other accomplished artists were considerably older than him, and they generally laughed when he approached them with his request to have a jam session. Enough decided to humor him, however, and they were always amazed at the talent of the scrawny kid with the shaggy hair. Soon he was writing songs for mixed ensembles, and loving every minute.

It was the next summer that Shelby got sick, and life as they knew it fell apart. Leukemia. The very word sounded ugly and hateful to Dylan. After several months of tests and treatments the doctors in Melbourne could do no more to help her, so his parents moved them to the States so she could get the very best care from respected specialists in the field. They tried everything—experimental treatments, conventional medicine—but she was getting sicker, and there was soon little doubt that she would succumb to the disease.

Dylan found a new musical niche in America. There was a different sound here, a different vibe, especially in the city where he got his first real tastes of soul, blues, and jazz. He loved the blend of colors and cultures that made up the music scene, and even though he was only seventeen, he usually managed to find ways to slip into clubs to soak in the new sounds.

His parents found a new niche, too. Doctors, hospitals, home health care nurses, more doctors, specialists; and none of them could rid Shelby of the disease that was consuming her. They'd sold their house and leased out the business back home; but the medical bills were staggering, and his dad had to find work to make ends meet, leaving Shelby's care primarily in his mom's hands. She had no time for her art; her daughter had become a full time job; one that would never bring any fulfillment.

Their days now included acting on a regular basis as well—his mom was so insistent that they keep the atmosphere of the house lively so as not to upset Shelby that no one could ever show true emotion—they communicated their fears instead with pained eyes and subtle touches. But Dylan had walked in on his mother many nights, crying alone at the kitchen table when Shelby'd finally drifted into a fitful sleep. He'd hold her silently and let her cry until his dad stumbled in after a long day of work, exhausted, to take his place.

For Dylan's part, he used his music to help Shelby through her days. He'd play the music he'd heard in the previous days at her bedside, working his voice to try and achieve the gravelly soulful sound of the heavy-set black men who he'd seen perform. Shelby understood blues—she lived it—and often confided in Dylan that she hated seeing their mother work so hard to be cheerful when they all knew she was going to die. Dylan became her confidant, and he often got stabbing looks from his mother when he and Shelby would sing songs they'd written together; songs titled, *"Cancer's Got me Down,"* and *"The Leukemia Blues."*

It was just a few months later that Shelby asked him to write her good-bye song, and he sang it for her on her fifteenth birthday, after over a month of trying to get it right. Three days later, she was gone.

His parents moved back to Australia to bury their daughter, rented a small house, and tried to start their lives again. There was still love in their home, but there was a huge hole where Shelby used to be, and they all felt it in very personal ways. After America, the music scene in Melbourne seemed stagnant to Dylan, and he decided to go to England to study music. There, he was introduced to punk rock, and added a whole new dimension to his inner musician. College fizzled—he didn't have the heart to study theory when he could be working on application, and he stayed in London for a few years, playing random gigs, working solo, starting a band, and attending festivals and concerts by the dozens.

It was at a little pub outside of London that he first met Bo Collins. He'd come from America and was doing a small tour with a couple of other guys. Dylan liked him at once—drummers didn't usually have much of a stage presence being all tucked up behind their drum kits and all, but this guy drew in the crowd. He had a friendly smile, was built like a truck, and pounded the drums like no one Dylan'd ever heard play before. After the show he'd bought the drummer a beer, and they'd hit it off immediately. Dylan joined his band the next day for a jam session, and ended up playing a few dates with them. Before Bo returned to America, he extended Dylan an invitation.

"Listen, Strummer Boy," he said. "If you decide to come back to the States—and I'm completely serious about this now—you look me up." Dylan swelled with pride at the confidence the talented man had in him. "You got somethin'—somethin' special, and I really think we could make somethin' happen, you and me." He left Dylan with his numbers in New York, and slipped out the door.

Dylan turned it over and over in his mind for the next few weeks. He was doing OK in London, he thought, but most of the musicians he knew were hoping to make it in the States. They spent more money on music and concerts in the U.S., and the tours were huge elaborate productions at immense venues, packing in tens of thousands people a night. He called Bo on a Tuesday, and was on a plane to New York City by the end of the week.

Dylan got a job bartending at a club that was known for its live music, and it wasn't long before he was performing there too, between acts. Bo had dumped his old band, and they played with different people, making connections and tasting all the music New York had to offer. They found fits—musicians who blended in with their personalities seamlessly, the first being Angelo. He was playing at the club while Dylan was tending bar and Bo was nursing a beer, and when Angelo hit the stage and started making the sax scream, they shared a knowing glance and a smile. They begged him to join them on stage for a number before the opening act was scheduled, and they clicked immediately.

That weekend, Angelo introduced them to his friend Ty, and the four of them met in Angelo's basement and started laying down some tracks. They all felt the electricity in the room that night, Dylan said, and started practicing together furiously, writing original songs and finding a style uniquely their own. They started touring, the four of them sleeping in an old van and toting their own equipment in a little U-Haul, playing everywhere they could, gathering a small, but ever-growing following. They met Tommy in Seattle, and it was then that they decided their band was complete. They were signed to a major label after a grueling year of constant touring and bombarding record execs with demo tapes, and the album went platinum in six months. The rest, as they say, was history.

"Wow," Tia said, exhaling on the word. "That's quite a story." She reached up and laid her hand on his cheek. "Thank you for sharing it with me...and I'm still so sorry about your sister."

"I know," he said, putting his own hand over hers, and sliding it over to kiss her palm. "It feels good to talk about it though. So," he added, "I guess you know it all now."

"Oh, I doubt that," she smiled. She wanted to know everything, but sadly, knew she wouldn't have enough time. "So what about your parents?" she added. "Are they doing OK?"

"They're great," he said with a smile. "They're really wonderful people. They healed, in time, although I don't think you can ever really get completely over losing someone you love, especially your own child." He looked into her eyes intently. "You understand."

"Yes, I do," she said quietly.

Dylan's phone chirped twice, startling both of them, but no voice followed. Dylan looked at his watch. "Shit," he said. "We need to have the pre-show meeting, but I haven't gotten a clear air report yet. I guess we'll need to have it in here, but I don't think the guys even know where I'm at."

Tia stood up. "I'll round them up for you. Penelope Valentine isn't looking for me, so it doesn't matter if I'm out and about."

"That would be awesome," he said. "Tell them to come staggered so it's not too obvious. Have Bo come first, since his name is on the door."

She gave him a quick kiss. "I'll send them in, and then I'll go meet Lexi at our seats. There's no way we'll all fit in this little room."

"I'll see you on stage, then," he said, pulling her in for a more intimate goodbye.

"I seriously cannot wait! I'm so excited!" she said, and she slipped out the door into the hallway.

She was just rounding the first corner when she walked right into a very agitated Penelope Valentine, who was obviously still hunting for Dylan and seriously pissed off that no one had found him for her yet. She was every bit the Hollywood diva, dressed in form fitting designer pants, a daringly low cut blousy top and staggering stiletto heels. Her blonde hair was long and flowing, and her make-up overdone. Her face, although pretty, wore an unattractive scowl. "Oh, sorry," Tia said apologetically.

Penelope grumbled something under her breath and walked past, but then she turned around and said, "Hey, you."

Tia turned around and looked at her. "Yes?"

"Where did you just come from?"

Tia motioned to the hallway behind her. "From that way," she said simply.

"Well, duh," her face scrunched up incredulously. "I'm looking for Dylan Miller. Have you seen him?"

"I saw him earlier," she replied, honestly. "In his dressing room."

Penelope made a face that could only be described as disgust. "Did you really," she spat, "and what are you, some sort of groupie or something?"

Tia tried not to be offended by her tone and the look on her face—even Bo had said she seemed like a bitch, but it was obvious that she thought she was above Tia, and that she looked down on her with distaste.

"Why, is that what you're hoping to be?" she replied coldly.

Penelope's chin rose, pushing her perfect fake nose into the air. "Certainly not," she said haughtily. "I have more class than that. I'm sure you know who I am. Everyone does."

Tia looked at her hard, as if she were trying to place her face. "Wait a minute," she said with fake awe in her voice. "Aren't you an actress or something?"

Penelope rolled her eyes as if she couldn't believe it took Tia so long to recognize her. "I'm an *Oscar nominated* actress," she said with an air of conceit.

"Hold on," Tia commented, shaking her finger as if she were trying to pull something from her memory. "Weren't you in that movie *Spring Moon*? I didn't see it—it was only in theaters for a couple weeks, I think."

Penelope harrumphed at being reminded of her box office disaster, and then stuck her nose back into the air. She was obviously offended, and went on the defensive. "Yes well, the director really screwed that up," she said quickly, and then changed the subject. "Now have you seen Dylan Miller or not? I have important business to discuss with him, and I don't need to waste any more time on someone like you."

"Someone like me?" she questioned, looking offended.

Penelope waved her off, dismissing her. "Forget it, I'll find him myself," she said, walking off the way Tia had just come.

Tia shouted back over her shoulder, "Good luck with that," she smiled, her voice sweet but condescending. Penelope didn't miss the tone, and turned back to give her one more disdainful look before turning the corner.

Tia could hear her knocking on doors, and went to find the guys, to send them on to the pre-show meeting.

Chapter 14

"Oh thank God, you're finally here!" Lexi exclaimed as Tia slid into her seat. "You missed a hellova opener, I'm telling you. Talk about making it just in time!"

"Sorry Lex," Tia replied. "But you knew I wouldn't miss InHap for anything!"

"Oh shit, Tia, I'm still all freaked out!" she took Tia by the shoulders and looked straight into her eyes to enunciate her point. "I'm dead serious when I tell you that Dylan Miller looked right at me. I seriously thought I was going to pee myself! I really think there's a chance we can get backstage! What do you think? Maybe I should flash him, or something."

Tia laughed. "Please don't do that. That would ruin our chances for sure!"

"What are you saying? That I haven't got it anymore? I'm telling you, he was looking right at me!"

"I'm sure he was, Lex. But maintain some control, OK?" She changed the subject. "So... how about these seats? Is this awesome, or what?"

Lexi turned to her and hugged her. "I know, right? It gives your cowboy a couple more notches of respect, I'll say that."

"Enough that you'll come out with us tonight and meet him?" Tia asked coyly.

"No, no, I didn't say that. I'm sorry, sweetie, but I just can't," she whined. "Think about how uncomfortable that would be for me when you're trying to score with some guy and I'm sitting there by myself; or worse, with the rest of his band. Ick." She made a face and shook the thought out of her head.

Tia smiled to herself. "I just want to be absolutely positive that there's absolutely nothing I can say that will change your mind. You are definitely not coming out with us."

Lexi took her arms and looked into her eyes again. "There is nothing you can say to change my mind. I am not coming out with you." She dropped her arms. "Besides, I'm getting backstage with Dylan Miller. I'm going to cash in on my gimme, have freaky hot sex with him, and there's absolutely nothing you could say that would change my mind about that."

Tia turned her head sideways in confusion. "Cash in on your what?"

"You know—my gimme. The one guy that I could have wild, unabashed sex with for one night without any regret or repercussion."

Tia shook her head. "Seriously? And does Ryan know about this?"

"Of course he does."

"So then, does he have a gimme too?"

"Yeah, he does. His is Alexis Janice."

Tia pretended to ponder this for a moment. "Not a bad choice," she admitted. "But you can't really be serious."

"We put the rule in place a long time ago. It's not like either of us ever thought that we'd ever have the chance. But I just might have the chance right now, and I'm going to go for it!"

Tia stopped for a minute. "Really, you think so?" she asked, trying to hide her smirk.

"I'm telling you, he looked me in the eye, smiled, and tipped his head toward backstage. I think he wants to meet me!" she sang, dancing like a kid in a candy store.

"Do I need to remind you that you are an engaged woman? With a wedding being planned as we speak?"

"Nope, you don't need to remind me about that, but..." she pulled off her engagement ring and dropped it into her wallet, zipping it in. "That's helpful!" Tia shook her finger at Lexi, scolding her.

"Don't rain on my parade, Tia! This would be a once-in-a-lifetime shot, and if the offer is out there, I'm taking it. Wait til you see him up close—he's even hotter in person!"

"Maybe you should let me have him then," Tia teased, "since you already have someone and I'm all alone in this world."

"Sorry," she smiled, "he's already tagged me."

"I swear, if you do anything to embarrass yourself, or embarrass me, I'm going to have to beat you," Tia stated.

"Fine—I'll keep the girls tucked away. But I'll do what I have to do if it means I might get to meet Dylan Miller live and in person! Besides, you'll be going out with your new cowboy and his band, so I'll have him all to myself. How'd it go with the cowboy, anyway?" she asked, changing the subject.

"I wouldn't call him a cowboy, exactly," Tia mused. "In fact, I wouldn't call him a cowboy at all, and neither would you, if you gave him a chance." She smiled. "But we had such an awesome day. I really like him, Lex."

"That's great, honey. You know I really do want you to be happy right? Wait a minute," she said, looking over Tia's shoulder, "isn't that—holy shit, it's that actress who was in that one movie, what's her name?"

Tia turned. "Penelope Valentine," she replied, and she watched Penelope's scowl with amusement as she was led to her fourth row seats. Tia tossed her the friendliest smile she could muster and threw her a little wave. *Groupie, indeed*, she thought. *I was making out with him while you were unsuccessfully hunting him down.*

"Shit, we have better seats than her!" Lexi exclaimed. "She looks pissed!"

"I'm sure she's used to getting the extra star treatment. It's pretty obvious that the seats *my* Dylan arranged for us aren't part of the regular seating chart." She turned to look at Lexi. "You know, my Dylan, the one you refuse to meet. The one I really really like."

But Lexi was too preoccupied by the hateful looks being shot at them by the Hollywood hotshot. Never in a million years did she think she'd upstage a megastar! "Wow, she really does look downright livid," she said. "She's still staring right at us."

Before Tia could reply, the lights dimmed, and the band stepped out onto the stage. The audience was immediately on its feet, roaring and whistling for the start of the show. Tia was full of energy and emotion, and couldn't wait to see how it would play out with Lexi. Dylan strutted to the front of the stage and addressed his adoring fans.

"Good evening Chicaaag-o!" he howled into the mike. The crowd answered with a deafening roar. "It's always good to be in this beautiful city..." he turned and looked down at Tia "...full of beautiful people! I hope you are having a good evening so far!" They pounded into the intro for *Seepage,* and the crowd roared their approval.

"See!!" Lexi yelled over the crowd. "What did I tell you? Did you see that? He's looking right at me! Damn, he is so hot! I told you he's even better looking up close!" She reached out her hand toward the stage. "God, I could almost touch him right now!"

"How do you know he wasn't looking at me that time?" Tia questioned. "I'm pretty sure he was looking at me."

"You weren't even here when he came out with Outcast! It was like he was looking for me in the crowd!"

"We'll see," Tia said knowingly, but the song was kicking into high gear, and they lost themselves in the music.

The more I look the more I see/ Both the left and right are the enemy/

You think you are but you're not free/ Time to open up your eyes...

Dylan was amazing. It was like seeing him in an entirely new light. He was still the rock-god persona, but, tonight at least, he belonged to her. She tried not to imagine what it might be like a year from now, seeing him on tour again from the middle of the second pavilion, wondering about what could have been and having him totally inaccessible to her. Would she join the pathetic throngs of women outside the stage entrance hours before the show, begging to be allowed backstage? Would she ever see him again after this weekend, or even this night? But, if there was one thing she learned from losing Nick, it was that you had to make every moment, every second, count, and she was determined to do that until she said goodbye to him and he was nothing more than an incredibly sweet memory.

As the notes from the first song faded out, Dylan looked down at her and smiled. She smiled back and cheered with the rest of the crowd as Dylan strummed the opening chords of *Into the Blue*, another of Tia's requests.

She turned to Lexi. "I think they might sing *Pull You Up* tonight—I just have a feeling," she said.

"Yeah, I wish!" she yelled over the crowd. "But it's not going to happen—sorry honey. You know they've never played that one live. Ever." Tia worked to hide her own smirk. Dylan hadn't told her that he would definitely play it; in fact he'd said 'no promises' again; but she was pretty sure that he would. It was written in the raised eyebrows when the rest of the guys read the set list Dylan handed them after dinner. She was thinking that he wanted to surprise her with it.

They danced and swayed with the music, and now the guy who'd been trying to dance with Lexi was vying for her attention, as well. She ignored him and kept her focus on Dylan, who was wowing the crowd with his incredibly versatile voice and raw passion for the music. Lexi was working really hard to get his attention, and Tia could see the laugh behind his eyes. He still didn't know that she'd kept him a secret, or that Lexi had no idea that he was the reason she was in the first row. Soon, though, all would be revealed, and she couldn't wait to see the look on Lexi's face when she figured it out.

When *Into the Blue* faded off, Dylan stepped up to the mike and addressed the crowd. "Thank you very much Chica-go!" he crooned. "This next song is very special to me," he said over the crowd noise, "but we've never played it live, so bear with me, OK?" The crowd responded as if he'd just agreed to play at their private parties. "Last night, in your beautiful city, a beautiful woman taught me a lesson about moving on," he continued. He hesitated for just a moment as the crowd quieted. "I haven't played this song in a very long time and never for an audience—so I might be kind of rusty—but tonight, the time has finally come. This night is for you, Tia, beautiful girl—and for you, Chicago." He strummed the first notes of *I'll Pull You Up* on his guitar, and the crowd went absolutely ballistic.

He smiled down at Tia, and she returned it with a blown kiss.

Lexi stood stunned; slack jawed, as the pieces of the puzzle came together in her mind. *I met him at Last Stop...his name is Dylan...he's in a band...he has connections with the management of the venue...he's only in town a couple days...I'm spending the day with him...I'll be there before InHap hits the stage...I can just see you dancing right now, trying to get the band's attention...*

Her jaw remained unhinged as she watched the exchange between her best friend and the man on the stage. Dylan Miller. Their eyes were locked on each other, and he was singing right to her as if no one else existed at the moment—as if there weren't fifty thousand other people in the stadium. She was stunned, to say the least, and missed most of the song as she watched her friend, obviously hypnotized and rightfully so, at the intimate words being sung right to her. When the song finally ended and Dylan had strummed the last note on his guitar, Lexi watched Tia bow to him, blow a kiss, wipe a tear from her cheek, and mouth a thank you at him. He bowed back to her, and then to the crowd as he soaked up the adulation that was due him after such a spectacular and unexpected performance.

It took Lexi another moment before she finally regained some of her composure and she was able to comprehend what she'd just seen. Dylan Miller had just sung to her best friend from the stage, and it was a song he'd never sung before in concert. He was her cowboy.

Tia didn't see the shove coming, so when Lexi hit her, she bumped into the dancer guy full force. When she turned to face Lexi, she could see the comprehension on her face.

"What the fuck!?" she yelled. "Dylan Miller?" She paused to catch her breath. "Dylan fucking Miller? That's who you met last night, are you kidding me??"

The look on her face was priceless, and Tia was instantly glad she hadn't told her sooner. She would remember that stunned expression forever, and laugh every time she recalled it. She smiled back sweetly at Lexi and merely shrugged her shoulders.

"You met Dylan Miller—last night—at that dump, and then you neglected to tell me about it?"

Tia smiled at her mischievously and tipped her head, raising her eyebrows. "It was just so much more fun watching you discover it for yourself!"

"You're such a bitch!" She shoved her again. "I can't believe you!"

Tia saw Dylan's look of concern as he looked down on their exchange and she smiled to reassure him it was OK. "Well," she said with a sly grin, "I told you he was looking at me!"

Lexi's mouth couldn't seem to remember how to close, but Tia said, "You can yell at me later. Right now, I have an entire InHap concert dedicated to me, and I plan to enjoy it."

"Thank you very much," Dylan said to the crowd with his eyes locked on Tia's. "I know it's kind of rusty, but it felt good to get it out."

The crowd exploded in another round of adoring applause, and Bo started hammering out the beat for the next number, which began with a long sax intro. Lexi turned back to her, her mouth still hanging open.

"I can't believe..."

"Yeah, I couldn't believe it either," Tia exploded, unable to keep her calm composure a minute longer and jumping up and down, exclaiming, "He's such a great guy Lex! He's open, and honest, and genuine..."

"You met Dylan Miller. At *Last Stop*." It was more of a statement than a question.

"Yeah, I did," she said, grinning.

"Holy shit." She spoke the words slowly, reverently.

"You can say that again," Tia teased. "You know, though, it's really too bad that you absolutely refuse to come out with us after the show, and that nothing I could say would change your mind. Because I wouldn't want you to feel like a third wheel, or anything, or be stuck with the rest of the band while I get to know my 'cowboy.'" She pulled the laminated "All Access" pass out of her bag and dangled it in front of Lexi. "I wonder how much I could get for this backstage pass, since you positively won't be joining us for Bo's party?" she said with a sardonic grin. "I bet your little dancing partner would pay big bucks for it." She pulled it out of Lexi's grab radius. "Think I could get a few hundred bucks? I didn't get Bo a present, so I could use the money for that..."

"To hell with that!" she yelled. "Oh my God—you're diabolical! You obviously knew all along that I would go!" she said, grabbing it from Tia's hand and turning it over in her hand. "Holy crap," she said reverently. "All access. This thing is like gold!"

"It is. And, of course I knew without a doubt that you'd go out with us—I won't even make you beg on your knees in front of all these people—but for that you'll owe me big! However," she added firmly, "I most definitely draw the line at gimmes. That man is mine."

"Dylan Miller," she said, dumbfounded. "Your man. Seriously!"

Tia's voice fell when she had to admit out loud what she didn't want to even think about. "Well, for tonight anyway. They have one more show tomorrow, then he's finishing up in the US and heading to Europe for the summer. Then he's going to film a movie in New Zealand."

"New Zealand? Could that be any further away?"

"I don't think so. Pretty much the other side of the world. So I probably only have tonight."

"Oh my God, so are you going to..."

"I don't know," she interrupted. "I'm definitely not that kind of girl---but it's hot, Lex, really hot between us. He keeps reminding me that he can't make me any promises, and I know that." She stopped to take a breath. "But I've thought about it, believe me! A lot. And when he kisses me, I have a hard time keeping my control..."

"Oh my GOD! You kissed him?"

Tia nodded, her smile taking over her face. "Numerous times," she added slyly, amused when Lexi's eyes widened. "But," she added, "it might hurt more to take it to that level and then have to say goodbye."

"Holy shit—how could you not? That would be an amazing level! Oh God, I can't wait to tell...everyone!"

Tia grabbed her arms and pulled her close, her tone turning serious. "Absolutely not. You tell no one. NO ONE! Not even Ryan, got it?"

"You're kidding, right? You can't possibly mean that. This is way too good to keep under wraps!"

"No Lex," Tia said forcefully. "I do mean it." Lexi pouted out her lower lip, and Tia continued. "First of all, it's my story to tell." Lexi nodded in deference, dropping her eyes. "Second, look at how you reacted. I don't want everyone and their mothers asking me to get them autographs, tickets, backstage passes, meet and greets for sick kids they know..."

Lexi looked at her with chagrin. "How can you possibly expect something like this to be a secret? He just dedicated the show to you in front of 50,000 people! You don't think there's anyone here who knows you? Probably half the students you've ever had are here tonight."

"That isn't the point. I'm sure I'm not the only Tia in the audience." She raked her fingers through her hair in frustration. "Hell, there is no point, really. I just know that I probably only have tonight with him, and maybe tomorrow at best. If he walks off and I know I'll never see him again, then it'll be different. I'm not even daring to hope for anything more. Once he's gone," she choked on the words, "I'll tell people, and so can you. Until that time, though, it's my secret; one that I've shared with you because you're my best friend. Plus, I'm letting you come out with us tonight and you get to meet the whole band. But," she added sternly, "I just want the little bit of time we have together to be just the two of us. And you, for the party."

"Aaww, Tia..."

"You have to swear to me, Lexi Marie." Tia looked intently into her eyes. "I mean it."

"I can't even tell Ryan?"

"Not unless you want me to tell him that you tried to force your gimme and not if you want to remain my best friend." Lexi looked stricken. "Swear to me. Swear it right now."

Lexi looked down at the ground and shook her head in defeat. "Damn it, alright. But how am I not going to tell people what I did tonight? This is already so incredibly awesome, and it's still going to get better."

"You'd better think of a way, or it's not *going* to get any better. I mean it, Lex. Swear it."

Lexi extended her pinkie to Tia and exhaled sharply. "OK, fine. I swear it. But I can tell people on Monday, right?"

"Probably, but you say nothing to anyone until I give you the OK. That's the deal."

"This is going to be so freaking hard!" She dropped her head and surrendered. "But OK. I swear."

They shook pinkies in the old grade school way, and Tia knew that her word was good. She could trust Lexi with her life; in fact had over the past year.

"Oh, I can't wait for you to meet him! He's just so awesome, Lex—he's not just incredibly sexy and a great performer—he's a really great guy."

"I can't believe you were just screwing with me this whole time," she said, shaking her head in disbelief.

"Yep, pretty much. And it was so worth it to see the look on your face."

"You can be a real bitch, Tia."

"I know. But you love me."

"God help me, I do." She pulled Tia into a hug. "Welcome back, girlfriend."

"It's good to be back."

Chapter 15

Being at a good rock concert is almost like a spiritual experience—there's something hypnotic about being part of a huge crowd gathered by the common bond of music. The pounding of the bass, the beat of the drums, and the soulful and passionate singing of talented performers brought people from all walks of life; all ages and colors; into one mass of humanity united for a single purpose—to have fun. InHap was known for its consistent, incredible performances and the loyalty of its fans, and Tia had never gone away from one of their shows without having been blown away. Tonight, however, was different than anything she'd ever experienced before. She was still part of the crowd; screaming, dancing, and singing along to the familiar tunes, but she was part of Dylan, too, and he was part of her. He was in fine form and he was in complete control of the audience—he owned the stage and he knew it, strutting around with his guitar, saying all the right things between songs, varying the set with the right mix of popular songs, standards, ballads, and rousing numbers that had the crowd roaring when he broke into a little shuffle step. He crooned, he growled, he was serious and funny, and the fifty-some thousand fans who had gathered were completely at his mercy.

Tia was lost in the music, and in the fact that he was doing this show for her. Every one of her selections was on the set list, and Dylan's mike was right in front of her, so that whenever he was singing, he was singing right to her, meeting her eyes and smiling at her constantly.

The band visibly enjoyed playing together, and all of them had several solos throughout the set designed to highlight everyone's musical talents. Each received rousing ovations, but Dylan, as the front man and voice of the band, was the one they'd all really come to see. She felt her heart swell with pride hearing the cheers for him, and watching him humbly accepting the adulation of his fans. Then he'd return to his mike, throw her a smile, and belt out the lyrics. "I hope you're havin' a good time tonight, Chicago," he'd say between numbers. "Tia, I hope you're havin' a good time—this one's for you."

Every time his eyes met hers and he sang down at her, she felt the crowd melt away and she was back at *Paddy's*, in his arms, his voice next to her ear. Tonight was for her—Dylan had said so more than once in front of the 50,000 that had gathered. But more than that—knowing it—was a feeling she had never even dreamed. She was flooded with so much emotion that she was caught up in the music, and the crowd, and the enormity of it all. She hadn't felt so good in what seemed forever, and she tried to forget that it was just for one night and live in the moment—this incredible, amazing moment. She checked her emotions and turned to Lexi and they danced; part of the crowd, but separate from it by her connection to the man on the stage.

It was over two hours later when InHap left the stage for the requisite break before the encore. Two hours of dancing, connecting, and feeling a part of something that Tia sadly thought she'd never feel again. When the band left the stage, Lexi immediately asked, "So do we go back there now?"

"Not yet. They're coming back for the encore. Dylan's going to give me a signal when they're almost done with the last number. Then we go back to meet them."

Lexi was positively giddy. "Then I get to meet them all?"

Tia nodded. "And Outcast, too. They're also pretty nice guys."

"You met them too? What the hell?"

"Of course. We all had dinner together." She smiled at Lexi's jealous smirk. "And, I saw them play, or at least part of it. I was watching you from backstage when I called you. I have to say, you were positively shameless."

Lexi laughed. "I was, wasn't I?" she smirked. "Wait a minute—so you were watching me, from backstage, while I was panicking that you weren't going to show? You were here the whole day?"

"Yep," Tia replied. "I hung out back stage, and even helped with the sound checks. I actually stood on that stage and sang into those mikes!"

"I'll say it again. You can be a real bitch."

"And I'll say it again. You love me anyway."

"Sometimes I wonder why, but I do," she teased, and InHap retook the stage and they continued dancing to the incredible music that surrounded them like a soft blanket.

When Dylan gave her the nod, she tapped Lexi and they hopped the fence that blocked the front row from the security tunnel. Lexi kept shoving her pass in the guards' faces as they passed. "All access!" she exclaimed. "Coming through!"

When they reached the backstage door, Lexi grabbed Tia's arm and spun her around. "I really can't believe this! We're actually going backstage and seriously meeting the band?"

"I've already met them," Tia reminded her, "and they're all very cool. Watch out for Bo, though, he's kind of a flirt." The guard opened the door for them and they slipped inside. "Come on," Tia told her. "Maybe you can have a tour later; even though there's not much to see. We're going to meet them in the common room since the stage hands will be all over the place at the end of the show checking sound equipment and swapping out instruments for tomorrow."

Lexi's eyes swept from one side to the other, taking it all in. She was still trying to get over the fact that her unassuming friend, the schoolteacher, had gotten her here; backstage at an InHap show not only about to meet the band, but to attend Bo Collins's birthday party at some swanky downtown club. Suddenly she wished that she'd dressed nicer, but when she'd come, she'd been sure that she wouldn't be going with Tia to hang out with her new boyfriend. She should have had more faith in Tia, she thought. It wouldn't be like her to hook up with a loser. Tia chose her friends carefully, and Lexi was proud to be among the best. But Dylan Miller? She still couldn't wrap her mind around that one.

From the common room they heard the last of the notes fade from the air, and the final, "Thank you! Goodnight Chicago, we'll be seeing you again tomorrow!" in Dylan's husky, sexy voice. Lexi was positively giddy, and couldn't contain her excitement.

The guys burst into the room, high-fiving each other and mopping their faces with towels. As soon as Tia saw Dylan, she rushed over to him and opened her arms. He put out his hand, palm out, and started, "I'm pretty disgusting right now, you might want to..." But she didn't care, and wrapped her arms around him, feeling the heat radiating from his body and inhaling the musky scent of his work. "Oh, Dylan," she whispered. "I don't know what to say...you are so amazing."

He wrapped her in his arms and pulled her up for a kiss. "You liked, it then?" he teased. "I'm so glad." He lifted her off the ground and found her lips, kissing her slow and deep while Lexi stared, her mouth once again hanging open.

Bo walked in last after handing off his drum sticks to excited fans, and nearly ran into them. "Damn that's hot," he said taking them in. "I think I might need a cold shower after seeing that!"

Dylan set Tia down and wrapped his arm around her shoulder. Bo noticed Lexi then, and his famous grin lit up his face. "Speakin' of hot," he mused, taking Lexi's hand and turning it over to kiss the back of it. "You must be my birthday present."

Lexi giggled like a schoolgirl and Tia introduced them. "Oh my God," she said. "Oh my God. You guys were so awesome! I'm such a big fan; I just love your music! I'm coming to your party," then she realized she was blathering like an idiot and visibly checked herself.

Star struck, Tia thought. It was the only way to describe the look on Lexi's face. The look in her wide eyes was giddy, doe-like, and confused all at once; the antithesis of her usual calm control. Her gaze darted around as she tried to take everything in at once, but she was having a hard time believing what she was seeing. It was the look Dylan talked about, the one that often made him feel uncomfortable. She felt confident that Lexi would get over it quickly, but just seeing it confirmed that she wouldn't be telling anyone about Dylan. Not yet. Not until he was gone, and they couldn't ask anything of her.

"I can't wait to see what you got me," Bo winked, and slipped out the door toward the dressing rooms. Lexi giggled again, and seemed to have a hard time controlling her own body. She shook visibly, and then put her hands to her face to feel the heat rising there as she blushed uncontrollably before regaining her composure and looking back at the couple who remained.

Then Lexi's eyes were locked on Dylan and her best friend, still wrapped up in each other. She'd seen the kiss too, and was still having a hard time believing what she'd seen with her own eyes. Tia had said that things were hot between them, but that was an understatement. She could feel the sexual tension in the air when they kissed; could almost reach out and touch it. Her brain was having a hard time seeing them as a couple, even when they were just a few feet away. She was staring, speechless, and that didn't happen to her very often.

Tia stepped forward. "Lex, this is Dylan," she said, even though introductions were not at all necessary. Lexi felt her knees go weak and struggled to move toward Dylan's outstretched hand. "Oh my God, oh my God," she said again. "I'm sorry, I don't know why I keep saying that, but, oh my God!"

Dylan laughed. "Nice to meet you too, Lexi. Tia's told me a lot about you."

That comment broke her trance, and Lexi found her voice again. "Really? Well she certainly didn't tell me anything about you!" She glared at Tia with exaggerated anger.

"That's what I figured," Dylan smirked, "when I saw you shove her back three rows. I have to say, the look on your face was...indescribable."

"Shock! It was shock! She told me she met someone at that dump she went to last night, so of course I assumed he was some sort of loser cowboy and that she was making a huge mistake, but I never dreamed it was you, but then when I saw you look at her and you dedicated that song..." she was blathering again, and had to stop and reign in the wide range of emotions flooding through her.

"I just thought it would be more fun to watch her discover it on her own," Tia grinned. "And it was. I know I'll never forget that face. I wish I had a picture of that."

"I'll check around," Dylan said. "We've always got guys filming stuff, for videos and all that. Maybe someone got it. I agree, it was...interesting."

"Don't you dare!" Lexi snapped, but she was laughing too. "OK, I just have to say this. I'm a huge fan, and being in the front row was so amazing—I just had the best time!"

"I'm glad," Dylan smiled. "Now if you ladies will excuse me, I'm in desperate need of a shower." He turned to Tia. "I need 15 minutes, tops. Can you meet me with the car at the side entrance? Jessa will show you where to pull in." He planted another kiss on her lips.

"Yep, see you in a bit," Tia answered and turned to Lexi as Dylan left the room.

Lexi grabbed both of her arms and stared into her eyes. "Oh. My. God!" she squealed excitedly.

"So you keep saying, but I know!" The two of them jumped up and down together like school kids. "He's just so awesome—in every sense of the word!"

"Yeah, and what you said about things being hot between you?" She waved her hand toward Tia in the "get outta here" gesture. "It's intense! I could feel the tension like it was a physical thing in the room. Like a volcano about to erupt."

"I know," Tia smiled, blushing. "Believe me, I feel it too. I don't know if it's because we both know that we have such a short time together or what, but things keep bubbling up and I don't know that I could stop them if they got much higher. I don't think I want to stop them."

"Oh my..."

"Shut up Lex."

Lexi laughed. "Shutting." She put her hand over her mouth and shook her head to regain control. "But OK, so about tonight. If Dylan's riding with you, you obviously don't want me tagging along. Do you want me to follow you, or what? Where are we even going?"

"Icon," Tia answered. "But actually, we thought that there'd be room in the limo since Dylan won't be in it, and maybe you'd want to ride with the guys. They're going to go schmooze with the fans outside for a little bit first before they head over, so we'll just meet you there. The limo can bring you back for your car after."

Another presence burst into the room. They both turned their heads, and Penelope stood in the doorway, hands on her hips, shooting daggers from her eyes. "Are you still here?" she spat. Tia smiled back at her and shrugged. "I guess you must be Tia, then." She said Tia's name as if it left a bad taste in her mouth, and her expression could only be described as ominous.

"Oh my God," Lexi gushed once again. "You're Penelope Valentine!"

"Obviously," she said with apparent disgust. She turned back to Tia. "I hope you enjoyed your little dedication. God knows what you had to do to get it." She raised her nose in the air. "So where is he now? I need to speak with him urgently, so don't play games with me again."

Tia looked at Lexi with a warning in her eyes to keep her quiet. "All the guys went back to their dressing rooms to shower and clean up."

She'd barely finished the words before Penelope turned on her heel and walked out in the direction of the dressing rooms without another word to either of them.

Lexi looked at the door. "Ooh, she seems like kind of a bitch," she said.

"She is," Tia agreed. "She's been hunting Dylan down all day. That's why I didn't see the whole Outcast set—after he got off the stage we found out she was looking for him and spent the rest of the time hiding out in his dressing room."

"Hiding out, huh? That sounds sexy," she crooned.

"Oh it was, believe me!"

"So what does she want?"

"Aside from being crowned queen of the world?" Tia said with a smirk. "Who knows? She just showed up and demanded to see him." Tia smiled. "Obviously, she didn't. She demanded front row seats, too, but that didn't work out for her either."

"Well, she's going to find him now," she answered. "Shouldn't you go and protect him, or something? She's a big Hollywood star!"

"Don't worry," Tia smiled knowingly "She won't find him. But if she tries to talk to you again, don't tell her where we're going, OK? He doesn't want to deal with her, so we definitely don't need her showing up uninvited again at Icon."

"No problem," Lexi nodded. "Not a word from me." She looked down at her casual outfit and frowned. "I'm already going to be upstaged by everyone in the place. I wish I had a change of clothes—I don't look hot enough for Icon!"

"Well, I guess next time you'll have a little more faith in me," Tia said simply. "You should know that I have pretty high standards when it comes to guys."

Lexi opened her mouth to protest, but quickly closed it. Tia was right, and she felt honestly bad that she'd questioned her integrity. "I'm sorry," she said softly, meaning every word, "you're absolutely right—I shouldn't have doubted you. But still, never in a million years did I imagine that you picked Dylan Miller up in that dump!"

"Yeah, well, life is funny sometimes, right? Incidental Happenstances, and all that? Now I'm going to head out to let Jessa know Penelope's on the prowl again and then go get the car. You OK riding with the guys?"

Lexi grinned sarcastically. "I think I can handle it. Might be tough, riding in the limo with them and all, but yeah, I'll manage."

Tia added, "Cause I really wouldn't want you feeling like a third wheel or anything, you know, on my first date. Hanging out with a bunch of strangers..."

Lexi pushed her middle finger up and laughed, humbly remembering their conversations from last night and earlier in the evening. Tia smiled back, and headed out to collect her car.

***

Dylan stood under the cold stream of water but still couldn't seem to cool himself. How had this woman gotten so deeply into his head, he wondered, and in such a short time? He loved Bo, and it was a tradition for them to spend birthdays together when they were on the road, away from family and other friends. But just this one night, he wished he could skip out, and spend the evening with Tia. They'd have no alone time tonight. The celebration would go late, they always did, but maybe it was better that way. The more time he spent with her the more time he wanted, and the fact was that he was leaving, and not coming back for a long time. If they took that next step, and then he had to go...his imagination took over, and suddenly all he could think about was that next step. He had to crank up the cold faucet to try and temper the rising that was occurring despite the goose flesh that covered his body. It wasn't fair to her, it just wasn't. But his mind and body battled on and when it came down to it, he wasn't at all sure which would win. He'd already decided he'd ask her to spend tomorrow with him—he could be free until about six when he'd have to start preparing for the show. He could invite her to the show, too, but then, by tomorrow afternoon, he'd have to decide whether he was going to dive into this thing head first without knowing how deep it was, or walk away without ever testing the waters.

His thoughts were interrupted by a sharp knock at the door.

Penelope knocked. She could hear the shower running inside and smiled to herself. She'd found him, finally. It was time to turn on the charm and get this party started. When she heard the call to come in, she turned the knob and stepped inside. She could still smell the stink of the show in the room, mixed with the light fragrance of earthy-smelling soap drifting through the cracked bathroom door.

"Finally, I found you," she said sweetly. "I've been looking for you all day, you know. I have something really important to discuss with you."

"Is that Penelope? I'll be right out," the voice answered, muffled in the sound of the water. "Just give me two minutes."

She smiled. He'd been waiting for her after all. "Maybe I could just come in?" she oozed sweetly. "I'm just dying to tell you something, and I don't know if I can wait another minute."

"Yeah, OK," the voice answered, as she slipped into the bathroom. "Hand me that towel, would you?"

She reached over to the rack and picked up a fluffy towel. This was going to be perfect, she thought, and she got herself prepared for her first act. "Need anything else?" she said suggestively.

"I can think of a couple things!" The curtain flew open and there stood, in all his naked glory, Bo Collins, grinning at her like the Cheshire cat.

There was one moment of frozen terror on her face before Penelope dropped the towel. "Oh!" she exclaimed, completely unprepared for this scenario. "Oh my God! I thought this was Dylan's room." She tried hard to divert her eyes, but he seemed to fill the whole room, and her legs refused to move.

"It is," Bo grinned. "But there was a spider in my shower—a really big one, and since Dylan was done anyway, I borrowed his." He looked at her lecherously. "Now, do you think I can have that towel, or," he said with a waggle of his eyebrows, "should I turn the water back on so you can join me? I think I might have missed a couple spots on my back..."

"Oh God!" she exclaimed again, scooping the towel from the floor and tossing it at him, fleeing from the room in the same instant.

He called after her, "Aw, honey, no need to be like that! It's my birthday, you know!" He laughed out loud as he heard the door slam and the frantic footsteps moving down the hall. Damn, he just loved putting people off like that! That chick was freaked! He couldn't wait to tell the guys. He started to whistle as he toweled off and got dressed. It was already shaping up to be a great night.

Jessa stepped into Dylan's dressing room and spoke through the closed bathroom door to let him know that Penelope was backstage again, still hunting him down, and that Tia was pulling the car around to the side exit, which so far, was clear of fans. They were all waiting by the main backstage entrance, she told him, and the other guys were going to make an appearance there. Dylan thanked her and toweled off, pulling on his clothes and whistling the opening lines of *I'll Pull You Up*.

Chapter 16

Icon was set up differently than most clubs in the city. The VIP room was elevated over the main floor, with some private rooms and booths, but a bar and dance floor were open to the rest of the club below so stars could mingle with the fans if and when they chose without actually having to make physical contact. When Dylan and Tia arrived, the place was already hopping. It was nearly midnight, and the music was pounding as hundreds of bodies moved and pulsed to the beat. Already seated in the VIP section was a group of Bears players, a table of baseball players with their wives or girlfriends, a country singer who'd had a show at another venue, and a smattering of people that Tia didn't recognize. After some handshakes and greetings to the other celebrities, she and Dylan slid into one of the private U-shaped booths, a dark and luxurious cave that provided adequate relief from the insistent beat of the music. He pulled her close to him and a waitress appeared immediately to take their drink orders. Her eyebrows rose when she saw Dylan seated there, but she'd obviously been well trained not to harass the clientele and took their orders professionally, appearing with their martinis in just a couple minutes. They'd entered through the back door, so the crowd below was oblivious to the fact that he was there. Celebrities could also opt to enter through a special front door, however, where they'd be publicly announced before walking a long red carpet that led to a set of stairs to the VIP lounge.

Tia turned to look Dylan in the eyes. "Listen Dylan," she said. "I keep saying there's no way I can ever thank you for everything, but that show tonight?"

He smiled at her. "I got all your requests in, didn't I?"

"And then some. But you played *Pull You Up*. For me."

He lifted his glass and tapped it against hers. "I did. But it was for me too, Tia, and it felt really good." He snuggled her closer and his voice dropped to her ear. "You feel really good."

Her insides did flip-flops again as he tucked her hair behind her ear. "Let me ask you something," he said. "Before it gets too crazy in here and the rest of the guys show up, I want to know if you'll see me again. Tomorrow."

Her heart leaped in her chest. "Absolutely!" she smiled up at him happily.

"I've got some free time, actually, and I do love this city. I was thinking we could spend the day doing some museums, maybe one of those Segway tours, grab some Chicago deep dish...just a normal day. A real date."

"I'd love it. It sounds wonderful!" she answered.

"But," he added quickly. "If I'm going out in public and we want to have our own fun, it'll mean I have to go in disguise again."

She laughed. "Oh no, not the mullet again!" she exclaimed. "Don't you have something a little less 80's Bono, Billy Ray Cyrus?"

"I do have other looks, you know," he smirked. I save the mullet for special occasions."

"Well if that's the case, I might be afraid to see the other ones. Let me guess. Homeless guy? Transvestite?" she giggled at the thought.

"They're all designed to be people repellant, I'll give you that. But," his eyes sparkled, "you've just given me some new ideas. Transvestite, eh? That might be fun." He looked her up and down appraisingly. "What size do you wear?" She slapped him playfully on the arm.

"You could never be repellant to me," she said.

"No?" he said, cradling her face in his hands. "Then that's all that matters, isn't it?" He brushed a soft kiss against her lips. "Seriously though," he continued. "How do you feel about dating a punk rocker tomorrow?" She raised her eyebrows at him and he raised just one back. "Nothing too obnoxious—spiky dark hair, faded Sex Pistols t-shirt, torn jeans, maybe a little eyeliner."

She pondered openly. "Eyeliner, huh? Sounds kind of sexy, actually."

"Yeah, you like that one?"

"It's definitely better than the mullet! Of course, that means I'll have to do something to match up with you so we look like a couple." She raised her eyes in thought. "Yeah, I think I could put something together for that."

He squeezed her against him. "OK, now you're getting me all excited! This is going to be really fun!" He added, "Would you come to the show again tomorrow too? Just you?"

"I was hoping you'd ask," she answered as he leaned down and kissed her.

"Were you?" he murmured between kisses, smiling down at her. "Were you really?"

"Yeah I was really," she answered, kissing him back.

Tia and Dylan knew the instant the rest of the band arrived. Bo, loving the attention of the adoring public, opted to enter through the front door and make his way ceremoniously to the VIP staircase. The music stopped and a voice came over the speakers, announcing the arrival of members of InHap, while cheers sounded throughout the place. They could hear Bo greeting the guests and slipped out of the booth to watch their grand entrance from a vantage point just out of view from the crowd on the main floor. Lexi held Bo's arm, strutting alongside him, looking as if she belonged there. She was just loving this, Tia thought, and was glad to see that the star struck look had finally left her eyes. The boys had had the same effect on Lexi that they'd had on her, then, and she was finally realizing that they were just a bunch of good guys. They heard a couple of people shout, "Where's Dylan?" and Bo told them that he'd probably be along later, but that he was shy, and avoided the limelight; to the obvious delight of the patrons.

By the time the group made it up the stairs, a table had been set for them, partially in and partially out of the view of the main room, and several bottles of champagne had been popped and poured.

Lexi rushed over to Tia. "Oh my God, these guys are so great!" she exclaimed. "They're just so nice, and fun, and Bo is so charming!"

"Yeah, he could charm the scales off a cobra," Dylan teased. "But he's basically pretty harmless."

Lexi turned back to Bo. "Oh, you have to tell them your Penelope Valentine story!"

They sat at the table—Dylan and Tia opting for seats on the private side—and Bo recounted the story, complete with vivid descriptions of the look on Penelope's face when she found herself standing in front of a 300 pound naked black man instead of 'heartthrob Dylan Miller,' as Bo put it. He was quite the storyteller, and by the time he finished, they were all laughing hysterically. Then Dylan raised his champagne glass, and proposed a toast.

"I say it pretty much every birthday, every celebration that we have to have far from home. We chose this life of vagrancy, and we revel in it. But all of it would mean nothing if I didn't have you bunch of ass holes to share it with." They all raised their glasses toward him as he continued. "Seriously though Bo, you are without a doubt one of the best friends I've ever had, and I couldn't have survived this crazy ride without you, mate. Happy birthday!"

"Happy birthday!" they all joined in, clinking glasses and taking turns hugging Bo.

A cake loaded with sparklers was carried to their table and they sang the requisite birthday song, with the patrons below joining in. Bo grinned from ear to ear, savoring every moment.

After they'd done their thing with the group, Dylan and Tia slid back into their private booth. Lexi was doing fine on her own, dancing with the guys in turn and stopping to flirt with the Bears' quarterback. She was a natural, Tia thought, wondering what her life would be like in a couple days with Dylan gone. She really felt like she didn't have to act with him, didn't have to try to flirt, and she hadn't been able to even imagine that she could feel so comfortable with another guy. She hadn't believed that could happen for a long time, anyway.

They hadn't been sitting alone for ten minutes when the music stopped again, and the crowd began cheering. They heard a voice announce, "Good evening Icon patrons! Looks like we have another special guest joining us this evening! Help me welcome Penelope Valentine, star of stage and screen, Oscar nominee, and very classy lady!" The cheers continued as Penelope obviously made her way to the VIP staircase.

"Damn it," Dylan said dejectedly, "looks like she found me. I guess there's no avoiding her now."

"Guess not," Tia agreed. "Any hope that she's given up on finding you and just showed up accidentally?"

"Hope so, but I doubt it," Dylan answered. "She seemed pretty determined that she had to talk to me about something. Might as well let her say her peace, and then get rid of her."

He'd no sooner gotten the words out of his mouth then she appeared at the end of their booth. "Well, well. Dylan Miller. You certainly are a hard man to track down," she said with honey in her voice.

"I heard you were looking for me," he answered politely. "Sorry I missed you at the arena, but I must have had my phone off, or something, and then I was anxious to get to Bo's party. I guess you found me now, though."

"It wasn't easy," she smiled, "believe me. I had to get a whole team working to track you down to find out where you went after the show!"

She extended her hand to Dylan and he shook it courteously. "So, what can I do for you Miss Valentine?"

"Oh please, just Penelope is fine," she smiled sweetly. "I have the most exciting news, and I was in town anyway, visiting a friend, and I wanted to tell you myself, in person." She turned to Tia and motioned with her head toward the main VIP room. "Would you excuse us, please?" she asked politely. "This is personal business."

"We don't have any personal business, Miss Valentine," Dylan replied. "She can stay right here," Penelope looked shaken for a moment, but maintained her flashing smile.

"Well alright, then," she said, sliding into the booth and sidling up to Dylan. "If you insist. Like I said, I have exciting news."

"Yes?" Dylan said, impatiently.

Tia could see that Penelope was working hard to hold her little 'nice girl' act together. She smiled sweetly at Tia, but it was easy to read the scowl in her eyes.

"I'd hoped we could have this conversation privately, but...." She looked around as if she was about to share a huge secret, then leaned into Dylan suggestively. "It's not going public until tomorrow, but guess who your costar for *Ambient Rain* is going to be?"

Dylan looked bored. "Let me guess. You?"

"Yes!" she sang, her face lighting up. "I'm so excited to be working with you! I love your music of course, and I've seen your films, and can't wait to bring the story to life with you!" She clapped her hands under her chin in a display of pure excitement. It was obvious to Tia that it was all an act, and not even a very good one at that. One look at Dylan told her that he wasn't buying it, either. "It was a great show tonight, actually," she added as an afterthought. "Thanks for fitting me in." Inside she seethed that she'd been given only fourth row, but she forced her smile and batted her eyelashes at him without any regard for the fact that he sat with a date at his other side.

Tia's stomach sank a bit at the news, but she wasn't really surprised. She'd heard Jessa tell Dylan that they'd be announcing his costar within the next couple days, and she'd guessed that might be why Penelope was so adamant about seeing him. It meant that she and Dylan would be filming and pretty much living together in New Zealand, on the other side of the world, for months. And she'd be sitting back in her fifth grade classroom, hanging out at the country club with Lexi and Ryan, and still trying to get her life back on track. It pulled something inside her out of whack, and she suddenly felt very dejected as the reality of the situation sunk in. She couldn't help the fact that some of the happiness she'd been feeling lurched out of her, and jealousy, sadness, and emptiness crept in. Dylan sensed it, and put his arm around her, pulling her closer to him.

"Well, that's great, Miss Valentine," he said, purposely ignoring her invitation to be on a first-name basis. "I look forward to working with you. I've seen some of your work, too. I'm sure it'll be fun." He kept his hand protectively around Tia as he said it, as if to reassure her of her own place. "Thanks for coming to tell me, I appreciate it, but we're sort of in the middle a celebration here..." His voice trailed off and his eyes wandered toward the main room. The meaning was obvious—he was inviting her to leave.

"Oh," she said, her eyes dropping just for a moment. "I was actually hoping that we could get to know each other a little, spend some time together. I think that we could have great chemistry, you and me, and thought maybe we could explore that a little bit, see where it takes us..." She put on her sexiest pout, hoping to drop the hint a little deeper.

Dylan responded by squeezing Tia even tighter and looking at Penelope with that one eyebrow raised. "Well, that's...interesting," he stumbled, unable to come up with a better word, "but that's why they call it acting," he said. "There doesn't have to be any chemistry. I think we've both done enough of it to make it work when it needs to."

"But why waste the opportunity?" she soothed. "I'm here, and you're here, and we have some pretty hot love scenes in the film, you know—I just finished reading the script." Actually, she'd skimmed it, looking specifically for those scenes. She looked at Tia with contempt. "Look," she pouted, "I didn't want to say this except in private, but if you're looking for some fun tonight, why waste your time with some groupie? Why not take your chances with someone who's more at your level?" She dropped her voice to a seductive whisper and looked at Dylan through drooped lids. "I think you'd find we have a lot in common." She tried her best to sound sexy, but to Dylan, she just sounded desperate.

Dylan physically felt Tia stiffen beside him, and when he looked at her, he could see the hurt in her eyes. Although he tried to contain his anger, his eyes and his words were full of venom. He flashed a sardonic smile and shook his head. "You've really got some balls, lady," he said. "Look, Miss Valentine. I appreciate that you came all the way out here to tell me the news in person, but you've just insulted my date, someone I care about, and I'm going to have to ask you to leave." Penelope started to speak, but Dylan continued firmly. "I'm going to ask you to leave *now*. I will see you in New Zealand, and we'll do a movie together, with lots of *acting*, and that'll be the end of it." Penelope was backpedaling, trying to save face, but Dylan wouldn't give her an opportunity to speak again. "Goodbye, Miss Valentine. Please don't expect any tickets for tomorrow's show or any other."

Bo chose that exact moment to sidle into the booth next to Penelope. Her eyes widened when she saw him and all the cool she was trying to portray slipped off her face.

"Well helooo, Miss Valentine," he said in a low, slow, and smooth voice. "I was hoping you'd come to my party. You left so suddenly before…"

"That was just a mistake," she stammered. "I was looking for Dylan—it was his name on the door! You were in his dressing room…"

"Now see, I don't believe in accidents," he said, his voice dripping with obvious undertones. "I think that things happen for a reason. Incidental Happenstance, and all that." He looked directly into her face, dropping his eyelids in a suggestive gesture. "And I can't help but wonder what that reason might be."

Penelope tried to maintain her composure, but her voice faltered when she spoke. "I don't… I think I just need to go now."

"Now come on, sugar," he whispered, laying it on thick. "It's my birthday. You've already seen me naked, so the least you can do is give me a dance," he put his arm around her shoulders and gave her a squeeze.

Penelope pressed herself even more against Dylan, but Bo just slid in closer, and twirled a lock of Penelope's hair around his finger. She was really looking desperate now, like a caged animal seeking an escape, and despite her mixed emotions, Tia almost laughed.

"I've got to go!" she exclaimed, winded. But it was obvious that Bo wasn't moving. Finally, she climbed over Dylan and Tia to escape out the other side of the half-moon booth, jabbing Tia in the thigh with the tip of her spiked heel. She winced at the pain, and Dylan's hand was there immediately, covering her protectively. Penelope nearly tripped getting out of the booth, and made a less than graceful exit. Bo and Dylan shared a smile and a knowing look.

Penelope brushed down her skirt and tried to regain her dignity. She wasn't used to being rejected this way. She wasn't used to being rejected at all, and it really pissed her off. None of this had gone the way she'd planned it, and it was all because of that stupid bitch, that little girl who was way out of her league and taking all Dylan's attention when it should have been hers and it wasn't fair, not fair at all, and she wouldn't be put off this way.

"Goodbye, Miss Valentine." Dylan replied coldly. "I'll see you in September." Penelope tossed Tia a hateful glare before quickly approaching the table of football players, her hand out in greeting and the sweet smile planted once more on her face.

Dylan immediately turned to Tia. "Look at me," he said, putting his finger under her chin and forcing her to meet his gaze. "Don't you for one minute worry about a single word she said," he whispered to her. "She doesn't have a fraction of the class you have, and she knows it. I'm here with you tonight because I want to be—she couldn't hold a candle to you."

Tia looked up at him and fought the emotions that raged inside her, but he could see the deep shadow in her eyes. Penelope's words had hurt her, and she pulled away from him, stiffening under his touch.

"It's true, you know," she said sadly, "pretty much everything she said."

"Now I won't hear any talk like that," Bo interjected. "Come on, little lady, it's time for you to give me my birthday dance."

Tia looked down at the table, "Sorry Bo, but I don't really feel…"

"Nope. Won't take no for an answer. Give her up Dylan; I need to talk some sense into this little thing." He slid out of the booth and came around to the other side of the U, taking Tia's hand in his, pulling her up to him and putting his arm around her shoulders. She looked back at Dylan, who shrugged. "Can't argue with the birthday boy," he said, raising his eyebrows.

Tia felt deflated as Bo led her to the little dance floor. He wrapped his big arms around her and she sank into him, not quite trusting her own legs. Bo took her face in his huge hands, pulling her up to meet his dark eyes, which blazed with intensity. "Listen, little girl," he said scolding her with his voice. "I heard what she said to you, and I watched your face literally fall off your head."

A single tear slid down her cheek, and he caught it with his fingertip, wiping it away. "It's true, Bo. Everything she said. I don't know what I'm doing here—I'm way out of his league."

"Hey now," he soothed. "I've known Dylan for a long time, and I can tell you, he doesn't have a league. He's the most down to earth person I know, and believe me; he's got it something bad for you." He settled his hands on her hips and swayed with her to the music. "Have you heard the story about how he and I met?"

"He told me tonight actually," she answered, "while we were hiding out from Little Miss Hollywood."

"Well, I'll bet his version and mine are a little bit different. Tell me, did he make me out to be the hero of the story? The one with all the talent who graciously allowed some skinny little white boy to play with his band?"

Tia smiled a little, in spite of herself. "Yeah, it was something like that," she said.

"Well let me tell you the real story," he said as Tia settled into the comfort of his bulk and they continued to sway to the music. "It was a Friday night, you see, and my band and I were sitting around a table in a little pub outside London after a gig—and I'm talking a very little pub *way* outside of London. He bought us a round and asked if he could join us, and started gushing about our performance—mine in particular; he said he'd never seen a drummer with such a huge stage presence." He leaned down and whispered in her ear, "I don't know if you've noticed, but I'm kind of a big guy."

"The thought had crossed my mind," she smiled in spite of herself, feeling her mood slightly lifted.

"So anyway, he tells us he's a fairly accomplished guitarist—that's what he said, 'fairly accomplished,' and he says he would be honored if he could have the chance to jam with us. I look around at my boys, and they're all smirking and shaking their heads, looking at this little punker boy with his messy, spiky hair and ripped jeans, but I figured, what the hell? We had a practice set up the next day at the pub we'd be playing that night, so we decided to humor him. We all figure that there's no way this boy—he couldn't have been more than twenty then—was going to be able to keep up with our bluesy sound, and guessed we'd jam for an hour or so and laugh about it later.

"So he shows up with his guitar slung over his back and I say, 'Show us what you got, Little Strummer Boy,' much to the amusement of my boys. Dylan says, 'You guys just go ahead and play, and I'll jump in.' We all smiled at each other, and pounded into a song. Dylan listens for about eight bars, eyes closed, nodding his head, and then dives in, perfectly matching the tempo and the sound. We all looked at each other, our eyes poppin' out of our heads—we'd never thought that kind of sound could come from an acoustic guitar or blend so perfectly with what we were trying to do musically. It was like he could draw a mood out of his instrument, an actual emotion, and we were completely blown away."

"It was because of his mom, and her art studio," Tia commented.

"Exactly!" Bo agreed. "So after a couple more tunes, we were thoroughly impressed, and I asked him if he did vocals. And I tell you, when that boy opened his mouth and started to sing, I knew he was going to the top. Instantly. His voice—well, you know—it was honest, open, and he could weave the lyrics as well as he could the guitar." Tia nodded—she knew exactly what he meant.

"We asked him to join us on the stage that night, and from the look on his face, you woulda thought we'd invited him to the queen's castle for tea. He honestly didn't realize how good he was, and thought we were doing him a favor. But that night, on stage, he just took over the show—not intentionally, but just by being himself—and the audience loved it. He joined us for the rest of the tour, which was only four more shows; but by the end of that week, I knew I wanted to work with him again. Not only was he a great musician, but I liked him as a person too, and knew he'd be a great friend. I practically begged him to come back to the states, and left him with all my numbers and a promise that I could hook him up with a place to stay and some steady work if he did."

Tia settled into him and listened with interest—she knew so little about Dylan in his younger days, and loved hearing Bo talk about him with such admiration.

"It was weeks before he called, but when he finally did, I managed to convince him to give it a shot. He slept on my couch for six months, working in a music store during the day, bartending in the early evenings and playing gigs at night. It was obvious to me who the talent was—hell, I like to think of myself as a pretty good beat man, but we all know that drummers don't do solo tours—a good band needs a good front man. Dylan had it all—talent, good looks, charisma—but he was just humble enough not to fully realize it, which kept him honest. I knew I could go to the top with him. We even wanted to name the band for him;" he added, "we wanted to call it the *Dylan Miller Experience*, because being with him *is* an experience, and we all knew it would be him that took us all the way. But again, the man is humble. He shook it off, said it was just incidental happenstance that we all met the way we did, and the name just stuck."

Tia understood the 'experience' part perfectly. "He has so much respect for you, though, Bo—you know that."

"I do, and that's another reason why I love the man. But the point of the story is that Dylan doesn't put himself on a pedestal like so many other famous people do. He doesn't think he's better than anyone else—he'd be just as happy playing in little pubs as he is playing on the big stages. It's about the music for him, always has been. He's never gone in for all that Hollywood bullshit. Hell, he lives in Colorado, for chrissake, on a ranch in a tiny little town. He's never tried to be some hotshot celebrity—he purposely avoids that scene as much as he can. And he keeps us humble, too, knocking us back down to Earth if things start going to our heads. He's our reality check, in a way. Why do you think he goes out in disguise? He misses being a normal person. It's just that singing and music are in his blood and he doesn't have a choice but to do it. The celebrity just comes along for the ride."

Tia whispered, "Oh, I know all that, Bo, I do. It's one of the things I like so much about him; that he's so down to earth and open. But what does it matter anyway? I'm living in a fantasy world here. He'll be gone in a couple days and then what?"

"Listen. I can't predict the future, but I can tell you that the boy is in deeper than even he realizes. I know I'm the jokester and the prankster of the band, but I'm also kind of the bartender —I hear more of their shit than I care to, sometimes," he said with a sarcastic chuckle. "Dylan's my best friend in the world, Tia, and I know him better than anyone. I see the way he looks at you—the way you look at each other. I hear the way he talks about you and see the way he lights up when you walk into the room. He's never dedicated a whole show to one person, and he played every song you wanted, even the one that was hardest for him play. You're bringing out all the things in him that he thought he'd lost, and I for one appreciate it. Damn, I don't know what's gonna happen tomorrow or the next day or next month, but I do know that you have to make the most of every minute and let it work itself out. Don't give up the time you do have worrying about time you might not get later. That would be a waste."

Tia hugged him tight. "You're right, Bo, I know you're right. I just don't know what I'm even doing here, and I'm scared." She looked up into his face and stretched up on her toes to kiss his cheek. "Thanks," she whispered. "You're pretty great, you know that? I'm so glad I could come to your party."

"Me too," he grinned back, giving her a little squeeze.

Dylan appeared beside them. "I really think I need to cut in, mate," he said to Bo.

"But of course," he replied, bowing and offering him Tia's hand. She stepped into Dylan's arms and he held her close, pressing his lips against the top of her head. "I'm so sorry, Tia, I'm so sorry."

"For what? For being you? You can't apologize for that Dylan. You didn't do anything."

"No, but she hurt you, and that really pisses me off." She felt him stiffen, and heard his exhale as he tried to tramp down the anger that still coursed through him. "You do know, don't you, that you've got more class in your little finger than she could ever hope to have? She's got nothing on you. You're the one I want to be with."

Tia sighed wistfully. "I just can't help but think..."

He interrupted her. "Don't think that way. I know it's hard, it's hard for me too." He ran his fingers through her hair and gently pulled her head back to meet his eyes. "Bloody hell," he said, clearly aggravated. "This isn't at all the way I wanted to ask you this, but I don't know how else to..."

She looked up at him with uncertainty in her eyes as he paused before continuing. "I had Jessa look into something. I wanted to know the latest time I could leave Chicago and still get to Cleveland in time for Monday's show. It looks like I can catch a private flight at 3:00 and still make it in time for sound checks."

Tia looked up at him, not quite understanding. "Damn it," he continued, glaring over at Penelope who was now perched on the quarterback's lap. "She's really fucked this up. Listen. Never once since I met you did I consider you a potential notch in my bedpost, or anything even close to that." He pulled away slightly and ran his fingers through his own hair, grunting with agitation. "Shit, I don't know what I'm doing here. This isn't fair to you, and it damned sure isn't fair to me, but I really do care about you, Tia. I know I just met you yesterday, but you've kind of gotten under my skin." He cradled her face in his hands and stared deep into her. "I want to spend as much time as I can with you before I have to go. Part of me knows that it'll just make it even harder, but I really like you, and I want every minute I can get." She smiled up at him, and he planted a soft kiss gently on her lips.

"I got a suite at the Hilton for tomorrow night. It's two bedrooms, and I swear it isn't about trying to get you into bed." He kissed her again. "Although I'd be lying if I said I haven't thought about it. A lot." He looked frustrated as he glanced over at Penelope again, still blatantly flirting with the quarterback and continually looking back to see if Dylan had noticed. "I just want to spend as much time with you as possible. I want to have breakfast with you and have you be the last person I see before I leave Chicago." Tia's eyes widened as she took it all in. He thought about being with her a lot? He got a suite at the Hilton and wasn't leaving until Monday afternoon? Her stomach was doing flips and turns while her mind imagined what that could lead to.

"I'm asking you to spend the night with me, Tia. Not in my bed, because I couldn't bear it that you'd always wonder if that was all I wanted from you from the start, but just to be with me, because I just can't seem to get you out of my head."

Tia breathed deeply and exhaled on a sigh. "You really mean it, don't you?" she asked, incredulously. She didn't need an answer; she could read the truth in his eyes.

"I absolutely mean it," he answered, stroking her hair softly. "I promise I'll be the perfect gentleman, but I also promise that it won't be easy—might be the hardest thing I've ever done—but I won't put you through that." He buried his hands and face in her hair and whispered, "Will you stay with me?"

She didn't hesitate for a second before answering, because even though she knew that saying goodbye to him would be horrible, she couldn't face doing it sooner. "Oh yeah," she said, finding his mouth and kissing him. "I absolutely will."

Chapter 17

Tia looked in the mirror one more time, satisfied with the final result. She'd teased up her hair, added some blue highlights that framed her face, caked on heavier than usual makeup, and practiced her scowl in the mirror. Her clothes were leftovers from a Halloween costume a couple years back, punk rock to the core but not over done, and when she looked at the finished product, she figured that even her students wouldn't quite recognize her. She hopped in her car and went to pick up Dylan at the Hilton; where she'd be spending the night with him in his suite. In a room right next to his. She was thinking about that a lot, spending the night with him without actually *spending the night* with him. He was worried about overstepping boundaries, but her passion for him kept growing, and when she was with him she always had the feeling that she was standing on a precipice from which she could easily fall at any moment. She didn't know what to think about it, but she wasn't afraid of the fall—just the aftermath. Being with him that way might make it harder to say goodbye, but not being with him might fill the rest of her life with regret. She'd always wonder if taking that one more step would have changed the course of her future. But, no matter what Bo and Dylan told her, the spiteful words of Penelope Valentine kept coming back to haunt her. That horrible woman would be spending months alone with Dylan in a foreign place where they didn't know anyone else; filming intimate love scenes and spending a lot of their time together. Tia didn't put anything past that woman, and it was obvious that she was hot to get her claws deep into Dylan.

She slapped her cheeks to ward off the negative thoughts. Bo's words came back to her over and over too, and his were much more pleasant to recall. He said Dylan was in deeper than even he knew, and that was comforting to some degree. The wisest words, though, were that she had to stop worrying about tomorrow and concentrate on today. It would be hard, since tomorrow would definitely take Dylan away from her, but she was determined to enjoy every minute of her time with him, trying to convince herself that if nothing else ever came of it, she'd still had the most amazing weekend of her entire life and she should be satisfied with that.

Dylan was waiting in the lobby, slouched against the wall and generally smirking at everything around him. Tia observed people looking at him out of the corners of their eyes, or lengthening their paths through the lobby to give him a wide berth. Repellant was the word he used, but as always, she was drawn to him, and she put on her own best smirk and sauntered over to his side.

"Hey, good lookin'," she said in her best British accent, which wasn't very good.

"Bloody hell, you look brilliant!" he mused. He held her shoulders at arm's length and looked her up and down. "I approve," he said, smiling. "It could be a new look for you. I bet your students would love it. You'd be the coolest teacher ever!"

"I'm already the coolest teacher ever," she said firmly, then broke into a grin. "Now are you ready to freak some people out, or what?"

"I'm all yours," he smiled, but in the back of his mind and hers, they thought simultaneously, *for today, anyway*.

It was an incredible day in the city. The sky was clear, the day was unusually warm, and the constant wind that often bellowed in from Lake Michigan had taken its own holiday. They started with an architectural boat ride down the river, cuddling up under a blanket at the back of the boat and learning about the history of Chicago between stolen kisses. They chased each other around the city on Segways, snacked at little street side cafes, and wandered aimlessly around the Art Institute, where Dylan fidgeted in the Modern Art Gallery. "I just don't get it," he said, "it's just a few colors tossed on the canvas. Maybe I'm in the wrong line of work. I could just throw blobs of paint at a wall, and I wouldn't have to spend nine out of twelve months away from home every year."

"You're not supposed to always get it," Tia said. "You're just supposed to appreciate it."

"You forget that I grew up with an artist, someone who created things of beauty—pieces that meant something," he said, shaking his head. "I get the Monet's and the Renoir's and the Degas's, but this is rubbish."

She laughed, and they wandered around the classics before catching a cab to head up to the 96th floor of the Hancock building for a quick drink, where they enjoyed an incredible view of the city. The elevator operator eyed them suspiciously as they ascended, and they got similar looks from the hostess at the bar. Torn jeans and Sex Pistols t-shirts were definitely not the fashion choices of most of the patrons at the bar, but a casually placed bill in the palms of the right people assured they were treated with respect, albeit with an eye of suspicion. Everywhere they went people tended to either ignore them or look at them with sideways glances, and they both enjoyed the reactions. If they only knew.

"Wow," Tia said as they sipped martinis next to the large window that looked out on the city, "repellant is a good word. I don't think anyone's looked me in the eye all day."

"That's the whole point," Dylan explained, "we can go anywhere and do anything, and no one wants to look directly at us. It's the only way I can blend into a crowd—by being completely separate from it."

"Yeah, but it's kind of sad in a way," she reflected, "because you only get to be on the fringes of it, not really a part of it, you know what I mean?"

"It's the story of my life," he said with sadness in his voice, "if I want any sort of normalcy."

They satisfied Dylan's craving for Chicago deep dish at Gino's, penning their names on the famous graffiti wall inside a little heart, and then it was time to head to the arena for the introduction of Outcast and the pre-show meeting. Tia sat in the common room with Jessa, and shared with her the fun they'd had that day.

"It sounds absolutely wonderful!" she said. "I'm glad you two had such a good time. Dylan really does love Chicago, but he hardly ever gets to do those sorts of things. I'm glad he had you to share them with Tia, really."

She was riding another high all through the show. It was so incredible to watch Dylan on stage—no matter how many times she'd seen InHap play, it was different every time and amazing to be a part of the experience. She couldn't help but think though, that in a couple short hours she'd be alone with Dylan in their suite, and that there would be some serious choices to be made. Every time he sang to her from the stage, she imagined his voice whispering in her ear, and felt the little rolls of her stomach that were way beyond her control every time their eyes met.

When they met up in the common room after the show, the weight of the rest of the evening began to settle in on both of them. Soon they'd be alone in the suite, and they'd both have either some big decisions to make or some huge battles to wage. As the boys wrapped up the evening and gave instructions to the stage hands who were already tearing down the drum kit and backdrops to load them on the trucks for the trip to Cleveland, Tia's mind and body were waging a battle of their own. Every time their eyes met, the questions hung between them, even from across the crowded room. Would this be the night? Would tonight be enough? Dylan tried to sound light, but his voice was gruff when he finally asked, "So. Are you ready to blow this place?"

Her answer was barely a croak, "Uh huh." It was all she could manage when she saw the fire flare up in his eyes. She drove them to the Hilton in silence, her hand resting in his during the short drive to the hotel.

The suite was incredible. It was all marble, wood and soft rugs that begged to be walked on barefoot. Tia was battling nerves from all directions; if he was going to try and be a gentleman she owed it to him not to push things, and if he wasn't...well, it had been so long since she'd been with a man that she worried about her lack of practice. This, after all, was a man who could literally have any woman he wanted and if he actually did want her...she just couldn't help but wonder if she was worthy.

The tension in the room was intense. It was just past midnight, so they still had a lot of evening ahead of them. Dylan went to the wet bar and pulled a bottle of white wine out of the chiller, motioning to her to have a seat on the couch. She sat, enveloped by the luxurious fabric and soft cushions. Dylan brought two glasses, poured, and then sat a measurable distance from her on the sofa. They raised glasses, and he said, "Here's to..." the unspoken words hung between them like a chasm. He cleared his throat, and finished, "...a great day." They drank, and then an uncomfortable silence fell over them. Tia finally broke it.

"Hey," she said simply. He looked at her with that one eyebrow look and forced a smile. "Whatever happens, Dylan," she continued, "I definitely don't want things to be awkward between us."

"I agree," he commented immediately, relieved that she was feeling it too.

"You've made me feel comfortable every minute we've been together—and at times, I know that hasn't been easy."

"Aw, Tia."

"Let me finish. When I was dancing with Bo last night, he said something that really made me put things into perspective. He said that it was stupid to waste a single minute of our time together worrying about what's going to happen tomorrow, and I mean to stick to that."

"He is a wise man," he joked, flashing his sideways smirk. "And I agree. I don't want anything to get in the way of our..." he almost said, 'last night together,' but caught himself just in time, "...evening." He scooted over to her and pulled her in so that her head rested on his chest. There were so many things he wanted to say to her, but all of them sounded like goodbye, and he wanted to put that off as long as possible. Again, she came to the rescue, picking up their conversations from earlier in the day—light topics; books he'd read, movies he liked, and soon they were laughing and talking again like old friends, their legs and fingers intertwined as they rested easily on the couch. *I can do this*, he thought, but in the back of his mind he added, *I could do this forever*.

After a while, they decided that it was safe, and even important, that they move the conversation to the hot tub that sat on a balcony overlooking the lake. Tia was very aware as she changed into her swimsuit that they'd both be seeing more of each other than they'd seen before. She'd brought a one piece and a bikini, just in case, and opted for the bikini with a cover-up until she got to the tub. Dylan was already soaking when she stepped out onto the balcony, and her breath caught in her throat. He was incredibly sexy, the contours of his body smooth and well defined with just the right amount of light brown hair swirling on his chest and creeping down his flat stomach beneath the water. The lights in the tub illuminated him from below, and she felt a now familiar tingle as she looked at him. He had more wine poured, and she slid off her cover up and perched one leg over the side of the tub. She was very aware of Dylan's eyes on her as she slipped slowly into the hot bubbling water, testing the temperature. She heard a low sound come from his throat, and he said, "Damn, that bikini sure makes this a lot harder. Literally and figuratively."

She smiled. "What, this old thing?" she laughed, submerging herself into the warm bubbles. "You like it?"

"Oh, I like it, alright." He'd like it a lot better off, he thought, but he'd made a promise, and he meant to keep it.

He handed her a glass of wine and draped his arm around her, pulling her close. Damn, he thought, looking down into the bubbles that churned and pulsed with light and seeing the swell of her breasts floating just below the surface. He massaged her neck, and felt the tiny string that with just a little tug would release them to his gaze, his hands, and especially his mouth. This wasn't going to be easy, he thought. If it wasn't for that bitch of an actress planting the seed that all he wanted from her was night in the sack, he wouldn't have this problem. He'd let things move at their own pace, and worry about the consequences later. But he'd seen the look on her face when that Valentine woman said the hateful words, and had seen just a moment of question and hesitation in her eyes. He respected Tia, and wanted her to know it, so even when his finger tangled in the string, he wiggled it free without releasing the knot. It might have been easier if she hadn't worn a bikini, but he doubted it. She could be in ski pants and a bulky coat right now and he'd still want her. And when she moaned with pleasure and leaned back into the slow relaxing circles he was rubbing into her shoulders, kissing her wasn't an option. He had to do it.

She felt him shift just a bit and knew the kiss was coming. She'd been half hoping that he'd pull the string of her bikini and send it floating to the other side of the hot tub, but apparently he was determined to be the gentleman. What she really wanted was for him to take her right there, to put out the fires that burned inside her. The feel of his skin against hers was distracting, to say the least, and she knew she wanted him; knew that if he started things she would continue them and follow through all the way to the end. But was it enough? She'd been wrestling with the thoughts all day, and still didn't have a good answer. There wasn't any good answer, really. It would be only hours now and then he'd be leaving and she knew he had to go; didn't have a choice, but wondered if it would be different if he was just some random guy that she'd met who lived in the area. She was sure that it would be, and that was the hardest part. If they had time to really get to know one another, she felt quite certain that they would at least give a relationship a shot.

One night with him, she thought, would never be enough. And if they were as hot in bed as they were out of it, she'd spend the rest of her life longing for something that could never be, and then she'd never get herself back on track. Even without that next step she knew that she'd compare every guy she met to Dylan, and she was truly afraid that no one would ever measure up. But on the other hand, if she didn't take the chance, she'd spend the rest of her life wondering what it would have been like, and she'd still compare every guy to him. She'd see him on the covers of magazines and from a distance at his shows, or from a theater seat or her couch as she watched one of his movies—and the longing would be there, always, out of reach and out of her league.

Oh, but when he kissed her, when his soft, full lips brushed hers as she closed her eyes to enjoy the feel of his hands on so much bare skin, she could push that all aside and just enjoy the moment, splaying her hands along the contours of his chest and swirling her fingertips through the hair that curled in the water. She pressed herself closer, and heard his breath catch and his breathing change and knew that he was feeling this too, that maybe it was beyond their control, his hands sliding down her back as she turned to return the kiss, and as he reached around her to touch her bare stomach, there was no thought, no compromise, no regret, no tomorrow, and the volcano that had been brewing inside of her since their first kiss erupted. She kissed him back feverishly, and rolled over to press herself against him. It had been so long, and her body was responding on its own with no direction from her brain, knowing only that it craved contact, intimacy, lovemaking, and she was just about to surrender everything when Dylan put his hands on her waist and pushed her away, gasping for breath.

She could see the conflict in his eyes and the fire that blazed there, and tried to move closer to show him that it was OK, she wanted this too, but he stood up and stepped out of the tub. "Bloody hell," he whistled under his breath. "It's getting hot in here. I think I need a shower," and he rushed off before Tia could say a word, closing the sliding door and stepping into his own room.

For a moment she just sat there, the bubbles continuing to churn around her now aching body, hoping the heat would relax her tensed and coiled muscles but knowing now that Dylan either didn't want to take the next step, or was determined to keep his promise to her. She knew that ice was the only thing that was going to tramp down the fire that burned inside her, and she slipped out of the tub and into her room for her own cold shower.

When she finally stepped out of the marble stall, shivering, she contemplated the outfits she'd packed for the night, sadly putting aside the lingerie in favor of a pair of old sweats and a faded InHap t-shirt and returned to the couch and her now warm glass of wine.

Dylan stood under the icy water for a long time, letting it drip into his face, but with his eyes closed, all he could see was Tia in her tiny bikini and that wasn't helping his situation any. God, he wanted her so badly, and he was so close to losing control. He could see her eyes, the droopy, half-lidded look of passion she'd worn as he just managed to pull away from her before he lost himself completely. He could almost feel the steam rising from his naked flesh, and the heat that raged within him couldn't be tamed by the cold water. When he finally emerged, he decided that the only thing to do would be to call it a night. It was pretty late; nearly three in the morning, but he hadn't planned on sleeping much tonight knowing that they'd be saying goodbye in just a few hours. But being close to her was not an option if he was going to follow through on his promise to be a gentleman—he'd lose control for sure and didn't want to leave her with any regrets—it wasn't fair to either of them, really. In the morning things would look different, he'd be leaving, and they'd have to say their goodbyes.

That dark cloud hung on him like a storm, and he wondered if he'd be able to deal with it any better when the time actually came to walk away. He seriously doubted it. He pulled on a pair of old lounge pants and a t-shirt, and stepped back out into the living room. She was already on the couch, her hair wet from the shower and her face scrubbed clean. Thankfully, she wore baggy sweat pants and an old InHap shirt, and he remembered he had a little gift for her and went back into the room to retrieve it. It was nothing, really, just a concert t-shirt from this current tour that would make a little souvenir—he'd figured he'd sign it with a nice message, which seemed really stupid now. It had his name written across the front, with the band name beneath and a picture of his guitar. As if that would be enough to remind her of their time together. As if they'd had enough time.

He tossed the shirt to her. "That shirt's like, five years old. How about a new one?"

She held it up in front of her. "Thanks," she replied. "It's great."

This is awkward, he thought. He figured he'd better say goodnight now, before he changed his mind. If he was going to keep his vow, it was the only way.

"So, I'm pretty wiped," he said. "What do you say we plan for an early breakfast in the morning so we can have..." he paused, "...some more time?"

"Yeah, OK," she replied softly, respecting his wishes. If he was determined that they not spend the night together, she'd have to find a way to deal with it. "Goodnight, then." She rose from the couch and gave him a soft kiss on the cheek, then went into her room without looking back. It was all he could do not to grab her and pull her back—but he watched in silence until she closed the door, then turned and entered his own room.

Bloody hell, he thought. He ran his fingers through his hair and stared out the window at the Lake in the distance and the Chicago skyline to the north. There was no way he was going to get a wink of sleep tonight, not when all he could think of was the woman in the next room.

He'd never met anyone like her. Hitting it big at a young age had its disadvantages. He found out quickly that you couldn't trust women when you were constantly in the limelight. There was always an agenda. None of them cared for him, not really. Penelope was right about one thing—it was damned near impossible to have normal relationships when you were a star.

But Tia was different. He'd never felt so comfortable with a woman, even in his younger, awkward days. He was able to be himself with her, and he trusted her honesty completely. Before meeting her, he couldn't remember the last time he'd laughed so openly, or just been silly with someone. It was so easy to let his guard down with her, and he was certain that she would never make him sorry for it. It just felt plain good to be with her—it felt so right to hold her hand, and holding her brought out something in him that he'd often feared he'd never feel.

And she was in the next room. In bed. Every fiber of his being ached to go to her—to take things to the ultimate level and to feel safe doing so. God, it had been so hard to walk away from her tonight. But he'd made a promise that he wouldn't take advantage, and he'd just barely managed to pull himself away before that promise went out the window. He could feel the energy of her in the next room, and still had the scent of her on his skin from their brief goodnight; the taste of her in his mouth.

He peeled off the t-shirt, leaned back on the bed, and picked up his guitar. Usually, playing soothed away any bad feelings and lifted him to a different place. He strummed a few notes. Maybe he'd write a song for her, about her, but all the words that came into his mind had to do with making love to her, holding her, kissing her, and just thinking about it made him feel even worse. The only thing worse than not having her here with him in his bed was knowing that tomorrow he'd have to walk away. He thought of her going back to her life without him, back to the country club with Lexi and *Paddy's*, back to her job...

He bolted upright as an idea suddenly sprouted in his mind, and he wondered why he hadn't considered it before. He'd been so busy thinking about telling her goodbye, that he hadn't been thinking about anything else. It lifted his spirits immediately, and he made the decision instantly. There was no question in his mind—he couldn't just walk away from her tomorrow and let her be gone from his life. He'd ask her in the morning, and hoped to God that she'd say yes.

But perhaps a bit of tea now, to maybe stop his blood from boiling and allow him a couple precious hours of sleep...

Stupid, stupid! Tia thought. She'd completely blown it. Now Dylan was in the room on the other side of the suite; so close, but so far away. She was still raging inside, and she peeled off her clothes and climbed into the huge bed, so empty with just her in it. But the soft Egyptian cotton was torture against her erect nipples, and she climbed out and picked up the t-shirt Dylan had given her. He must have had it in with his own things, because it smelled of him, and she held it to her face and inhaled his scent deeply before slipping it on.

She stood in front of the mirror and looked at her reflection. She could see the flush in her cheeks—she felt as though she were on fire. Across her chest read Dylan's name, and she imagined "Property Of" being written above it. She was, now. She felt as though she belonged to him. But she had to make that feeling go away. There was no sense in feeling it when he was going to say goodbye in the morning and she might not ever see him again. She felt so conflicted—she wanted him desperately, and wanted to give herself over to him, but he was right, and he was stronger than she was, obviously; if they took it further it would be even harder then to watch him walk out of her life, probably forever.

He'd made a promise not to use her for a notch in his bedpost, so to speak, but that wasn't the way he made her feel. When he held her, she felt as though there was no other woman in the world, and she trusted her heart to him. Should she go and knock on his door? Oh, God, she was so tempted to do just that—she was falling for him. *Yeah right*, she thought, she'd already fallen. And she'd known him what, a little over 48 hours? She'd thought it would take months, maybe even years to feel this way about another man, and now she wondered sadly if she could ever feel it again for anyone else.

There was little chance that she would sleep tonight, with him just a few feet away, alone in his own bed. She paced the room, and decided that maybe some tea would help to relax her anxious heart. There was a tea service right outside the rooms—surely they had something herbal and decaffeinated to help her at least lie still for an hour or two. She'd have to figure out the rest tomorrow, when they said their goodbyes.

Chapter 18

She stepped out into the corridor and set the tea maker on heat. It took only a couple minutes for the water to boil, and she placed a chamomile tea bag into one of the large mugs that sat on the table. No sooner did the heater begin to sound that it had completed its cycle than Dylan stepped out of the far door, shirtless and wearing lounge pants that hung low on his hips, accentuating his flat stomach and the 'v' that led the fine line of hair down into his waistband. Damn, he was incredibly sexy, his eyes lidded and lips slightly parted.

He stood in the foyer for a moment and just stared at her, the intensity of his gaze pouring over every part of her and leaving no doubt about the desire that simmered there, just below the surface. Her breath quickened and the volcano bubbled, her blood pulsing like hot lava through her veins. The air in the room suddenly sizzled with electricity—she could almost hear the crackle and could definitely feel the hum vibrating against her skin. She stared back, unable to pull her eyes from him.

Oh God, he thought. She was just standing there, looking back at him with her lids drooping and his name emblazoned across her breasts, a tiny v of sexy black silk just visible below the t-shirt. One word pounded in his brain like a heartbeat. *Mine.* His breath caught in his throat on a low moan and his heart hammered against his chest. In an instant, his entire body reacted as if she were already in his arms.

It seemed that neither of them moved, but suddenly they were joined in the middle of the room, locked in a passionate embrace. He murmured, "Oh hell," and they were connected, his mouth taking hers hungrily, possessively. He wrapped his arms around her, cradling her ass in his hands and pulling her against him roughly, and she clearly felt his own need—hard and heavy—pressing insistently against her stomach. There was no pulling back now, for either of them, as the passion grew and desperate need flooded them both. Their tongues melded in the smolder of their embrace, and the heat rose to immeasurable proportions. Tia felt herself give way; felt the dampness in the scant panties that she wore underneath the thin t-shirt that barely contained her swollen breasts.

The kisses drove deeper, and Dylan's hands were everywhere at once, sliding up the t to stroke her tensed nipples with the rough pad of his thumb, skimming down her back, grazing up her throat where her pulse hammered to tangle his fingers in her hair, pulling her in deeper still until the heat that was rising in her threatened to explode. Suddenly, Dylan pulled away and his gaze burned into hers, the heavy lids betraying the passion that consumed him.

"Oh God, Tia," he murmured. "If you don't want this, you need to walk away right now and lock the door, because I'm all out of self-control."

She looked into his burning eyes, fiery flakes of amber sprinkled amongst the blue. She couldn't walk away now, she knew that, and if this was all she could have of him, she would take it, gratefully, and worry about the rest later. "I want this," she whispered. "I *need* this," she added in a voice that sounded nothing like her own, and he responded in an instant, sliding his hand beneath the panties to find her wet, willing, and ready. She cried out the instant his finger slid into her, pushing herself against his hand to drive him deeper. He moaned deep in his throat and she responded with a low growl that seemed to vibrate through her entire being. Her body was responding too fast, too naturally, and she tried to rein back the intensity as she clung to him, sliding her hand down to his core to feel his own need, stroking him without inhibition, wanting nothing more than to feel him inside of her to fill her with what she'd been missing for so long.

"I want you in my bed," he growled against her ear as he scooped her up and carried her into his room. She cried out softly, "Yes, Dylan," as he tossed her on the bed and crushed against her, his weight both a comforting warmth and a frantic fever pitch against her own skin. He peeled off her t-shirt and pressed himself against her naked breasts, kissing her deeply and causing her to cry out in purrs and moans; and she was lost to everything but the sensation of his hands, his mouth, his hunger. His lips moved to her neck, and then he kissed his way down and suckled her nipples, taut and sensitive to every touch and swipe of his tongue. She tugged at the string of his pants, wanting to feel him against her and inside of her, and he reached back and tugged them off, laying his full length against her inner thigh. He shifted and his lips and tongue moved lower, swirling between her breasts then around her belly and reaching the top of her panties as he slid them slowly down her legs and dropped them to the floor. There was nothing between them now, except skin, and she lost herself completely when he took her with his mouth and swirled his tongue in slow, delicious circles, luxuriating in the exchange, and moaning his own desire.

When she came it was like the ocean, wave after wave of pleasure pitching and rolling over her entire being; every nerve in her body fully alert as she fisted her hands in the sheets and cried out his name. He made his way back to her lips, and kissed her again. "Are you sure, Tia?" he growled insistently against her ear, "I need you to be sure, and to know that you are not a notch in anything."

She responded in the only way she could, pushing herself against him and whispering, "I'm so sure, Dylan, I need you inside me," and then he was, effortlessly sliding into her and bringing her to instant climax with a groan that could only be described as pure bliss. He moved with her, into her, matching her rhythm as she ran her hands through his hair, dug her nails into his back and called out his name until they both fell breathless into the soft pillows and he lay against her, entirely spent and breathing as if they'd just been drowning in the deep sea that was their desire.

He pulled her into his arms and kissed her head, her cheeks, her lips, muttering all the while, "Oh my God, oh my God," and she could only respond in turn, whispering into his ear, "That was so incredible. You are so incredible."

They lay for a while against each other, each holding desperately to their own needs, and to something that could be taken from them both in just a few short hours. Finally, he pulled back enough to bring his lips to hers and kissed her tenderly. He stroked her cheek, and then ran his fingers along her back, over her breasts, and back down her body. She had always thought he had bedroom eyes, the kind that, at half mast, looked incredibly sexy and desirable. And his lips, God his lips, full and perfectly shaped and beckoning...she reached up to kiss them again, and he responded fully.

"I can't say goodbye to you," he whispered. "I just can't. You've gotten inside of me, and I haven't gotten enough."

"I know," she whispered, stroking his face. "I just found you, and you'll be gone too soon. I don't know how I can just go back to my life like this never happened."

He sat up and looked down at her, staring deep into her eyes. "I don't want this to end, Tia, not when we're just getting started. When are you done with school?"

The question took her by surprise; work was the furthest thing from her mind as she lay in his arms, but she realized that she'd be going back tomorrow, and that this weekend would be just a memory. "Umm," she stammered, trying to gain control of her brain, "we go until next Wednesday with the kids. I have to work a half-day on Thursday to get grades done, and then that's it."

"So you're off the whole summer then?" he asked.

She nodded her head.

He took both her hands in his, and pulled her close, mesmerizing her with the intensity of his gaze. "Come with me, Tia. Come with me to Europe on the tour. I'll have to work, but we've planned it out so we have some free time to spend in a lot of the places we play. We could spend the summer together, and see where this takes us...I'm just not ready to say goodbye to you."

Her heart started dancing in her chest—he wanted her to spend the summer with him! She could think of nothing that would be better than that, and she smiled and kissed him. "Oh Dylan," she whispered, barely able to find her voice. "You mean it? There's nothing in the world I want more than time with you."

"Listen," he whispered. "I know this has been a whirlwind for both of us. I don't know where this'll go, but I know I want to find out." He released a sigh. "We'll take it day by day, and if at any time things don't feel right and you want to go home, you can go...anytime you want."

She squealed in excitement as her brain processed his proposal and pulled him closer, her smile taking over her face. "But I can stay the whole time with you?" she asked, kissing his cheeks and running her fingers through his hair, down his back, "because I can't imagine that I'm going to want anything else but that!"

He smiled back at her and kissed her lips. "That's what I'm hoping for too," he said. "I'll have Jessa get with you to take care of all of the arrangements." He pulled her down to lie on his chest and stroked her hair. "Oh God, I don't know where this is going to lead, Tia, but I know that right now I want it to lead somewhere. I can't let you go."

She rose up to kiss him full on the mouth. "I can't wait to see where it goes," she whispered against his chest. "It's been in the back of mind since the first night—I didn't know how I could bear saying goodbye to you, Dylan. Not when I just found you."

He responded by rolling on top of her. He was ready again, and she was ready still. They took it slow and sensual this time, kissing and fondling and staring into each other's eyes. Finally, spent, she curled into the warm and protective cocoon of his body and they slept, both finally dreaming happily of what tomorrow could bring.

Too soon a knock at the door woke them both, and they looked into each other's eyes, limbs still entangled, acknowledging all that had happened and all that was yet to come. They smiled at each other, and he rolled over in the huge bed.

"I ordered breakfast," he croaked, circling her nipple with the tip of his finger. "But I think I'm hungry for something else at the moment." He kissed the top of her head and rolled over, climbing out of the bed and slipping into his pants. "I'll just have them leave it in the foyer." She rolled over too and went into the bathroom, splashing some cold water on her face. Her image in the mirror gave her momentary pause—she was flushed and healthy looking, and even the complete lack of sleep the night before did nothing to diminish the glow. She looked happy—was happy, and it was reflected back to her and made her heart sing. Dylan was already waiting for her in the bed, and stared at her intensely as she glided naked back to his arms.

"You are so beautiful," he whispered, patting the bed next to him. She slipped in beside him, and he handed her a cup of steaming coffee. "I don't know about you, but I definitely need some caffeine this morning," he smiled. "What did we sleep, maybe an hour or two?"

"At best," she said with a smile. "I kept having this delicious dream, but then I realized that I was awake and in your arms. I was afraid to sleep and then find out that you were just a dream."

He took her coffee cup from her hands and set in on the nightstand next to the bed. Then they satisfied one hunger before moving on to the breakfast that sat cooling in the foyer.

When the phone rang in the room, Tia's heart sank. She knew it was the call that would take Dylan from her, and although she'd see him again in less than two weeks, it suddenly seemed like an eternity. It was just one o'clock, but expected holiday traffic in the city meant he needed to allow extra travel time—he was cutting it very close to the wire and needed to be in the air by three. He pulled her close and held her tightly in his arms. "I'll see you soon," he whispered against her ear. "And I'll call you."

"OK," she whispered, unable to trust her voice to say more without cracking. He kissed her deeply, and then grabbed his bag, waving as he walked out the door. She went back into the bedroom and lay on his side of the bed, inhaling the scent of him and their lovemaking, trying to hold on to something that would last until she saw him again. Emotion rocked her—joy, elation, emptiness, anticipation—and she lay on his pillow, going over it all in her mind. Had it really been just three days ago that she was taking the first steps toward getting her life back? Meeting someone had been completely out of the realm of possibility, and now here she was, anticipating spending the entire summer with Dylan. She'd be lying if she said she wasn't nervous—they still had so much to learn about each other—but the excitement of the prospect well outweighed the apprehension. She rolled over in the bed and smiled, inhaling Dylan's scent once more from the pillow, and said aloud, "I'm going to spend the summer with Dylan in Europe!" It was still hard for her to believe that it was true.

Another knock at the door of the suite pulled her back to reality, and she rushed to open it, hoping that he'd come back for one more embrace. Instead, sitting on a silver cart in the hall was an enormous bouquet; tropical flowers in impressive shapes and beautiful vivid colors. The card read simply, "Miss you already, D."

"Oh, you got me flowers," she whined, and then the tears started. She held the flowers to her face and breathed in the exotic scent. It was another half hour before she managed to get herself together and head toward home.

She called Lexi as soon as she sat in the car, and she picked up on the first ring. She didn't say hello, just started shooting questions in rapid fire in a frantic whisper. "Oh my God, tell me everything! Did you do it? How was it? How was he? Holy crap. Please, can I tell people now? You know I'm dying here!"

Hearing the excitement in Lexi's voice helped to pull Tia out of her fog. There was a lot to do in the next two weeks, plenty to keep her busy until she saw Dylan again. She leaned back in the seat and smiled to herself, answering Lexi very simply. "Yes, incredible, amazing, no."

"Yes, incredible, amazing, no, what?" Lexi barked "Yes you did it? Start right there, and spare me no details!"

"Oh shit, Lex. I just had the most amazing night of my life," she crooned. "I have to drive home, but I can't seem to get my head out of the clouds."

Tia heard voices in the background. She heard Lexi tell Ryan that she was on the line and said, "Ryan says 'hi.'"

"Hi back."

Tia heard Ryan's muffled voice, and then Lexi returned to the phone. "He just said Jace was looking for you. He called Ryan a little bit ago and asked if you were here."

She remembered her last conversation with Jace and scowled. He was the furthest thing from her mind, and she wanted it to stay that way. "That's just what I don't need right now. If he calls again, just say

I'm out for the day and you have no idea where I am. And don't give him my cell number."

"Got it. Hold on a sec. Let me get somewhere quieter." Tia heard her relay the information to Ryan in case he got another call from Jace, and then heard the smack of the kiss she planted on him. Lexi came back on the line after a minute, breathing heavily. "OK, I'm all ears and uninterrupted. Best night of your life, huh? Please, please, tell me quick!"

"There's nothing quick about it. Where are you, anyway?" She looked at her watch and saw it was just past two o'clock. "It sounds like a party."

"I'm at the damned Memorial Day picnic. At the club? Are you coming? Then you could tell me all about it, and we could tell everyone here about your weekend. I can't wait to see the looks on their faces..."

"No, sorry Lex," Tia interrupted. The club was the last place she wanted to be today, especially if Jace was looking for her. Plus, her parents would be there, and she had to figure out how she was going to explain to them that she was going to be spending the summer in Europe with a guy she'd just met. She needed some time to wrap her own head around the whole thing first. "I'm not coming to the picnic."

"Aw, Tia..."

"I didn't sleep at all last night. I'm completely wiped."

"Holy crap!" she shouted. "No sleep at all? Sounds positively wonderful!"

"Oh man, it really was," Tia crooned. "But it gets even better—oh shit, I can hardly believe it!" She paused, trying to comprehend it herself, and took a deep breath before continuing. "You're never going to guess what he asked me," she said conspiratorially.

"Tell me!"

"I know this is going to ruin your day, but you still can't tell anyone about us."

"Please don't tell me that—I'm close to bursting already, and I've only been here for an hour!" She hesitated, and then asked, "Wait a minute--why can't I tell? What did he ask you?"

Tia dropped her voice to an excited whimper, "You can't tell because I'm going to see him again!"

Tia had to hold the phone away from her ear as Lexi screamed. "OH MY GOD! Seriously? When? Isn't he headed for Cleveland, or something?"

"Yeah, he's on his way there right now. Oh God, Lex. I still can't believe I'm saying this. I can't believe I'm living this!" She took another deep breath before continuing and pushed her fingers through her hair, willing her heart to beat a normal rhythm and failing miserably. "He asked me to go on the summer tour with him!" she nearly squealed.

"No fucking way! In Europe? That's the one in Europe, isn't it?"

"Yep. Fifteen countries in ten weeks. And I get to spend it all with Dylan!"

"You are the luckiest bitch on the planet," she breathed. "I mean, except for..." her voice dropped off.

"I know, right? I'll always love Nick; he'll always be a part of me. I never in a million years dreamed that I'd meet anyone so soon, or that I could ever feel this way again about anybody. But Dylan is so...oh God, I don't even know a word strong enough to explain it!"

"I'm so happy for you Honey! The whole summer touring Europe—with InHap? Wow! But I'm miserable for me you know—this is killing me! I thought for sure that I could start telling people today—wait—are you telling me that I can't say anything for three whole months? I don't know if I can stand it!"

"You can stand it. Especially if you want to join me for ten incredible days of the tour—Dylan suggested I invite you so we could hang out and so I wouldn't miss home too much."

"No way!" she exclaimed. "Seriously? He wants me to come?"

"Seriously. He's even picking up the tab. First class and everything!" She held the phone away from her ear as Lexi squealed excitedly at the news.

"Holy *shit* that is one fine man you've got yourself there! When can I come? Which country?"

"We're spending a full week in England, and then going to Amsterdam for three days. Dylan lived in London for a few years when he was first starting out, and they've got a big following there. He's got some old friends, too, that he's going to get to see while we're there. They've got a bunch of publicity stuff to do too, you know, like interviews, radio and TV spots, that kind of thing, so they'll be pretty busy. You could meet us there and we could shop, sightsee..."

Tia could hear Lexi losing it on the line, and just knew that she was about to burst, probably dancing around the lawn. "I'm going to London," she was singing into the phone.

"Calm down before someone hears you!" Tia warned, but she couldn't help but laugh. Lexi started singing her chant more softly, "I'm going to London!"

"OK, now get your head back on straight and get serious for a minute." She waited for Lexi's breathing to settle down before continuing. "I've been thinking about this a lot, Lex, and I still really don't want anyone to know about Dylan and me yet. I obviously can't just disappear for three months without an explanation, but I think I'm just going to tell people I'm studying over there for the summer or something—I haven't come up with my story yet, but I'm working on it. I'm sure I will be studying somewhere along the way—the museums there, the architecture...I just don't want any weird attention because I'm dating someone famous, and... " She stopped herself and gripped the steering wheel tight enough to make her knuckles go white. "Holy shit, I can't believe I just said that. I'm dating Dylan Miller!"

"I know! How incredible is that?"

"Incredibly incredible!" she said, singing. "I still think it might be a dream. Although I do still have the marks from last night..."

"Oh yes, please, get back to those details, will you already? I'm dying here!"

"First give me your word that you can keep quiet about this—even while I'm gone."

Lexi sucked in a loud breath. "It's going to suck eggs, but I promise. You're studying, that's all," she repeated with a pout.

"Who knows how the summer is going to go? We may decide we're not as compatible as we think we are; and there's still New Zealand coming up in the fall. He'll be 10,000 miles away for months, and I'll be back at work. I don't know what's going to happen, and until I do, I don't want to say anything. I have no problem saying I'm seeing someone, I just don't want to tell anyone exactly who it is right now, OK?"

"Fine, Fine," Lexi complied, "But tell me this--were you compatible last night?" she asked with an evil grin in her voice.

Tia's tone changed immediately. "Oh yeah," she gloated. "Extremely compatible."

Lexi squealed into the phone again. "You know I'm jumping up and down right now, right? I can't contain myself! But I swear I'll keep your secret. It may kill me, but I'll do it. And I get to come meet you in London? When?"

"Jessa's going to email me the itinerary. I'll have dates for you by tomorrow."

"And details! How many times do I have to ask for them? Spill!"

Tia grinned. "Let's just say it was incredibly awesome, in the truest sense of the word. He is so incredibly hot—especially naked—and his talents are many." She giggled, and couldn't help but to blurt out the bad joke. "He definitely played me like a finely tuned instrument."

"OOHHH! God, I'm so jealous! I don't even know what to say!" Her voice dropped. "Shit. Ryan's heading my way, probably to see why I'm making such an ass of myself in front of all his country club friends. I'm serious, I'm close to bursting! Are you sure you won't come for just a little while? We could find a quiet corner to talk."

"All I want to do today is go home and get some sleep. Maybe take a hot bath. Plus, I need some time to absorb all this. It's been one hellova weekend, and I've got a ton to do over the next couple weeks, including finishing out the school year, which is always a pain in the ass. I can't even believe that I'm going to be back in my classroom tomorrow—I have no idea how I'm going to be able to concentrate on work after the weekend I just had! Then I don't even know how to begin packing for a ten week trip. Not today, Lex, sorry. Want to come over for dinner tomorrow? It'll be simple, but I can throw something together."

"I'll be there, definitely—and don't worry about cooking; I'll pick up some Chinese on my way. Now I better go before Ryan gets to me and reads it all on my face—I'm so excited right now!"

Chapter 19

Tia barely remembered the ride home. She was on autopilot, weaving through heavier than usual Memorial Day traffic while her mind raced a mile a minute, much faster than the traffic allowed her car to go. Europe! For the whole summer! With Dylan! Her mind kept going back and forth between elation and disbelief. By the time she pulled into her driveway, all she could think about was a cup of tea, a hot bath, and her bed. She would rest up today, and start planning her summer tomorrow with Lexi's help. She reached over to the passenger seat and grabbed her overnight bag and the enormous vase of flowers. She'd only taken three steps toward the door when the voice stopped her.

"It's about time! Where were you?" the voice asked accusingly.

She turned to see Jace slamming his car door and strolling toward her. In his hand he held a cheap grocery store bouquet of daisies and carnations. *Oh crap*, she thought. She didn't want to have to deal with this right now—or ever, for that matter. She turned and set her bag and Dylan's bouquet on the stoop next to her door and turned back to him, hands on her hips.

"Jace, what are you doing here?" she asked, trying not to sound too irritated.

His eyes widened and darted around as if he couldn't believe her question, then he opened his mouth and snapped it back shut before speaking. His eyebrows were raised in question. "I came," he said slowly as if to emphasize every word so that she would understand, "to pick you up for our date! You were so adamant that all our dinners together didn't count for anything, and that I never officially asked you out for a real date..." The look of surprised disbelief seemed glued to his face. She looked back at him incredulously, not following a word he was saying.

He shrugged. "The picnic? At the club?" He was still shrugging, waving his hands, palms up, waiting for her to get it.

Tia looked him straight in the eye. "I don't know what you're talking about Jace. We didn't have a date today." He still looked stricken. "I think I'd know."

"I called last night and left you message? I said I'd pick you up at one, and now it's" he moved the cheap flowers to the other hand to look at his watch. "Almost three o'clock. I've been sitting here waiting for nearly two hours!" He crossed his hands over his chest, nearly crushing the bouquet, as though waiting for her to give him an explanation.

Tia shook her head in disbelief, and had to put her short temper in check before she responded. She was tired, elated, nervous, and the last thing she wanted to do was to deal with this bullshit. Who did he think he was? Just because he was some high-powered attorney with money, he thought that everyone should jump at his whims? She couldn't help but think that Dylan had at least a hundred times the money and influence Jace had, and he would never stoop to this level. She was pissed, and she didn't really know the guy that stood in her driveway right now. He certainly wasn't the Jace that she knew from the club; full of himself, for sure, but at least a halfway decent guy. She had no idea what he was capable of, but the anger in his eyes was very real, so she held herself in check. Sort of.

"Wait a minute," she said. "Are you telling me that you asked me out on my answering machine, told me what time you'd be here, and just expected that I'd be sitting here waiting for you?" The 'aha' look on his face only served to further fuel her anger. He was looking at her like she was a child, finally comprehending something she'd been told a dozen times. She turned his own tactic back on him. "You have a lot to learn about women, Jace. Asking someone out is a question, hence the 'asking' part." She made air quotes with her fingers around the word. "There can be two answers to that question—yes, and no. My answer would have been no even if I had gotten the message." His mouth fell open, but the anger still flared in his eyes. She continued. "I have no intention of going to the picnic today, and I am not interested in dating you, now or in the future." She spoke the words clearly, hoping he'd get the hint and walk away. Instead, his eyes turned to the bag and flowers on the stoop, and his nostrils flared.

"Wait a minute. You didn't even *get* the message, isn't that what you just said? Is it because you were too busy whoring it up with some guy you just met two days ago? Are those flowers from him? Is that the bag you carried your slutty lingerie in?" His face turned even more hostile as the realization sunk in. "Holy shit, you're just getting home, aren't you?" He spat the questions at her like venom, and his eyes widened in disbelief.

His words hit her like a slap, not because they hurt, but because there was so much menace behind them. She backed up toward her door and fumbled in her pocket for the keys.

She looked him square in the eye and tried to relay a confidence that she didn't feel. "Listen, Jace. This conversation is over. It is absolutely none of your business who I see, what I do, or when I get home. Like I told you the other night on the phone, you have never been anything more than an acquaintance to me, and I still can't believe that you would think there was anything between us, especially since you've had a girlfriend for the past year." Her cell phone rang in her pocket, and she snatched it. Dylan's name showed up on the display. "I'd like you to leave now, and I would like to forget that this ever happened. Do not call me, do not come to my house, and do not think for a minute that I am not completely serious."

The phone chirped its second ring. Jace exhaled sharply, threw the flowers on her driveway, stepped on them, and turned to strut back to his car. She tapped her phone and tried to hide the agitation in her voice.

"Hey!" she answered, trying to sound cheerful.

"Hey yourself," Dylan answered smoothly. "Did you get my flowers?"

"I did, and they're so beautiful! Like a rainforest, thank you."

"That's what I thought too. Pretty and unique, just like you."

"I just love them," she said.

Just then, Jace stomped back across the street. "Is that him?" he yelled. "Is that the ass hole you're sleeping with?"

Tia tried to push the key into the lock, but her hands were suddenly shaking. Jace reached her, put his hand on her arm, and spun her around. "Is it?"

Tia tried to cover the phone. "Get out of here Jace, I mean it!" she whispered fiercely through clenched teeth. Jace panted like a caged animal, but finally dropped his arms. "Whatever! He can have you, then!" Jace growled back. Then he sprinted to his expensive sports car, slammed the door, and floored the motor, squealing down her street in a frenzied escape.

She could hear Dylan yelling from the phone. "Tia, are you OK? Talk to me!"

She took a deep breath and tried to control the shaking of her voice. "I'm here. I'm OK."

"What the hell was that?" he demanded.

"Nothing, it was nothing," but he could tell by the sound of her voice that it was definitely not nothing. "Hang on a sec. Let me just get in the house." She managed to get the key in the lock, scooped up her bag and the vase, and locked the door behind her. Instinctively, she went to the front of the house to look out the window and make sure Jace wasn't coming back.

"Talk to me Tia," Dylan demanded. "Are you sure you're OK? What's going on?"

She shook her head to rid herself of Jace's angry face and plopped onto the couch, curling her feet beneath her. Hearing the concern in Dylan's voice helped to calm her, and she took a deep breath and released it. "It's just this guy," she said, trying to sound stronger than she felt. "It's nothing, really."

"Like hell it's nothing! He sounded pissed!" His voice dropped then and he said, softly, "Is he your boyfriend Tia?"

"No. No!" she replied instantly, insistently. "But I guess he thought he was."

"What do you mean?"

"He's Lexi's fiancé's best friend," she explained, feeling calmer. "I've known him for a long time, and during the past year, when I spent a lot of time with Lexi at the club he'd sometimes join us for dinner or drinks. We never had a date, never even talked to each other except when we were part of a group, and he never once put any kind of move on me. Not once. But all of a sudden, when he heard that I'd met someone, he got my phone number and started freaking out on me, asking me how I could do this to him when he'd been waiting for a year for me to get over what's-his-name."

"Sounds like a real prick," Dylan said, the concern still heavy in his voice.

"He's always been really conceited—he's a partner at a big law firm, drives a BMW, thinks he's all that—but for the most part, he was always a nice enough guy. Not my type; I never even considered that I'd ever go out with him, but he and Ryan played golf and tennis together and he was just always there. I've never seen this side of him, before today."

"What happened today? Why was he at your house?" He paused as the realization dawned on him. "Oh shit, was he there waiting for you when you got home?"

"Yeah, and he was waiting for hours, so he was pissed." Tia explained the call she'd gotten the day before, and how she'd told Jace that she didn't want to date him. She included the fact that he'd been dating someone else the whole time, and how it'd never crossed her mind that he was interested in her. Talking to Dylan calmed her, and she laughed when she told him about the cheap grocery store bouquet and the look on his face when he saw the exotic flowers she'd gotten from Dylan.

"Tell me the truth, Tia," his voice full of genuine concern. "Should I be worried about you?"

Just hearing the caring tone of his voice relaxed her shoulders, and she felt her calm returning. "No, Dylan. You don't need to worry, but it's sweet that you would. I'm going to be way too busy the next couple of weeks to even go to the club, and other than that, we don't run in the same social circles. I was more than firm with him—actually I was downright pissed—and I think it would hurt his pride too much to try and pursue me and have me shoot him down again. Then, I'll be with you, my fearless protector, far far away. He'll forget all about me by then."

"Don't underestimate the effect you have on men, Tia, I'm a victim myself," he said with a smile, trying to lighten the tone. "Don't underestimate men, either. Especially ones who are used to getting what they want. If he shows up again, I want you to call the cops."

She smiled, and twirled her hair around her finger. "That's really sweet. And I will call the cops if he shows up again, I promise. I really don't think he will, though."

"OK then. Keep me posted. I want to know about anything he does." Dylan changed the subject. "Listen, I was calling for a couple reasons." His voice dropped to a husky whisper. "First, because I miss you already and needed to hear your voice."

Tia felt her stomach roll over at his words, the delicious tingle in her center starting to bloom. "I miss you too," she whispered.

"I'm glad," he said softly. "Second, Jessa was supposed to have emailed you a possible itinerary for the summer. I need you to check the times and dates, and make sure they work for you before she books anything. We'll already be there by the time you get out of school, so I'll have to arrange for a car to pick you up and all that. I'll have her arrange a car to collect you from your house, too, to take you to the airport on your end." She could hear the smile in his voice when he added, "I want to be sure to get you all locked in before you can change your mind."

"No chance that's going to happen," she smiled. "I'm coming whether you like it or not. Even if I have to swim there."

"Oh, believe me, I like it," he said, and the growl in his voice got her stomach rolling again. "Listen, though, I have to cut out now—I'm on the tarmac, and the pilot is getting anxious. I'm going to try to sleep on the plane—you kept me up all night."

"Yeah, I'm going to have a bath, and then I'm sleeping too."

"Mmmmm, I like the image I have in my head of you in the bath. I'll have to be sure to get some rooms with big tubs while we're across the pond."

"Do that—definitely—it sounds wonderful. See you soon, Dylan."

"Not soon enough," he answered sweetly, then clicked off the line.

Chapter 20

Waking up on Tuesday morning to go to work was a cruel reality check for Tia. She sat on her patio with her morning coffee and watched the birds as they chattered at her feeders and filled the morning with their own music. She sipped slowly, enjoying the feeling of summer's return, while she reflected on her incredible weekend. Her goal had been to ease into living again, and in just three short days she'd found a whole new life. She was flooded with emotions and joy, and wanted desperately to tell everyone she met the reason behind the smile on her face. Dylan. He was such a surprise, such an unexpected, wonderful new part of her, and she wanted to share her happiness with the whole world. She could just picture the looks of disbelief she'd get from her friends, family, and colleagues, and even her students if she were to tell them that she was dating Dylan Miller. Lilly would be the most vocal, she knew, jokingly accusing Tia of stealing her real husband. But she knew in her heart that she'd made the right decision to keep his identity to herself. After the initial shock wore off, people would look at her differently, and treat her differently, too. The individual identity she was working so hard to achieve would be even further out of her grasp because she wouldn't just be Tia Hastings; she'd be the girl who was dating rock and roll's sexiest bachelor.

Some of them would undoubtedly want things from her. Autographs, pictures, concert tickets, meetings; she wondered if even Sean, one of Nick's best friends in the world, would recall how Dylan had liked his singing and use her to try and get a demo to him. None of her real friends would purposely impose, but she knew that it could create some uncomfortable situations. She remembered Dylan telling her how people came crawling out of the woodwork when you had celebrity, and that it was sometimes hard to know who your real friends were. She knew a lot of people in her community, and word would spread quickly, she was sure of that.

Honesty was important to her too, though, and she hated being deceptive, especially with people she cared about. She decided that she'd stick as close to the truth as possible, and try and be vague with the details. There was no doubt that she'd tell people she'd met someone special over the weekend, and she'd use his real first name;

even mention that he was in a band. He did more than sing, however, so using the line Dylan had given to Sean—that he was in the business end of the entertainment industry—should be vague enough, but close enough to the truth. She'd even include him as part of her trip to Europe—she wasn't anywhere near having clear details yet, so she could beg off those questions and just say that he would be playing a few shows between business; with all the interviews and appearances Dylan had scheduled, that would be factual as well. Once she got all that straight in her own head, she left the birds to their breakfasts and went in to get ready for work. Thank goodness that she had Europe to look forward to—she couldn't imagine how differently she'd be feeling this morning if they'd said goodbye forever and she was facing a long empty summer.

Lilly noticed the change in Tia as soon as she walked in. "Well now don't you look like the cat that ate the canary?" she smiled as Tia stepped into the office. "The look on your face gives away the answer, but I'll ask anyway. Did you have a good weekend?"

Tia couldn't contain her grin. "The best," she said. "I can't even believe how good it was!"

Lilly leaned forward. "Oh, I'm so glad to hear that! So what happened to put such a huge and genuine smile on your face?" she asked, honestly interested. She'd known about Tia's plan to get back out in the world over the weekend, and had been one of her confidants at work over the past year. "Don't tell me you actually 'found yourself' in one weekend."

Tia stifled a giggle. "Not completely," she smiled, "but I'm a lot closer. Actually, somebody found me. I met someone."

Lilly stood up. "No way! Really? A guy someone, perhaps?"

Tia blushed. "Yes, a guy someone," she said shyly.

"Oh, I gotta hear this!" she exclaimed, pointing at the bench that sat in front of her desk.

Tia sat and leaned toward Lilly. "His name is Dylan," she continued. "I met him on Friday night—the night I was going to be a fly on the wall." Her smile lit up her face, and she could feel the heat rising in her face just from saying his name. "He's just…incredible! I can't even begin to tell you."

Lilly stood and pulled Tia into a hug. "Way to go, girl," she said sincerely with a huge open grin. Her wide white smile against her cocoa skin and the way her eyes crinkled when she grinned reminded her for a minute of Bo. "I know it's been a long hard year, but it's about time that you start living again." She gave Tia another squeeze and let her go. "Speaking of Dylans, didn't you go to the InHap show on Saturday? How was that?"

Now Tia really had a hard time containing her smile. "Oh, it was so great. They always are. But Saturday's show was especially amazing!"

"I was at Sunday's show, and it was amazing too, as always. They actually played that song that they never play live—talk about blowing an audience away! My real husband was in fine form that night, I tell you!" She exhaled a breath in a 'whew!' and fanned at her face with her hand. "Now wait a minute—don't you be tellin' me that that's the Dylan you met? I'd be crushed if you were runnin' off with my real husband," she said with a wink.

Tia laughed it off. "Now that really would make for an awesome weekend, wouldn't it?" She didn't confirm or deny, but her tone made the suggestion sound preposterous.

"I'd have to put that out over the announcements, right before I died of jealousy!" Lilly laughed. "Oh honey, I'm just so happy you found someone to help you through the weekend," she said, concerned. "I was worried about you. What about the memorial, did you go?"

"I did, and I'm so glad I went. In every way this weekend was more than I could have even hoped for. It was closure, acceptance, and a new lease on life, all in three days."

"I'm so glad for you, Tia." She put her hands on Tia's shoulders and gave them a squeeze. "Really. It's so good to have your real smile back."

Lilly didn't have to put anything over the announcements for everyone to hear about Tia's new guy. All staff members checked in at the office when they started their days, and Lilly was sure to deliver the message personally, telling them all to stop by Tia's room to ask about her weekend with a wink and a smile. She told the story again and again, and never got tired of it. She worked with a great bunch of people; they hung out socially fairly regularly and kept track of each other's lives. They were great to her after Nick died, taking turns bringing her dinner, stopping by with groceries, dragging her out for drinks or meals; and they supported her throughout the next school year, knowing she was still hurting. The happiness they felt for her was genuine, and that made her feel a twinge of guilt that she wasn't telling them the whole story.

By the time her students arrived, she was riding on a cloud. Even they noticed her giddiness, and it turned out to be a pretty good day, after all. Still, she was counting down the days until she'd be going to see Dylan again. Concentration was eluding her, and she had so much to get done in the next ten days. Jessa had sent the itinerary the night before, and there was a flight leaving for Prague at 9:45 PM on the last day of school. She could sleep on the plane, and wake up to see Dylan. She'd need to have her classroom packed away for summer, and have everything done by noon that day, plus have her luggage ready to go. When she replied to Jessa's email, she'd asked for the car to collect her by 5:00 to give her time to get to the airport for the requisite three hour check in for international flights.

Lexi didn't end up being a calming presence. She showed up at Tia's door at 5:00, her arms loaded with travel brochures, excursion pamphlets, and lists of stores and spas they simply had to visit. She had maps of the city, the tube station and surrounding areas, and three Chinese take-out bags dangling off her wrists. She dumped the contents of her arms unceremoniously onto Tia's living room coffee table and plopped onto the couch.

"Oh my God," she exasperated. "Do you have any idea how much there is to do in London? There's the Tower, the London Walks, the museums, the shopping, the castles... I don't know if one week's going to be enough time!"

Tia laughed, and poured them each a glass of wine. Lexi grabbed hers and downed it in one tip of the glass, immediately handing it over for a refill. "Don't freak out on me now, Lex," Tia mused. "I'm freaking out enough as it is! I'm counting on you to keep me grounded over the next couple weeks. There're a million things I'll need to get done."

"I need to know what nights the concerts are," she continued as if Tia hadn't spoken. "I know you and Dylan'll want some alone time, so I have some solo activities I can do while you're busy, but I want to plan everything! I've already told them at work, so I'll be set as soon as I have the dates. Did Jessa send you the info yet?"

"Yeah, it was here before I even got home yesterday. She's really good at her job."

"Ooh, so when do I come?" she asked excitedly.

Tia picked up the printout she'd made of Jessa's timetable. "Let's see...we arrive on the afternoon of the 14th of July. The 15th is a Saturday, so you could come in that day. We stay for the week, and leave the following Saturday for Amsterdam. We'll be there until the 26th, but we're leaving that morning for Paris. That's..." she counted on her fingers, "...11days."

"I just can't believe this!" she said, punching the dates into her Blackberry. "And Dylan's really buying my ticket to get there?"

Tia snickered. "Yes, I already told you that. First class all the way. And, he's springing for a room at the Ritz—just for girl time."

"You need to hold onto that man, I'm telling you!" she crowed.

"I miss him so much, Lex! It seems crazy that we only had three days together. You aren't supposed to get that attached to someone so fast. But I am. I can't wait to see him."

"What's the countdown?" she asked.

"Nine days. Then an overnight flight. Prague is six hours ahead of us. I leave here at 9:45, and arrive around noon the next day, Czech Republic time." She took a sip of her wine. "I don't know how I'm going to make it."

"Oh, you'll make it, don't you worry about that. So listen, I've decided that you don't have to try and pack for the whole summer. There are so many designers out in Europe that you can just buy new things when you get there, and then ship them back home as you wear them. Just in London we're going to..."

"Have you forgotten that I live on a teacher's salary?" she interrupted. "I can't afford designer clothes."

"True, but you're lucky enough to have a best friend who makes tons of money," she said, indicating herself with her finger. "And when your boyfriend flies me out first class for an all-expenses paid trip to London and Amsterdam, the least I can do is take you on a shopping spree. Consider it my birthday present to you."

"Holy crap," Tia said, realization dawning on her. "I'm going to spend my birthday with Dylan. In freaking Paris!"

Tia hadn't even thought about the fact that she'd celebrate it in Europe--what a way to spend a birthday, in the most romantic city in the world, surrounded by the lights and energy of Paris. Better yet, she'd be spending it with her man.

"Could you imagine a more perfect present?" Lexi asked enthusiastically. "I know I couldn't!"

"Dylan doesn't even know when my birthday is," she said. "We still have so much more to learn about each other." She dropped her head and turned to Lexi. "Oh God, Lex, this is getting really intense."

"Yeah, but that's the fun part," she stated, matter-of-factly. She clapped her hands and rubbed them together. "Oh, this is going to be so amazing!"

The last few days before she left were like a tornado, and Tia kept so busy that the time actually seemed to pass at a somewhat normal pace. Aside from everything she had to get done at school, she also had to arrange for a service to cut her lawn over the summer, her mail had to be stopped, she had to install timers on her lights, empty her fridge and freezer so she could unplug them, get international calling for her cell phone, and a dozen other loose ends that filled a lot of her time. She had to have dinner with her parents, too, and explain to them why she was going to Europe for the entire summer with a guy she'd just met and who they hadn't met at all. She felt especially bad not telling them exactly who she was dating, but she wanted that specific information in as few hands as possible and as much as she loved her mother, Tia knew she enjoyed gossip more than most. In the end, they took it better than she thought they would. They were thrilled to see her happy again, and trusted her to make the right decision about how to move on with her life.

Packing for the trip was the hardest part, and she had precious little time to do it. She spent most of her evenings pouring over her wardrobe, deciding on items that could be mixed and matched in different ways. She also packed three boxes that Lexi could send to different destinations, and she planned to ship some of her more worn items back. It was a daunting task, but she figured that she could take her vacation fund money with her as well, and fill in with some new clothes while she was overseas—there were some amazing shops in some of the cities she'd be visiting, and she relished the thought of splurging at least a little bit.

Finally, she said goodbye to her students for the last time and sent them off for their summer vacations. She spent most of the evening at school, packing away textbooks, covering her class library, taking down bulletin boards and cleaning up the room. She didn't sleep at all that night, thinking that the next day she'd be on her way to see Dylan. Even with the lack of sleep, though, she skipped into work on Thursday, eager to get through the next couple hours so she could put work behind her and start what she anticipated would be the best summer of her life. They had their last staff meeting of the year, and shared around the table how they'd be spending their summers. Tia so badly wanted to blurt out exactly what she'd be doing, but kept her plans just vague enough when she told them she'd be spending most of it in Europe, visiting a number of cities, and seeing Dylan when she could. They were all excited for her, and extracted promises for emails and postcards, and lots of pictures when she returned. She hadn't shared a picture of Dylan with them, and they were all curious about him. She made her promises, hugged them all goodbye, and finished up her year, running out the door as soon as the clock struck noon.

The car picked her up at precisely 5:00pm, and she left her house with two huge bags plus a carry-on. Her heart pounded the whole way to the airport—she was merely hours now from seeing Dylan again, but neither the over-the-counter sleep aid nor the cushy accommodations of British Airways first class did much of anything to relax her. She slept fitfully, fighting the medicine all the way to Prague, and when she finally stepped off the plane, her heart was pounding in her chest and she was riding on adrenaline. It was nearly impossible for her to keep still as she stood in the customs and immigration line, and when she finally made her way to the luggage carousel, her heart sank just a little bit when she saw Jessa holding a placard with her name on it. She tried not to show her disappointment—did she really think she was going to see Dylan standing in the middle of a public airport?—and gave Jessa a hug.

"It's so great to see you!" Jessa said happily, hugging her back enthusiastically. "How was your flight?"

"Not quick enough," Tia joked. "No matter what I said, the pilot wouldn't fly any faster."

"I totally understand," she smiled, "and I know you're anxious too, so I won't keep you here. You can just head out to the car and I'll collect your luggage and bring it out to where you're staying. How many bags?" she asked. "Do they all look like this one?" she added, motioning toward her carry-on.

"Two," Tia said, nodding. "Big ones—are you sure you want to handle them by yourself?" She was shaking with anxiety and the luggage hadn't even started appearing on the carousel yet, but she felt bad leaving the job to the tiny woman.

"No problem," she said. "I'll get one of these big strong guys to help me," she waved her hand toward the many porters who stood around the fringes of the crowd waiting to offer their services. She handed Tia the placard with her name on it and pointed at an exit door to the right. "They can't park at the airport, of course, so just go out to the line where the limos are cruising through and hold this up so the driver will know when to stop.

"Aren't you riding with me?" Tia asked, unsure of what to do next.

"No, I'm pretty sure that Dylan would think three's a crowd," she replied, smiling.

"He's here?" she squealed, looking in all directions at once and hopping from one foot to the other in anticipation.

"He's in the car," she laughed, "and very anxious to see you. Just give me your…"

But Tia had already dropped her carry-on at her feet and was sprinting for the door. She saw the line of limousines drifting slowly by and held her name up over her head. When his limo pulled over to the curb, the door opened before it even stopped and Dylan leaped out, a smile lighting his entire face. "Heey!" he said, reaching her in seconds. He lifted her off the ground and spun her in a slow circle. He hugged her to him, and planted a soft kiss on her lips. "I've missed you," he said simply, looking all sexy in baggy jeans and a t-shirt. "I'm so glad you're finally here!"

Tia wrapped her arms around his neck and nuzzled her face into his shoulder. "I'm so glad to be here!" she said. "Oh Dylan, it's so great to see you!"

"Come on," he said, "let's get out of here before we attract attention." He wrapped his arm protectively around her and led her to the limo. The driver was standing there already, holding the door. They climbed into the car and tangled together, trying to make up for two weeks apart.

"Mmmmm," he sighed, taking her face in his hands and kissing her. "I've really missed this."

"So have I," she murmured against his lips. "I thought the plane would never land—I think it was the longest nine hours of my life!"

"But you're here now, and we have the whole summer ahead of us," he smiled.

"Oh, it's going to be so amazing," she said, pushing her fingers through his hair and pulling him close.

A few minutes later, the driver's voice came over the speaker. "Mr. Miller, sir? We're approaching the city now." Dylan hit a button and thanked him, then hit another, opening the expansive sunroof overhead.

"Check this out," he said, standing on the seat and poking his head through the sunroof, inviting her to do the same. "We're going to take a little tour of Prague."

Tia stood too, and the two of them took in the sites, Dylan pointing out landmarks and famous sites, and Tia adding what she'd learned during her research. She'd tried to learn about the places she'd be visiting; as a teacher, she had a keen interest in culture, art, architecture, and history; but she'd only had enough time to get the basics. Lexi had helped, gathering travel brochures and doing some research on the internet for her, and reading the literature on the plane helped her get at least a little background info on the cities she'd be visiting. There were so many, though, that it was hard to keep them all straight.

Prague was a beautiful historical city, and she and Dylan pressed against each other as the breeze lifted their hair and they weaved slowly through Old Town Square past the amazing architecture that made the city unique. They chatted easily about the past two weeks, her last days of school and the gifts and notes she'd received from her students; Lexi's uncontrollable excitement about joining them for a leg of the tour, the cities the band had already visited and Tia had missed. Dylan quieted suddenly, and just looked at her.

"What?" she asked, smiling.

Dylan kissed her gently and said, "It's downright embarrassing how much I missed you! It's just so damn good to see you again."

"Me too," she said, resting her forehead against his lips and running her hands down his back. "I can't believe I'm finally here!"

They pulled onto a side street and stopped in front of a little house covered with ivy and tucked away from the main line of traffic. "Home sweet home," he said, motioning to the doorway as the limo came to a stop and Dylan ducked back into the car. The driver was there in a moment, holding the door for them. Dylan thanked him and shook his hand, and from the look on his face when he checked the bill Dylan had tucked into his palm, he was tipped generously.

"Thank you very much, Mr. Miller," he said grinning. "Enjoy the rest of your stay in Prague!"

He looked at Tia as he answered, "I certainly will—it just got a whole lot better—thank you."

They entered the little house and Tia looked around. From the outside, the house had old world character and charm, but the inside had been modernized and was beautiful and quaint. There were flowers everywhere, the beautiful tropicals like those in Dylan's first bouquet to her, and candles were lit, bathing the rooms in a soft glow against the pulled curtains. There was a bottle of champagne chilling on the counter, and two glasses had already been poured. Dylan picked them up and handed one to Tia, clinking glasses and offering a simple toast, "To reconnections, and getting to know each other a whole lot better."

They sipped, and Dylan put his arm around her shoulders and led her on a tour of the little house. When they reached the bathroom, Tia saw petals sprinkled on the floor and more candles burning. A large claw-foot tub sat in the center of the room; full and steaming and inviting, with more flower petals floating on top of the water.

"Do you know how hard it is to find a place in this city with a tub big enough for two?" Dylan asked as Tia looked at him smiled. "But I just couldn't get that image of you soaking in a bath out of my head, and I had to find one. I thought maybe you'd like to clean up after being on the plane all night." He leaned down and nuzzled her neck.

"It's definitely big enough for two," she said slyly, "and I couldn't think of a better way to start off the summer than right here."

He took his time undressing her, running his fingers over her skin as he exposed it, planting little kisses that drove Tia crazy. All her weariness left her, and she slipped into the hot water, watching as Dylan undressed and climbed in beside her after pushing the button that turned on the jets and sent the water churning around her entire body. Then she was in his arms, all slippery skin and bubbles, and the past two weeks melted away as they kissed and explored each other, hands sliding easily and greedily over the contours of their melded bodies. Dylan pulled back, cupped his hands under her, and lifted her hips out of the water, taking her with his mouth. The swirl of his tongue coupled with the swirl of the water was an incredible sensation, and she gave herself to it fully, every nerve in her body on fire as she rolled into an intense and shuddering climax. She moaned when he entered her, reveling in the slipperiness between them and the way their bodies came together in rhythm with the churning water. When they were spent, he grabbed a bottle of scented wash and sponged her all over, washing her hair and massaging her scalp as she leaned back against him. She felt herself completely relax for the first time in two weeks, and exhaustion finally caught up with her. They stepped out of the tub and he toweled her dry, and tucked her into the soft bed, lying next to her and lightly massaging her shoulders.

"It's so good to have you back," he whispered against her ear. "Sleep a little now, and I'll wake you in a few hours."

"Mmm hmm," she murmured, drifting off. There was a show tonight, she knew, and she planned to be there. Wrapped in his arms, she slipped off into the best sleep she'd had in weeks, the smile she wore never leaving her face.

Chapter 21

With each leg of the journey Tia found herself more enamored with Europe, and much more enamored with Dylan. Every city had its own flavor of cultures, food, drink, art and architecture, and she drank it in like a thirsty sponge. They spent a good deal of time together, but Dylan had his work, too, and his schedule varied greatly from day to day. Naturally, Tia attended all the shows, and it never got old watching Dylan and the rest of the boys do what they did best. Occasionally, she'd attend a taping of an interview or TV show, but Tia was determined not to get in Dylan's way or to be constantly underfoot, and she had no problem wandering the streets of places like Vienna, Geneva and Munich, on her own. With her tourist maps in her bag and her camera at the ready, she quickly mastered the art of public transportation, and enjoyed exploring the cities at a casual pace.

She wanted to remember every minute of this summer, and had brought several journals that were filling up more quickly than she'd imagined. Many afternoons she sat in parks or at sidewalk cafes and wrote about her experiences, the places she'd visited, and her ever-growing feelings for Dylan. She loved watching the people that strolled through the cities; the tourists and locals from each place she visited gave every destination its own character. Sitting alone, she sketched the scenes on empty pages and sent emails and pictures to her friends, creating vivid descriptions of each place. The shops were incredible as well, and she enjoyed picking up unique little souvenirs for everyone back home.

Every day brought her and Dylan closer together—they discovered many things they had in common and others that were uniquely their own. They both loved architecture, and enjoyed touring the many cathedrals and castles that stood sentinel over the cities they visited. Neither was into the club scene—both preferred quiet strolls and occasional shows to the crowds and pulsing beats of the European nightlife. They shared a similar sense of adventure and a love of the outdoors as well, and spent time hiking in the Alps while in Vienna, soaking up the early summer sunshine and enjoying a picnic lunch of wine, bread and cheese in one of the most beautiful settings in the world.

The boys had planned the tour so that they'd have some free time in each of the cities they visited, and whenever Dylan had a free day, he and Tia made it a point to see the highlights of each place. In Geneva they strolled arm in arm through the cobbled streets of Old Town past the tall grey stone houses and past the Rue Fontaine to visit the Temple de la Madeleine, a beautiful gothic church at the center of the square. In the afternoon, they hiked on Mont Saleve, through the woods and up to the expansive meadows filled with summer colors. In Stockholm they took a breathtaking hot air balloon ride over the city and the tiny islands that created the amazing archipelago, soaking in the sights while sipping champagne and nibbling on caviar-laden crackers. They both fell in love with the casual atmosphere of Munich, and spun through the city on Segways, excited to find a Segway tour after having loved the one they'd taken in Chicago. Later in the day, they visited the English Gardens, sharing a maas at the world-famous Chinese Pagoda. They sipped fresh German beer from huge steins at street side cafes and watched the crowds strolling through Marienplatz, the large public square.

They were growing closer all the time, and enjoyed each other's company and their similar sarcastic humor. Each of them took hundreds of pictures, and Dylan added some sketches and notes of his own to her journals. She knew that they'd be treasures to her forever, and loved the quirky drawings and comments he made that she'd read over and over while they were apart in the fall.

She'd grown to love the rest of the band, as well. Tia became a regular fixture back stage, and they'd gotten to know each other pretty quickly. She even talked Bo and Ty into having lunch with her once in a while when Dylan was busy doing solo interviews or guest appearances.

Often, when all the boys were busy, Jessa joined her for little adventures, and they became fast friends. They reveled in discovering the local flavors of tiny street cafes and bakeries, always bringing something back for the boys to enjoy. It was at the sidewalk café at Hotel Adlon, overlooking the Brandenburg Gate in Berlin, the fifth stop and three weeks into her visit, that Jessa blurted the question. They'd been pouring over maps and coffee, nibbling warm strudel, and planning out their afternoon, when she said softly, "You're in love with him, aren't you?"

The question took Tia by surprise, and she stopped mid-sip. "Excuse me?" she stammered, obviously flustered.

"I'm not trying to be nosey," she added quickly. "But it's pretty obvious from where I'm sitting. I can see the way you look at him. And the way he looks at you."

Tia exhaled sharply. She'd known Dylan only a little over a month, but the question had been nagging at the back of her mind for some time now. She tried not to think about it, about what it could mean to be in love with someone like him. It was an incredible feeling, but one that scared the crap out of her at the same time. Now that it was on the table, though, she couldn't deny it. "Oh God, it's true," she breathed, and Jessa grinned. "But I don't know, Jessa, what am I supposed to do about it? Things are so great between us, but I don't know what he's feeling, exactly, and anyway, what kind of future do we have? He's going to go away to film a movie on the other side of the planet, and I'm going to go back to my fifth grade classroom. He's going to go to a Hollywood premier as the star of the red carpet, and I'm going to be doing report cards and hosting parent conferences. Hardly a match made in heaven—our lives are so different." She'd gone over these words in her head a thousand times, and it actually felt good to finally voice them aloud.

"So what?" Jessa said matter-of-factly. "Love is love, and if it's meant to be, it'll work itself out." She lowered her voice to a conspiratory whisper. "I'm rooting for you, you know."

Tia leaned over and hugged her. "I'm glad to have you on my side," she giggled. "I'm already beside myself worrying about him spending months alone with that horrible Penelope Valentine. She wants to sink her teeth into him, and they're going to be really involved with each other while they're in New Zealand..."

"Never gonna happen," Jessa answered. "Trust me, he sees right through her. He can't stand her type of person—she doesn't stand a chance with him. Besides, I'll be there too, and I'll be sure to mention you at least...oh, twenty times a day or so. But even if I didn't, it's not like he could forget you. Like I said, I see the way he looks at you, and he talks about you constantly. He's really done a lot behind the scenes to make sure you have a good time on this tour and that you always have something to do. It's working out for me, that's for sure—part of my job while I'm here is making sure you enjoy yourself, which is guaranteeing that I'll have some fun too. He's worried that you'll get bored and want to go home."

"You're kidding, right?" she mused. "I can't believe he'd even think that! I'm loving every minute here, whether it's with you, by myself, or with him." She smiled at the sideways smirk Jessa threw her way. "OK, I fully admit that the times with him are the best, but I haven't been bored for a minute—how could I be, when I'm surrounded by all this?" She motioned to the beautiful public square, sipped her coffee, and sighed. "Oh Jessa, I'm completely out of my mind over him, and it scares me to death. I've only known him a little over a month, but now it's hard to imagine my life without him. But I have no choice in the matter—he's going to be gone for a long time. I'm trying not to get too attached, but I'm afraid it's already too late."

Jessa reached over and patted her hand. "The feeling is mutual, I'm sure of it."

"You know," Tia confessed, "when I first met you, I was so jealous that you got to spend so much time with him, and got to travel with him...I have to say, I wondered if there was something between the two of you. I'm so glad I got to know you. I like knowing that he has you to look after him."

Jessa laughed. "Oh, there's a lot between us, I assure you," she confided. "In some ways, I know more about him than I want to." A smirk touched her lips. "But none of it's beyond a professional relationship, and it never was."

"I know that," Tia added quickly, "I do. He loves you too, you know."

She smiled. "Yeah, I do know. He's a great guy, and you're a great couple. I like you so much better than all the other girls he's dated. Believe me when I say he never cared about any of them the way he cares for you. Take it from someone who knows him."

Tia looked her in the eye. "You won't tell him, though, right? If he doesn't feel the same way..."

She interrupted. "Of course not!" she said, surprised that she'd even suggest it. "But I really think you should."

Tia thought for a minute before answering. "I'm sure I will eventually, but not yet. I just now admitted it to myself, and no matter how comfortable we are with each other, we've still only known each other a short time. If I told him and he wasn't feeling the same way, it would be awkward and I couldn't stand that. Things are perfect right now, and I don't want to do anything that could mess that up."

"I understand," she said. "You'll know when the time is right—I just like you both so much, and I like what you do for each other. I really want you both to be happy."

"I am *so* happy!" Tia exclaimed. "And I like you too, Jessa—you're an awesome person, and I'm so glad to call you my friend."

They finished their strudels and coffee and bought some snacks to take back to the boys, then strolled casually around the square, taking pictures of the historic gate, before heading back to the hotel. *We really bonded*, Tia thought happily, and she felt as if she had a new true friend, one who understood where she was coming from, and one she could trust with her true feelings about Dylan.

As much as she was coming to love Jessa, and enjoyed their time together, Dylan turned out to be right about her missing home. As the time for Lexi's visit grew closer, Tia found herself looking incredibly forward to seeing her old friend again and sharing London with her. Just another week and a half, four more cities, and then she'd have a whole week with Lexi in London and then a few more days in Amsterdam.

The time difference and their schedules made it difficult to keep in close contact, but she and Lexi talked at least a couple times a week and emailed regularly. Dylan had booked them a room to share to have "girl time," and Lexi had already planned a host of activities around the InHap shows to experience the magic that embodied London. With the boys they'd planned a couple of private tours with London Walks, including a Jack the Ripper tour and a haunted pub crawl, and she insisted they visit the Tower and Buckingham Palace. It was going to be a busy week, and Tia couldn't wait.

When the day of Lexi's visit finally arrived, Tia found herself full of nervous excitement over seeing her best friend. She waited at the luggage carousel holding Lexi's name above her head. When she appeared, Tia shrieked and ran to hug her, and they spun and looked each other up and down and embraced again. "Europe agrees with you, Tia," she observed, "you look amazing!"

"Oh, it's so good to see you Lex!" Tia exclaimed, hugging her again.

Lexi looked around. "Where are my boys?" she grinned. "I expected Bo to show up, at least."

"They're over at Wembley," Tia answered, "setting up for the show tonight. It's kind of tense tonight, actually. Ty's having throat troubles and might not be able to sing back-up. It's the first of two sold out shows and the place is huge—they might be the biggest shows of the tour."

The English audience had always been tremendous supporters of InHap. They'd embraced them as their own, perhaps because Dylan was a native Aussie who'd lived for a time in Northampton. The Wembley shows had sold out in less than an hour, and they were playing in two other cities as well during their stay in the UK. They had a heavy agenda, with a bigger than usual number of television appearances, interviews, radio shows, and even an audience at Buckingham Palace with the crown princes, who were longtime fans. Tonight's show was a big deal, and having one of the band members not able to give 100% would really disappoint the fans. Tia knew that Ty had been drinking honey-lemon tea all day and had seen a doctor, and although he felt well enough to perform, his voice was gruff and crackly.

"Poor guy," Lexi said. "I can't even imagine having a job like that to do when you don't feel well. It's got to take a lot of energy to be up there on that stage." She changed the subject. "We do have front row seats though, right?" Lexi pleaded.

"Of course," Tia replied, struggling to pull one of Lexi's enormous bags off the carousel. "Shit, what do you have in here, rocks?" she grunted.

"I think that's my shoe bag," Lexi smirked. "Hey..." she said when Tia glared at her from the corner of her eye. "Don't give me that look. It's not every day a girl gets an experience like this one, and I intend to look good doing it!"

Tia just laughed at her and tugged the bag off to the side. "I've got a taxi waiting out front. We'll drop your bags at the hotel and head over to Wembley—the boys are planning dinner with us backstage."

"I'm so glad you're my friend, Tia," Lexi crooned. "You get me into all the right parties!"

Tia draped her arm over Lexi's shoulder and gave her a squeeze. "I missed you, Lex. It's so good to see you."

"Right back at you, girlfriend. I can't even tell you how jealous everyone back home is that I'm here right now."

"You didn't tell anyone...about me and Dylan though, right?" she asked cautiously.

"No, no, don't worry," Lexi placated. "But it's been so hard, you know, covering all the bases? I just told people that your new boyfriend was playing with InHap—which isn't a lie—and that we had preferred seating and we'd get to hang with the band after the show. Ryan is beside himself, thinking that I'm going to cash in on my gimme."

"I thought you told him you had a new gimme," Tia said suspiciously.

"I did," she answered, "but he doesn't believe it. It was Dylan for so long, and without telling him the real reason I had to cross him off my list, he just wasn't buying it. It's cute, actually," she giggled, "since I told him I was coming and that I'd get to meet Dylan, he's suddenly all jealous and protective. I've never gotten so many flowers in my life, *and*," she said, holding up her wrist where a diamond tennis bracelet sparkled, "he gave me this last night before I left—so I wouldn't 'forget how much he loved me,' he said."

"It's gorgeous!" Tia gushed, relaxing her shoulders. She trusted Lexi completely, but felt better knowing that even Ryan didn't know the truth. If she'd kept it from him, the secret was safe. "You can really play this to your advantage—for a while, anyway."

"I know, right? I've got my eyes on some earrings, and I dropped a little hint before I left. I expect I'll have them in my hand shortly after I get home."

"You are shameless," Tia laughed.

"I know. I'm a lawyer—it's my job, and I'm pretty damned good at it. Manipulation is quickly becoming second nature," she joked as she wrestled the last of her overstuffed bags from the carousel.

Lexi was positively giddy by the time she stepped into the hotel. Tia had arranged for the taxi to take the scenic route, and every time Lexi saw a structure she recognized, she let out a little squeal and got more excited. The Ritz itself had a worldwide reputation, but nothing can truly prepare a person for stepping into the doors and experiencing the marble elegance that welcomed one from the street, or the luxuriously appointed rooms that held no pretenses. "Damn, I feel like a princess!" she exclaimed.

"You'll feel even more like one tomorrow," Tia said. "We're doing high tea downstairs at two, compliments of Bo. It's a British tradition, and it's supposed to be quite an experience."

"Well, I guess I owe him one big kiss!" she exclaimed. "I just love that man—he's so adorable!"

"Yeah, he's a sweetie," she replied fondly. She'd come to love the man too—he was funny and obnoxious on the outside, but was really a very insightful and intelligent person. Tia had grown to trust him a great deal with her feelings and fears.

"Dylan has arranged a day at the spa for us on Tuesday," she added. Lexi's eyes lit up immediately—a day at the spa had been at the top of her 'to-do' list, and Tia knew it. "But I'll be the one to deliver *that* kiss. You can just say thank you and shake his hand." She wagged her finger at her friend when she saw the look of mock surprise on her face.

"Aw, you can suck the fun out of a circus," she smirked. "But I'll be good, I promise." Lexi took a quick shower—three hours in the airport and eight on the plane practically required it—while Tia unpacked one of her bags, hanging her things in the closet and smiling inwardly at the clothes Lexi'd brought on the trip. Everything she pulled out screamed 'sexy and available,' and there were incredibly few casual choices. When Lexi stepped out of the bathroom in a perfectly accessorized low cut fitted pant suit, Tia took one look at her and said, "No wonder Ryan's worried. If he saw the clothes you packed for the trip, he'd think you were planning to get yourself a booth in the Red Light District. Did you even bring any jeans? You can't go sightseeing in any of this stuff!" She held up a stiletto heel. "Do you realize how many of the sidewalks here are cobblestone?" she added. "You'll break your neck if you try to walk around in these things."

"The smaller bag is my casual stuff," she smiled. "I told you I was going to look good on this trip."

Tia shook her head in exaggerated disbelief and said, "You do look gorgeous, by the way."

Lexi performed a little three-point catwalk turn and smiled back over her shoulder. "So, I'm ready—let's head over to the stadium—I've never seen a sound check before! Who's opening for them, by the way?"

"Tandem Obsession." Lexi squinted in question and Tia continued. "They're pretty hot on the Brit scene right now, but they haven't hit it in the U.S. yet. They're pretty good though; they opened in Glasgow last week. Kind of punky pop, with a bluesy attitude."

"I like the name," Lexi pondered. "Any hotties?"

Tia rolled her eyes. "What do you mean, 'any hotties'?"

"You know exactly what I mean. I obviously need a new gimme, and this is just the place to find one. I just love the vibe here; I could feel it as soon as I stepped off the plane."

"It's called jet lag," Tia joked, "and you are impossible, Alexis Marie."

"You know I hate when you call me that. You sound like my mother."

"Yeah, well I should call your mother and tell her you're trying to get in a quick lay with a Brit punker. She'd love that. So would Ryan."

"Yeah, whatever," Lexi smirked. "So I ask again, any hotties?"

"Definitely none hotter than mine, so I can't really say," she grinned.

"Well, duh!" Lexi bubbled. "Only one of us can be dating the sexiest man in the world." She stuck out her lower lip in a pathetic pout. "I hate that it's you."

"I just bet you do." Tia smiled at her best friend in the world, linked elbows, and led her back to the lobby to catch a taxi.

Ty was still losing his fight with laryngitis when they arrived—apparently honey and lemon weren't enough to push it back. After rushed greetings and an over exaggerated exchange between Lexi and Bo that had everyone's eyes rolling, the girls took their seats in the front row to watch the boys sync mikes and instruments. Tia looked forward to introducing Lexi and Jessa, but Dylan's assistant was busy running errands and getting things together for dinner, and couldn't join them yet.

"This is so exciting!" Lexi exclaimed. "It's kind of weird being in an empty stadium." She looked around the vastness of Wembley, eyes wide. "This place is enormous—how many people does it hold?"

"Ninety thousand," Tia answered as Lexi whistled through her teeth, "and every one of these seats will be full in a few hours. Both shows sold out in less than an hour."

"That's a shitload of people!" Lexi exclaimed. "I'd be scared to death in front of an audience that big!"

Tia laughed. "Are you kidding me? You'd love every minute of it."

Lexi smirked. "Yeah, you're probably right. Having that many people chanting your name and screaming for you—it's got to be seriously awesome!"

"Hey Tia," Dylan called from the stage. "Can you help get Ty's mike through sound check? We can run through *Lost in You*. He still sounds like shit."

"Absolutely!" Tia mounted the stage and took Ty's place at the mike. Lexi watched from the floor as they ran through the intro and her eyes widened as she heard how Tia's voice blended with Dylan's in perfect harmony. "Wow, you guys sound amazing together!" she exclaimed breathlessly. "I've heard Tia sing before, but...wow. It sounds great from here!"

The sound guy Neil agreed with two thumbs-up, but Dylan wanted to be certain. "Let's run through *Over the Hills* once, just to be sure," he said into his own mike. And they were off again, their voices rising and falling over the music as if they were one.

"I'll say it again," Lexi yelled toward the stage. "Wow."

Ty was silent during dinner, hoping that resting his voice would be enough to get him through the night. The rest of the guys harassed him relentlessly, well aware that he'd taken a self-imposed vow of silence. At the preshow meeting, however, it was evident that he wasn't going to be able to sing backup vocals.

"I guess we'll have to scrap *Lost in You* and *Pull You Up*," Angelo said. "Unless you want to do them acoustic?" he looked at Dylan.

"I hate to scrap them;" he said, "they were both really big over here. And now that we've started doing *Pull You Up*, we'll hear about it if it isn't on the set list. They're not as good without the harmony, but I think we'd better keep them. Acoustic is better than nothing."

They finished off the meeting and Bo motioned Dylan over to a corner. "A quick word?" he said, and the two huddled for a moment, glancing back at the girls. Dylan smiled, and they nodded to each other. The boys gave each other a pre-show pep talk, and Dylan planted an enthusiastic kiss on Tia before she and Lexi left to take their seats.

They watched the crowd filing in, and were in awe at the number of people packing the stadium. "Damn," Lexi said, "it looks even bigger when it's full—I don't know if I've ever seen so many people together in one place!" They looked around their immediate area, front and center to the stage, and pointed out all the people they recognized. There were other celebrities, members of Parliament, and even the princes with their dates were just a dozen seats down, surrounded by their entourages.

The crowd rose to its feet immediately when the lights dimmed, the roar deafening. The boys walked casually onto the stage and waved, inciting more cheers from the audience. Tia was, as always, mesmerized by Dylan onstage. He owned the audience, and no matter how many times she watched him perform—twelve, by her count, just on this tour and at least twenty before that—it never got old. Every show was different, unique, and tailored to the audience and the songs that were most popular in that region. They started with a bang, Bo pounding the bass drum and everyone else jumping in with a song that kept the audience on its feet, moving as one and singing along to the familiar tune. Tia and Lexi danced with them, pulled into the common bond that great live music delivered by talented performers forged for an evening. Dylan growled, howled, wailed and crooned into the mike, and delivered song after song in his unique and enthusiastic style. When the fourth song ended, Dylan spoke to the audience.

"Hellooo, London!" he yelled gruffly into the microphone and the audience responded with a deafening roar. "It's so good to be back in this amazing city—one that I'll always call home! You've been so great to us, and we love you!" More screams and applause met his words. "Thank you very much! Now this next song is one of our absolute favorites to play live…" more screams and hollers, "…but unfortunately, Ty's voice is a bit under the weather today, and he's not going to be able to sing for you tonight…" the tone of the audience changed to something that could only be described as collective sympathy, ninety thousand voices sighing, 'aaaww.' "But if you'll be so kind," he added, "I have a beautiful lady in the audience tonight who knows this song, and if you could help me persuade her, perhaps she'd join us on the stage and grace us with her amazing harmonies…" The roar of the crowd filled Tia's ears and her heart began to beat a mile a minute as Dylan looked down at her and extended his hand. "Would you help us out, Tia?" he said with a grin, nodding toward the mike that a stage hand had just placed at his left side.

"Holy shit," Lexi wheezed on panting breath, "he wants you to…"

"Yeah, holy shit is right!" Tia bellowed. "Oh my God, I can't do this! There're 90,000 people in this place!"

"Oh yes you can!" Lexi hollered, propelling her forward toward the guard that stood ready to help her mount the stage. Dylan encouraged her with his eyes, and before she could even think about it, she found herself being lifted onto the stage, into the harsh glare of the spotlights and to Dylan's side. He planted an encouraging kiss on her cheek and slid into the intro.

Time stood still. Tia knew the song inside and out, and had sung harmony just this afternoon at the sound check, plus hundreds of times before that. She took a deep breath and remembered the first night they'd sung this song together—their first night together—at Sing-a-long-Cassidy's, in front of less than a hundred people. They'd come so far together on this journey, yet here they were, back where they'd started, and Dylan was winding up the intro and starting to sing…*Lost in you, don't know what I'm gonna do, every day is an eternity, every minute an hour and I'm searching, searching, for what I lost in you*, and Tia fell into the music on autopilot, sliding in at just the right moment, her voice more clear and steady than she could have believed, and there, in front of the sold out stadium, she and Dylan sang together, weaving their voices like a complex net, ensnaring the audience with the words and harmonies. She'd never felt so alive yet so completely vulnerable, but then Dylan was at her side, smiling at her, singing to her as he looked into her eyes and strummed the melody, and it was only the two of them in the whole world as they finished the song, holding out the last note as he coaxed the final chords from the guitar. At once the applause from the audience was deafening, and she was jerked back into reality, thousands of voices screaming their approval and Dylan was stepping back and motioning for her to take a bow. She absorbed the applause like a drug, hardly able to believe it was for her. "Thank you very much!" Dylan said to the crowd, "and thank you, my lovely lady, for helping us out!" The crowd cheered again, and Tia took one more bow. Then, just as swiftly, she was swept back into the audience and back to Lexi's side.

"Holy shit!" Lexi bellowed as soon as she'd retaken her seat. Strangers around her were patting her on the back and congratulating her on her performance. "You were awesome!" she cried as Tia tried to catch her breath. She looked up and saw Dylan smiling down at her. Then Bo hit the snare in a familiar opening and the crowd exploded again as InHap belted into the next number.

"Oh my God!" Lexi yelled over the crowd. "You just sang in front of 90,000 people! And you *rocked* it!!"

"Holy crap, I did, didn't I?" she yelled back elated, unsuccessfully trying to get her heart to beat a normal rhythm. Her breath was still coming in gasps; she could scarcely believe what she'd just done.

"That's my girl, Tia!" Dylan exclaimed into the mike. "Give it up for her one more time!" Again the crowd answered enthusiastically, and Tia broke into a huge grin. Dylan blew her a kiss, and then added his guitar to the drums and keyboards on stage as the next number exploded from the speakers. But as much as she appreciated the applause, she was even more excited that Dylan had just told ninety thousand people that she was 'his girl.'

Tia rode the rest of the evening on a high that she couldn't put into thoughts or words. She and Lexi danced, sang, and high-fived all the spectators eager to get closer to the girl who'd been called up to sing on stage with InHap. She passed on a thought to Nick, who was surely cheering more loudly than all of them, proud of her and what she'd done.

It wasn't until the encore that Dylan played the first chords of *I'll Pull You Up*. He'd played only three notes before the crowd recognized it and went ballistic. He stopped playing, and the crowd quieted immediately, waiting for him to speak.

"This next song is special in my heart," he said softly. "We've only recently started playing it live, and I could use some help with this one too—it isn't the same without the harmony." He looked down at Tia and raised that one eyebrow in question. This time she didn't even hesitate, and she was lifted once again to the stage where she took her place beside Dylan, sharing his mike, as he wound into the intro for *I'll Pull You Up*. They swayed together as the music wound around itself, creating an other-worldly sound and as Angelo joined in with the sax, Dylan poured out the first lyrics, *"You lie dyin' and I'm left here cryin'... nothin' I can do to save you, but who's gonna save me? Thought that I could be so strong but you've been leavin' me for so long...now there's nothing left but this hole...* Tia joined in, soft and slow, *I'll pull you up, from your darkest fears...when the world's tryin' to drown you in your own tears... take my hand, and hold on tight...I'll pull you through this dark, dark night...The sun's still shinin' on the other side...have no fear, I'll be your guide... through heaven's pearls or the gates of hell...inside my heart you'll always dwell... You'll never be too far from me...don't lose your grip, we'll make it you'll see...When the skies are gray and stormy, I'll pull you through the clouds, so you can see the sun's still shining, above the earth's dark shroud... I can't you on take this journey, and that we've always known, but in my heart I know you have the strength to get there on your own...*

They ended the song resting their foreheads against each other, much like they had when they first sang together just over a month ago. Something was so different this time though; they shared the common bond of loss and survival and were both stronger because of it. Their relationship had grown immensely in a short time; spending so much time together over the past couple months had given them a sort of crash course in each other, and they were finding that they were incredibly compatible in all the ways that mattered. There was a comfort that passed between them, and at that moment, there was no crowd, no cheering, no pressure, just a sense of security and connectedness that they both felt strongly. He tossed his guitar over his shoulder and put his arm around her waist and bowed with her, then stepped back and motioned with a sweep of his arm for her to once more receive the adulation of the audience. Reality hit hard when her eyes swept across the crowd and she saw the immense sea of faces there, and her knees went weak, heat rising to her face and her breath was gone again, but Dylan was back, pulling her into an embrace and kissing her before handing her back over to the security guard who helped her back to her seat.

Lexi just stared for a moment, then her whisper was lost in the sound of the crowd and the music but Tia read it on her lips, "Oh my God, Tia, you are so amazing together," and she pulled Tia into an embrace and said into her ear, "I am so blown away by you right now!"

Tia hugged her back, welcoming the support as she was trying to settle her heart, breathing and body temperature into some sort of normalcy. Again, the people around them were patting her back, rubbing her head, and doing anything they could to get more connected to what was happening on the stage. A big bear of a guy spun her around and pulled her into a hug, and as she laughed, she saw, four rows back, Penelope Valentine, glaring at her with a look that was downright hostile.

Penelope seethed in the fourth row—again. She'd had her agent get the tickets for her and her assistant so she could catch Dylan off-guard after the show and maybe get a little time to get to know him. This time she'd done her homework, and knew the kind of person that Dylan needed her to be, and she had every intention of playing the role like it was for another Oscar nomination. She'd never for a moment considered that he wouldn't be here alone. The first few songs had her up and dancing with the rest of the crowd, and she was feeling almost giddy watching him on stage. He had such an amazing presence and he couldn't be sexier, and she imagined that this time, he'd be lonely and glad to spend some time with her. Then her entire fantasy came crashing down around her when he plucked that little bitch out of the audience and had her singing with him on stage.

Penelope found it absolutely pitiful the way she was behaving, craving the limelight one minute and feigning shyness the next, just to get applause. Worse though, was the realization that things could actually be serious between them—Dylan had obviously thought enough of her to bring her to London, and maybe even for more of the tour. She'd hoped that he'd have forgotten about her by now, and that showing up 'accidentally' in Europe would jump start things between the two of them. It hadn't figured into her plans that she might still have competition for his attention.

Patience was never one of her virtues, but she knew when it was time to drop back and wait. This Tia person was a schoolteacher, for chrissake. She'd be back to grading papers and wiping snotty brats' noses in the fall, and Penelope would have Dylan all to herself. They'd be far from his little commoner and from Hollywood, and then they could take things to the next level. It was all a matter of timing, she told herself, and this wasn't the right time. She'd just have to kick things up a notch later, have a good plan in place and follow through in just the right order. She was an Oscar nominee—she knew just how to play the part—and Dylan was part of it. He just didn't know it yet. There was a positive side to this little encounter, though—now at least she knew there could be another hurdle she'd have to get over, and she could plan for that too. That little girl was deluding herself if she really believed she could hold on to a man like Dylan Miller. She had no idea what she was up against, and Penelope smiled as she leaned over and whispered something to her assistant. They needed to get on this right away; there were only a few weeks left before she'd have him all to herself.

InHap finished off the show with two more rockers and an extended jam that had the audience jumping in unison and singing along. When Dylan gave her the nod, she and Lexi waved to the people around them and headed for the stage entrance. She was sure to flash a smile at Penelope, who had to know she wouldn't be welcomed backstage.

There was no waiting in the common room this time. Tia threw her arms around Dylan the minute he stepped off the stage, but he spoke before she had a chance to. "You were brilliant!" he yelled. "Thanks so much for stepping in—I knew you'd be incredible!"

"You're thanking me?" she squealed, astounded. "I can't believe you did that! I can't believe I did that! It was so incredible!"

"It was Bo's idea, actually," he said, folding her into his arms, "but we thought if we told you ahead of time, you might chicken out."

Tia recalled the two of them head to head at the pre-show meeting, and the look they'd thrown her way. "I probably would've!" she exclaimed. "I would've been so freaked out the whole time...oh, but it was so...I don't even have words for it!"

Ty hugged her next. "You saved my ass tonight, Tia," he rasped in a voice that still sounded like sandpaper, "and you were nothing short of awesome. I'm sure glad you can't play bass, or I'd be out of a job!"

"Yeah right," she exclaimed. "That'd never happen." She threw her arms in the air and wiggled excitedly. "It was an incredible feeling though—how do you do it night after night and not let it go straight to your heads? I feel like I'm dancing on clouds right now; it was so much fun!"

"And you," Dylan said, slinging his arm over her shoulder and kissing the top of her head, "were nothing short of spectacular. You know, I think we sound pretty damn good together, you and me," he said with a smile.

"I completely agree," Lexi chimed in. "I've obviously heard her sing before, but I still couldn't believe it was her on that stage! The audience loved it, too."

"Yeah, well, I'm not giving up my day job just yet," Tia laughed. "But this certainly goes down as one of the best nights of my life!"

"Mine too," Lexi added. "Even though I can't tell a soul about it."

A shadow crossed Dylan's face. "What do you mean?" he asked.

Lexi held up two fingers in the Girl Scout salute. "I am sworn to secrecy when it comes to who Tia is dating," she said. Dylan looked over at Tia with a question in his eyes.

"It's just easier that way," she said. "First, it isn't her story to tell…" she stuck her tongue out at Lexi and she responded in turn. "Second, I only knew you a few days when I left, and I only had a couple weeks to get everything together to come here. I didn't have time for the extra attention I'd get if people knew I was coming here to see you, and it's not the kind of news you send in an email…"

"That was actually a good idea," Dylan agreed, although he was amazed again that she'd keep him a secret. Most women wanted the notoriety of dating a celebrity, but she was too down to earth to see it as an advantage. It was actually more of a disadvantage to her—he knew that, but he was surprised to see that she realized it too. "I just hope there weren't paparazzi in the audience snapping your picture while you were on stage. You could be all over the British tabloids tomorrow morning."

"I didn't see any big cameras," Tia said, "but I did happen to see our little friend Miss Valentine in the audience tonight."

Dylan frowned. "I'd heard she was in Europe," he said, "but I didn't know she was here. At least she had the sense not to try and get back stage again. Now that she knows you're here, hopefully she'll keep her distance."

"Yeah, she doesn't like me very much," Tia agreed, "and that suits me just fine."

Bo walked in then, always the last to leave the stage, and handed Tia two drum sticks. "I kept the real ones for you, sweetheart. A little memento of your InHap debut." He smiled, and she hugged him. "You were spectacular, by the way. You did us proud."

"Thank you very much," Tia said in her best imitation of Dylan, which wasn't very good. "I am humbled and honored to share the stage with such a fine bunch of gentlemen," she added with a flourish and a bow.

"Well now, I wouldn't go that far," Bo added with a grin. "But you can sing for me anytime."

Tia and Lexi sat in the common room while the boys flirted with fans who waited patiently outside the stadium for a glimpse of their idols. Jessa finally joined them, and after introductions and more gushing about Tia's stage debut, the girls popped the tops off a few Stellas and toasted each other.

"Seriously," Lexi said. "You said that things were pretty intense between you and Dylan, but seeing you on stage together—I thought I was going to melt from all the heat!"

Tia just laughed, but Jessa leaned in toward Lexi and whispered, "They're like that all the time—you can just feel it whenever they're in the same room together. And when they aren't together, Dylan is always worried about what she's doing and who she's with. I say it's love."

Lexi shook all over as she took it in. "I knew it!" she exclaimed. "I just knew she was holding something back! Whenever we talk it's all like, 'we're getting closer, I really like him,' but it's more than that, isn't it?"

"I think so," Jessa said. "I've known Dylan for over a year now, and I've seen the way he was with other girls. It's totally different with Tia."

"So it's him too, and not just her?" Lexi asked.

"Uh, hello?" Tia chimed in. "I'm still here, remember? Could the two of you refrain from making decisions about my love life until I'm at least out of the room?"

"Ah hah!" Lexi burst. "You just said 'love life.' You are in love with him, aren't you?"

Tia took a deep breath and let it out slowly, bowing her head in resignation. "Yeah, I just can't help myself." Lexi and Jessa high fived each other over the table, but Tia was quick to scold them both. "Not a word from either of you—got it?" Lexi and Jessa shared knowing smiles. "Listen, girls. If he's going to hear it from anyone it's going to be me, and I'll never forgive either of you if you say a word to anyone. I have no idea if that's what he's feeling, despite Jessa's insightful guessing. We only have a few more weeks before he goes away to make that damn movie, and I have no clue what's going to happen then. He could forget all about me once he's wrapped up in the Hollywood scene again."

Lexi leaned across the table, resting her chin on her fist and turning to Jessa. "What do you think, Jessa? Is he going to forget all about my friend here and just go on as if they never shared anything?"

"No way," Jessa agreed. "There's something between the two of them. Something that isn't going to just go away."

"You see?" Lexi turned to Tia. "Don't give up before you give him a chance. You aren't the only one with a say in this, am I right?" she said, turning again to Jessa.

"Oh, I think he'll have a lot to say about it," Jessa replied, and Tia chewed that over in her mind until they were interrupted by the return of Ty and Bo.

"Who has a lot to say about what?" Bo asked, pulling Lexi up into a hug. "I do hope you're talking about what you and I are going to be up to later, beautiful," he waggled his eyebrows at her obnoxiously.

"Well yeah, of course," Lexi teased, "how could we be talking about anything else?"

It was a public evening, out and about at London's hottest clubs. This was part of the job, Tia knew, but she felt a tugging at her heart every time a female fan wanted to get a picture with Dylan or wanted him to autograph a part of her body that Tia had no desire to see. They flirted with him unabashedly, pressing themselves against him and whispering what she could only assume were suggestive comments into his ear. He turned to look at her often, pointing to her and then himself and then interlocking his index fingers to indicate that they were connected. It helped ease her some, but it still gave her a bad feeling in the pit of her stomach when she realized, not for the first time, that he could have any of these women any time he wanted. Even though Jessa had said that she thought Dylan's feelings for her were beyond a little fling, she felt that damn pang of jealousy again. She held her ground, though, and tried to focus on all the good points of the evening—her singing on stage, her best friend by her side getting along famously with her new friend; and she forced herself not to interfere with his work.

She and the girls sat off to themselves when they first arrived at each place, sipping British beers and laughing amongst themselves while the boys did their thing. They made a great threesome--Jessa and Lexi hit it off almost too well— and they couldn't stop joking about Tia not being able to focus on anything else but Dylan.

When the boys finally called it a night, Dylan pulled her close. "I'll miss you tonight," he whispered. "My bed'll be cold and lonely without you in it."

"It better be," she snapped, and was immediately sorry she'd said it.

"Oh Tia," he soothed, smoothing her hair with his hand. "Don't you know that there isn't anyone else here for me but you?"

"I'm sorry," she said immediately, meaning it. "It's just so freaking hard watching all those girls literally throwing themselves at you all night long." She exhaled sharply. "It isn't my business, I know," she added sadly, "but it is *your business*, and I have no right to be upset."

"I *am* your business," he replied, pulling her chin up to meet his gaze, "and I think I'd be bummed out if you weren't a little jealous. This is just part of the job, that's all, and I never even remember the faces I see night after night. They're all the same to me. You're the only one I want to be with. I won't be able to think of anything else but you all night."

She leaned against him and held him tight. "I'll miss you too," she said.

"Well, you girls'll have fun tonight. It's obvious Lexi missed you."

"Yeah. It's really great to have her here. And you were right—having her here is like a little bit of home. I didn't really realize I'd missed it until she got here—thanks so much for bringing her. But you and me..."

"Shhhh," he whispered. "We have lots more time. And I'm pretty exhausted. I'm going to have some tea and hit the bed—alone—and I'll see the two of you at the stadium, tomorrow afternoon, right, after your little tea party?"

"Definitely," she said. Jessa and Lexi had already decided that the night wasn't over yet, and Tia watched Dylan and the boys go as she went back to join the girls.

Lexi said, "So who's the third wheel now?"

Now that it was just the girls, Tia put herself into party mode. "Not you, Lex. Never you."

Lexi and Jessa raised their glasses and Lexi made the toast. "To Hollywood's new power couple!" she exclaimed. "I could cut the sexual tension with a fucking chainsaw right about now."

Tia laughed and raised her glass to toast her friends, ready to enjoy a girls' night out. It was great to be with them, and how often did she get to go clubbing in London with such amazing people? They hit the dance floor, ignoring the men who tried to cut in on their trio, and made an already incredible evening even more unforgettable.

In the end, there was an article in the tabloids, but all the pictures were too grainy to really make out Tia's face. "Beautiful Mystery Woman Becomes Sixth Member of InHap at Wembley," the headline read, and the article went on to wonder if "sexy heartthrob Dylan Miller is taking his name off the Most Eligible Bachelor List," quoting that he'd called Tia "my lovely lady" and that he'd kissed her before she exited the stage. They got her name wrong, though, calling her 'Tina,' and although they didn't know her identity, readers could be assured that a team was 'on the case.' Tia bought ten copies.

Chapter 22

Walking into the spa was like walking into a fantasy—it was all marble, soft colors, incredible smells and total comfort. Dylan had insisted Jessa join them for the day as well—and the girls donned their thick robes and headed first to the steam room. They'd finished the two Wembley shows; thankfully Ty's voice had come back enough to perform the second show, and they had a couple free days in London before going up north to Manchester to play two more gigs at the end of the week. Dylan was spending the day with some of his old friends in Northampton, an hour and a half outside of London by train, and he had a lot of catching up to do. He figured he'd likely spend the night—sleeping on someone's couch, he'd said, just like the old days. Tia was thrilled to have a spa day and time with the girls, and wanted Dylan to have his guy time, too, but she was well aware that it was already mid-July, and that their time together was growing short.

"Oh, this is the good life," Lexi moaned as she lay back on the warm wooden bench, stretching her arms over her head. "I kind of like this guy you're dating, Tia—he knows how to please a woman."

"You can say that again," Tia smirked. "And he has good ideas for girls' day out, too," she said, adding a wink.

"You going to be OK being without him for a whole day?" she teased.

"Funny," Tia said. "I think I'll survive, but if I have to be without him, I think I can handle spending it this way."

Lexi turned to Jessa. "What do you think, Jessa, is she really going to have fun, or is she going to be pining all day and just pretending?"

"We'll just have to make sure she has fun," she answered, "and I think we have that pretty well covered." They shared a knowing smile.

Tia sat up. "What?" she asked suspiciously, eyeing the looks on her friends' faces. Their expressions suddenly turned falsely innocent, and they shrugged at each other. "Spill it—now." Tia said, folding her arms across her chest and giving them scolding looks.

"What, and ruin the surprise?" Lexi replied secretively.

"You have a surprise for me?" Tia asked. "Now why would you do that? You know I hate surprises!" When that didn't elicit a response from either of them, she tried whining. "Come on, tell me! Please?"

Lexi stood. "Maybe in the hot tub—isn't that our next stop?" Lexi bolted out the door and the girls followed. They showered off and slipped into the deep tub that had wonderfully scented bubbles rising a foot off the top of the water.

"Mmmmm," Lexi moaned." This is already a great day, and it's barely even started."

"Alexis Marie, tell me my surprise!"

Lexi looked at Jessa. "Hmmm, what do you think Jessa? Should we tell her?" she asked innocently. "Or make her wait?"

Jessa shrugged, "I don't know," she pondered, "I keep remembering that first night in Chicago when she let you figure out that she was with Dylan by watching him dedicate the show to her from the stage—seems to me she can dish it out, so maybe she should be able to take it, too."

"Exactly!" Lexi agreed. "I'm still pissed about that! You are a wise woman, Jessa, maybe we should make her wait."

But Tia wouldn't have it. "Listen girls," she said. "Neither of you would be here if it wasn't for him, so leave Dylan out of it." She stuck her lower lip out in a pout and lowered her head. "Don't make me beg!" she said. "Tell me!"

"Oh, alright," Lexi drew out the words as if she'd just surrendered, but Tia knew she wouldn't have been able to keep the secret from her for long. "After the spa, we have a personal shopper set up for us at Harrods—it's time for your birthday present!"

Tia could hardly contain her excitement. "Oooh, seriously? That's going to be so much fun! I can't wait! But you know you don't have to do that Lex, it's too much, really."

"Oh stop it," Lexi scolded. "You'll let me do this, and you will enjoy every minute of it, or I'll kick your ass."

"I will enjoy every minute!" she exclaimed, "and since you're being such a smart ass about it, I'll make sure it costs you!"

"I'm counting on it," Lexi smiled. "But Jessa set the whole thing up for me, so you have to thank her too."

"You are pretty awesome," Tia said to Jessa. "I can see why Dylan keeps you around."

Jessa smiled. "Happy birthday, by the way. When is it, exactly?"

"July 28th," Tia said, and immediately added, "but not a word from either of you about it to Dylan!"

"You mean you still haven't told him about your birthday?" Lexi asked.

"Why in the world not?" Jessa added.

Tia just glared at them. "Hello? Could the man do any more for me? We're all sitting here enjoying this pampering because of him. This entire summer is a gift to me—I couldn't ask for more. But if he knew it was my birthday, he would do more, and I don't want him to feel obligated…"

"Obligated?" Jessa interrupted. "I think he'd want to know. It'd be up to him if he wanted to do something special, and I think he'd be ticked off if you didn't let him make that decision for himself!"

"How has that not come up in conversation?" Lexi asked. "You know that he hates cauliflower, for God's sake, and you don't know each other's birthdays?"

"I don't know," Tia defended, "but it hasn't, and I'm not going to go tell him and look like I'm asking for something else from him. If he asks, I'll tell him, but I'm not making a point of it, and neither should you. It's absolutely enough for me that I get to spend it with him—and in Paris no less! That's the best gift I could have."

Lexi and Jessa rolled their eyes simultaneously and then laughed at each other and at Tia. "Fine, whatever," Lexi said, "subject closed. Now let's get back to shopping, shall we? I was checking out their website from home and Harrods has designer everything—I'm going to do some serious damage to my credit card, there's no doubt about that!"

"I've wanted to go there since we got to London," Jessa agreed. "I'm so ready to splurge a little, and I couldn't think of a better place to buy overpriced clothes and shoes!" she said, doing a little happy dance through the bubbles.

"We're all going to get decked out in new digs and then hit the town tonight," Lexi said. "Here's to girls' night out!"

The next three hours were heaven--massages, manicures, pedicures, haircuts and make-up. By the time they left, they were all feeling pampered and spoiled, and they grabbed a black taxi to Harrods. The store was enormous, and they rode the Egyptian escalator up to meet their personal shopper.

Dylan hopped off the train and looked around at the familiar station in Northampton. The one thing about the old cities in England, he thought, is that they never changed much. They'd stayed pretty much the same for hundreds of years, and it was like stepping back into his past. He hadn't bothered with much of a disguise today, just a sweatshirt with the hood up and a pair of dark sunglasses. He'd gone unrecognized on the train, but as he scanned the station, he caught a familiar pair of eyes that recognized him right away. "Dylan, mate, it's great to see you!" His old friend Max grasped his hand and then pulled him into an embrace.

"You haven't changed a bit," Dylan remarked, clapping him on the back. "You look great!"

"Yeah? Well you certainly have," his old friend commented. "Big hotshot celebrity now, aren't you?"

"I guess it had to happen to one of us," Dylan grinned. "I'm damn sure glad it was me!"

"Ah," Max said, shaking his head. "Some things don't change, though; I see you're still full of shit!"

They laughed together and headed out of the station, Max's arm slung companionably over Dylan's shoulders.

"This place hasn't changed at all," Dylan said, "it still feels like home. So what's on the agenda?" he asked, adjusting his backpack. He'd brought a change of clothes and his punk rock disguise, in case the guys decided they wanted to be out and about. It was a college town, and he'd be sure to be recognized at a public club.

"Actually, we thought we'd have kind of a private party," he said, "if that's OK with you. Collin's uncle is giving us the pub for the night—it's a Tuesday anyway and summer break, so business isn't exactly booming right now. Besides, he knew we'd fill the place and buy plenty of beer."

"That sounds perfect!" Dylan agreed. "Who's going to be there? What's everyone up to? It's been so long since I've seen you guys—I can't believe you're all still stuck in this little town!"

"Yeah, well, not all of us get to run off to Hollywood and tour the world, you know, but a lot of us are still playing. We'll have the stage at the pub—maybe we could jam."

"That'd be great." It would be, too, he thought. He couldn't wait see some of the guys from his early bands, and it would be fun to play with them again.

"A bunch of the guys are there setting things up," Max said. "Collin, Les, Chad, Brett, Dex and Leroy should be waiting for us. Leroy's married, you know—he's got two kids."

"I did hear that—I think you emailed me. I sent a gift."

"I'm sure I did. Danny, Andy and Will are going to show up a bit later—they couldn't get the day off work. Who else," he pondered, "Gina and Margo will be along tonight, and probably Juliet and Scott—they're a hot item right now. There'll be a few people you don't know, but we tried to keep it pretty private. We know that if we bring you out in public, we won't get two seconds with you! We're catering food in and everything."

"That's perfect," Dylan said, recognizing the names and looking forward to seeing them all. "I really just want to catch up with everyone—it'll be a long time before my path crosses this way again."

"So, tell me about the tour. What's it like to be adored by tens of thousands of fans every single night? The Wembley shows got great reviews."

"That part of it's pretty awesome—you know the feeling, and then multiply it by a thousand. The pain in the ass is that I can't go out in public anymore. Sometimes I envy the simple life."

"Yeah, but then you park your Porsche in the garage and walk into your mansion and the feeling goes away, right?"

Dylan smiled. "Yeah, something like that," he laughed.

Underground hadn't changed a bit either. Same worn wooden bar stools, same jukebox in the corner, same dusty decorations on the walls. When he walked in he was greeted like an old friend, and everyone queued up to hug him and welcome him back. They'd known him before he was famous and refused to give him the celebrity treatment, which he appreciated immensely. The last time he'd felt so comfortable in a public place was at *Paddy's*, when everyone in the place was lined up to greet Tia, and he wished suddenly that he could introduce her to his friends. She needed a girls' day, though, and he understood how much having her own identity meant to her. He didn't want to smother her.

He'd barely greeted Collin and Brett before someone pushed a beer into his hands. Most of the rest of them already had pints, and they raised their glasses to welcome him home. He teased Les about his receding hairline and congratulated Leroy on the birth of his second child. When he'd made the rounds, he sat at a table with his former band mates and settled in to shoot the shit. They chatted easily for an hour, reliving old times and catching up on each other's lives.

"So which Hollywood starlet's heart are you currently breaking?" Collin teased. "I read that you're doing your next movie with Penelope Valentine—she'd be pretty easy to wake up to in the morning!" The rest of the guys agreed, and bumped their glasses together.

"I'm done with starlets—have been for a while," Dylan said. "They're nothing but trouble."

"So you're still living the bachelor life, eh?" Chad replied. "Gina'll be glad to hear that. She was beside herself when I told her you were coming out."

The thought of seeing Gina again bothered him, just a bit. She'd taught him one of his first hard lessons on dating celebrity style. They'd been dating almost a year, and his band, *Slingshot*, was opening for *The Tuesday Warriors*, a popular London band perched to make it big. He'd gotten Gina back stage, and within a week of the show, she'd dumped him for their lead guitarist. Two months later, he dumped her, and she came begging Dylan to take her back. It was painfully obvious to him that it was the guitarist's celebrity that drew Gina in, and he wanted no part of it, and refused to continue their relationship. Over the next year, they slowly rebuilt a tentative friendship; she even played with his band for a while, but he knew he could never trust her again.

"I didn't say that," Dylan said. "I'm pretty involved with someone right now—I've actually brought her with me on the tour."

"Wait a minute," Max interjected. "The mystery Wembley woman! I read about her in the paper—she's the one, right?"

Dylan smiled, remembering Tia's reaction when she saw her picture in the tabloids. "That's her. Her name is Tia," he said.

"What, and you didn't bring her to meet your oldest and dearest mates?" Brett said. He held his hand over his heart. "I'm crushed. Aren't we good enough?"

"Obviously," Dylan teased. "One look at you blokes and she'll wonder what she ever saw in me!"

The guys took the ribbing easily and Chad continued, "Really though, she's come with you for the whole tour? What is she, a bloody heiress or something that she can run off for the whole summer?"

"Actually, she's a school teacher," Dylan said, "so she has summers off."

"A school teacher!" Collin exclaimed. "How in the world did you hook up with a teacher?"

For the next half hour, Dylan recounted the story of him and Tia; the first crazy night, the whirlwind weekend, their first night together, the first month and a half of the tour so far, and when he finished, the guys were all staring at him gap mouthed, incredulous looks on their faces. "What?" he asked, taking in their stunned expressions.

"Bloody hell," Chad spoke up. "Miller's in love."

Now it was Dylan's mouth that hung open. "What?" he said again.

"It's brilliant!" Max said, taking in Dylan's look. "It's written all over your face, mate."

Dylan's mind raced. Was he in love with Tia? He'd been so busy trying to balance all the aspects of the tour—the shows, the interviews, guest spots, meetings, trying to make sure he had time to spend with her and that she wasn't bored when he couldn't. Their relationship was progressing quickly, and he felt completely comfortable with her; they were a natural fit, and seeing her was always the highlight of his day—but was he in love? He hadn't really had time to think about it, but now that it was out there, smacking him in the face, his mind was turning a mile a minute.

"Well that settles it then," Chad said. "You've got to call her right now and invite her out—we've got to meet the girl who's going to set hearts all over the world to breaking."

Suddenly Dylan did want her there. He did want her to meet his old friends, and he hadn't seen much of her the past couple days since Lexi arrived. They had so few free nights together; it really was a shame to waste one.

"OK," Dylan said standing and pulling out his phone. "I'll call the guys too—we can make this a real party!"

The girls were walking out of Harrods, dressed in hot new finery and struggling under the bulk of their many bags. The shopping trip had been a huge success, and they were all going to cringe when they got the bills. They all wore new dresses, new shoes, and carried overpriced handbags. With their hair and makeup done and their bodies pampered from the spa, they were feeling like a million bucks. The plan was to drop the bags at the hotel and head out for dinner and a night on the town. They'd just gotten into the taxi when Tia's phone rang. She smiled when she saw Dylan's name on the display.

"Hi!" she answered brightly.

"Hello, beautiful," he responded, "how was your day at the spa?"

"It was pure bliss," she answered dreamily. "I don't think I've ever felt so spoiled." Lexi and Jessa were both mouthing 'thank-you' at her to pass along to him. "Lex and Jessa say thank you, and so do I. It was a great day!"

"I'm so glad you liked it. What are you doing now?"

"Well," she said, "we're just heading back to the hotel. We've had a bit of a shopping spree at Harrods and have dozens of bags to drop off. We're looking pretty hot right now, I must tell you—we got some gorgeous new things. Then we're heading out on the town—I'm not sure where we're going; I think Jessa has it planned out."

"How would you feel about a change of plans?" he asked.

"I could definitely be open to that, if it means I get to see you," she said.

His mind raced again at her words, and the 'L' word was nagging at the back of his brain. "I was hoping you'd say that. I'm at this little pub with my friends, and I was talking about you, and they're insisting that I invite you out so they can meet you."

"You were talking about me?" she asked sweetly.

"Of course," he replied matter-of-factly. "How could I not?" he could almost feel Tia's shy smile through the phone line. "I called the guys, and they're all coming too. There's a train leaving in half an hour from Euston station, and they could meet you there..." he hesitated a moment before continuing, "I don't want to ruin your plans, though, if you were set on a girls' night out."

"Hold on," she said, and he heard her voice as she spoke to the other girls. "How do you guys feel about a little party in Northampton?" she asked excitedly. "The rest of the boys are going to go—we could meet them at the train."

Dylan heard the sounds of agreement from Jessa and Lexi, and smiled. He needed to get to the bottom of the thoughts that were running through his head, and having her here would hopefully make things more clear.

"We'll be there!" she said, coming back to the line.

"Great!" he answered, "I'll see you in a couple hours then. I'll call Bo and let him know you'll be meeting them at the station. They'll have your tickets for you."

"We'll see you in a bit then!" she said, then lowered her voice. "And Dylan? Thanks. It means a lot to me that you want me to meet your friends."

Again, she caught him off guard, and he felt his heart skip a beat. "Yeah, well we'll see how you feel about it after you've met them— they're an interesting lot. But I'm glad you're coming—see you soon."

Dylan was on his way back to the table to tell the guys that they were on their way when Gina walked in with Margo. She wore a little black dress, and little was the operative word—she was all leg and cleavage, and she looked good for herself. Her eyes swept the room as she stepped in, and immediately stopped on Dylan, a smile spreading on her face. Dylan knew that smile, and saw right away that he'd have a situation to diffuse. She ran up to him and jumped into his arms, pressing herself seductively against him and grinding her hips into his in an all too familiar gesture. "Oh Dylan, it's been ages!" she whispered in his ear. "I've missed you, you know—you look great!"

Dylan put his hands on her hips and gently pushed her back. "You too, Gina, you look...just the same as always. It's good to see you." She tried to press against him again, but he stepped away and reached for Margo. "And you," he said, pulling her into a friendly embrace, "look great too. How've you been?"

"Good!" she answered, giving him a peck on the cheek. "Whatever possessed you to come out slumming? Big star like you—we thought you'd forgotten all about us."

Dylan smiled. "How could I forget you guys? I had a lot of great times here; it's good to be back."

Gina interrupted, winding her arm through Dylan's and leading him to the bar. "Buy me a pint?" she asked sweetly. "I'm just dying to catch up with you!"

He got them a couple of beers, and she sidled up to him next to the bar. "I really have missed you, Dylan," she whispered. "I've been following your career—you're doing amazingly well! I can't wait to see the Manchester show! How'd Wembley go? I haven't seen the papers."

"They were great!" Dylan answered, gently sliding her hand off his thigh. "It's great to be back here, too. So you're doing well?"

"Same old thing," she sighed. "I've thought about you a lot, you know. We had some great times together, the two of us."

Dylan slid over a couple inches as she tried again to press herself against him. "I have a lot of great memories from Northampton," he said vaguely.

"We were so good together, you and me—I've never gotten over you, you know." She brushed her tongue against his ear. "It's never too late for a fresh start, you know--after we're done here, want to head over to my place, relive old times?" The look in her eyes left nothing to the imagination.

Dylan stepped back. "Sorry, Gina," he said kindly, "but I'm not available for that. I'm involved with someone—pretty seriously."

Gina looked around the room and then back at Dylan. "Well I don't see her here right now—it could just be our little secret. We lit the world on fire you and me—don't you ever wonder what would have happened if you didn't decide to take off to the States? I think about it all the time."

"You mean what might have happened if you didn't run off with what's-his-face?" Dylan asked.

She pouted, and added, "Oh Dylan, I knew it was a mistake from the minute I did it and I was so sorry, but you just couldn't forgive me."

"I couldn't trust you, and that made all the difference," he said. "But that was eons ago, and we've both moved on, so it shouldn't matter anymore. Not after all this time."

"Then maybe we should give it just one more shot," she said, leaning over to nuzzle his neck, her breasts nearly spilling from the black lace.

He backed away from her, and looked into her eyes. "Look Gina," he said, "it's great to see you, really, but I'm not interested. My girlfriend's on her way here right now, actually, but even if she wasn't, I wouldn't do that to her. Even if she never knew, I would."

Gina pouted again, but she quickly bounced back and smiled. "I'm glad to see you haven't lost your sense of honor, Dylan. It's one of your best qualities. Oh well, it was worth a try, anyway, for old times' sake. She must be something if she's got you. You're still a great guy," she added. "She's a lucky girl."

"I'm pretty lucky too," he answered simply. "So now that we have that awkwardness out of the way, how have you been? What's life been dealing you the past few years?" She was the same old Gina, he saw, taking life as it came and making the most of it. They chatted easily like old friends, and she didn't try to come on to him again. She understood the score, and knew Dylan well enough to know that he meant what he said. They caught up for a while, then Dylan went back to join his old band mates, who had another pint waiting for him. He took a seat that faced the front of the pub, and watched the door anxiously.

The minute Tia walked into the pub, he knew. It wasn't just that she looked amazingly sexy in a smoking red dress that showed a lot of leg and just the right amount of cleavage, or that she had new highlights in her hair. When she met his eyes and smiled, from across the room, he knew instantly. He was in love with her. His stomach did a little turn and his breath caught for a second—this was big. It was huge. He realized that he should have known it all along; or at least he should have figured it out weeks ago. He stood up and made his way to her, pulling her into his arms and kissing her mouth. "You look so incredibly hot right now," he growled in her ear. "I'm so glad I didn't set you loose on the streets of London—you'd be fighting off every guy in the city."

Tia blushed, "Well, thank you," she said sweetly, "but there's only one guy in the city that I wanted to see tonight."

"Please say me, please say me," he said hopefully, teasing, fingers crossed and eyes closed.

She threw her head back and laughed, wrapping her arms around his neck and kissing his cheek. "Actually," she teased, "I was thinking about that guy over there," tossing her head in the general direction of the bar, "but you'll do."

"Good enough for me!" he smiled, but his head was clouded and his heart was beating too fast. He was in love, and it rocked him to the core. He swept her toward the table to introduce her to his former band and the rest of his friends.

Tia was enjoying herself. Dylan's friends were all great, and she loved hearing their stories about him in his reckless younger days. Finally Max asked, "So, Big D, we gonna jam, or what? A *Slingshot* reunion, what do you say?"

"Hell yes," Dylan replied, smiling, and they leaped from the table to take the stage. Lexi, Jessa and Bo took the emptied seats.

Slingshot had been mainly a cover band, one of Dylan's earlier groups, and they easily fell into a familiar old pub favorite.

"This is so fun!" Lexi exclaimed. "So much better than the loud clubs—I'm glad we came."

Bo agreed. "I'm glad you came too, gorgeous, how about a dance?"

"You got it, handsome," she said, jumping from her seat. Their unabashed and innocent flirting was now familiar to all of them, and they all just rolled their eyes. Soon, other couples were taking to the dance floor, and the mood of the place was lifted to new heights. One of Dylan's friends--Danny, Tia thought, asked Jessa to dance and she raised her eyebrows at Tia as she stood up to join him. Tia looked around the room and felt complete contentment. Dylan smiled at her from the stage where he was obviously having a blast playing again with his old friends, Angelo, Ty and Tommy were laughing and having a good time, and her girls were being twirled around the dance floor. The song ended, and the group cheered for their old friends. Then Max pounded a beat on the drum, and they moved into another number. Gina squealed from the floor and jumped up to join them on stage, grabbing Collin's mike and sliding over beside Dylan with a knowing smile on her face. Tia felt a pang of jealousy—the girl was beautiful; blonde, built, and sexy, and she was obviously on very familiar terms with Dylan. Tia had heard her name mentioned in more than a couple of the stories told by his old mates, and she'd been pointed out, although they hadn't yet been introduced. Again, she fought back the jealous feeling at the pit of her stomach. She really needed to get over this if they were going to have any kind of relationship. She had to have a lot more trust than the average girlfriend—very few people had boyfriends who were voted the sexiest man on the whole damn planet.

Dylan invited her tonight because he wanted to be with her, and she had to trust that. He'd never given her any reason to doubt him, and she had faith in his integrity. She pushed the feeling down and watched the two perform together. It wasn't the first time, obviously, and they sounded good together—her voice had a raw edge to it and she knew how to work the stage. Tia cheered just as enthusiastically as the rest of the group when they finished and took a bow.

Chad plucked the first notes of Van Morrison's *Brown Eyed Girl* on his electric guitar, and the crowd cheered, nearly all of them jumping to their feet to hit the dance floor. It was an obvious favorite, and Tia watched them, smiling, as they danced and spun to the song. Dylan sang the first couple lines, then put his mike in Chad's stand, leaving the stage and sauntering over to Tia, his hand extended. She smiled and put her hand in his as he led her, hips swaying seductively, to the dance floor. He pulled her into a sensuous dance, their bodies moving together in slow circles, and he thought to himself, *I love this girl!* The thought both thrilled and terrified him, but right now, with her in his arms, he was feeling mostly the thrill. He led her in a spin, then dipped her back, kissing her as he bent over her. He sang to her, changing the words to "green-eyed girl," and she laughed at his exaggerated dance movements. The entire crowd sang the last verse, getting louder and singing to each other with huge smiles "sha la la la la la la..." Dylan spun Tia, slow and easy, she tossed her hair and smiled—she felt on top of the world, and then she was back in his arms, pressed against him and swaying until the song ended, and the whole crowd broke into enthusiastic applause and began hugging one another.

"Whew!" Tia said, "I didn't know you were such a sexy dancer!"

"Well, some of it might be that dress," he smiled seductively, "you sure know how to bring the sexy into a room!" He put his hand on her cheek and looked her in the eyes. "I'm really glad you came, Tia."

She smiled warmly at him, pressing her cheek into his hand. "Me too."

They headed back toward the table, but Tia took a detour to the ladies' room. When she walked in, Gina was standing in front of the mirror, putting on lipstick. Their eyes caught in the reflection, and Tia smiled at her, extending her hand for an introduction. "Hi," she said. "We haven't met yet. I'm Tia."

"I'm Gina," she said, taking Tia's hand and shaking it.

"I've heard a lot about you," Tia said, and Gina raised her eyebrows.

"Really," Gina said, somewhat suspiciously.

"A bunch of the guys were telling stories about when Dylan lived here, and your name came up a lot. You were great by the way, on stage. You've got an incredible presence and a great voice."

"Thanks!" Gina said. "I always loved singing with Dylan. It's really great to see him again."

"I'm sure he was glad to see you too. I know how excited he was to come and see all his old friends," she replied. "This is a great party they put together for him."

Gina hadn't planned to, but she couldn't help but like this girl. Her face was honest and open, and she was being genuinely nice, even after seeing her and Dylan on stage together. She didn't detect any animosity or jealousy, and could instantly see what Dylan saw in her. Plus, she'd seen the look on his face when she walked into the pub, and how he looked at her while they were on the dance floor—like there was no one else in the room; or the world, for that matter. She knew that look, and in her younger days she was always hoping that he'd look at her that way. They'd had some amazing times together, but he'd never looked at her with that kind of pure adoration. She decided to be straight with her.

"You know, Tia, everyone was so excited when he said he was coming," she began, "but maybe no one was more excited than me." It was Tia's turn to lift her eyebrows in question, and Gina continued. "Listen, before you hear it from someone else, you might as well hear it from me."

Tia swallowed and nodded her head. "OK."

"Dylan and I dated back in the day—for a while; I thought he was the one."

"I see," Tia said, having pretty much figured that out already.

"I'd even hoped that seeing him again tonight might rekindle something." Tia's face dropped a bit, but her eyes remained steady. "I hit on him pretty hard when I first got here, but he pushed me back in no uncertain terms." Tia inhaled deeply, instantly relieved. "He told me he was serious about someone, and I could see it as soon as you got here—his whole presence changed, you know? I've never seen him that way with anyone—including me, and well, you seem really nice, and I didn't want any hard feelings."

Tia smiled, thankful for her honesty, and secretly thrilled that Dylan had told her that their relationship was serious. "I appreciate you being straight with me," she said, "and there aren't any hard feelings, don't worry." She stuck her hand out to shake Gina's again, and she said, "Nice to meet you, Tia. You know you're pretty damn lucky, right?"

"Luckiest bitch on the planet," she smiled, recalling Lexi's words. Gina laughed again and agreed completely, then left to rejoin her friends at their table.

When Tia approached their ever-growing group, Max was busy persuading Dylan to do one of his songs. "Come on Dylan, give us one of yours," he said.

Dylan looked at Tia and asked, "How about it? Will you sing with me? We'll do *Pull You Up*. Just you, me, and the guitar."

"I could do that," she agreed immediately, and the crowd applauded appreciatively as Dylan stepped up behind the mike.

"Can I just say," he began, "that this has been a bloody brilliant evening, and I'm so glad to see all of you again!" His friends toasted him and clapped in total agreement. "Max has been bugging the shit out of me to play one more, so I hope you don't mind..." more applause and whoops of encouragement, "and I'm asking my special girl to sing with me." He strummed the first chords, and slid into the song, Tia closing her eyes and getting lost in the music, singing in her clear, cool voice. The more Dylan sang that song the more he loved it; and he really loved singing with Tia, as well. It was another thing they had in common, and for him, it was one of the most important qualities he needed in a girlfriend. Music was his life, and he needed his partner to share that passion with him.

When they finished the song, Dylan kissed her, and put his arm around her so that they could share a bow. The group was enthusiastic with their appreciation, and Tia felt as though she were dancing on a cloud. Gina caught her eye and gave her two thumbs up, and Tia smiled back.

It was getting late, and since there were now eight of them instead of one, they decided they'd catch the last train back to London. It took a half hour to say goodbyes. When Gina hugged Dylan, she whispered, "She's a keeper," and he replied simply, "I know." He bid farewell to his old friends, knowing it would be a long time before he'd see most of them again. He handed out tickets for the Manchester show to his old band mates and whoever else wanted them, and they headed back to the station to catch the last train back to London.

Tia fell asleep on the train, her head resting against Dylan's chest. He looked down at her and felt his heart swell. He was in love. He needed to tell her, obviously, but he wanted it to be special, and private, and as long as Lexi was here and the girls were rooming together, it wouldn't be. After Amsterdam they'd be going to Paris, and he couldn't think of a more perfect place in the world to give her his heart; not that she didn't have it already. Lexi leaned over and whispered something in his ear, and he smiled—the perfect plan forming in his mind.

Chapter 23

Tia woke up in the luxurious bed and rolled over to look out the huge window from which she had an incredible view of the Eiffel Tower. It was her birthday, and she sang softly to herself as she soaked in the city below her. The conversation hadn't come up, so Dylan still didn't know, and she certainly had no intention of springing the information on him today. This entire summer had already been the best gift she could ever imagine—the chance to spend more time with him and an entire season on one of the most incredible continents in the world. It was more than enough for her that she'd be able to spend the evening with the man she loved.

Dylan had slipped out sometime earlier; she knew he had some business to take care of this morning including a live appearance on a talk show, a taped performance with the rest of the guys for a late night show, a radio interview, and an audience with the mayor. The sun was shining and she felt wonderful; she was satiated from their lovemaking the night before, and more than content with the way things were going between the two of them. She had so enjoyed her time with Lexi in London and Amsterdam, and was still enjoying every minute of her summer. Her only regret was that it would be coming to an end in just a couple weeks. After Paris they had only Madrid, Lisbon, Rome and Florence before she'd have to say goodbye to Dylan for a very long time. But, today was her birthday, and she refused to feel sorry for herself for even one minute. This was going to be a day to remember, with the beauty and magic of Paris at her fingertips.

Tia threw the curtains open wide and stepped out onto the terrace to stare down at the city that spilled at her feet. Even Jessa had a full schedule today so she had most of it to herself, and she reveled in the idea of wandering aimlessly around the Louvre and through the Tuileries Gardens before meeting Dylan for a quick lunch at a little café on the Champs Elysees between interviews. Her afternoon would be full of shopping on one of the most beautiful and trendy streets in the world, and she'd decided that today would be a good day to splurge on something incredible. InHap wasn't playing until tomorrow night, so Dylan had planned a late dinner at the Jules Verne, on the second level of the Eiffel Tower, a spectacular site for a quiet birthday dinner and an excellent reason to buy a fabulous new dress.

The one she picked out was a knockout—so was the price, but she gritted her teeth as she handed over her credit card, knowing she'd freak out all over again when she got the bill—a sapphire blue silk with a plunging neckline and slits up the sides, beaded on the bodice with almost invisible iridescent pearls. It seemed to swim over her curves in little ripples when she moved, and to twinkle, just slightly, when light hit the beads. It reminded her of the Tower at night, sparkly against the deep sapphire sky. She returned early to the hotel to soak in a tub full of deliciously scented oils she'd picked up at another boutique, and took her time doing her hair and makeup. She wanted tonight to be extra spectacular.

***

There were no disguises tonight—the Jules Verne was exclusive enough that Dylan would be one celebrity among others; and those who could afford to dine there were not easily awed. He looked incredibly sexy in his dark gray Armani suit, and when he came out of the room and stopped short, staring appreciatively when he saw her in her new dress, she felt positively dizzy with delight. He pulled her into his arms and nuzzled her neck, whispering, "Maybe we should just stay home tonight, Mademoiselle, and I will show you the new French I learned." She whispered an incredibly sexy reply in French into his ear—he had no idea what it meant, but it made parts of him stir uncontrollably just to hear her voice breathing the words. In the end, though, he'd gone through an awful lot of trouble to plan this evening, and he wasn't about to lose a minute of it. When they got home, however, he would make sure to get a translation.

It was late in the evening, but the city still buzzed with excitement and lovers strolled through the streets arm in arm, oblivious of those around them. The plan was to go to the top of the tower first, on one of the last and least crowded ascensions, before heading down for an elegant and romantic dinner. Tia couldn't imagine a more perfect night—the sky was clear and the city was illuminated, the Tower twinkled and flashed against a full moon, and the air held the usual Paris crispness. The streetlights cast just enough shadows that they were able to remain anonymous and enjoy the walk to the Tower alongside other tourists and the handful of locals that hadn't yet fled for their summer holidays. Tia had been looking forward to this all day; looking out over the city of lights from the most incredible vantage point that Paris had to offer; so she couldn't hide her disappointment when they reached the gates and read the sign that said the Tower Observation point was closing early that evening; sorry for the inconvenience. It was their only free night in Paris; there would be a show tomorrow and they would leave the following afternoon, so it was the only chance they'd have to go to the top together.

"Oh, no," she said sadly, "The top of the Tower's closed? Why tonight?"

But Dylan kept walking, right up to the entrance for the lift, where an older gentleman was standing. "Bonsoir, Monsieur Miller," he smiled. "Mademoiselle," he added, nodding at Tia. "Everyzing is in order," he continued in heavily accented English, "après moi, s'il vous plaît."

Tia glanced over at Dylan with a question in her eyes, and he smiled down at her with a glimmer of knowing in his own. "What did you...?" she asked, as they were whisked into the lift and began their ascent up the Tower. He pulled her into an embrace and whispered into her ear, "I managed to reserve us a private viewing," and he held her against him as the streets and fountains fell below their feet and their eyes swept over the top of the city. Paris was spectacular at night, all lights and shadows with the incredible architecture rising in peaks and spires. When they reached the top, the gentleman handed Dylan a small device and said, "Simply beep when you are ready, monsieur. Enjoy the view," They stepped out of the lift and the man tipped his head as he began his decent.

Tia stepped out onto the platform and ran to the edge to take in the city below. "We have the whole thing to ourselves?" she said excitedly, pulling Dylan to the edge with her. "I can't believe it! Is there no end to the influence you have?"

"I had to pull a couple strings, believe me," he smiled, "it was part of my meet and greet with the mayor today, but just seeing your face right now makes it all worth it."

"This is incredible!" she exclaimed. "Look! There's the L'arc de Triomphe! I can't believe how tiny it looks from up here!" She turned to him and kissed him on the cheek. "It's the most beautiful thing in the world!" she exclaimed.

He looked deep into her eyes. "You're the most beautiful thing in the world," he said, pulling her to his mouth.

"Oh Dylan, this is more than I could have dreamed!" she said, spinning in small circles and coming back into his arms. "You make me feel so special, and I'm just so incredibly lucky to be able to share all this with you. You're pretty amazing, do you know that?" She wrapped her arms around him and rested her head against his chest. "I couldn't ask for a better night!"

He led her around the circle of the platform for another perspective on the city. "But if I wanted to make it even better, you'd be OK with that, right?" he asked mischievously. She was just about to tell him that it couldn't get any better, but as they rounded the next curve, she saw a table set for two looking out over the Seine. A bottle of champagne rested in a silver chalice, and two glasses were already poured, perched on the edge of the table.

"Oh my," she breathed, stopping and staring. "You weren't kidding. Is this for us?"

"Happy Birthday, Tia," Dylan smiled warmly. When she looked at him with confusion in her eyes, he answered, "Lexi told me. Why didn't you?"

"I..." she stammered, flustered. "I didn't want you to feel obligated to... Oh Dylan, you've given me so much; this whole summer is more of a gift than I could have ever hoped for..." He laughed at her and handed her a glass of champagne. "It would have been the best birthday I've ever had, just being here with you, in Paris of all places! I didn't need anything else to make it special—this is already as good as it gets!"

"You are a lady of mystery," he said. "You always keep me guessing." He clinked the rim of his glass against hers. "To you," he said. "I'm so glad to be spending your birthday, and this summer, with you." They drank, and Tia suddenly giggled and ran to the edge of the platform, yelling out over the city, "I have the most wonderful man up here, Paris! Best birthday ever!"

Dylan laughed, and removed the domed lid from the silver platter on the table. On it was an assortment of crackers, olives, and nuts—the aperitif, Tia recalled; the first in the long procession of a typical French meal. "Mademoiselle," he crooned, bowing, pulling out her chair and spreading her napkin on her lap. "Dinner is served, in typical French birthday style."

They nibbled on crackers and olives while they talked about their respective days. She gushed about seeing the Mona Lisa—much smaller than she'd ever imagined, and the Venus de Milo and the incredible paintings, sculptures and historical pieces that had filled her day. She showed him pictures of the gardens, and the glass pyramid at the Louvre, and they both agreed that it just looked out of place next to such grand ancient architecture. He told her about his interviews and his meeting with the mayor, where he'd agreed to perform a couple songs at his daughter's wedding next year in exchange for a private dinner on the top of the tower. "A small price to pay to see the look in your eyes tonight," he told her, then added, "I hope that you'll be my date for the wedding, Tia."

Her heart jumped in her chest. He still hoped to be seeing her next year! She couldn't control the smile that took over her entire face when she gladly accepted.

Dylan hit the button on the device the elevator operator had given him and within a couple minutes, two waiters appeared to whisk away the crackers and bring the entree: warm cheese soufflé, French onion soup, and a carafe of Sauvignon Blanc. The waiters greeted the couple warmly, and then disappeared back to the lift. "Seriously?" she said. "You just hit the button and they come flying up the elevator to take care of your every whim? Must be hard to get used to that kind of treatment," she added sarcastically.

"Not so hard," he replied with a smirk. "There are some perks that come with celebrity that are pretty damn nice." He took her hands in his and looked at her seriously. "There are sacrifices, though too, Tia, always remember that. Sometimes there's a pretty big price to pay."

"I know," she whispered. "That part is incredibly hard; I see how you struggle with it." She kissed his fingers and then picked up her fork. "Tonight, though, we have the easy life."

He smiled. "And I'm all for enjoying every minute of it." He speared some soufflé onto his fork and fed it to Tia across the table. They ate that way, sharing bites and sipping wine, talking about everything and nothing. They'd reached a certain comfort level with each other now, and the silences they shared were as easy as the exchanges. Time passed slowly; the leisurely pace of the French dinner and the quiet of the city view allowing them to relax and enjoy every moment. The waiters appeared after each course and with polite efficiency cleared their table and set up the next round of incredible food paired with just the right French wines. She sipped slowly, not wanting anything to cloud her mind on this perfect night. They got up and walked around the platform occasionally, taking in the views arm in arm and walking off one course before starting on another. It was a delicious evening, unhurried, elegant, casual, and she didn't want it to ever end.

Dessert was mousse au chocolate, complete with a sparkling candle in the center. "Make a wish, Tia," he whispered, and there was no question in her mind what she would wish for, what she'd been wishing for ever since she'd met Dylan, and she closed her eyes and blew out the flame. His intent gaze met her own as she opened her eyes, and she knew that he could read her wish in them.

"I'll be right back," he said, and went around the curve to the left, coming back with his guitar slung over his shoulder.

"You're going to sing happy birthday to me," she said, touched and amused.

"Something like that," he replied and moved his chair out from the table, facing her. He began with the Happy Birthday tune, singing the words slowly, smoothly, turning it into something she never thought it could be. But when it ended, he kept strumming and said to her, "I have something for you, Tia. I've been working on it for a while now, and finally I think it's ready." He began with a hum, low in his throat, smooth and sensual, that wound around the soft sounds of the guitar, building in intensity and complexity. It was nothing she'd heard before, and when he started to sing, her heart absolutely melted.

When you looked into my eyes/and saw through my disguise/no one was more surprised than me...It took a little while/but it was written in your smile/you make me what I want to be...We took a spin around the stars/and now the universe is ours...It's impossible to hide/the love I have inside/there's a real kind of magic when our worlds collide.
You amaze me, entertain me, mesmerize me, recognize me... See right through me, how you do me, with you I need no disguise... You elate me, and inflate me make me see what's there inside... Just like heaven/ all this love /that I find when our worlds collide.

As he held out the last note and strummed the final chord on the guitar, he raised his eyes to hers and saw the tears that spilled there. He saw in her tears everything that he felt, everything that he poured into the song, and he leaned the guitar against the wall and pulled her into his lap, wiping her tears and kissing her damp cheeks.

"You wrote me a song," she whispered. "I can't believe that you wrote me a song. It's the most beautiful thing I've ever heard." More tears slid down her cheeks and she held his face in her hands and looked into him. "You are the most amazing man, Dylan Miller. I still can't believe I found you. I..." she hesitated, catching herself before she said more than she should. "...don't know what to say. Words can't describe what this means to me. What you mean to me."

He stood them both up and walked over to the edge, looking over the city of lights. "I have some more words for you, Tia." He kissed the top of her head and took a deep breath. He couldn't remember the last time he'd felt so nervous, even though he was quite certain she felt the same way he did. "Every word in that song rings true and it was so easy to sing it. A bit harder to say it." He cradled her face and met her gaze. "I guess I suspected it right after I met you—that first night. Probably when you made me work so hard at getting you to go out with me." He smiled, remembering.

"Sean asked me what you meant to me that night at *Paddy's*, and at that exact moment you looked over at me and smiled, and without a thought I blurted, 'I could get lost in her.'" Tia's eyes melted and a smile touched her lips. "You challenge me, Tia, and you make me a better man, and you..." he kissed her softly on the lips. "...You take my breath away every time I look at you." The intensity of his gaze held her. Her mind was reeling, taking in every word. He stared straight into her soul. "I'm in love with you, Tia. Hopelessly, helplessly, completely in love with you."

She felt her knees go weak, and her heart seemed to soar out over the city, but somehow she managed to keep her legs. "Oh my God," she said breathlessly, taking his face in her hands. "I'm in love with you too, Dylan. So incredibly much!"

He brought his face closer and kissed her, soft, gentle and deep, his gaze never leaving hers. They held each other for what seemed a long time, caressing, kissing, and whispering things they'd waited so long to say. Finally he led her back to the table and they sat. He picked up his wine glass and she raised hers. They touched glasses and he said, "To the woman I love," and she cried all over again and climbed into his lap. "I can't believe this," she whispered, "I'm so happy!"

He knew she had some hard truths to face before she could commit to a relationship with him, but not tonight, he thought. Tonight was a happy night, and they were in the city of lovers. He intended to make the most of it, for both their sakes. He pulled a square box from his pocket. "Happy birthday, my love."

"Oh Dylan, I can't possibly accept anything else from you! You've just given me the best gift I could ever hope for. You love me, and there's nothing else in the world I could possibly need!"

"I do love you—God it feels good to say that!" he said, kissing her again. "But I saw this, and I just couldn't resist. It's just a little something to remind you of this night," he said, pulling the lid off the box to reveal a diamond-crusted Eiffel Tower hanging from a delicate gold chain. "I was hoping it would help you remember how much I love you, even when I'm far away—I want you to remember that you're always close to my heart."

"How could I ever forget this night? It's been the best night of my life!" She giggled. "I guess I say that a lot when I'm with you don't I? But this has most definitely been the best so far." She turned around so he could fasten the chain behind her neck. "It's so beautiful, Dylan, thank you. But I don't need anything to remind me of this night. I'll be playing it over and over in my head every day and see it in my dreams at night. And my song—you have to record it for me so I can listen to it while I'm missing you and hear your voice singing just for me. Oh God," she thought aloud. "Are you going to put that on a CD?"

"That's the plan," he mused. "The guys liked it. Bo's got a rough recording and is working on laying down the beats for it as we speak. We go into the studio after the movie wraps. I was thinking it could be the title track, actually. I like the name, '*Worlds Collide*.' Kind of has a double meaning, you know?"

"Oh! A song written for me that I'd hear on the radio? That I could put on my iPod? That gives me goose bumps!"

"So, what do you say we have our traditional after dinner drink and get out of here? I can think of another way to show you how much I love you, and it starts with getting you out of that gorgeous dress." He looked at her and raised that one eyebrow, and her heart immediately fluttered in her chest.

"And here I didn't think this night could get any better," she smirked, "but I think you just figured out a way."

The moment they entered their suite, Dylan swept her into his arms and carried her to the bed, laying her down and looking deep into her eyes. "I love you, Tia Hastings," he whispered.

"I love you, Dylan Miller," she breathed back.

They made love, slow and easy, each feeling the new intensity that came with knowing that they were going to build a future together. The glittering Eiffel Tower around Tia's neck sparkled in the moonlight that drifted in from the window and they fell asleep in each other's arms, each dreaming of what that future might bring.

Tia woke up the next morning curled in Dylan's embrace and smiled, reliving the incredible night they'd shared. He stirred, and pulled her closer, whispering sleepily in her ear, "No, it wasn't a dream—I am in love with you." He kissed her head and she rolled over to face him, smiling sleepily.

"Oh God, I love you, too," she said, her smile getting bigger. "I've wanted to tell you for so long and it just feels amazing to be able to say it! I don't think I could ever get tired of saying it--I want to shout it from the balcony and have it tattooed on my arm. I love you, I love you, I love you!" she said, kissing his cheek, his forehead, his nose.

He wrapped his arms around her and just enjoyed the feeling of her naked body pressed against his own. He glanced at the clock over her shoulder and frowned—he had an interview later this morning, and as much as he didn't want to do it, he needed to make sure Tia really knew what she was in for with him if they were going to go forward in their relationship. Putting it on the table now would give her some time to think about things while he was out, and she could make an informed decision. He was hoping that she'd decide to give it a go, but it wouldn't be fair to her not to let her know the harsh realities before it was too late for either of them to go back.

He pulled back, running his hand down her arm and settling it on her waist and said, "Listen, baby, there are some things you need to know, before you decide if you really want to give us a go. Some of them aren't easy to say, or to hear, but I have to say them."

"There isn't anything in the world that would change my mind about wanting to be with you Dylan," she said firmly. "Nothing."

He smiled at her thinly, then sat up and got out of bed. "Let's do this over coffee, shall we? Once again, you had me up all night and I need some caffeine."

When they were seated on the balcony nursing steaming mugs, Tia looked at him. "Don't try to scare me, Dylan—there's nothing you could say to me that would make me feel differently about going forward. I love you."

"I love you too," he started. "It's not so easy, though Tia, being in love with me. You have to think about that."

"What do you mean?" she asked. "It's the easiest thing in the world. Completely natural," she smiled.

He shook his head and scooted his chair closer to hers, putting his arm around her. "We still have some hard realities to figure in, though," he said sadly, tucking her hair behind her ear and kissing her cheek.

"Yeah, I guess we do, huh," she conceded.

"I'm so glad it's easy for you to love me. I feel exactly the same way—like it's such a natural fit with us. Being in love with someone like me though...has complications. Tough ones, sometimes. I think you need to know what you're in for if we..." his voice trailed off, and he pulled her closer.

"I know," she said. "It's hard to go out in public, I lose my privacy, you're traveling all over the place, women are constantly throwing themselves at you...but as long as we love each other, I could learn to deal with it."

"But that's not all. The paparazzi are relentless. I live on a ranch to try and keep them at bay, but even so, they have these long range cameras, they go through my trash, they lurk in hotel lobbies and outside restaurants... I avoid them as much as I can, but they're always there. I absolutely never talk to them or give any statements; I don't buy the tabloids, and don't try to attract their attention. But I'm in the public eye and they're determined to give the public as much gossip as they can—especially after that 'sexiest man' thing. And when they don't have any real stories, they make them up. They try to link me with other celebrities, fabricate relationships—there has to be a whole different level of trust between us than the usual relationship."

"I do trust you Dylan. I'm not going to lie and say I haven't had a few pangs of jealousy here and there, but I fell in love with the person you are, and I have complete faith in you."

He kissed her again, and smiled. "I'm glad you know that, and I'd never betray your trust; but it still isn't easy when you see articles in those damned magazines that allude to things that aren't real. People believe them, and they can be awfully hurtful. When they find out about us they'll pick your life apart, baby. You'll be a story—the girl who landed the sexiest man alive," he said, making air quotes with his fingers. "They'll dig up info about you any way they can—they'll talk to your co-workers, former students—anyone who'll give them a crumb of information. They'll find out about Nick—are you prepared to have that dragged through the media? To have them say that I was your rebound relationship?" Tia looked pained, but she had to know it all in order to make the right decision for her.

"You don't always know who your true friends are, either," he continued. "People suddenly come climbing out of the woodwork pretending to care about you, but all they really care about is what they can get from you. Believe me; I learned that lesson the hard way, more times than I can count. They could make life uncomfortable, at least for a while. Of course, there is the travel aspect of my job too. This tour is different, and I've chosen to spend the money so that we could spend quality time together. But when we tour the States it's totally different. Mostly we sleep on the bus when we travel between cities and it keeps me away for months at a time." He sighed, and pulled her closer. "It's a lot to think about, I know," he said, "but you do need to think about it. I'll be gone for a few hours today, so you'll have some time to make an informed decision," he finished, kissing the top of her head and resting his lips there.

Tia moaned deep in her throat. "Oh, it's not fair!" she exclaimed. "I said it on our first night—why can't you just be a normal guy? And you said, 'I am a normal guy, Tia, I'm just not in a normal situation.' I know it's going to be hard sometimes, Dylan—I've seen the tabloids and the TV shows. But it all comes down to the same thing anyway, don't you think?" She hugged him tight. "If we love each other, we work it out. We just figure it out as it comes. Because I do love you, and can't imagine my life without you in it anymore. I just can't."

"I know—I feel exactly the same way. I just need to give you all the facts in case you…" he didn't want to finish the sentence; didn't want to give her an out, but he had to be fair, "…decided that it wasn't right for you," he finished.

Tia sat up straight and looked into his eyes. "I don't need a single second to think about it, Dylan Miller," she said, taking his face in her hands and kissing him gently. "*You* are right for me, and life without you wouldn't have any meaning. I'm sticking, and you'll have to get used to it. I do trust you completely—I'm working really hard to get over the jealousy thing, and I will. We'll face whatever happens together, because you are my life now."

Dylan felt relief sweep through him and he planted gentle kisses on her cheeks, her forehead, her nose, her lips, running his fingers through her hair and down her back, pulling her to him. "I was hoping you'd say that," he whispered. "Because I want you to be mine, Tia. Exclusively."

"I've been yours since the start, Dylan. Didn't you know?"

"And I've been yours. It's just that I'm a guy, and it took me a little longer to figure it out," he said with his famous half-smile.

She entwined her fingers through his. "I'm so glad you finally did."

"Me too," he said, kissing the back of her hand. "But there's one more thing we should talk about. Something else we need to get figured out."

"What's that?"

"I was thinking, that since you've already made the decision to keep me a secret…"

"I'm not keeping you a secret, Dylan. I'm telling people *about* you, I'm just not telling them exactly who you are."

"And I think that was a smart decision on your part. The last thing I want to do is make your life difficult. This is going to get tricky for you, Tia, and going public with our relationship right before I go off to make a film on the other side of the world would definitely create problems for you."

"That was the main reason I made that decision. I want to tell everyone in the world that I love you, but I'm afraid of how some of them will react. I knew I didn't want to deal with the hassle when I thought I might only have a couple days to spend with you, and then I had so much to do to get ready for this trip..."

"I want to tell the whole world, too. But it's going to a big story, and the paparazzi will be all over you; and I won't be there to help you deal with it. I was thinking we might wait until I've finished the film before we go public—how do you feel about that?"

Tia didn't have to think about it for long—she'd been considering all of these things since the first day she met him, and had no desire to deal with the publicity alone. "I think it's a good idea too," she agreed. "I definitely want you by my side when I have to deal with that."   "You could tell your friends, though," he said smiling. "While you still know who all your real friends are. I don't have to be a big dark secret."

"I could," she said, noncommittally. She wanted to desperately, especially now that she knew he returned her love and that they had a future together. But she was still nervous about how much her life would change once that knowledge was out there, especially when she'd have to face it alone until spring. She'd cross that bridge when she came to it, she figured.

Chapter 24

August came way too soon, and the realization began to sink in that they were going to have to say goodbye long before either of them wanted to. Tia's last stop was Florence, and although it was a beautiful city, it was a bittersweet part of the summer for her. Mostly bitter. InHap still had two stops left in Europe before wrapping up the tour, and then it was on to New Zealand for Dylan, who had barely a week to spend with his family in Melbourne before filming began.

On their last night together, they held each other in silence as each dealt with the reality that they wouldn't see each other for months. Tia's schedule didn't allow her any significant time off until Christmas break, but Dylan had invited her to Melbourne to meet his family and spend Christmas with him in Australia. She knew that her own family would miss her over the holidays, but was confident that her parents would want her to follow her dreams and to be happy, and she gladly agreed to join him. She was nervous about meeting his family, but thrilled that he wanted her to. He'd send her plane tickets in November, he said, once he had his own schedule worked out and knew exactly when he'd be able to get away.

There were no more words to be spoken between them—they'd said everything they'd needed to say over the past three months—so they just held on, wishing the minutes would tick by more slowly as her departure grew ever nearer. Neither of them slept but a couple winks, and even those were spent entangled in each other anyway. Parting was something neither of them wanted to do.

"It isn't goodbye, remember that," Dylan whispered as he rode with her to the airport. It was hard for her to believe that the next day she'd be back at work, setting up her classroom for another school year, on the other side of the world from the man she loved. Somehow, putting up bulletin boards and designing lesson plans seemed the furthest things from her mind, yet it was her reality.

"I know," she whispered. "It's just going to be so long before I see you again...oh God, I don't know how I'm going to go through the motions."

"I know, I know," Dylan said softly. "It's going to be the same for me, you know. I'll be thinking of you all the time and we'll talk, and email..." but they both knew that was going to be difficult. There was an eighteen hour time difference between Chicago and Auckland, and with both of them working, it would be tough to stay connected. Somehow, she thought, she had to get through the next four months without him. She'd become so accustomed to seeing him every day, spending the nights with him in their shared bed, and now she would go home to the boring normalcy that was her life before she'd met him. There was no plan for how she was going to make it—there just didn't seem to be an easy way. She also didn't know how she was going to talk about the amazing summer she'd had without bursting at the seams. She was in love with the most incredible man and wanted to tell everyone, but she still didn't know if she should tell anyone who the love of her life really was.

Dylan went in disguise to the airport, so he could spend every possible moment with her before she had to go through the security line and out of his sight—out of his life. They held each other until the last possible minute, kissing and whispering "I love you" until it was time for her to go. One last kiss, and then he watched her as she constantly looked back to him, tears spilling freely down her cheeks, until she turned the corner and was out of sight. It was going to be a rough few months, he knew, and he would miss her terribly, but he felt certain their love was strong enough to survive time and distance; and there sure would be plenty of both.

The tears wouldn't stop as she turned the corner and Dylan was out of her sight. For months. Her breath hitched in her chest and she had to wipe at her eyes just so she could read the signs and find her departure gate. She finally found the right place and fell into an empty seat while the people around her either openly stared or glanced at her from the corners of their eyes. She didn't care that people were staring—she was going to have to ride out this wave of emotion—it was pointless to try and stop it.

A woman about her age sat across and a few seats over from where Tia had landed, surrounded by half a dozen purses and backpacks. She rose from her seat and handed Tia a tissue. "Are you OK?" she asked tenderly.

Tia nodded and croaked, "Not really, but I'll be alright eventually. Thanks."

"Is there anything I can do? Anything you need?"

Tia was grateful for the kindness, but knew that there wasn't anything anyone could do to make her feel better. "Thanks," she said again, "but there's nothing." She wiped the tears from her face and added, "I just had to say goodbye to my boyfriend, and I won't see him again for four months." More tears spilled, and she dabbed at them with the already sodden tissue.

The woman reached into her purse and pulled out a travel-sized pack. "Oh, that sucks," she said, handing Tia the package. "You're probably going to need the whole pack, then." Tia took the tissues gratefully and the woman nodded sympathetically and went back to her seat.

Tia did the only thing she could—she pulled out her iPad, popped in her ear buds, cranked up some of Dylan's music, and started scrolling through her pictures. It didn't make her feel better; she could feel the sense of loss becoming a physical hole; but she had his voice in her ear and his images in her hand; two empty hours before they started boarding the plane, and a whole pack of tissues.

Each picture was a treasured memory and she was still amazed that they had done so much in just two and a half months. She took in the pictures slowly, savoring each memory: the two of them hiking the Alps near Vienna, Dylan leaning casually against a tree with the majestic mountains in the background, them zipping around Munich on Segways and walking the English Gardens. Other shots showed Dylan in his punk rock disguise, scowling at the Brandenburg Gate; in front of the Kibble Palace glasshouse; her smiling with the whole band back stage in Glasgow...

She was so engrossed in pulling forth the details from each picture that she didn't notice the small crowd that had gathered behind her; hadn't heard the first exclamation from the guy who'd inadvertently noticed, over her shoulder, the primary subject of her photos. A light touch on her shoulder jerked her from her revelry and she flinched, turning to see the interested expressions on the dozen or so faces that had been watching from behind her. She clutched her iPad to her chest and pulled out her ear buds, Dylan's voice suddenly tinny and distant, and looked at the strangers questioningly.

"That's Dylan Miller, isn't it, in your pictures?" a scrawny young man asked reverently.

There was no point in trying to hide it, Tia thought, they'd obviously already seen that it was. "Yeah," she answered.

"Holy hell!" Tissue Woman exclaimed. "He isn't the boyfriend you had to say goodbye to...is he?"

Tia just nodded. Part of her was thrilled that she could actually tell someone about Dylan, but the way they were all staring at her was making her uncomfortable at the same time.

"Whoa, wait a minute..." the scrawny guy interjected. "You're the mystery woman—from the London show—the one who sang on stage with Incidental Happenstance—I saw you on the monitor; I thought you looked familiar!"

"You were at the Wembley show?" Tia asked, surprised that she was running into him now, in Italy.

"We spent the summer backpacking," he said, indicating with a toss of his head an equally scrawny and scruffy looking companion, "and pretty much followed them around, catching as many shows as we could. It was you, wasn't it?"

"Yeah," Tia admitted, "it was me."

"You were really good, by the way!" the companion added.

"Thanks." She was feeling crowded and anxious now; several other people had heard the exchange and were expanding the group, and they started firing questions at her all at once.

"What's he like?" "You were on the whole tour with them?" "Do you know the rest of the band?" "Are they all as cool as they seem?" "Was he really here, at the airport?" "Can we see the rest of your pictures?" And dozens of others that were lost in the din.

Tia held up her hands to stop them. "I'm sorry," she said, "but I'm really emotional right now, and I just want to have a little pity party for myself. I will tell you, though, that Dylan is the most incredible person I've ever met, and that all the guys in InHap are awesome."

She started to put her ear buds back in, hoping they'd get the hint and leave her alone, but they weren't swayed so easily.

"Wait!" another voice called from the crowd. "Today's my sister's birthday and she's like, totally hot for..." he caught himself, and changed his tone. "I mean, she's a huge fan of his. Do you think you could get him to call her and wish her a happy birthday? It would mean the world to her, really."

Tia was flabbergasted that some total stranger expected that she'd just call him up and ask him something like that. Before she could answer though, another voice rose up. "Maybe you could call him and we could pass the phone around—that would be so cool!"

"Sorry," Tia said, "but he's on a plane right now on his way to Greece." Or at least he would be very soon. She wouldn't have done it anyway, but it made it easier for her that she didn't have to come up with a story or be rude. Of course, she thought it was incredibly rude for a complete stranger to ask that of her, but that was the kind of thing that would happen always, she realized, when you were dating someone as well-known and popular as Dylan, and it would become her reality as soon as their relationship was public knowledge. She instantly had a better understanding of his need to go out in disguise—it was kind of creepy having a bunch of people who didn't know you crowding in on your personal space. They were fans, of course, which would be flattering, but they were strangers, nonetheless.

"Hey, do you think I can I get a picture with you?" the tissue woman asked.

Tia's face scrunched up in question. "Why in the world would you want a picture of me? I'm not the one who's famous."

"Not yet," she answered, "but if you're seriously dating Dylan Miller I'm sure you will be eventually."

Tia was floored, and as she glanced around wide-eyed at the sea of interested faces, it dawned on her then that she couldn't share Dylan's identity with the people back home—not yet. If total strangers were unabashedly asking her to impose on Dylan for their own whims, what would her friends do? Dylan would do pretty much whatever she asked of him—he'd gladly signed a picture for Lilly—but he'd said so many times that one of the biggest drawbacks of his celebrity status was that everyone seemed to want something from him, and she'd never take advantage of their relationship that way. Once they went public all her real friends would meet him; he'd probably even go with Sean to poker night when he could; but she'd tell them beforehand in no uncertain terms that they needed to treat him like a normal person.

She knew all too well that it only took one slip of one tongue to spread juicy news like wildfire and unfortunately, there were tongues at both work and at the club that she didn't trust; and one of them was her own mother. They wouldn't betray her purposely, she truly believed that, but this kind of news could prove too good to keep, and she definitely didn't want to deal with this kind of attention on a regular basis—not without Dylan by her side.

Tia grabbed her carry-on and hastily stood up. "Sorry," she said, "but I really just need to be alone right now." She made her way quickly to the first class lounge. She hadn't wanted to go in there while she was having her emotional meltdown, but now she pushed through the door and went up to the bar, ordering a drink and taking a seat at a little table in the corner with her back to the wall so no one could look over her shoulder. She waited for the final boarding call before she slipped onto the plane, knowing she'd be one of the first ones off and that she could quickly disappear at JFK when she caught her connecting flight. Her seat was like a little private cocoon, and she sank into it gratefully, ordering a glass of red wine and popping in her ear buds.

    She'd saved the videos for last. There were hours of them—she was really glad she'd spent the extra money to get the most storage space on her iPad—and she had a nearly 12 hour journey ahead of her. She watched them in order, and marveled at how obvious it was that she and Dylan were falling in love as the trip progressed. She saw what Jessa had seen—the way they looked at each other, the comfort level building, their shared experiences bringing them closer. She watched Dylan performing the song he'd written for her and sung atop the Eiffel Tower—the first time he'd told her he loved her. He sang it for her camera sitting shirtless on the balcony of their suite in Madrid and she smiled as she remembered how she'd gone to him after and they'd made love. When it ended, she hit play again and watched it three more times, smiling through her film of tears. It wasn't until the very end that she saw Dylan had left her with a goodbye video, knowing that she'd see it after she was gone. She touched the play button, and his voice filled her head while his image held steady on the screen.

    "Ah, Tia," he said, his voice full of melancholy, "you're sleeping in the next room right now, and I just couldn't shut my eyes for even a second. I've been watching you sleep, and thinking about how tomorrow night I'll be in yet another strange bed, but you won't be with me; and you'll be too far away for me to reach you. You snore, you know, but it's just tiny little sounds that you make and it's really cute." She smiled, tears once again spilling over her cheeks. "Sometimes you murmur my name in your sleep," he continued, "and it makes my heart sing every time you do it. I know you'll see this—I'll be pouring over my pictures and videos too, reliving the incredible summer we just spent together—and I want you to know that I love you more than I can say, and that we're going to have a lot more incredible times together. I dread saying goodbye to you tomorrow, but I know that our love is incredibly strong—God, how did that happen in just a few short months?" He did that one eyebrow thing that she loved, "—and that we'll be together again. That's what I'm going to be holding on to, you know, the sound of your laugh and the feel of your lips against mine and the...well, you know," he waggled his eyebrows. "We're pretty great together in every way, don't you think? I just wanted to tell you one more time that I love you, that I'll be thinking of you every minute while I'm away, and that I'll be counting down the days until I can see you again. You have my heart—don't doubt that for a minute—and I trust you'll keep it safe. I miss you, and I'll be thinking of you all the time—I already said that, didn't I? You are by far the best incidental happenstance to crash into my life, and I'm so glad that we found each other. So anyway, my love, think of me too, OK?" His image on the screen turned toward the open door behind him. "Well, I'm going to get back to watching you sleep—I want to hold you as much as I can before you have to go; so I'll say farewell, but not goodbye, because we'll be together again."

Dylan's image blew her a kiss, and then froze, the play arrow obscuring his face. She hit the button again, and watched the video over and over, tears falling freely and silently. She reached into her purse and pulled out a notepad and immediately began writing him a letter. She'd write him constantly, she figured, and that would help her through the next four months—at least a little.

Arriving back at O'Hare sent Tia's spirits in a downward spiral that was beyond her control. She called Lexi, who was circling the airport, waiting for her, and met her at the arrivals lane. She dumped her suitcases unceremoniously into the trunk and jumped into the car. Lexi hugged her, but the look on Tia's face said that she was less than thrilled to be home.

"Oh, sweetie, you miss him already, don't you?" she asked rhetorically.

"From the minute I left him," she said. "I knew it was going to be hard, but right now it seems damned near impossible."

"But you'll see him at Christmas, right? It's not so far away."

"Christmas is four freaking months from now—it's still summer!" She pouted, but she'd cried herself out on the plane. There were no more tears left. "And then when I do see him again," she added, "it's not going to be just the two of us; I'm going to be meeting his whole family. That part already scares me to death—I'm just a flipping elementary school teacher—how am I going to measure up?"

"Measure up to what?" Lexi asked. "The fake people he's dated in the past? Do you even know if he's introduced any of his other girlfriends to them? Just be yourself—who can help but love you?" She leaned over and kissed Tia on the cheek. "You know I do."

"Yeah, and that's worth a lot," she barked. It came out sounding really bitchy and she instantly regretted saying it. "I'm sorry, Lex, I don't mean to take it out on you. I just can't get my head in the right place. I have to go over to school tomorrow and start setting up my room for another year. After the summer I had, I can't even imagine going back to my simple little life. Alone again."

"But you're not alone!" Lexi soothed. "You still have Dylan; you just aren't in the same country right now. It's different than with Nick. You and Dylan'll be together again, it's just a matter of time."

"God, I hope so," Tia said. "I just can't seem to wrap my head around how long it's going to be before I see him again. We've been living together for three months, for chrissake, and now I'm not even going to see him for longer than that."

"I know, honey," she said sympathetically. "But you'll still talk to him and be in touch—and the time will fly by. Just keep busy, and take it day by day, and you'll be back together before you know it."

"And what about after that?" Tia moaned. "We'll have a couple weeks together before he has to go to Bora Bora to finish the movie, and then he won't even be in the States again until February. And then he has to go into the studio, which is in Seattle..."

"Stop it!" Lexi yelled. "You can't do this to yourself. You can't keep worrying about the next obstacle that you're going to have to face. When you're in love, you work things out. The two of you'll figure out something that works."

"Oh I know it, I do." But she was going to worry about it, just the same. "I'm just feeling really sorry for myself and I have to get over it. It's just going to take some time, that's all. Right now all I want is a bath and my own bed, and to sleep away at least a little of the time."

"Actually, I was thinking we could swing by the club for a drink or something. Your parents'll be there, and they'd be glad to see you. It's only six o'clock."

Tia instantly thought of Jace, and didn't want to go anywhere near the club. "Maybe here, but not on my time clock," she sighed. "I'm still on Europe time." She yawned as if to prove her point. "I'm exhausted already, and the last thing I need is a drink. Not tonight," she said yawning again. "I'll call them when I get home and meet them for lunch tomorrow or something. I have to get over to school for at least a little while tomorrow—I'm already a few days behind schedule."

"OK," Lexi said. "I'll just take you home, then."

"Thanks. Speaking of the club, what's going on with Jace—is he still with Ditzy?" She wanted to know up front if she should expect any problems with him.

"Yeah same as always, but I have to tell you, he was incredibly interested in my little trip this summer and what you've been up to. He's been asking about you constantly, according to Ryan. He keeps asking when you're coming back."

Tia shook her head. "Shit. Listen, if he asks again, tell him I became a gypsy and ran off to Poland, or something, OK? "

Lexi laughed. "A gypsy, eh? Now there's a picture," she said sarcastically. "I'm sure no one'll have any trouble believing that."

"I just don't want him getting any ideas, especially if he finds out that I won't be seeing Dylan for such a long time." Lexi's eyes dropped, and she looked at Tia apologetically.

"Oh crap, he already knows that?" Tia asked, her voice tense.

"It just came up in conversation," Lexi said. "I didn't think it was a secret. He would've found out eventually, anyway."

Tia shook her head. "Shit, I guess you're right," she conceded. "Did you at least happen to mention that I'm completely in love?"

"I did tell Ryan that you two were completely in love, so I imagine he passed on the message. Maybe that'll be enough of a hint for him."

"God, I hope so," Tia said, "I definitely don't need to deal with that right now."

"OK—don't be pissed, but I have to ask," Lexi said. "Can I tell people now? You guys professed your love at the top of Eiffel Tower, so it's official, right? That'd shut Jace up real quick—even he's not full of himself enough to think he'd be able to compete with Dylan Miller."

Tia sighed and shook her head, and told Lexi about what happened at the airport in Florence.

"Seriously?" Lexi exclaimed. "Some total stranger in the airport asked you to have Dylan call his sister? That takes some serious balls, if you ask me. What was he thinking?"

"I know—I couldn't believe it either! And if that's how complete strangers reacted, I don't even want to know how people who actually know me will take it. We're going public after the movie—it's just easier to present ourselves as a couple when we actually are one, you know? I decided that I'm still keeping him to myself, for now."

"Damn it!" she said. "You can't keep doing this to me! Do you have any idea how hard it's been not to tell everyone about the incredible experiences I've had?"

"Believe me," Tia said sadly, "I know it all too well." Irritation crept into her voice. "Don't you think I want to tell the whole world who I'm in love with? I had some pretty incredible experiences too, you know. I have about a thousand pictures and videos of them—including the song he wrote just for me—and I want to share them with everyone, but I can't! I want to put it on the fucking news, but I can't! Dylan said the paparazzi would be all over me, and after seeing what telling just a few people in the airport did, I don't doubt it for a second. Sorry Lex, but no one's going to be suffering more than me. I'm going to have to deal with it, and so will you."

Lexi softened immediately. "Oh Tia, I'm so sorry; you're absolutely right. Of course this is going to be hardest on you." She reached across the console and took Tia's hand. "I'll do whatever I have to—don't worry about anything."

Chapter 25

    Tia rolled out of bed at four the next morning; jet lag holding a firm grip on her senses. She dragged herself to school at five and sat at the desk in her classroom looking around at the empty bulletin boards and bland walls. It would be just a week before the room was filled with students again, and she would start another year of working to get them to love reading and writing, and helping them to find their own individual strengths. Usually she loved this time of the year—the anticipation of meeting her students and getting to know them, the sounds of children's laughter, the unabashed love and trust they eagerly and freely gave. She'd missed her friends here too, and was looking forward to hearing how they'd spent their summers; even though she was seriously bummed out that she couldn't share all of hers. The halls were still quiet, but she knew that in just a couple hours, the building would be bustling with teachers, moving from room to room to catch up on everyone's summer adventures and getting reacquainted.

    It felt completely different this year, as she knew it would. There was a whole different kind of anticipation running through her veins, and she worried that she wouldn't be able to get back to a normal level of functioning after the excitement of the past few months. The summer had changed her—she was no longer a simple school teacher in a small town outside Chicago, and she'd come to accept that she never would be. She'd toured practically the entire continent of Europe, stayed in some of the world's most luxurious hotels, had shopped in the most exclusive stores, partied with celebrities, sung on stage at Wembley Stadium and had her picture in the tabloids—thank goodness the photos weren't clear enough for her to be recognized at home—and in six months or so she'd be announcing to the world that she was paired with one of the world's most eligible bachelors. The tour would have been enough in itself to throw her off-kilter, but toss in falling madly and deeply in love, and kick in the fact that her new guy was mega famous, mega rich, and the sexiest man on Earth, and that just pushed it into overdrive. She realized that she was going to have to be an actress, too, pretending that she was the same old Tia who'd just had a wonderful summer with her new guy. It was going to be exhausting, she thought.

When the clock hit 7:00 AM, she wandered toward the office to see Lilly, who had just arrived to take up her place at the front line of the school. As soon as she saw Tia, her face lit up in a huge grin and she put out her arms for a hug.

"Whoo whee!" she said. "I was hopin' you'd be in, girl!" She held Tia at arm's length and looked her up and down, nodding. "I can tell by the look on your face that you had a good summer—tell me, is that smile still from the same guy?"

"It is," Tia announced. "And we had the most amazing summer." She looked around secretively before blurting out, "I'm in love!"

Lilly hugged her again. "That-a-girl!" she said, genuinely happy for her. "Have a seat and tell me all the juicy details!"

Tia plopped onto the bench that spanned the office and crossed her legs. "Well," she began, "he had a lot of business in Europe, and he took me with him..."

"Europe!" she exclaimed. "You know I was jealous when I heard you were going. What cities did you see?"

"We were all over, actually—I got to see a bunch of them." Lilly kept nodding, encouraging her to continue. "My favorites were Munich, London, Paris and Tuscany," she continued, "but I was in a few others, too. It was so awesome—every place is so different, and there's so much to see!"

"Wow," Lilly exhaled on a long breath, "my friend, the world traveler! Now what kind of business is that boy of yours in that he gets to visit all those places? I want a job like that!"

"Tell me about it," Tia agreed. "Part of the reason he was there was that his band was doing a tour, and he was taking care of other business in between. I got to see the best shows!" Tia opened the manila envelope she'd carried in with her and said slyly, "Actually, I brought you a little present."

Lilly waggled her fingers in anticipation. "Ooh, a present for me? Well, give it over; you know how I love presents!"

"First, a little background," Tia teased, pulling the envelope just out of her grasp. "Like I said, his band played some dates over there, in lots of different places. You know the Aid Tour for Africa? It's one of those huge festivals?"

Lilly nodded. "I saw some of it on TV—InHap was playing, so of course I TiVo'd that part." She stopped, and her eyes widened. "Don't tell me you were there!"

"Not only was I there," Tia said slyly, "but my Dylan's band played on one of the stages and we had all access passes...we actually got to hang out with a lot of the other bands."

Lilly held her hand to her ample bosom and looked at Tia, wide-eyed. "You didn't. Tell me you didn't meet my real husband live and in person, or I might just die of envy!"

Tia smiled. "I did," she said, handing her the picture of Dylan. She'd taken it just as he'd turned to look at her during a pre-show meeting—it was the perfect image of him, all smiling and happy, slumped casually on a couch. "We got to hang out with them a lot during the three days of the festival, and I just knew you had to have this exact picture."

Lilly fanned her flushed face with the photo. "Oh my God, you met my real husband!" she breathed. "Damn, that man is fine!" she held the picture against her breasts before holding it out to look at it again. "Oh, you have to tell me. What's he like?"

Tia couldn't control the grin that took over her face every time she talked about Dylan. "He's so nice, Lilly. Down to earth, friendly—everything you'd want him to be." *Everything she wanted him to be, that was certain.* "He's just an amazing person—talking to him; you'd never know he was so famous. He's got a great sense of humor, too—kind of sarcastic."

"I just knew it! Sometimes you can just tell about a person, even if you never met them. But you did meet him, and I am so incredibly jealous! Your Dylan had to be beside himself worryin' that you'd run off with this one. I know I'd run off with him—in a heartbeat! And you got me his picture!"

"Look on the back," Tia prodded.

Lilly looked at the message scrawled on the back, made out to her, with Dylan's autograph. After his signature he'd put, 'RH?'

"What's this 'RH' mean?"

"Real husband, of course!" Tia smiled.

"Oh my," she panted, catching her breath. "You actually mentioned me to him?"

"I told him that I couldn't possibly show my face to you and tell you I'd met him without having something to give you. He insisted he sign the picture for you."

Lilly fanned herself with the photo again, catching her breath. "Hot damn, this is a treasure, Tia, thank you! I can't believe you met him! And what about the rest of the band? Are they amazing too?"

"They're all great guys, but besides Dylan—who is positively dreamy of course—I have to say I just fell in love with Bo—you know, the drummer? He's just awesome. Actually, he reminded me of you a little. He's got a big heart, he's a shameless flirt and he's always smiling."

"Me, a flirt?" she said smiling coyly. "Well, if it wasn't me who met him, it couldn't have happened to a nicer person." She pulled Tia into another hug. "Thank you so much—you know I love it! And I'm so glad to see the real you back, Tia. I missed you, you know. We all did. I'd like to thank that man for bringing you back—you tell him that for me, OK?"

"I know, and I will. And I love you guys for all the help and support you gave me last year—I couldn't have made it without you. It feels great to be happy again, except for the fact that my Dylan is still working overseas. I won't see him until Christmas."

"That's not so far away," she soothed. "It'll be here before you know it."

"That's what everyone keeps telling me, but I want it to be here yesterday," Tia said.

"But you're in love, and love conquers everything! Tell me how that happened!" she said, carefully tacking the picture of Dylan to a place of honor on the bulletin board alongside her desk.

"Wow, it was so romantic Lilly! He told me he loved me in Paris," she exhaled on breath as light as air, "at the top of the Eiffel Tower."

Lilly swooned. "Now that is a man I'd like to meet. You gotta have a picture of him, right? Let's see." She held out her hand and waggled her fingers.

"I'll bring it down later," Tia said. "I was too excited to give you your picture first." The official photo of her and Dylan that she would share was a picture of him in disguise, in the punk rock getup. He didn't look obnoxious, but she didn't think anyone would recognize him in the photo. It was from a bit of a distance, and there were enough shadows to cast a doubt as to his true identity.

"Oh, honey, you just made my day. No, my month. Maybe even my year, judging from the number of parents already calling about classes and such. It's gonna be busy." She turned back to her desk and indicated the mound of paperwork already piling up.

"Well, I'll let you get to it. I've got a lot to do myself. It's my first day in."

"I know that," she said with a wink. "I've been lookin' for you every day for the past week. You're usually in sooner than this."

"I just got home yesterday," she confessed, "and I have to admit, after the summer I had, I'm having a hard time getting my head on straight."

"I can believe that," she replied, "but I know you, and you'll be back on your game by the time those little ones come traipsin' through the door."

Tia left her to her work and went to continue her own. Throughout the day, just about everyone stopped in to hear about her summer in Europe and her new love. One thing about Lilly, she knew how to dish the gossip. Tia enjoyed telling the story over and over, and no one seemed to suspect that she was holding anything back. She shared the picture of Dylan, which she'd tacked to her own bulletin board, with everyone who came in, and they were all thrilled for her. She wanted to put up one of her pictures of Dylan without the disguise as well; everyone would know she'd 'met' him from Lilly's. She worried though that someone might see the resemblance if she had them too close together, so she tucked one in her desk drawer, where she could see it any time she wanted.

She did get some work done, but not nearly as much as she'd hoped to before meeting her parents for a late lunch. They were thrilled to see each other, of course, but she felt guilty sharing her edited photo album with them, the one that contained only pictures of Dylan in disguise. It was even more depressing that she couldn't share the majority of her experiences, including Dylan singing her song, *Worlds Collide*, her singing on stage at Wembley, and even smaller events like their hot air balloon ride over Stockholm.

She ran into her front door exactly at 3:00. When the phone rang, she answered it before it finished its first ring.

"Oh Dylan, it's so good to hear your voice!" she said softly.

"How are you, my beautiful girl?" he asked, his voice low and husky.

"I'm better now, that I'm talking to you," she said, and added, "I miss you something awful."

"Me too," he whispered. "I can't believe it was just yesterday that I saw you. It feels like months already."

"I was back at work today," she said. "Talk about a mood breaker. I couldn't get my mind focused on anything—part of me still thinks I'm in Europe."

"I sure wish you were," he replied.

They chatted easily for the next hour and they both tried to keep the conversation light and cheerful. They'd gotten matching calendars in Florence and were crossing off the days together, counting down to their reunion. Dylan teased that he'd get to cross off two once he got home—they were nearly a full day ahead there. When it was time to say goodbye Tia felt the emptiness settle in on her, but somehow she managed not to cry until after she hung up the phone.

Tia forced herself into autopilot to get through the next few days, which were spent in a flurry of putting up bulletin boards, preparing lessons, creating name tags, passing out books, doing inventory, attending meetings, and preparing for the start of a new school year. It kept her busy, which was a blessing. At first, she brought her InHap discs and played them while she was working, but she soon found that she couldn't focus on her work when Dylan's voice was all around her. She switched over to internet radio which helped some, but when an InHap song came on she'd stop instantly, reveling in the sound of his voice; her mind conjuring up images from the tour.

On the nights when there weren't InHap shows, she'd run out at one or two o'clock and rush home to wait for a call from Dylan. He had another week in Europe, and then he'd be going to spend some time with his parents in Australia where the time difference between them would jump from seven to seventeen hours, making it even more difficult to stay in touch. They talked or video chatted for hours, the distance between them shrinking with the contact. Sometimes, they'd watch the same movie together on speaker phone, talking and sharing like they were on a date.

When Dylan wasn't available she'd go out with one of the girls from school, hang out at *Paddy's*, or meet up with Lexi after work. She completely avoided the country club and a possible run in with Jace, but so far she hadn't heard anything from him, so she hoped that he'd gotten the message that she was in love and no longer available; not that she hadn't made it incredibly clear that she was never going to be available to him regardless. It was the nights that were hardest, though, when she was alone with her thoughts. She spent much of the time at her computer, putting together pictures and videos from her summer, creating a documentary of their time together, using Dylan's music as a background. It would be gift for him at Christmas, she thought, and was a gift to her now. At least it made the empty hours pass by.

***

Dylan woke up, grabbed some coffee, and wandered into his mother's studio where she was taking advantage of the early morning light streaming in through the huge windows. It was a sunset landscape she was painting—a replica of a picture Dylan had sent her from Italy. He recognized the scene as soon as he saw her canvas, and remembered Tia sitting beside him as he captured the explosive colors of dusk with his camera. His thoughts drifted to her and he picked up his guitar and began strumming the opening chords of *Worlds Collide*. His mother was deeply engrossed in her work, but she turned to him and smiled warmly, indicating with a finger that she'd be ready for a break soon.

His arrival the night before had been a flurry of activity; aunts, uncles, cousins and friends filled the house to welcome him home and it had been a great evening. It had been more than a year since he'd been back—recording and touring had been constant, and the distance was too great to travel for short periods of time. He usually liked to spend a month, but he had less than a week here now before he shot south to New Zealand for the movie. Spending time alone with his mother in her studio was therapy for him and he relaxed into the song, knowing he couldn't set a more perfect mood for what she was painting.

"That's something new, isn't it?" she asked. "It sounds polished."

"It's pretty complete, I think," he answered.

She put down her brush and wiped her smeared hands on her stained work pants. "You seem pretty complete, too, Dyl," she smiled. She stood and pulled her boy into an embrace. "It's so good to have you home," she whispered.

"I'm glad to be home," he said, "I just wish it could be a longer stay."

"But you'll be here for Christmas, and I couldn't be happier about that." She curled herself into the huge wicker chair alongside Dylan's and smiled at him. "Now," she said. "Tell me about this girl who's got my baby's head and heart all tangled up."

Dylan smiled back at her and leaned his guitar against the wall, settling in himself. He'd always loved having heart-to-heart talks with her in here—it was such a warm and inviting space, and his mother was completely at ease in it.

"She's the one, Mum," he said simply, his grin widening. "There's nothing tangled about it. I'm bringing her here for Christmas, and I can't wait for you to meet her. I just know you're going to love her too."

She reached out her hand and he wrapped his own around it. "I can see it all over your face," she said. "You told me on the phone, but I couldn't be sure until I saw it in your eyes." He smiled at her again, and she saw the sparks there. "And there it is. My baby's in love! I'm so happy for you Dyl—it's the one thing you've been missing in your life; I know." She squeezed his hand. "And if you love her, I'm sure we will too."

"I know you will. She's just an amazing person in every way. Come on," he said, pulling her up from the chair. "It's easier to show you. I've got about a thousand pictures and videos to share with you—you'll see exactly why I fell for her."

Chapter 26

Penelope was sitting in a lounge chair outside his trailer when he arrived at the enormous camp the studio had set up for the cast and crew. It looked like a small town, and Dylan tried to take it all in as a crew member drove him to his new accommodations in a golf cart. "Well, look who decided to show up," she smiled, extending her hand. "Nice to see you again, Dylan."

He was a bit surprised at her casual greeting after the way she'd acted when he last saw her, and hoped it was a positive sign. "And you as well," he replied formally, shaking her hand.

"I've been here a couple days already, so I can show you the layout," she said.

"Is there a map or something?" he joked. "This place is huge! I don't even think I could find my way back to where I came in."

Penelope giggled. "Well, it's not actually as crazy as it seems," she said. "The Village is set up kind of like a wagon wheel, and each spoke is assigned to a different group. Like, one spoke is for the camera people, one for producers and directors, one for lighting and set design—you get the idea. Our spoke has twelve units, and the best view," she swept her arm across the expanse of empty field that ran in front of their accommodations. Dylan could see the line of another spoke, but it was a fair distance away. "Your trailer is right here, the one next door is for your assistant, mine is the next, then my assistant, then Bruce Dinsmore and his assistant, Sadie Cochran and hers, Trent Savage and his, then wardrobe and make-up." She pointed down the line of little boxes.

"There's kind of a common area in the middle of the wheel," she continued, "everyone's just calling it 'The Hub,' and there's a little store there with some basic staples like bottled water, bread, milk, eggs, pop, canned stuff—that sort of thing. We're a half-hour drive from town, so it'll come in real handy. There're some people from the store who'll be going into town regularly, so if you bring them your lists, they'll pick things up for you. There's a bonfire pit and some barbeque grills there, too, and people are already starting to hang out there in the evenings, so it's best to do your shopping in the morning."

"OK, well thanks," he said, stepping inside his trailer and looking around the little box that would be his home for the next several months. He turned back to Penelope, who'd kicked off her shoes and taken a seat on his sofa. He couldn't believe that she thought it would be OK to just get comfortable in his space after the encounter they'd had in spring, and he didn't intend to allow it to happen. "I don't mean to be rude," he said, "but I've had a long day, so I'm just going to..." his voice trailed off and he motioned with his hand toward the door, indicating that she take her leave.

She jumped up off the couch. "Oh, OK, I didn't mean to intrude or anything..." she started out the door, then turned back. "Dylan? There's just one thing before I go," she said softly. "Let's get this out in the open right away because I don't want it always hanging between us. I really want to apologize for our first meeting. It was wrong of me to..."

"Forget about it," he said curtly. "Ancient history." He was going to have to work with this woman for the next few months; at times in smothering proximity; and he needed to keep things civil. He was already dreading the love scenes they'd have to film, but it would be even worse if there was hostility between them.

"No, I can't," she replied. "Please just let me have my say, and then we can put it all behind us."

"Fine." He wandered around the tiny trailer—luxurious by general trailer standards, but a little box, just the same. His bags had already arrived and he unzipped his duffle, pulling out a picture of him and Tia in Paris that he placed on a little shelf alongside the love seat that made up the main area of the trailer. He put a picture of his parents next to it, and continued unpacking, waiting for her to say what she needed to say.

Penelope glared at the picture over Dylan's shoulder and took a deep breath before continuing, gritting her teeth. "That night in Chicago I was totally out of line about a lot of things, and I'm terribly embarrassed by my behavior. I was so excited about getting the part and then even more excited when I found out I'd be working with you. I've followed your career, both of them, actually, and have a lot of respect for you being able to juggle them both without going crazy." She laughed, "I have a hard enough time just dealing with the Hollywood drama." She waited for a response, but all he gave her was a little grunt that indicated he still might be listening as he continued to unpack.

She wanted to force him to look at her—she'd worked really hard to plaster just the right look of apology on her face, but she was forced to try and convey it with her voice. "There's no excuse for the way I acted, but I'd just come off a really rough couple months; a box office nightmare and a bad breakup; and, well, you know how it is. People think they know me because of the roles I play. For you, they think they know even more because of your music. They think you are your songs, and well, I guess I was a little guilty of it as well. I started listening to your music—I'd heard it before of course, and have all your CDs—but the more I listened, the more I thought we could be connected."

Dylan finally turned to her and looked her right in the eye. "We *cannot* be connected," he said firmly.

"I know," she rushed. "It was stupid of me. I insulted your girlfriend," she had to work to keep a straight face when she said 'girlfriend,' "and I really regret it. I can see by that picture that you're still together, and I had no business interfering."

"I'm in love with her," Dylan said frankly, "and what you said to her was inexcusable, selfish, and rude."

"I couldn't agree more, and I'm so sorry. I'd be happy to apologize to her myself, if that would make you feel better."

"No need. I'll pass on the message." He could just imagine calling Tia and handing the phone over to Penelope Valentine. Tia'd climb through the phone to wring her neck, he thought, then instantly thought that it would be worth it if she could really climb through the phone and into his arms. He returned to his unpacking, glancing back up at the picture they'd taken at the top of the Tower, shortly after he'd told her he loved her for the first time. There was so much joy in both their faces, and it always warmed his heart to look at it.

"I just want you to know that I wasn't myself that day—that's not the kind of person that I truly am, and I really regret that your first impression of me was such a bad one. I really hope that we can start over and be friends, and that once you get to know the real me, you'll feel differently. It's going to be a long few months away from everyone we care about, and it would be so much easier if we were OK with each other. That's all I ask. No pressure."

He turned back to face her. "As long as you understand that friends are all we can ever be," he said, "we won't have any problems."

"Great!" she smiled, her demeanor changing. "You won't be sorry, I promise! So then, as your friend, I've made you a list of the best delivery places in town—which remember is a half hour away, so be prepared for some hefty delivery fees—and have taken the liberty of stocking your fridge with some staples and making you dinner. A peace offering, if you like."

"I'm not really hungry," he said. Although he was actually famished after the flight and the journey to the set, he definitely didn't want to spend his first evening having dinner with Penelope.

"I'll just leave it for you," she said, "and I'll get out of your way so you can unpack and get settled. I've already eaten, actually, but I thought you might be hungry after the long day of traveling. That flight is a real bitch." He didn't remind her that he'd only come from Melbourne, just a three and a half hour flight, for fear that she'd take that as an invitation to stay. She left, and returned less than a minute later balancing a large platter covered with aluminum foil. "Let me know if you need anything else—I'm just two trailers down. I'll see you for rehearsal in the morning," and with that, she left and walked toward her own trailer.

Dylan unpacked a few more things, hanging clothes in the tiny closet and tossing some jeans into the miniscule dresser. He pulled his large envelope of pictures from the summer tour out of his carry on and started sticking them in places where he'd always be reminded of Tia—in the corner of the bathroom mirror, under magnets on the fridge, propped up on the nightstand next to the bed, along the edges of frames hanging on the walls that held generic landscapes designed to make the box feel more like home. Finally, the aroma coming from the plate started getting to him and his stomach insisted he peel back the foil to check out the contents. He moaned hungrily when he saw a T-bone, a baked potato, and some mixed vegetables—it was just what he needed to put his angry stomach to rest. He nuked the plate, pulled some butter and sour cream out of the little fridge, and reveled in finding a few bottles of cold beer. He put together his makeshift dinner and glanced at the picture of him and Tia. It was going to be a long few months, he thought as he sat down to eat alone.

Penelope went back to her trailer and flopped onto the couch. Her first act had gone well, she thought. She could see the look of confusion in Dylan's eyes when she apologized so openly, with just the right amount of humility thrown in for good measure. That was the first part of the plan—keep him guessing—win his trust in bits and pieces without being too obvious. She hadn't been sure that Dylan would still be involved with that woman, but after seeing them in Europe; she'd considered it as a possibility and written a contingency plan. It put a few different twists on things, but it was nothing she couldn't handle. She'd let them have their long distance relationship for now—she was the one who got to see Dylan every day, after all, and that had to drive the bitch crazy. Tia had to know there were some steamy love scenes involved in the movie—Penelope was willing to bet the little teacher had read the book and maybe even the script. She'd give it a few weeks, maybe a month to gain his trust, and then she'd enlist her accomplice to blow things out of the water, if she needed to. Her hope was that spending time together would make Dylan forget about what's-her-face and that he'd fall for her on his own. A lot of time had gone into researching how to be his perfect mate, but she was an Oscar nominee after all; she could play any role, and this was very possibly the biggest of her life. Either way, by the time Christmas came Dylan would be hers; they'd build their romance in Bora Bora, and by the time they finished filming, they'd be Hollywood's hottest couple and she'd be back on top of the world.

Penelope showed up at Dylan's door at eight the next morning. He could feel the thick fog that came from lack of sleep in a strange bed as soon as he opened his eyes, and he rolled out, pulling on the jeans and t-shirt from the night before as he made his way to the door. It was only a few steps, but he'd spent enough time living on tour busses to appreciate that at least he had the place to himself.

God he looked sexy right out of bed, Penelope thought when he opened the door. His long blonde hair was mussed and tumbled around his face and the shadow of a beard gave him a rough-edged look that she found more than a little appealing. Soon, she thought, she'd be waking up next to him every morning, and the mental pictures she was conjuring sent shivers up her spine. "Good morning!" she said brightly. "Did I wake you?" Dylan grunted something incoherent and she was quick to apologize. "I'm sorry," she said sweetly. She held up a casserole dish. "I do come bearing breakfast though—French toast casserole. We have a cast meeting at ten, and I thought maybe we could go over some of our lines for the afternoon rehearsal."

Dylan swung the door wider and motioned for her to come inside. He was barely awake and felt like he hadn't slept at all in the rock hard and tiny bed that would be his for the next few months, but his stomach rumbled at the spicy smell that wafted from the dish. He was going to have to rehearse with her, he knew that, but he didn't want to get into the habit of sharing his meals with her. Her apology and casual air the day before gave him some hope that she'd given up on the idea of them having 'chemistry,' but he knew if she started pushing things with him romantically, he'd have to lay down the law. It was the first day, though, and he figured he'd give her the benefit of the doubt; plus his stomach was rumbling once again. He'd have to put together a list and drop it off at The Hub today so he could at least fend off starvation on his own until Jessa's arrival in two days.

He motioned to the little table that served as dining, desk and storage, pushed his laptop out of the way, and went into the tiny bathroom to splash some cold water over his face and run a comb through his hair. After brushing his teeth he felt a bit more human, and he stepped out to see that Penelope had already started coffee and set the table for two.

"Coffee," he grumbled. "I need some of that before I can even think."

"It's almost done," she said cheerfully. "I figured you might need some."

"Thanks," he managed as he dropped himself into one of the chairs.

She jumped up as soon as the pot was full and poured two cups. "Cream or sugar?" she asked.

"Not today," he said, holding out his arm palm-up. "Can you just put it right in a vein?"

Penelope giggled and sat down opposite him, handing him a steaming mug and pulling out her copy of the script. "Did you have a chance to look at the filming schedule?" she asked. "I just got mine a few days ago. We're going to start with the beginning and the flash-backs, then you're off to do your wilderness scenes—hopefully by late next month, then it'll be my city scenes—there're a bunch where I think I see you in a crowd, so you'll need to be there. That should take us up to the Christmas break, and then we have a couple weeks to finish up here before we head to Bora Bora for the big reunion scenes." Dylan cringed a bit—that was where they'd film some pretty steamy action. Penelope, though, brushed right over it and continued, "I figured we'd run through the back story; then focus on the scenes we need to shoot next. Is that OK with you?"

"That's fine," Dylan answered, taking a big pull from his mug and helping himself to a forkful of the casserole. "This is pretty good," he said.

"Thank you," she said proudly. "It's my favorite aunt's recipe. It's always a hit, and it gives me a little comfort of home, you know what I mean?" She'd actually had her assistant, Angela, pick it up from one of the bakeries in town the day before and had thrown it in the oven before she headed over, but he didn't need to know that. Besides, she had to plant the 'favorite aunt' early, as she was part of a back-up plan and could potentially die in the near future. Figuratively, of course, since she didn't really exist.

"So, the back story?" Dylan prodded, scooping more casserole out of the pan. It was sweet, infused with cinnamon, and sprinkled with nuts; coupled with the strong black coffee, it was exactly what he needed and he felt the fog finally begin to lift.

"Of course," Penelope answered, and launched into her work. In some ways it was the typical story, boy meets girl, boy loses girl, boy finds girl again; but there were some twists and turns that kept it fresh. Dylan's character would be kidnapped by an angry drug cartel after witnessing a murder and being mistaken for someone else, then he'd be dragged into the wilderness where he eventually escapes and has to fight the elements and try to find his way back to civilization. Penelope would play the estranged wife who has to help the cops crack the case and falls in love with her husband all over again in the process. It would be billed as a chick flick, Dylan knew, but there was enough action that it would make for a good date movie. Although he was too humble to admit it out loud, he couldn't help that his head swelled just a bit knowing that it was his accolade of sexiest man that the production company was counting on to pack the theaters.

Acting was a completely different kind of work, and Dylan enjoyed the occasional break from the music scene. Lonely nights far from home were part of filming in a remote location, and Dylan usually took advantage of the down time to work on new music. The recent influx of emotions—meeting the girl of his dreams, falling in love, having to say goodbye—had all kinds of thoughts rolling around in his head, and he looked forward to sinking into the creative process of going from idea to actual song. For right now though, he tried to shake thoughts of Tia out of his head—that wasn't help his concentration any—and ran through some lines with his co-star before heading out to the first day of many filled with meetings, rehearsals and filming.

Chapter 27

Tia skipped into her front door on Dylan's first full day in New Zealand—they hadn't been able to talk for days and he'd said he'd take a break and call her at 4:00 her time. She held the phone in her hand, willing it to ring. When it finally did, her heart leaped in her chest.

"Hi!" she said, falling onto the couch.

"Hey gorgeous," he replied casually, "miss me?"

"It's what I do best these days," she replied. "I can't seem to keep my head on much else."

"Well, I don't mean to brag, or anything, but it's already tomorrow for me, so I got to cross another day off the calendar."

"Not fair," she pouted, smiling to herself. "So how's New Zealand?" she asked.

"Lonely," he answered simply. "But I'm trying to make the best of it. It's actually really beautiful here, though; lots of wide open spaces and wilderness. I could see taking a trip here sometime just for fun. You'd like it," he added.

"I know I would," she said. "I've seen some shows on the nature channels that were filmed there, and it does look gorgeous." She changed the subject. "So, I have to ask—how's our little friend?" She was more than a little curious to know how Penelope had reacted to Dylan's arrival.

"So far, she's fine," he said. "Believe it or not, one of the first things she did once I got here was to apologize for her behavior. But you'll like this even better—she even offered to call and apologize to you personally, if you wanted her to. I fielded that one for you, though. I really didn't think you'd want to hear her voice, so I just said I'd pass along the message."

"Thanks," she said. "You're right about that. Hearing her voice would ruin any day of mine, even if she were apologizing. Somehow, I doubt the sincerity of anything that passes through her lips—unless she's on a rampage, of course; then I believe everything."

"I thought so too," he replied, "and I take it with a grain of salt, but it was still more than I expected."

"I just hate that she gets to see you every day, and I don't," Tia pouted.

"And I hate that I see her every day instead of you," he said, "but remember, you're the one I'm madly in love with, so you have nothing to worry about."

"I'm so glad to hear that."

"I sent you a letter—I don't know how long it takes to get there, but I'll keep writing, and email, and call when I can—but I just bugged out at the very start of our first cast meeting to call you, and I got some pretty scary looks, so I'd best get back to work. Wish I could talk longer, but—it's so good to hear your voice, and now I can get through the rest of the day."

"I wrote you too," Tia replied, "and I understand, even though it sucks. I'll talk to you soon—whenever you can—I know the time difference is going to be hard."

"I love you Tia, and I'm thinking of you every minute."

"I love you too, Dylan."

The call ended too fast, and Tia was left with the entire night ahead of her. She sat down and wrote Dylan another letter, telling him how much his call had meant to her and filling him in on the details of her first full week back at work. It was six pages long by the time she finished, and she tossed in a couple pictures of her in her classroom and with her students as an afterthought.

Meetings and rehearsals went smoothly, and the director laid out the schedule for filming to the cast. He hoped to start shooting some short simple flashback scenes the next day, which meant that Dylan would have to spend some time with Penelope that night running lines. She offered to bring dinner over to his trailer so they could run through scripts over the meal then rehearse right after. He still didn't want sharing meals to become a habit, but he'd never made it over to the damn Hub to drop off his list and still had nothing decent to eat at his place, so he gratefully accepted. "How do you do it?" he asked. "We've been here all day, and now you're going to cook?"

"Oh, my assistant Angela is just a dear. She does the shopping for me and helps me put things together. It'll be no big deal, really. I'm just going to throw a salad together, cook up some pasta and garlic bread...I'll be over in an hour, if that's alright with you."

"Sounds fine," he said, glad that he'd have some time to scribble another letter to Tia. He included some pictures he'd just had printed of the two of them in Prague. He figured he'd send a few from one of their destinations with each letter to remind her of the amazing summer they'd had. Hopefully it would fill in the gaps a little bit until they were together again at Christmas. He also included some pictures of the trailer and his immediate surroundings, including the expansive open field that was now his front yard. In the picture of the empty bed, he wrote over the blanket, "Wish you were here."

He addressed the envelope and set it on a little shelf next to the door, and then snagged a golf cart and ran over to The Hub to grab some staples and drop off a shopping list. He was more than a little disappointed to find that he'd missed out on a shopper—someone had already gone into town that day and was already on the way back—and there wouldn't be another trip for a couple days. By that time, Jessa would be here, and she'd take care of it. The selection of food they had there was pathetic at best; he was going to be living on soup, cereal and eggs for two days; but he was determined to politely decline Penelope's offers to continue cooking for him. Maybe he could score some leftovers from tonight to hold him over.

Penelope arrived right on time juggling several dishes and a bottle of chilled wine. "The New Zealanders supposedly know how to make a good pinot gris," she said, passing him some of the dishes, "I haven't tried it yet, but it should go well with pasta."

"Oh, no wine for me," he said, "I don't drink before I work—at least not at the acting job. I'll forget these lines in a minute if I don't keep a clear head. Feel free to go ahead, though."

"We can save it for after," Penelope suggested. "A toast to our first day of filming."

"I don't think so," Dylan replied bluntly. "I've got some things to do tonight, and I really need to try and get a decent night's sleep..."

"Of course," she said, "I understand. We'll just save it for another time, then."

Dylan let it go. He didn't want to start trouble with her, especially on the first day. She may have been nominated for an Oscar, but he'd only been in two films and didn't know if he had it in him to pretend to be in love with someone on camera if he was having serious issues with her in real life. He put the dishes on the table that he'd already set and pulled a couple bottles of water out of the fridge, offering one to Penelope.

They'd planned to run through the scenes they were scheduled to film in the morning, but Penelope noticed the letter he'd written Tia perched near the front door, ready to post, and opened a conversation.

"I know I never gave your girlfriend a chance," she said. "What's her name again?"

"Tia."

"It's a pretty name. And you guys are pretty serious, huh?"

"*Very* serious," he said with emphasis.

Penelope sighed. "There's something about being in love that just makes the whole world brighter, don't you think?"

Dylan was surprised by her comment, but answered, "That's a great way to put it. I agree completely."

"How's she handling such a long separation?"

"It's hard for both of us," he answered. "She's back to work now, so keeping busy helps. Unlike me, she's home with her family and friends, so I might have the tough end of that deal, actually."

"You know I really do want to be your friend, Dylan." She saw his eyebrow go up in question and jumped back in immediately. "Seriously, really!" she exclaimed. "I said I was sorry for my behavior and I meant it. I'm not going to try to come between the two of you, and I want you to feel like you can talk to me about things—even her. We're going to be spending a lot of time together, and it'll be so much better for both of us if things are comfortable between us. I know we got off to a bad start, and that was totally my fault. I'm trying to make it up to you, and I promise not to pressure you into anything you don't want." She held up her index and middle finger in the Girl Scout salute, and then crossed her heart with her fingers.

Dylan was surprised again, but tried not to show it. He didn't have any reason to trust her, but he had several reasons not to. Still, she was trying to be nice, and he had to give her credit for that. It would certainly be a lot easier to get through the next few months without a lot of animosity between them. "As long as we're a hundred percent clear on that, I'm all for it," he answered.

"Great—I'm so glad Dylan, really. So just to prove I'm serious, why don't you tell me about Tia? It might make you miss her less if you can talk about her. How did the two of you meet?"

Dylan couldn't resist telling the story. It was such an unusual way to meet, and talking about her did make him feel better. Penelope sat engrossed throughout the story, shaking her head and smiling. "That sounds like a movie to me!" she exclaimed. He was surprised that it was so easy to talk to her; she was a captive audience who really seemed to enjoy hearing the story. She asked for details, gushed about how romantic it all was, and it was after seven by the time they started running lines. Two hours later, Dylan started yawning and insisted he get some sleep. Penelope picked up the envelope by the door and turned back. "Do you want me to have Angela take this into town for you in the morning? She's got to stop at the post office anyway."

Jessa was scheduled to arrive in two days, and her first order of business would be to go into town to do some shopping and run some errands, so she could take it in. He hesitated for a moment. The post office would be closed by the time Jessa arrived, so that would mean at least three days before the letter got in the mail. He figured it would be a statement of good will and trust on his part to have her assistant handle it, and the letter would then get to Tia three days earlier. "That'd be great, I appreciate it," he said, clenching his fist just a bit as she walked through the door with the letter in her hand.

"No problem!" she said. "Like I said, Angela's going in anyway. Do you need anything else? I can have her stop off at the grocery for you too, if you want."

Dylan definitely did want, thinking about the starvation rations he'd been able to gather that day, and he handed off his list, thanking her again and saying good night.

Penelope returned to her trailer and poured herself a tall glass of wine, downing most of it in one long swallow. Damn, it had been torture keeping the smile on her face while she was sitting there listening to Dylan tell about his love affair with the school teacher. She'd never be able to understand the pressure of being a star, the constant hunt for the limelight, the constant fear of falling from the pedestal that being famous required. Life just didn't work that way, and Penelope knew it better than anyone. He was kidding himself that it was going to work out between them in the end. She, Penelope, knew the stresses of being in front of the camera and in the public eye.

It had gotten a little easier, though, when she started imagining that he was talking about her with such reverence, and she mentally started inserting her own name whenever he mentioned Tia's. He talked about that girl like she was some kind princess; like he was the lucky one instead of the other way around. He kept saying how amazing she was, and how good they were together, and Penelope wondered if anyone had ever talked about her with such emotional admiration. She seriously doubted it, and it kind of stung. But she was more determined than ever that someday Dylan would be talking about her that way. She could already see why Susannah Atwald had said he was the best boyfriend she ever had—Penelope was already starting to like him.

She held the letter to Tia in her hand. She wanted nothing more than to tear it up into pieces and toss it into the trash, but it wasn't time for that yet. Instead, she put on a pot for tea that she never intended to drink. When the kettle whistled, she held the letter over the steam and carefully pried it open. She read the letter, frowning at his professions of love, but curiously satisfied that he'd said that she was more genuine than he'd originally thought—that meant that her plan was working so far.

She slipped a stack pictures out of the envelope and recognized Prague in the background of several. "Well aren't they just adorable?" she said to herself sarcastically. She selected one photo to keep and shoved the rest back into the envelope. She sat on the couch and started at the picture—Dylan looked so happy and his smile just lit up his face. If only the teacher wasn't in the picture, she thought, it would be perfect. From the kitchen drawer she pulled out a pair of scissors and carefully cut Tia's face out of the photo. It was an improvement, but now the picture had a gaping hole, which was distracting. She pulled her portfolio out from under her bed and found a picture of her own face that fit in the space, carefully cutting it out and sticking it behind the original photo. She pressed the altered image onto the first page of her photo book, and stared at it some more. "Much better!" she said out loud, and then she returned it to the shelf behind her bed before putting the rest of the contents back into the envelope and resealing it. She'd give it to Angela in the morning to drop at the post office. Satisfied, she sat back on the couch and took another large pull of her wine, feeling the alcohol course through her veins and into her head. It was all about patience right now, she told herself. It was going to be a long show, but so far, her performance had been flawless.

It was another six days before Tia's first letter reached him. Jessa delivered it as soon as it arrived, and he held it like gold before gently opening the envelope. It smelled of her; she had spritzed it with some of her favorite perfume, and his heart was lifted at seeing her neat and even handwriting on the page. He hoped that she'd gotten his first letter, and imagined her sitting at her kitchen table with a glass of wine, as excited to see his handwriting on the page as he was to see hers. He skimmed the letter quickly, and then sat to reread every line, hearing her voice speaking the words in his mind. Immediately, he sat down to write her again, and slipped in a few pictures of them from Geneva, with the Alps in the background. He smiled as he wrote on the back of one, "Can you still yodel?"

Over the next few weeks, Dylan and Tia each fell into their own routines, working at their respective jobs and finding a rhythm that worked for them. They talked whenever they could, sent emails constantly, and each got letters from the other every couple days. Sadly, the wireless service available at The Village wasn't fast enough to support video chat, so they both started including all kinds of recent snapshots with their long notes. Neither of them felt it was enough, but it was the best they could do.

Tia successfully avoided the country club, but when they held a charity dinner in her mother's honor, she had no choice but to attend. Worse, since her parents would be seated with the heads of the club and the charity, Tia was left once again to be a third wheel at Lexi and Ryan's table. Much to her dismay, she walked in and saw that Jace and Ditsy were sharing the table as well. She hadn't heard anything from Jace since she'd gotten back from the summer, so she was cautiously optimistic that she wouldn't have any issues with him tonight. Still, spending the evening with him and Ditsy was definitely not the highlight of her week.

"Oh Tia, hi!" Bitsy squawked in her high-pitched voice as soon as she approached the table. She rose to give Tia air kisses, one of the things about her that drove Tia crazy.

She smirked at Lexi over her shoulder as Bitsy planted the tiny kisses a fraction of an inch from her cheeks and took her seat at the table. "Hey Bitsy," she said simply, careful not to use the unflattering nickname given to her by Lexi, and then added, "Jace."

He nodded at her and tipped his drink toward her in acknowledgement, but didn't speak. Tia noticed two empty shot glasses sitting on the table in front of him.

Tia tried her best to be cordial to everyone at the table, but focused her conversation toward Lexi and Ryan. She hadn't seen him since she'd been back, and it wasn't long before he asked about her summer.

"Oh my God, Tia, that's right!" Bitsy spurted as they waited for the salads to be served. "I heard you spent your summer in Europe! I've always loved the south of France—did you go there?"

"No, I was in Paris, actually," she answered, catching the look of disgust on Jace's face from the corner of her eye.

"Oh, I love Paris too," she gushed. "Especially the Louvre." It came out Lou-vree, and Tia had to hide her own smirk. "Did you go there?"

"I sure did. I loved it too," she answered.

"That's where Tia's boyfriend first told her he loved her—at the top of the Eiffel Tower," Lexi interjected, and Tia shot her a look. She hadn't planned on broadcasting that information, especially not while Jace was still glaring at her.

"Well isn't that romantic," Jace drawled sarcastically, "and so original, too. He must be quite a guy." He downed his shot of cognac and ordered another.

"They're just the perfect couple," Lexi said to Bitsy, ignoring Jace's comment. "They're absolutely adorable together!"

Jace turned his back on Bitsy and turned his attention to Tia. "But he's not here now, is he? He's off on the other side of the world. What's he doing, I wonder?"

"Working, actually," Tia said, glancing at her watch. "It's two in the afternoon there right now."

"Playing with his little band?" he said sarcastically. "Breaking the hearts of girls all over the globe? Everyone knows about guys in bands. You really think he's being faithful to you?"

"Yeah, I really do," Tia answered softly. She didn't need to defend Dylan or herself to him, and she didn't owe him any more of an explanation.

"You don't know guys then, do you, Tia? You could have had a nice normal guy right here, but you had to go traipsing all over Europe with someone you barely knew. And now look at you, alone again, tagging on to Lexi and Ryan and spending all your nights alone waiting. He's not coming back, you know." His words were slurred around the edges—they hadn't even gotten salads yet and he'd already had too much to drink.

"I do know a little about *some* guys," Tia said angrily. "The ones who think they're better than everyone else and that the world should fall down at their feet? *Those* kinds of guys are a bunch of pricks." All the eyes at the table turned to Jace, but he seemed oblivious to the fact that she was talking about him.

Jace finished his fourth shot and handed his glass to the waitress who was placing salads on their table. "Fill this for me, will you sweetheart?" he said to her. Then he turned to Tia. "We'll see," he spat. "But don't expect me to be waiting around for you."

Tia glared at him as she watched Bitsy's face fall. He'd gone too far, and the pain was plainly written in her eyes. "If you'll excuse me, I think I'll go say hello to my parents." She started to get up, but Jace put his hand on her shoulder and pushed her back into her chair. Bitsy looked as if she wanted to climb under the table and disappear, and Tia could see the tears that were starting to pool in her eyes. Jace's next drink arrived, and he quickly downed it and motioned to the waitress for yet another refill.

"We haven't even started dinner," he said. "You can't go yet." She glared at him, and he pasted a pout on his face. "Aw, I'm sorry, Tia. Did I hurt your feelings?" he whined.

"No," Tia said, "but you certainly are hurting Bitsy's. And actually, I think I've lost my appetite. I'll just go say goodbye to my parents." She turned to Lexi. "Talk to you tomorrow?"

"Sure...yeah," she said, shooting daggers at Jace from her eyes. "I'll call you in the morning."

Tia took a few minutes to chat with her parents, congratulating her mother and feigning a headache, then slipped out the door without a backward glance. When she walked into the parking lot, she was more than a little annoyed to see Jace there, waiting for her. She tried to walk past him, but he put his hand on her arm, stopping her. He swayed on his feet, and his speech was slurred. "Oh come on, don't leave Tia," he moaned. "I'm sorry. I just always seem to say the wrong things around you—you get me so flustered I can't even think. I just missed you so much all summer, and you look so good, and I can't stand hearing you're in love with someone else..." He tried to put his arm around her, and she stepped away.

"Give it up Jace!" she answered shortly. "What the hell is wrong with you? You just left your girlfriend sitting in there by herself after you treated her like shit in front of a bunch of people. I can't believe you could be that rude!"

"She doesn't mean anything to me!" he bellowed. "I've told you that a dozen times!" His pathetic pout returned, and he lowered his voice. "It's you I want Tia, it's you I need." He drew the last word out, making him sound like a whining child.

"Damn it Jace, you just don't have a clue!" she said. "This isn't even about me—it's about you not getting something that you want—you just can't stand it, can you? I told you all this before. I don't want you." She enunciated every word and spoke slowly, making sure he had time to process each one through the fog of alcohol. A pained look crossed his face, but she continued. "You are not even close to being my type. You're pretentious, rude, conceited, and any girl stupid enough to date you better be happy with being second best, because your life is all about you. My being in a relationship isn't even a factor—don't you get it? Even if I didn't have Dylan, I wouldn't date you!"

"That's not fair, and you know it!" he slurred. "I was always very nice to you, and I always put your needs first—that's why I didn't make a move sooner. Your supposed boyfriend is on the other side of the world, and I'm here. We could be so good together if you just give us a chance. What can he give you that I can't, Tia? I'm rich," he started ticking off his qualities on his fingers, "I'm highly respected in my field, I'm good looking, I'm..."

"A complete ass," she finished for him. "And definitely not a guy I'd ever want to be with. Now get out of my way, Jace, and go back to your poor unfortunate girlfriend and start begging for forgiveness, before I have to yell for help."

"Fuck, why are you being such a bitch?" he growled, tripping back into the doors of the country club.

Tia took a deep breath and headed straight for her car, locking the doors and starting up the engine immediately. She thought she'd rid herself of Jace, thought that four months with no contact would deaden any attraction he had for her. She was wrong, apparently, and she vowed that she wouldn't be returning to the country club again for any reason.

Dylan's routine was simpler, and revolved solely around the movie. Filming was going well, and they were making pretty good progress. It helped that they'd set up a makeshift studio on the outskirts of The Village. Technology made it easy, too—they could film a lot of scenes in front of the green screen, and the techies could add backgrounds later. So far they'd filmed the flashbacks, which involved a lot of arguing with Penelope's character to tell the story of their break up. They'd also done a lot of the main story that involved her character, and he had to admit that she was a good actress. She could cry on command, go from happy to angry in the blink of an eye, and she was doing a great job portraying the character as she was in the book—the audience would love it.

Personally, she was keeping their relationship at a professional and friendly level, and he was finally starting to trust her; which was good, because he saw an awful lot of her. Bruce and Sadie, the other two actors who shared their spoke of the wheel, were now a hot item and were rarely around. Trent wasn't scheduled to arrive for a few more weeks, and then would only be staying for a short time, and characters with smaller parts were rotating in and out of another set of trailers. Which left Dylan, Penelope, and their assistants the only constant presences on their spoke of the wheel. It seemed to Dylan that Penelope had some kind of uncanny radar that alerted her to his whereabouts—whenever he walked out of his trailer Penelope was either already there—sunning herself in a lounge chair or reading a book—or she stepped out shortly after he did. The closest town held little of interest, and it was a pain in the ass to get there, anyway. He was feeling claustrophobic, and after two weekends of sitting in his trailer playing cards with the director and dodging Penelope's invitations to 'hang out,' he needed to get out and do something.

Being so far out of town, the cast and crew were forming their own little community, and it hadn't taken long for people to start congregating at The Hub on Friday and Saturday nights; sharing pot luck meals, telling stories of home and work over beer at a bonfire, and generally entertaining each other. It was Dylan's third Saturday, and they'd just finished running lines for tomorrow's scenes. He was done for the night, and Stan wasn't available for a card game, which was fine with Dylan anyway—he'd already lost enough money to him. So when Dylan stepped out and heard the guitar and singing drifting over from the direction of The Hub, he was glad that he wouldn't have to spend the evening alone or worse, listening to Penelope talk about how wonderful she was. He'd never met a more insecure person. She was constantly belittling others and talked down to everyone, and he was really getting sick of it.

Jessa had hung out at The Hub the previous week, and had said that the people were all pretty decent—they'd been in the business long enough not to flip out if a celebrity was walking around among them—and he decided to grab his own guitar and head down. He'd hoped to slip out unnoticed, but Penelope's radar was apparently working and she walked out just as he was tossing his guitar case into the back of the golf cart.

"And where are you heading off to on this beautiful night?" she asked sweetly.

"I thought I'd go down and check out what's happening at The Hub," he answered casually. "I hear a guitar, and thought maybe I could get a jam going. You know, get to know some of the folks we're working with."

"Seriously?" she said. "I thought maybe we could watch a movie, or just hang out," she pouted, making Dylan more even determined to spend some time with other people.

"I'm sick of the trailer already," he answered, "and we're going to be here for a long time yet. Might as well get to know some of the people living in our little town." He secured his guitar case into the back of the cart and climbed in. He wanted to just drive away, but the look on her face stopped him. He might as well invite her—there would plenty of other people around, and maybe he'd get lucky and she'd make a friend or two and give him some peace.

"Are you coming?" he asked, starting up the cart.

"Oh, I guess," she said drearily, not wanting to miss an opportunity to spend time with him. It was better than being alone, she figured.

When they pulled up, the music stopped and everyone turned toward them, silent for a moment before someone called out, "Hey! Glad you could join us! Grab a beer and pull up a chair!" He motioned to a row of coolers that had been set out.

Dylan left his guitar on the cart for now—he didn't want to upstage anyone who'd already been the center of the little group. He opened a couple coolers until he found a palatable brew, and took an empty chair between a girl he recognized from make-up and a dark haired older man he didn't know. Penelope glared at the girl until she stood up and offered her seat, much to Dylan's disappointment.

"We wondered if you'd ever make your way down here," one of the stage hands said. "We hoped you would," another person added shyly.

This was the part Dylan hated. He couldn't just walk down here, introduce himself, and be one of the gang. The assumption was always that he thought he was too good for them, and it ticked him off. But he knew he couldn't blame them for their opinions of movie stars. They'd been shunned by far too many of them to give him the benefit of the doubt.

"Well of course," Dylan said cheerfully, "we're going to be spending a lot of time together over the next few months, so we might as well make the best of it. Next time I'll bring the beer!"

They cheered him, and then the guy with the guitar said, "Maybe next time you could bring your guitar? It'd be so awesome to jam with you," he said, head bowed.

"Well actually, I was hoping you'd say that," Dylan replied, handing Penelope his beer and walking to the golf cart, pulling his guitar out of the case and slinging it over his shoulder. The buzz of the group rose to actual applause, and Dylan waved it away. "Hey," he said. "I'm not a rock star tonight, OK? I'm just one of the guys, hanging out, playing a few jams." He stopped, and added, "That's actually who I am every day, alright? None of this star treatment rubbish!"

They cheered him again, and Dylan grabbed his beer from Penelope and went to sit on the bench with the other guitar player who introduced himself as Gary. Dylan shook his hand warmly, and settled in to jam. Penelope's face wrinkled up in disgust as a young stage hand with long stringy hair took Dylan's seat and leaned toward her, smiling, to introduce himself.

Dylan started strumming a background rhythm in a simple G key, not sure how accomplished Gary was, but indicating that he take the lead. The guy was pretty good, he thought, and Dylan started singing softly, making up lyrics as he went along. His pace increased and Gary matched him, Dylan scatting along with the tune. When they wound down, the group had expanded, others coming out of their little temporary homes to join in the festivities. The audience burst into applause, and Dylan nodded slightly, indicating to Gary with his left hand. "You're good!" he said to the kid. "I'm impressed!"

Gary sat up straight, the pride obvious on his young face. "That means a lot coming from you, Mr. Miller. Thanks so much!"

"Hey, none of this 'mister' crap," Dylan teased. "I'm not that much older than you. It's just Dylan."

"OK!" he exclaimed. "Thanks, Dylan!"

Dylan started playing *Brown Eyed Girl*, figuring it was a song every guitarist would know. Gary jumped right in and the whole crowd sang along, dancing in the shadows of the bonfire and sharing the evening. Dylan's mind wandered to Tia, and the night they'd danced to this song—the night he finally realized that he was crazy in love with her. He smiled at the memory, and at the scene that played out before him. It really didn't matter how big or small the audience was—he loved bringing joy with his music. The crowd cheered when the song ended, and Dylan jumped into another popular dance number.

When it ended, Gary shyly shook his head, deferring to Dylan. "God, that was awesome—thanks so much Dylan," he said, blushing. "But that about does it for the extent of my talent. Maybe you could play something for us?"

The audience voiced its agreement, and Dylan sat back down on the bench. "I'd be glad to," he said. "This here's an old cowboy song," and he began strumming an intro. When his voice joined his instrument, a hush fell over the crowd. God, Penelope thought, he's really good. His voice was slow and deep, soft and melancholy. She couldn't take her eyes off him, and she noticed no one else could either. They were completely captivated, swaying slowly as one while Dylan wound his way through the words, his voice rising and falling, telling the sad tale.

"In the middle of the night under the deep dark sky... I see her sitting in black over my bones she'll cry...and I never got to tell her though I thought I would...that I didn't deserve her that I weren't no good...In the middle of the night under the big full moon... I was way too young and I went too soon... but I got too drunk and I done her wrong...couldn't stand to see her face cause I ain't that strong...So from the big long bridge I looked down and fell...God ain't gonna save me I'm goin' to hell...I want to tell her to go but I need her to stay...to let the warmth of her tears wash my sins away."

When his voice fell away hauntingly, and he had gently plucked the last note, there was a moment of silent appreciation before the ever-growing group burst into enthusiastic applause. "Thank you," he said, in true rock star form, picking up his beer and draining the bottle. He stood up to go, but they begged for one more and he gave it to them—one of InHap's more popular songs. The small roar of approval they showered upon him when he finished sounded just as good to him as it did in a big stadium; he was really glad he came.

Penelope took the opportunity to jump from her seat and throw her arms around him in an embrace from behind the bench. It would be good for these people to start seeing them as a couple, she thought, and she didn't like the way a lot of the girls were looking at Dylan, as if he were a mouse to their hungry cats. God knew he'd already fallen for a school teacher, so she wasn't taking any chances. Better stake her territory, she decided. Dylan just stood up casually and out of her embrace without acknowledging her and walked back to the cart, much to the audible disappointment of the group. They wanted more, it was obvious.

He turned back, grabbed another beer from the cooler, and faced the group, who were collectively watching him. "I said I'd bring the beer next time, and I meant it," he said. "I'll see you next Friday night right back here. But for now," he said, stretching his arms over his head, "I'm beat, and I've got an early shoot tomorrow." He climbed back into the cart, hoping Penelope would decide to stay, but she immediately jumped in beside him. She gushed over him all the way back, and he found himself wishing he had a faster cart.

Chapter 28

Tia woke up on Sunday full of anticipation. It was late October, and fall had painted the trees in dozens of beautiful colors. She sat on her patio with her coffee, wearing jeans and a sweatshirt to ward off the chill and watching the leaves drift lazily to the ground. The robins and hummingbirds had left, and the first of the dark-eyed juncos were just starting to arrive. She savored the bite in the air—she couldn't ever remember wanting winter to arrive, but now she couldn't wait for the first flakes of snow to start flying. Better still, she had flipped over three months on her calendar since she'd arrived home, and just two more flips would take her to the month when she'd see Dylan again. She was expecting a call from him, and he had a free day; so they could have a real conversation without interruptions.

"I miss you, baby," he said. "It's eight in the morning here—what time is it there?"

"Two in the afternoon—yesterday," she said. She had the time difference down now and no longer had to count the hours that separated them.

"I just crossed your today off on my calendar," he said. "This month's almost done. You doing OK?" he asked.

"Oh, Dylan, it's so much harder than I thought it would be. And I pretty much thought it would be impossible."

"Just another six weeks," he said. "And then we'll be together again. I have Jessa working on your tickets as we speak. I should have my days locked in by the end of the week, but it looks like I'll be home by the time you start your break, so she'll start looking for flights that match up," he said. "I want every minute I can get with you."

"I'll feel so much better when I have it my hand," she said. "Then at least I'll know it's real and that I'll see you again."

"You know I can't wait to see you either. Oh hey, before I forget," he added, "Bo said to tell you he's coming through Chicago next weekend. He wants to know if you want to do dinner with him."

"I'd love it!" she said. "It'd be great to see him!"

"I'll let him know and get back to you with the details. I think he said something about inviting Lexi too. I wish it was me meeting you though, I'm already jealous."

"I wish it was you, too. I always do."

They spent the next hour chatting about little things and remembering parts of their summer. Tia grilled him about his parents and the rest of his family, so she could be at least somewhat prepared. "They'll love you, don't worry," he said sincerely. "Even if I didn't love you, they still would; but I do, so I know they will too."

"I just can't wait to see you," she said.

"Expect the tickets in the next few weeks or so. I still haven't figured out how the mail works from here. What letter did you get last?"

"Copenhagen," she answered. "I love that you send pictures with every letter. It helps me relive the summer all over again, and they bring such good memories."

"I've already sent Stockholm and Oslo, so they should arrive soon."

"I can't wait."

"I love getting your letters too. They're the highlight of my day every time I get one. Don't stop sending them, OK?"

"No way," she said.

"I miss you my love," he whispered. "I've written two more songs for you—I can't wait to play them for you at Christmas."

"I love you," she whispered. "I can't wait to hear them."

***

Angela Barker was nothing but a fame hog, and she would do pretty much anything to get ahead. She was a competent assistant, but what she really wanted was to be a star, and Penelope knew she could use that to her advantage. God knew she'd stepped on enough toes and used a few people to get ahead, and she saw in Angela some of that same relentless drive she'd had when she was starting out. All Penelope had to do was dangle the right carrot, and in the end all it took was a promise to get her some auditions, and she was fully on board with the plan. It made it easier that Angela didn't really know Tia and that Dylan would never know just how he'd been played. She spent the good part of an evening laying it out for her, and explaining the role Angela would play.

"You know how celebrities are Angela, you're practically one of them," she confided, happy to see the gleam in her assistant's eyes when she heard the compliment. "We walk a different line than normal people, and no one else can really understand us, am I right?"

"Absolutely!" she agreed. "It's a completely different kind of life, and not everyone can handle it."

"Yes!" Penelope exclaimed. "You're going to survive it though, because you've got what it takes."

"You really think so?" Angela asked hopefully.

"Without a doubt," Penelope said with a wink. "I wouldn't agree to support your career if I didn't."

"And you'd help me get auditions? Real ones, for decent parts?"

"Honey, if you play this part right, and Dylan and I end up together, I will guarantee you at least a supporting role in a major production."

Penelope watched as Angela rolled the promise around in her head. She kept her face open, warm, and interested, and smiled to herself as the corners of Angela's lips turned upward in a sly smile.

"I mean, it's not like I'm hurting anyone, really, right?" she said, convincing herself.

"Well, let's be realistic," Penelope said. "I want you to go into this with a clear head and a clear conscience." She leaned over and poured Angela another glass of wine. *Just two girls sharing a secret over a bottle of chardonnay,* she thought ruefully. "We have to look at the big picture here."

Angela took a sip of the wine and looked at Penelope. She could be a real bitch sometimes, but she was big in Hollywood and she definitely knew how to get what she wanted. And if she wanted to help Angela along in her own acting career, it would happen. This movie would be good and Penelope would get a lot of the credit for that—she was a damn good actress. She had clout in the industry, and knew all the right people. A few months down the road, Angela could be looking at her own name in lights and she just knew that once she was out there, she'd hit it big. It was that first chance that was the hardest to come by, and Penelope could hand it to her on a silver platter. That was her big picture, and she liked the way it looked.

Penelope continued. "At first they're both going to be hurt, Angela, you have to be prepared for that. Dylan really thinks he's got a future with this girl, and he's not going to take a break-up easily." A shadow crossed Angela's face, and Penelope acted quickly to diffuse it. "But," she said pointedly, "we both know it's only a matter of time for them. Look at the track records of other celebrities who try to make it with average people. It just doesn't work. There isn't any way to make those two worlds come together. They're going to be hurt anyway, and probably more so after they've invested even more time and energy into each other."

Angela considered this. "Especially since he's in a band, too," she added. "He'll be away on tour all the time, and that makes it even harder."

"Exactly," Penelope agreed. "Plus, I really like Dylan, and I could make him really happy. I want to make him happy. I understand him and the world we both live in. He makes me want to be a better person—I'm really falling for him, Angie, and I just know we'd be so good together. This is my shot, while we're far from Hollywood, to really get to know each other. But it won't happen until he can see the possibility of *us*, and once he does, I'll make sure he's happier than she could ever make him."

There were still a few unsettling feelings rolling around in Angela's mind, but the prize was too good to pass up. She'd seen the way Penelope looked at Dylan, and she was certainly being a nicer person lately. He'd been good for her so far, and who knew? Maybe they could make it. "OK, I'm in," she said.

"Do you want to take some time to think about it, Angie?" Penelope coaxed. "If you do this with me, we do it all the way. I don't want you coming to me halfway through with a change of heart or a guilt trip—because that would mean all bets were off. If you betrayed me, I'd have to seriously reconsider my role in making or breaking your career, so you need to be absolutely sure that you can see it all the way to the finish."

There was little doubt in Angela's mind about how Penelope would deal with a failure to deliver. She'd added the little part about breaking her career for a reason, and Angela knew that she'd pursue that with even more vigor than she would in making it. She realized that just hearing about the plan put her in jeopardy—if she backed out now, she'd certainly be out of a job; Penelope wouldn't trust her not to fill Dylan in on the details. She'd be finished before she even started.

"I don't need to think about it at all, Penelope," she said, already playing the part. "It's the right thing to do, and I'm in one hundred percent."

"Excellent," Penelope smiled, and she began laying out the script.

The next day, Angela stepped into the camera shop in town and looked around. There were so many models to choose from, and she really didn't know squat about photography; her ultimate goal had always been to be in front of the camera, not behind it.

"Can I help you?" asked a voice from behind her.

"Hi, yes, I'm looking for a digital camera, but I confess I don't know a lot about them," she told the older gentleman who stepped up to help her. "I know that I need one that can take high quality distance shots, though, and one that's pretty simple to use."

"I can certainly help you with that," he answered kindly. "I have a few very good models," he said, pulling a few cameras out of their display cases and laying them on the counter. "Now you probably want at least twelve megapixels if you're doing a lot of long distance shots, and depending on what you're shooting, you may want to add on a telephoto lens. You'll definitely want HD video, and a good variety of photo settings…"

"Mmm hmm," Angela murmured, absently picking up one of the cameras and turning it over in her hand. She shrugged, showing him that he'd already lost her.

"Let's simplify things a bit," he smiled, "can you give me an idea of what you'll be shooting?"

"Birds, mostly," she answered, "and I really want to get nice clear shots. I'll be up in the mountains though, hiking, so I need it to be something that's durable and easy to carry—and easy to use," she added again, "I'm kind of a novice."

"Can you give me an idea of how much you want to spend?" he asked. "That can help narrow things down a lot."

"I just want the best there is," she replied, "I don't care how much it costs."

The old man smiled, showing a few gaps in his teeth. "I've got just the thing for you then," he said, reaching into the display again and bringing up a small, compact camera. "This one takes really excellent shots by itself, and has a better than average zoom. You can add on a telephoto lens when you really need the distance. It's got a lot of preset photo settings, so it's simple to use. I can run you through the basics, if you have a little bit of time, and you'll be a pro in no time."

"Perfect," she smiled, pulling out her wallet. "I'll take it."

The next step was for her to befriend Jessa, and to gain her trust. Since there were so few people on their spoke of the wheel, and Dylan and Penelope were working so closely together, it made sense for the two assistants to be friends. At Penelope's prodding, the girls worked out a kind of rhythm—they'd go into town together to run errands, schedule joint interviews around the filming schedule, and work together around The Village, scheduling hair, make-up and costume fittings. Penelope encouraged the girls to take some leisure time together, and they started spending their weekend evenings together at The Hub with the rest of the crew.

Angela was working out better than Penelope had hoped—she'd managed to become the postal worker of the group, and when they went into town, Jessa would go off to collect dry cleaning or groceries while Angela visited the post office. There was almost always a letter for Tia to mail, but Angela was always one letter behind. Once the girls parted ways, she'd slip the new letter into her pocket and remove the one from the previous trip—the one Penelope had already read and from which she'd stolen a picture or two for her collection.

Penelope's photo album was starting to fill up. She had pictures of her and Dylan in Prague, Vienna, Geneva, Munich, Berlin, Copenhagen and Stockholm. Mostly she took just one, but sometimes it was too hard to choose and she ended up with two or three. The teacher would never know the difference. It should have been her on that tour with Dylan anyway, not some two bit commoner who had no business being with someone like him. Angela was getting to be quite the photographer, as well, and Penelope had printed a number of pictures of her and Dylan from scenes they had filmed. Cameras weren't really allowed on the set, of course—the studio had their own photographers and sent out only what they felt would drum up public interest, but Angela had 'befriended' one of the security guards from the crew and he often looked the other way. She was also getting better at using the telephoto lens, and was often able to tuck herself away in little places where she wouldn't be seen while she shot. They'd already "leaked" a few preliminary photos to the tabloids, to set the stage. When Penelope was ready to move to the next and most crucial part of her plan, Angela would be ready.

Dylan had really taken to hanging out at The Hub on weekends. The Villagers were finally accepting him as one of them; although they still treated him with reverence—making sure he had a seat close to the fire, always having his favorite beer in the coolers, saving him a steak or burger when he arrived late. He figured that those things were a small price to pay for some normalcy in his life, and for evenings that involved someone else besides Penelope. She attended with him most nights, but he noticed more and more that she was starting to befriend others from The Village, and he was glad. She really did seem to be changing for the better—instead of looking down her nose at the crew, she smiled and joked with them, bringing dishes to share at the pot luck and trading recipes with some of the other girls. She even accepted an invitation to take a little shopping trip into Auckland, something he couldn't have imagined her doing a month ago.

The change was making her easier to be with—she just seemed lighter and more carefree—and they fell into a more easy friendship, although Dylan was always still a bit wary. He tried to be nice without being too nice, always feeling like he was walking a line with her. There was just still something about her that he didn't trust, but he couldn't put his finger on what it was.

At first, Penelope was put out that Dylan wanted to spend his weekends at The Hub, instead of with her. Reluctantly, she went, but she tried to hang close to Dylan and avoid contact with the other people there. Really, she thought, why would a star of her caliber want to hang out with a bunch of stage hands and costume designers? But when she started noticing Dylan's looks of disappointment when she refused to interact, she figured she'd better change her tune. He really seemed to enjoy hanging out with people, and never put himself above them. He laughed and joked, played guitar, shared the grilling and cleaning duties, and tried to be one of the gang. If she was going to be the perfect match for him, she'd have to learn to be friendlier to people too.

It was hard at first—having conversation with strangers didn't come naturally for her, but she slowly realized that she did have something in common with these people; that being the industry. She chatted about films she'd worked on and listened as they did the same. They dished about stars they'd worked with, and she found that they were pretty perceptive about what was going on behind the scenes. The more time she spent there the more comfortable she felt, and she began looking forward to meeting people who were honestly interested in her. She'd never had a lot of girlfriends, and she found herself actually enjoying hanging with a group of girls, talking about everyday things like clothes, travels and recipes. Some nights, she'd go an hour without searching Dylan out in the crowd. One of her favorite things, however, was the change in the way Dylan looked at her. Instead of the disappointed scowl he usually wore when he glanced over, she started to see him smile. She was making him happy, and that made her happy.

The thing was—the more time she spent with him, the more she really liked Dylan. He was so real, so different than the guys she usually dated. He found obvious pleasure in making people happy, whether it was pulling up to The Hub with a cart full of beer, ordering pizzas for the entire group, giving Gary guitar lessons in front of his trailer, or performing around the bonfire. He never sought credit for what he did;

he was just being nice. He was the kind of person that you didn't have to try hard with; conversation came naturally, he had a great sense of humor, and he was one hundred percent man. Without even trying he was sexy, masculine, and completely unconcerned with the incredible good looks he'd come by naturally, which just made him even more appealing. The more time she spent around him, the more she really wanted him to be hers for all the right reasons. It was easy to imagine spending her life with him—hell, she'd even move out to Colorado if that's what he wanted. She was beginning to see how shallow her Hollywood life was, and she could actually feel herself changing into a different person—the kind of person that he could love.

She felt a few pangs of guilt about what she was going to do to make that happen, but she was more determined than ever that Dylan would be hers, and that she could truly make him happy without even having to act the part. Once she finished this crucial role, she'd never need to be anything other than herself again—she could give herself to him and he could make her happier than she'd ever been in her life. They'd still be a power couple, of course, but people would look at her differently once Dylan loved her, and she'd have both the respect she deserved and the man of her dreams. It wouldn't be long now, and she could put her scheming behind her and move forward with a new life; the one she always longed for. When she found out that Dylan had been scheduled to film for nearly a week in a remote wilderness location without any access to phone or internet, she knew the time had come to begin the most important phase of her plan. It was time to get Tia out of the picture.

Chapter 29

Penelope's plan was complex, to say the least, but then, nothing worth having ever came easy, she knew that from experience. The first step of the master plan, as she called the next phase, was to get rid of Jessa, Dylan's faithful assistant. And she had just the thing. Dylan had Jessa's loyalty, but Penelope had Angela, and she was a proving to be a force to be reckoned with. A little girls' weekend in Auckland was just the thing to get the ball rolling, and Angela was happy to oblige.

"So, does Dylan ever let you get out, you know, to do your own thing?" Angela asked on a Thursday as they drove into town to run some errands.

"Sure," Jessa answered, "he usually encourages it, actually. Why?"

Angela got excited. "I was thinking of a girls' weekend, just you and me, out to Auckland. Could you get away? Maybe this weekend?"

Jessa shrugged. She didn't see any reason why Dylan wouldn't let her go; there wasn't a whole lot for her to do here in New Zealand besides be a gopher. There were only a few interviews and appointments to set up, and most of what she did was via email with people back home. She could take her laptop and do most of that in Auckland. "I don't see why not," she said.

"Great!" Angela sang. "I'm just so bored here without any of my friends, and there isn't all that much to do. I was hoping that we could be real, true friends, and I can't think of a better way to do it!"

"Sounds fun," Jessa said. "I'll talk to Dylan about it tonight."

"I'll make all the arrangements!" Angela gushed. "I'm thinking shopping day and spa day, what do you think? I'm in desperate need of a mani-pedi."

Jessa looked at her pathetic fingernails, cut short and unpolished, then shrugged. The last time her nails had been done was in England, over three months ago. "Sure, why not?" she said. "I'm up for anything."

Dylan was more than fine with it; in fact he insisted on paying for the spa day for both girls. Massages, mani-pedis, and facials, he'd insisted, and Jessa couldn't talk him out of it. They left on Friday morning in one of the studio's rented cars and drove into the city. On the way in they chatted about home and what they missed the most being so far away. Jessa traveled a lot more than Angela did, and she asked a lot of questions about the summer tour in Europe. Angela was interested in what Jessa had to say about Tia, Dylan's girlfriend back in the states, the one she was helping to purge from Dylan's life. Jessa talked about her as if she were a good friend, and couldn't say more about what a great couple she and Dylan made. To hear Jessa talk about it, they were truly in love and would find a way to make it work.

Angela felt a sudden touch of guilt over what she was about to do, but in the end, she decided, she had her own future to think about, and Penelope had warned her that she was going to have to step on a few toes. She felt bad about Jessa; she was a genuinely nice person, but she didn't even know this Tia woman, and it was obvious how much Penelope honestly liked Dylan—he really brought out the best in her. Angela had never seen her so happy, and Penelope had never been so easy to work for—she was starting to believe that they could actually be good together.

They checked into their hotel room and immediately hit the road to do some shopping. Jessa had never had an affinity to designer clothes; her tastes had always been pretty simple; but the Victoria Park Market practically begged to be shopped, just as Harrods had. The boutiques showcased unusual styles and unique items, and every window beckoned them inside. Angela fell in love with the Ariana Boutique and vowed that neither of them would leave without getting something nice for themselves. "We work hard for it, Jessa," she said. "We deserve to have some nice things."

Jessa settled on a beautiful and unique scarf, full of colors and textures she'd never seen before. It was more a work of art than an article of clothing, but she could match it with almost any color and it would make pretty much any outfit in her generally bland wardrobe really stand out. Angela insisted she buy it. "The colors are amazing on you," she said, "I know you'd regret if you didn't get it." Jessa took her one meager item to the counter, cringing when she signed the credit card slip—she was still paying off her shopping spree at Harrods—and the clerk wrapped the scarf in gold tissue before placing it into the bag.

Angela had considerably more in her arms, sweaters, scarves, a hat, a handbag—she was really splurging. "Hey," she suggested to Jessa. "Why don't you check out those two little restaurants we passed on the way here, and see which one would be good for lunch? I'll be a minute, and meet you over there."

Jessa nodded, and walked out into the clear spring day as Angela finished her business. "Oh, just one more thing," Angela told the clerk after Jessa left the boutique. "I want one of those scarves like the one my friend just bought. My little sister will just love it." The clerk wrapped it in the same gold tissue and placed in on top of Angela's heaping shopping bag. "Thank you!" she said brightly as she exited the shop to meet back up with Jessa.

The girls returned on Sunday afternoon, looking refreshed and happy. Both went immediately to Dylan to kiss his cheek and thank him for their day of pampering. They had the rest of Sunday to relax, officially on vacation from their jobs, and they spent it together, sipping wine they'd bought in the city and chatting comfortably. Angela had been to the Oscars, and Jessa to the Emmy's, where InHap had won for best live performance. They shared stories about after-parties, and giggled over which celebrities made asses of themselves after having too much to drink. Jessa left happy, glad that she'd found a new friend to pass the time with on this long trip away from home.

On Monday morning, Jessa's task was to collect some studio bigwig from the airport. She crawled out of bed, her head still a bit fuzzy from all the wine, but all she really needed to do was hold the placard with his name on it and guide him back to the limo where the driver would be waiting. She grabbed her new scarf, wrapped it over a fresh outfit, and contemplated her image in the mirror. It really did match with anything, and she felt elegant and confident as she drove a golf cart over to the little makeshift studio to meet the limo. She arrived at the airport to find that the flight had been delayed an hour, so she stopped off at one of the bookstores in the airport to grab a magazine, found a seat, and settled in to wait.

When the first call came in, Dylan and Penelope were perched in lounge chairs outside Dylan's trailer, running through the scenes for tomorrow's filming. She saw him frown as he looked at the display, obviously not recognizing the number, but he punched the keypad and took the call.

"Hello?" he answered.

She saw his eyebrow lift in that little way she had grown to love, and smiled to herself. She could only hear his side of the conversation, but it was more than enough to assure her that her plan had been set in motion.

"Yes, who's this?"..."Excuse me?"..."Hold on a second, how did you get this number?"... "What airport are you in?" he asked incredulously, shaking his head in disbelief and looking at Penelope, his face twisted into confusion. "No, I'm sorry to disappoint you," he said, thinking quickly, "but I'm not that Dylan Miller—this must be someone's idea of a joke." He tapped the keypad to end the call, and before he could even say a word, it rang again in his hand.

"What the hell?" he said angrily, hitting the talk button.

"No, this not that Dylan Miller," he replied, hanging up again.

Penelope watched as Angela approached, just as they'd rehearsed. Now it was time to see if she actually had any acting talent—she'd put a lot of faith into her assistant, but it couldn't be helped. She needed to be sure that her hands were clean in all of this, and that she was around to pick up the pieces when they started raining down.

"What is it, Dylan?" Penelope asked, her voice full of concern.

"I don't know," he said as the phone rang again. Penelope and Angela exchanged a knowing glance, and then looked back to Dylan, who punched the keypad hard with his index finger, disconnecting the call.

"Talk to me Dylan, what's going on?" Penelope asked again.

"I'm not quite sure, but it looks like my private mobile number just went public," he said, scowling at the ringing phone. He clicked the disconnect button again, and then shut off his phone. "It seems that a few of my fans are calling to chat."

"How in the world could that happen?" Penelope asked innocently.

"Damned if I know," he said. "The first caller said she got the number at the airport. The Auckland airport."

Angela inhaled sharply and dropped her eyes, shook her head the smallest bit, and began to slowly slink away.

Penelope looked at her with concern. "Are you OK, Angela?" she asked. Angela nodded, her wide eyes searching, but unfocused. "Wait a second, where are you going?"

Angela turned back toward them and there was guilt written all over her face. Penelope smiled inside, but maintained a look of genuine concern. So far, so good—Angela kept just the right distance and looked just uncomfortable enough to be believable.

"I...I," she stammered, "just remembered something." She tried to turn again, and Dylan and Penelope shared a look of suspicion.

"Wait a minute," Penelope said. "What's going on with you? Why do you look so flustered all of a sudden?"

Angela's eyes turned up and to the left—a sure sign that a lie was coming. "It's nothing," she said shakily, putting her hand over her stomach. "I just don't feel so well all of a sudden. I...I've got to go."

"Oh no you don't," Penelope said. "Angela, do you know something about this?"

Angela's face went from flustered to pained. "No, I..." she looked like a trapped animal ready to flee. Easy now, don't overdo it, Penelope tried to convey with her eyes.

Dylan spoke up. "Angela, what do you know?"

"Son of a bitch," Angela wailed. "I really don't need this right now!" She sank into a chair, looking defeated.

Penelope held up a hand to stop Dylan from speaking and sat down next to Angela. She put her hand on Angela's back and rubbed small circles there, her voice motherly and full of concern. "Listen, Angela," she said soothingly. "If you know something about this, you need to tell us—this is important. Look at me," she commanded. Angela raised her eyes, the look of pain clearly evident. "This is very serious, honey! If someone did this purposely it's a personal attack on Dylan, and it's incredibly unfair. You need to speak up right now, and tell us everything you know." Angela stammered something unintelligible and looked around for a way out. Penelope continued. "Now you've always been loyal to me Angie," she said softly, "but if I find out later that you knew something about this and didn't share it when you had the chance, I'm going to have to seriously reconsider your trustworthiness." Angela's shoulders hitched, and Penelope pulled her into an embrace. "It's OK, Angie," she said. "Just tell us what you know."

Tears began to slip down Angela's cheeks, and Penelope cheered internally for her trusty assistant who was playing the part even more perfectly than she'd hoped.

"But she's my friend!" she whimpered. "I don't get to have many friends, you know!"

"Come on, honey," Penelope prodded. "You just need to tell us." She scooted her chair closer to Angela's and put her arm around the sobbing girl.

"I'm so sorry," she breathed, "I never really thought she'd go through with it!"

Dylan sat bolt upright in his chair. "Who are you talking about?" he barked. "And go through with what, exactly?" he demanded.

"She told me when we were away over the weekend," she said between sobs.

"Wait a minute," Dylan interjected. "Are we talking about Jessa here?"

Angela nodded, and more tears fell. Penelope dashed into Dylan's trailer and came out with a box of tissues, which Angela gratefully accepted.

Dylan was having a hard time holding on to his patience, but he forced his voice to be smooth and even. "What did she tell you, Angela?"

"Oh shit!" she tried to force the tears down and make her voice work properly. "She said that you didn't know what was coming to you; that you deserved it for the way you've treated her this past year!"

"What are you talking about?" he bellowed. "The way I treated her? We get on brilliantly!" He shook his head quizzically. "I'm sorry, but I just don't get it," he said. "She loves her job—she tells me that all the time!"

Angela was shaking with emotion. "No," she whispered, "what she loves is *you*, Dylan; she's been in love with you for over a year and she always assumed it would just be a matter of time before you felt the same way about her. But then Tia came along, and she was so resentful."

"No," Dylan uttered, shaking his head. "No, that isn't true, it's just not possible—she and Tia are friends!" His face was twisted in pain and confusion, and Penelope sat back to enjoy the show. She patted Angela on the back, encouraging her to continue.

Defeat settled onto Angela's face and she looked up at Dylan with pained eyes. "She said that at first she thought Tia would be like all the others so she let it go. She said she knew you wanted a real down to earth person, and since you and Jessa spent so much time together, and got along so well, she figured eventually..." she broke into another fit of sobs, but then continued. "But all she ever heard about was Tia, and then you brought her to Europe, and Jessa had to make all the arrangements for fancy hotels and special dates, and she was so mad! She finally realized that her last chance to get you to notice her would be here, when your girlfriend wasn't in the picture." She took several deep cleansing breaths, and wiped her eyes with a tissue. "Over the weekend, she said she knew it was pointless, and that she had to get away from you before she lost her mind along with her dignity. She told me you'd be sorry you ignored her as a woman." Her breath shuddered in her chest and shoulders. "I'm so sorry, Dylan, I really didn't think she'd do anything like this—I thought she was too nice for that! I couldn't imagine her doing something so mean!"

"No way," Dylan said, staring at the ground and shaking his head. "I just can't believe that about her. She's doesn't have a mean or vindictive bone in her body, even if she was that angry. I trust her completely. It couldn't be her—it just couldn't."

Penelope put her arm around Dylan's shoulders and gave him a friendly squeeze. "Never underestimate a woman in love, Dylan; especially one who feels scorned. Desperation is a hell of a motivator."

Dylan shook his head violently. "I can't believe it. I won't believe it!"

"I'm sure you're right, honey," Penelope said, standing and putting her hand on his arm. "I really couldn't imagine her doing that either. She's incredibly loyal to you and has always been completely professional. So let's clear her name right now, and then we can figure out who actually did do it."

Dylan looked at her quizzically. "And how do you propose we do that?" he asked.

"It's simple," Penelope replied. "Just turn your phone back on, and ask the next caller who gave them the number—ask them to describe the person. They had to get it from someone."

Dylan nodded and turned his phone back on; frowning when he saw the display announcing that he had twenty seven new voice mail messages. The phone chirped almost the instant it powered on.

"Hello?" he said, trying not to sound too aggravated. "Yes, this is..." "Well thank you, thanks a lot, I really appreciate it..." "Listen, can you do something for me?..." "Thanks—I just really need to know how you got this number—did someone give it to you?..." "Can you describe them to me please?..." Penelope watched Dylan's face fall as the caller delivered the news, and shared a quick triumphant glance with Angela, who flashed her just the hint of a smile as Dylan's back was turned. "Thanks a lot," he said, "and thanks for being a fan."

The call waiting beeped before he finished the call. His heart fell in his chest, but he had to be sure, and hit the button to take the call. "Can you describe the scarf to me?" he asked the caller. "Yes, thank you very much. I'm glad to talk to you too." He turned the phone off again, and shoved it into the pocket of his jeans. "Bloody hell," he whispered.

"What did they say?" Angela asked urgently. "It wasn't her, was it? Please tell me it wasn't her."

"Did you see her before she left for the airport this morning, Angela?" Dylan asked. She nodded. "Did you notice what she was wearing?"

"Umm," she said, her eyes rising as if she was trying to recall the detail. "All I remember is that she had her new scarf on—the one we bought in Auckland? It looked so pretty on her that I didn't notice anything else, sorry."

Dylan's shoulders slumped as he collapsed into a chair. "What does the scarf look like, Angela?" he asked.

"Well," she said, thinking. "It's silk, but it's got some texture to it, you know? Kind of like feathers, almost. It's got lots of colors, kind of swirled around…"

"That's enough," he said sadly, dropping his head.

Penelope stepped behind his chair, giving Angela a thumbs-up before reaching over to gently massage Dylan's shoulders. "Was it Jessa, then?" she asked sympathetically, already knowing the answer.

"She described her to a tee," he sighed dejectedly. "Right down to the beautiful scarf she was wearing."

"Oh Dylan, I'm so sorry," Penelope whispered. "What can I do?"

Anger and disbelief boiled his blood as the realization set in. "Shit, I don't know what to do!" he exclaimed, getting up from the chair and pacing across the lawn, running his fingers through his hair in agitation. "What the hell can I do?" he yelled. "Bloody *fucking* hell!" He tried to collect his thoughts, but his head was positively spinning. "Oh Christ, I have no choice, do I? I have to let her go—it's pretty obvious that I can never trust her with anything again." He paced some more as the betrayal began to bubble into anger deep in his gut. "Shit!" he yelled, kicking a rock that bounced off the side of trailer with a sharp ping. "How could she do this to me?"

"It'll be OK, Dylan," Penelope said softly. "We'll work it out somehow."

"Really?" Dylan growled. "How do you figure that? My phone number is going to be in the hands of thousands of people in a matter of minutes, I've been totally betrayed by someone I trusted, and now I'm halfway around the world with no assistant! Then, I have to leave tomorrow for shooting in some god-forsaken place where there's no phone or internet reception, which means it'll be days before I can even deal with this whole situation—my number will be everywhere by then. How is that going to be OK?"

He was playing right into her hands, Penelope thought triumphantly. It couldn't be more perfect. It was time for her take some control. "Give me your phone, Dylan."

"Why?" he asked.

"Just give it to me. If I answer a few of the calls, and they hear a woman's voice, I can tell them that it's all a joke." Dylan handed her the phone. "We'll have to change your number immediately, of course, but that shouldn't be too hard to do. The little card in your phone has all your numbers stored—you just transfer it to the new one."

Dylan paced around the yard, his mind running a mile a minute. He couldn't believe that Jessa had betrayed him like this! How the hell could she be in love with him? She'd never once acted unprofessionally or shown even the hint of a suggestion that she had any romantic feelings for him. But why else would she do something like this? The evidence was staring him right in the face; the callers had both described her as a short, good-looking Chinese woman wearing a really pretty colorful scarf. He had absolutely no choice in the matter. He had to let her go immediately.

"As far as an assistant goes," Penelope continued, glancing over at Angela, "I don't have all that much for Angela to do while we're over here—she can take care of your business as well as mine without it being too much extra work. The girls were working together most of the time anyway, so she pretty much knows how you like things done." She looked over at Angela hopefully. "Would you be OK with that, Angie?"

Angela jumped up from her chair eagerly. "Oh definitely!" she exclaimed. "It's the very least I can do—I just feel horrible, Dylan," she said, shaking off another round of sobs. "I should have tried to stop her, or told you—but I really didn't think she'd actually do anything!" Her voice was pleading, repentant. "Please let me make it up to you. I'll take care of everything. I'll get your number changed for you and inform all your contacts. I can have it all taken care of by the time you get back—please let me do it—it'll make me feel at least a little better!" She looked at him and pleaded with her eyes, her hands folded beneath her chin.

Dylan ran his fingers through his hair again, stopping to massage the base of his skull where a nasty headache was brewing, and took a deep breath. Two months ago he couldn't have imagined a scenario where he'd be grateful for Penelope's presence, but she was really helping him out here; being a real friend. She'd taken control of the situation and gotten Angela to confess, and now she was graciously offering him her own assistant. There was no other choice, really, especially in light of the current situation. He couldn't possibly handle it all himself, especially since he had to leave the next day. He sighed. "I don't need too much either, and I wouldn't overwork you, so if you're sure, I'd be so thankful."

"I'm positive!" Angela brightened. "I want to do it! You won't be sorry, I promise! I'll go get on the phone with your cell provider right now and see what we have to do!" She sniffed, dabbed at her face one more time with the tissue, and gave Dylan a quick hug. "Thank you," she said hoarsely, "I won't let you down—anything you need, anything at all, just ask." She skipped off to Penelope's trailer to start working for Dylan.

Penelope was fielding call after call on his phone, playing the crank call victim perfectly. It didn't matter, though, Dylan thought, because every person who'd heard his voice mail message after he'd turned off the phone would probably recognize his voice and know it was his number. They'd forward the info to their friends, who would do the same. There was no saving it—it was already too far gone. Frustrated, he stormed into his trailer to grab a beer.

It only took a couple punches on the key pad to begin phase two. Penelope had seen the phone Dylan carried, and knew just how to access the information she needed. She scrolled through his contacts, found the one she needed, and punched the button for 'block caller.' Edit number was next, and it only took the change of a couple digits to make sure a certain call couldn't get through. He'd have to leave his phone off today, and by the time he got back from shooting the wilderness scenes, they could blame the 'error' on the phone company. The next phase of the plan was even more complicated, and success depended on several factors coming together at once. However, Penelope was more than satisfied with the results of this phase. She mentally patted herself on the back, watching Dylan come out of the trailer with two beers cradled between his fingers. The phone rang again, and she answered as she had the others, telling the person on the line that someone had played a joke on them. Dylan motioned her over with his finger, and handed her a beer.

"Just turn it off," he said. "It's too late to stop it; I'll definitely have to get the number changed."

Penelope accepted the beer, the first drink he'd shared exclusively with her since they'd arrived, and sat in the chair next to Dylan. "I'm afraid you're right," she agreed. "It became an avalanche with the very first person. Try not to worry too much though," she added quickly, "by the time you get back from the outback, it'll all be cleared up. Angela's good at what she does."

"God, Penelope, you don't know how much I appreciate that. You really saved my ass here—it's a real stand-up and unselfish thing, and I thank you."

She tsked her tongue at him. "Dylan, Dylan," she said with a waggle of her finger. "I told you I wanted to be your friend. I told you that the person you met in Chicago was not the real me. If anything, I should thank you for the opportunity to show you that I'm not the bitch you think I am."

"I don't think you're a bitch," he said.

She wagged her finger at him again. "Yeah, you did," she smiled, "but I hope that now that you've gotten to know the real me, you don't think so anymore." She extended her hand to him and he shook it. She pulled Dylan into a friendly hug and he didn't resist. "Now, quit worrying and let's just enjoy our beers—we can fix this." She sipped it happily, although she hated the stuff. The simple joy of sharing something with Dylan; a moment of trust and friendship; was well worth the bitter taste.

Dylan stewed for another two hours, drinking two more beers, before Jessa finally returned. His anger was reaching monumental proportions, but the betrayal weighed even heavier on his mind. Trust didn't come easily for him; he'd been burned too many times by too many people; but he'd had complete faith in Jessa, and that made it even harder for him to accept. He saw the car pull up, and his heart sank as he watched her get out, all smiles, wearing the damned scarf knotted loosely around her neck.

"Do you want me to go?" Penelope asked as Jessa made her way over to them.

"Actually, I'd like you to stay," he said, not taking his eyes off the approaching figure. "I don't want to lose my head, and I'm feeling seriously pissed off right now."

Penelope smiled. "Whatever you want, Dylan," she replied.

"Whew!" Jessa said as she approached. "The airport was crazy! The flight was delayed over an hour, and it was so crowded!"

Dylan worked hard to maintain control of his emotions. She didn't have an ounce of guilt on her face, and he was positively floored that she could be so cold and calculating. "Jessa," he said coldly. "I am shocked and incredibly hurt by your behavior today. I trusted you completely, and you betrayed that trust."

"What are you talking about?" her face fell into a puzzled look as she saw the menace in Dylan's eyes and heard the chill in his voice.

"Did you think I wouldn't know it was you?" he burst angrily. "That scarf is a little obvious, don't you think? One of a kind, you said?"

"Dylan, I don't have a clue what you're talking about! Talk to me, what did I do?" she was scared now; she'd never seen him look so angry.

"Oh shit, just stop pretending, Jessa—it's too late for that. I am shocked, hurt, angry—I have nothing else to say to you, except to tell you to give me your phone, pack your bags immediately and head back to the airport. I'll have you booked on the next flight out of New Zealand. You're fired, Jessa." His heart hurt just saying the words, and he couldn't look her in the eye. There wasn't any guilt there, only pain and confusion, and he wanted to take it all back and come up with some other explanation for this pile of shit he suddenly found himself in. But the evidence was too clear, too indisputable to ignore, and he had to just be done with it before he did change his mind.

"Fired?" she asked, astonished. "What are you saying, Dylan? Holy crap, at least tell me what it is you think I did, because I've never done anything to betray your trust! You know me better than that!"

Dylan shook his head. "I thought I did, Jessa, but I guess I didn't really know you at all."

Penelope interrupted as she saw Dylan's shoulders begin to shake. "We all know what you did, Jessa, and so do you. Angela didn't want to, but she finally filled us in on your little conversation over the weekend, and we were able to confirm everything."

"Angela?" she asked, searching her mind for something she might have said that was taken out of context or misconstrued but coming up with nothing. "I don't understand any of this! You know me Dylan," she pleaded. "I wouldn't ever do anything to hurt you. Just tell me, so we can work this out, please!"

"I think you just need to go, Jessa. Now," Penelope said directly. She could see Dylan was about to blow.

"But I..."

"Get out!" Dylan yelled, his face and voice full of emotion and heartbreak. "Just go—I have nothing else to say to you!"

Jessa looked from Dylan to Penelope, and saw just the hint of a smirk at the corners of her lips. "Oh my God!" she exclaimed. "You're behind this!" she yelled, pointing. "What the hell did you do, Penelope?"

Penelope looked right at her with daggers in her eyes. "Me?" she said. "You have the audacity to try and blame this on me?"

"You little bitch!" Jessa spat. "You've wanted to get your claws into Dylan since that night in Chicago! You're little nice girl act hasn't fooled me for a second! Do you really think getting rid of me will make Dylan fall for you? You're not even close to being good enough for him!"

"That's enough!" Dylan growled. "This doesn't have anything to do with Penelope, and you know it! Now give me the phone, and just go!"

Jessa jumped at the tone of his voice, handed over her phone, and ran back to her own trailer in tears. She turned back once and yelled, "She did something Dylan—figure it out before it's too late!" She was confused, angry, hurt, and didn't know what to think or say. Her mind was running a hundred miles an hour as she hastily threw her things into her suitcases and dumped them unceremoniously into the trunk of the rental car. How could Dylan fall for her line of bullshit, and what the hell did Penelope pin on her that had made Dylan so angry that he'd fired her? So angry that he wouldn't even listen to her? She got behind the wheel, unsure if she'd be able to drive through her tears, then jumped out and knocked on Angela's door. For a brief moment when she first appeared in the doorway Jessa saw sympathy behind her eyes, but they quickly turned cold.

"Angela, what the fuck is going on? Do you know that I've been fired?"

"Oh, I know all about it," she said menacingly. "I'm Dylan's assistant now." Then she burst, "How could you do it, Jessa? How could you hurt him like that? He's always been so good to you!" She didn't know if she still had an audience, but she was determined to play her role perfectly from start to finish. Her new career depended on it.

"Do what!?" she yelled back, the sound of disbelief desperate in her voice. "No one'll even tell me what I supposedly did!"

"As if you don't know," Angela spat. "Now get out of my sight. I can't believe I thought we could be friends!" She slammed the door in her face and clicked the latch, then watched from the window as Jessa climbed dejectedly behind the wheel and slowly drove away. She clapped her hands together once, up and down sharply, like a clapperboard and said to herself, "Scene one, take one, cut: that's a wrap!"

Chapter 30

Tia was surprised when she tried calling Dylan and kept getting a busy signal. Then, when she finally got through, the little electronic voice told her that Dylan's voicemail box was full, and that she should try her call again later. Maybe he had to go to the boondocks early, she figured, and she was saddened knowing that it would be at least a week before she could talk to him again. She sat down at her computer and sent him an email instead, knowing he'd see it when he returned from filming out in the wilderness.

Penelope sat down with Angela and praised her performance. "I've had a lot of assistants during my career," she said, "and all of them thought they could act; all of them thought they'd get famous through me. But you my dear," she said fondly, patting Angela on the back, "you just might have it. Keep this up, and I just might be able to get you that supporting role!"

Angela basked in her praise, especially thrilled to hear the words 'supporting role.' Her dreams could finally be coming true, and Penelope had the power to make it happen. In the back of her mind and in the pit of her stomach, however, she was bothered by the look she'd seen on Jessa's face. She hadn't known her long, but Jessa had been genuinely nice to her and had really tried to be her friend. "Thanks, Penelope. I really appreciate that a lot. But I do feel a little sorry for Jessa though."

"Oh no, don't you think that way!" Penelope interrupted. "You think it's easy to make it big in this business? You think there aren't people around every corner who want to knock you off your throne and take it all away from you? It's a cutthroat business, and you have to be willing to cut a few throats of your own along the way because there's always going to be someone looking to cut yours. You've got to look out for number one, and in order to get to the top, you have to have something to climb on."

"I know that," Angela said, "but..."

"Listen," she said, "you don't get anywhere in this business by being nice. Being nice is what gets you stepped on. That's a lesson you need to learn early on."

"But Dylan's nice."

She waved her hands in the air in exasperation. "Yeah, he is. But he's obviously an exception to the rule. He's blessed with natural good looks and a likable personality, and he doesn't have to work at it the way most of us do. Besides, it's different with music than it is with film. No one's competing against him to be the singer for his next tour like they'll compete against you for a starring role. Acting is an extra for him, not his first career. He doesn't have to be in movies to make his living, so he doesn't have the same pressure."

"Yeah, I guess you're right, but I..."

Penelope held up a finger to silence her and looked her straight in the eye. "Don't go getting all holy on me now Miss Angela—you knew what you were in for from the start of all this, and if you can't see it through to the end, then I'll find someone who will." There was no doubt about the message she was sending, and Angela got it loud and clear. "Jessa is good. She'll find another job—I could even make some calls on her behalf, if that'll make you feel better." She had no intention of doing so, of course, but the look in Angela's eyes changed just slightly, and it was enough.

"Look," she continued, "The hard part's over. Aside from Jessa, everyone wins in this situation. Dylan is much better off with me than with that schoolteacher person, and she's better off without him. We've gone over all this before—their relationship just won't work, and it's only a matter of time before she gets tired of waiting for him to come home or he screws up and bangs some groupie or supermodel and hurts her anyway. I can give him everything he needs, and the more I get to know him, the more I truly adore him and want to be with him for all the right reasons! I know it didn't start out that way," she looked into Angela's eyes, "but I'm in love with him, Angie, I truly am. I understand him and the world he lives in, so in the long run, this is what's best for everyone—I'm just giving it a bit of a jump start, is all." She put the carrot out there again—she held the power to make the girl's dreams come true. "Think about the prize, Angela," she said soothingly. "Think about what it's going to mean for you to be handed a role—that's way more than most people get." The girl's eyes brightened considerably. "Now I need to know that you're still with me on this, all the way."

Something inside Angela stopped. Penelope's voice was soft, but her face told an entirely different story; one in which only Penelope had a happy ending. Her eyes shifted between menace and what Angela could only describe as wistfulness, and she saw the danger in both. Angela clearly saw who Penelope was now. She was mean, dangerous, and more than a little off-balance. This thing with Dylan had become an obsession, she realized, and there would be no turning back. Angela had serious doubts that Dylan would want a romantic relationship with Penelope with or without Jessa and Tia in the picture. She'd heard Dylan talking to his girlfriend in hushed tones, heard him working on songs that were obviously about her, had seen how many pictures of the two of them he had scattered around his place, and she'd plainly seen how many letters he wrote her—fat ones with many pages and lots of pictures. He was in love with that girl. Angela had never officially met her, but had seen her in Chicago and London, and had seen the way she and Dylan looked at each other. On stage at Wembley there was an electricity between them that she could almost feel, even from the fourth row.

A sick feeling settled in the pit of her stomach as she fully realized the magnitude of her situation. The truth was, she didn't really have a choice—her entire future depended on helping Penelope with her sick and selfish plan. She could never again show any hesitation or guilt, because she knew that if she did, it would be her throat that Penelope would be cutting. Forcing back the lump in her throat, she flashed Penelope an award-winning smile. "You're right!" she said brightly. "You and Dylan make a great couple, you really do. I'm with you—all the way."

"That's the spirit!" Penelope confirmed, patting her on the back like a child. "Now we have to lay out the time frames for the next phase of our plan, because there's a lot to do in a short amount of time, so listen carefully..."

While Angela listened, the actress absent-mindedly pulled a shoe box from a shelf in her bedroom and slipped out three photos. She watched with amazement as Penelope cut Tia's face from them and replaced the empty spaces with her own images before carefully putting them into a photo album. Penelope then pulled out one of the letters that Angela had never posted, took some liquid paper from a drawer, erased Tia's name, and penned in her own. She'd often wondered why Penelope had insisted that she be given all of Tia's letters, and now she saw the truth. Her stomach rolled over on itself sickly as she watched Penelope casually press the letter onto another page of the album which was already nearly bursting from the binder. A shiver ran down her spine, and she had to work hard to keep a look of horror from showing on her face. She wanted out of here, but she couldn't leave without her prize. There was no choice but to finish this off, get her career on track and then get the hell away from Penelope and not look back.

Once she left Penelope's twisted fantasy world and returned to her own trailer, she lay restless in her bed, pondering whether she could go to Dylan and tell him the truth. Maybe he'd help her. She entertained that hope for almost a minute before realizing that it would never happen. Dylan valued trust very highly, and admitting her role in framing Jessa would also mean that she'd have to tell him that she hadn't posted any of his letters in well over a week, and that all along she'd helped Penelope to steal pictures that were meant for Tia. She also had two of Tia's letters to him that she'd never delivered hiding in a shoe box in her own trailer. He wouldn't be able to forgive her, and she really couldn't blame him. No, she didn't have any other choice—she was already in too deep.

It was going to be a rough few days, that was certain, if they were going to get everything into place before Dylan returned. She had to suck it up, cut her losses, and think about herself for right now—her entire future depended on how well she played her current role.

By the next morning, she was determined to get it over with as quickly as possible. Luckily, Dylan had left his trailer unlocked when he took off to film the wilderness scenes, and she collected his laptop before driving into the city and taking it into the computer repair shop.

The disinterested young kid behind the counter never took his eyes off the video game he was playing when she walked in. "Can I help you?" he asked absently when he heard the little jingle of the bell above the door. His dark hair hung over his eyes, greasy and unkempt, and he didn't look more than eighteen or nineteen years old. Aside from him, the shop was completely empty.

"I need a hacker," Angela announced. "A discreet one who wants to earn a lot of money for a little bit of work."

That got his full attention; the kid lay his controller down on the counter, forgetting the battle raging on the screen in front of him. He stood up and extended his hand. "I can help you with that," he said confidently. "My name's Steve. I'm the best, and I'm very discreet."

"Glad to hear it, Steve," Angela smiled, shaking his hand and placing the laptop on the counter.

She watched as his fingers flew over the keys, his tongue sticking out from the corner of his mouth as he stared at the screen with total concentration. It was a small matter to figure out the passwords needed, and a few mouse clicks on a particular email address was all it took to sever the communication superhighway. A new email address that would go straight to Penelope assured that she assumed control over said communication, and a tiny virus planted in an unassuming email held another little surprise. Less than an hour later, Angela walked out with everything she needed, and Steve became her new best friend. They would do more together, she assured him, much to his delight as he slipped a large bill into his pants pocket.

Her next stop was the cell phone shop, where they'd change Dylan's number. "I need the sim card transferred so the stored numbers will be in the new phone," she told the clerk.

"That's not a problem," he replied. "But can you pick it up tomorrow? I got a message from the States that you'd be coming by, but I have a few things I need to work out with their tech department before I can finish the job. It's the middle of the night there, so I'll have to get in touch with them later. You can come by say...any time after ten, and I'll have everything set for you."

"That's fine," she replied, leaving the store and heading back to The Village.

Penelope positively dreaded the thought of camping in the middle of nowhere; the idea of sleeping on a cot in a tent full of bugs and spiders sent shivers up her spine. But she needed an alibi so that she couldn't be connected in any way to the events about to unfold if for any reason things didn't go as planned. She knew that Dylan was the adventurous type and that he enjoyed the outdoors, so she figured it was just another thing she'd have to learn to like. She certainly wouldn't get a better chance than this one to show him her newly invented adventurous spirit, so she had no choice but to take advantage of it. It was only a few days, after all. She could handle just about anything for that much time. Plus, Angela was going to sneak in and take a few shots—she had some ideas that she thought they could send to the tabloids back home to get the rumors flying in Hollywood. Dylan wouldn't know about them—he absolutely refused to even acknowledge the magazines—and even if he did find out, he couldn't accuse her of taking the pictures when she was in every single one of them. She packed a bag, put on her best face and climbed into the van that would take them out to the middle of nowhere. Dylan raised an eyebrow at her when she tossed her designer suitcase onto the seat behind her.

"What are you doing here?" he asked. "You're not in any of these scenes."

She smiled at him, hoping that the look on her face showed excitement rather than the apprehension she was feeling. "I know, but I just love camping!" she exclaimed. "I used to do it all the time when I was a kid, and I didn't want to miss an opportunity to see the wilder side of New Zealand—who knows when I might make it back this way again?"

"Really," Dylan mused, having a hard time picturing her as an outdoor kind of girl. "I find that hard to believe, actually."

"Well, I guess there's still a lot you don't know about me, Mr. Miller," she smiled slyly. "I'm just full of surprises."

"I guess you are," he smiled, "but this isn't one of your Hollywood campgrounds, you know—it's going to be awfully rustic on this trip—no amenities at all."

"That's the way I like it best," she said, dreading the sound of his words. God, she hoped she didn't have to shit in the woods—that would really put her acting skills to the test. "Besides, it'll be good for me to see these scenes—it'll help me be in the right frame of mind when you return to me and we rediscover our love for each other. Stan thought it was a good idea," she added.

Dylan had been looking forward to a few days without her hanging around, but part of him couldn't help but be amused by the thought of her camping out. It could actually be quite entertaining. "OK then," he said, "I guess we're all going camping!" A few more people climbed into the van, greeting Dylan and looking at Penelope with amused faces.

"What?" she said, laughing. "I love camping!"

Dylan shared a knowing look with one of the crew members, and the caravan of vehicles began its journey.

It bothered Penelope a lot that Dylan hadn't yet shown any sign of returning her affection. He was always kind and considerate toward her, but he was pretty much that way with everyone. It was already November, and she'd hoped that by now he would have broken up with Tia on his own and made his way into her bed. Although she made sure to grab the seat next to his on the van, he laughed and joked with Bruce, his character's kidnapper, and the camera crew, and barely paid her any attention at all. When she lightly rested her hand on his knee, he gently but firmly removed it and went back to his conversation without so much as a glance in her direction. She had hoped that the plans that were already in motion wouldn't be necessary—there were a lot of facets and more margin for error than she was comfortable with.

Angela should be taking care of one of the major components right now, she thought, looking at her watch as the desolate wilderness slid by outside her window. She'd be driving out to meet her at the site later in the day, provided she could get everything done. Between worrying about that and dreading the isolation of the next couple days, it was all Penelope could do to maintain her enthusiastic attitude.

The trick for Angela was getting the right shot. It had to have Penelope and Dylan involved in some sort of intimate embrace, and since Penelope wasn't actually in any of the scenes, she didn't have a lot of contact with him. The two girls shared a small tent, and they went through the pictures she'd taken that day without finding anything tabloid-worthy. The next day, however, they filmed a scene where Dylan, after having escaped from his kidnappers, struggled his way across a river, crawling out exhausted on the other side. Penelope watched the scene unfold from a lounge chair in her tiny bikini, distracting the hell out of some of the camera guys but getting no reaction from Dylan whatsoever. She couldn't take her eyes off him as he played out the scenario.

God, he was incredibly sexy emerging from the water at the end of the scene, shirtless with a grizzled beard and his long hair plastered in soft waves around his face. His jeans clung to him deliciously, and he glistened in the afternoon sun, little rivulets of water making their way slowly down his muscled chest to disappear beneath his waistband. The water was freezing, Dylan said, but the air was unusually warm for late spring, and once the director called the final cut of the day, the crew decided to take a swim. Penelope eagerly joined them, while Angela decided instead to take a walk and "look for some wildlife." As planned, Penelope watched for the signal that she was in place—a little glint of a mirror reflecting the sun, and then she howled in pain, neck deep in the frigid water.

"What's wrong?" Dylan asked, making his way over to her while she choked on water and gasped for air.

"Ow!" she cried. "I stepped on something—I think I sprained my ankle!" She hopped on one foot, and then howled again. "Oh shit—the other one!" Her face slid under the water, and she pulled the string on her bikini top, pushing it to the bottom and placing a rock on top of it to keep it there.

Dylan was there in a moment, pulling her up. "Hey!" he yelled once her head broke the surface. "Are you OK?"

"I don't know," she rasped, coughing. "I don't think I can walk. I think it might be broken!"

Dylan grumbled, but he put his arm under her legs and swung her up, carrying her toward the shore. Penelope rested her head against his shoulder and wrapped her arms around his neck, pressing her bare breasts against him. "Ow, ow, ow," she moaned. "I'm sorry— my foot got jammed between some rocks and...ow!"

"Yeah, and you somehow managed to lose your top, too, I see," Dylan said suspiciously. "It's going to be fine, don't worry," he added, calling for someone to get a towel to cover her. As he made his way out of the water with Penelope in his arms, Angela began taking shot after shot from behind a clump of bushes a good distance away. No one noticed her as they ran to help Penelope into a chair to tend to her 'injury.' Supposedly hearing the commotion, Angela ran over to see about her boss, and although they could see no visible signs of swelling, it was determined that Angela should take Penelope back to The Village to be examined more thoroughly. That suited Penelope just fine—one night in a tent was more than enough for her, plus she could see to some final details before Dylan returned. They pulled off the road once they got out of sight and checked out the photos Angela had taken, smiling in agreement. Steve, Angela's new best friend and computer geek extraordinaire, could definitely do something with these shots, they were sure of it.

Chapter 31

The email came on a Wednesday morning, Tia's longest day of the week. She had no breaks from the kids, no specials, barely any time to use the freaking bathroom. She checked her mail every morning, a habit she'd gotten into since she and Dylan were in two completely different time zones. She sat at her kitchen table with her coffee and smiled when she saw his name in her inbox, but then stared at the screen while her coffee went cold, unable to believe what she was reading.

Tia, This is incredibly hard for me to say. The last thing I ever wanted to do was to hurt you. Believe me, it was never my intention. I know you've been through hell, and I never wanted to be the cause of any more pain for you. You'll always have a special place in my heart, and the time we spent together will always be full of good memories for me. But I've realized, now that we're apart, that things could just never work out between us. We're too different; our lives are too different. I never thought I'd say this, but it's time for us to move on. I'm with Penelope now, and even though I never dreamed it was possible, she understands me like no one else ever could. She lives the same life I do, and knows the demons I face. I wish you nothing but the best in the future, and I'm sorry that I can't be a part of it with you. But we both have to face the reality of our situation, and admit that in the long run, we would have hurt each other even more if we tried to force something that could just never be. I am so sorry, and will never forget you. I think it's best that we make a clean break—I've changed my number and email so we can both move on more easily. You are a great person, and I know you'll find someone who will make you happy—happier than I could ever make you. I wish you all the best, Dylan.

"Oh my God!" she breathed. "Dylan, no!" she whispered to her empty kitchen as tears burned in her eyes. "I don't get it!" she said aloud. "Why?" She couldn't take her eyes off the screen, reading the words over and over and trying to make sense of them as her tears spilled down her cheeks. But no matter how many times she read them, they didn't make a damn bit of sense. She'd just talked to him a week ago, and everything was fine—he'd told her he loved her and that Jessa was working on her tickets to go see him. Now she'd never see him again? How could everything have changed since then? How could he say that she would be happier with someone else? And maybe worst of all, how could he possibly be with that horrible conniving woman? How could Penelope have won him over? A million thoughts ran through her head, each more horrible than the last, and she was completely overwhelmed by her emotions.

She felt sick suddenly, and ran into the bathroom to throw up. She caught a glimpse of herself in the mirror; puffy red eyes, blotchy cheeks, mascara streaked down her face. God, she had to pull herself together and go to work—how in the world was she going to get through the day?

She fixed her face the best she could and sat back at the table. This couldn't be—it just couldn't. She picked up her phone and dialed his number, her heart breaking when she heard the recorded voice telling her that the number had been changed. She fell into a kitchen chair and immediately responded to the email.

Dylan, I don't understand! The last time we talked, we were discussing our plans for the holidays and you said you couldn't wait to see me and that you loved me, and suddenly we're through? Just like that? Please, just call me so we can talk. I need you to explain what's going on, how you went from loving me to dumping me with an email, for God's sake! I love you so much! We knew there would be challenges in our relationship with your job, but I thought we had it worked out—you know I'd do anything for you, just please call me. Please! Tia

She barely kept it together and as the day progressed, and she knew she'd be a wreck tomorrow. She put together sub plans for Thursday and Friday and planned to take the days off sick. Everyone noticed her red eyes and constant sniffles as she fought back tears throughout the day, so no one questioned that she wasn't feeling well. She had to get a hold of Dylan and fix this—there was no way she'd just accept that they were suddenly finished. When she got home and there was no reply to her email, she curled up on the couch in fetal position and called Lexi to come over.

"Oh God, he broke up with you in a fucking *email*?" Lexi shouted, reading it for the second time. "I can't believe it!"

"I can't either. Damn it, Lex, how am I supposed to deal with this? We were in love, Lexi—IN LOVE! And he pulls this 'Dear John' shit on me? He's done with me? Just like that? I just can't even process it!" The tears spilled down her cheeks freely, and Lexi pulled her into an embrace.

"You can't let it go like this," she said. "You just can't. There was something really good between the two of you, and that conniving bitch got her teeth into him? I gave him a lot more credit than to fall for someone like her. She's a snake! He's smarter than that!"

"What else can I do?" she sobbed. "Of course I tried to call him to get an explanation, but it's true, his number's disconnected. And if he changed his email too, I have no way to even get in touch with him—no way at all. He didn't answer my email today—I don't even know if he got it."

"There has to be something," she pondered. "You can still write to him."

"It takes something like two weeks for a letter to get there and another two for a reply. It'll be Christmas before I could even hope for an answer, if he even reads it! What do I even say in the letter, Hey, got your email, don't agree, what the hell is going on?"

"That about sums it up," she said, shaking her head. "I just can't believe that he'd write you off so easily! You guys were tight—it wasn't just some summer romance. Anyone could see it."

"Apparently not Dylan," she cried, the tears coming again. "Oh Lex, what am I going to do?"

"You're going to write to him right now and demand some answers!" she commanded. "And you are not going to give up on life again. You just got it back, for chrissakes!"

"I know," she whispered, defeated. "Listen Lex, thanks for coming, but I really need some time to get my head around this." She threw up her hands and gasped. "Oh God, I should have known! In the back of my mind this was always my biggest fear! He's always been out of my league! I thought he was different; hoped he could be, but it was always a fantasy for me you know—it was too good to be true."

"It was not a fantasy! I saw the two of you together! I saw the way he looked at you, the way you were together." She slapped the table with her hand. "I just don't get it!" she yelled. "That doesn't sound like him at all! I just can't imagine him doing this! Not to anyone, but especially not to you!"

"Well, he did," Tia said sadly. "So much for getting my life back on track." Tia eyes snapped open as the realization hit home. "Oh God, they'll be all over the tabloids. It's just what Penelope wanted. I'll have to see them together every time I go to the grocery store—I don't know how I'm going to do that!" She buried her face into Lexi's shoulders and let the emotions come. Her darkest fears had come true, and the life she was happily planning for herself had come to a bitter and abrupt end. "I need to go to bed, Lex. I need some tea and a quick escape from this whole thing."

"No way," Lexi said. "You are not going to shut yourself off from the world again like you did when you lost Nick." Her voice softened. "I know it hurts, honey, but I can't stand to see you like that again. It's not going to be easy, I know. Heartbreak never is. But he's a bastard to do this to you and an even bigger one for buying into that bitch's shit. She's behind this, not him—I still say it doesn't seem like something he would do! It stinks of Penelope!"

Tia was racked with a fresh set of sobs. "Oh God, I'll never even be able to get close to him again! I could never get backstage, couldn't even get someone to pass him a message! I'll never even talk to him again!"

Lexi just held her and let her cry. She was right, unfortunately. If Dylan was done with her, there was nothing Tia could do about it. She'd never get an opportunity to even get near him—he was too big of a star. Reluctantly, Lexi made her some tea and drew her a bath, and then she tucked her in as best she could and went to sleep in the spare room. There was no way she was leaving Tia alone tonight. She could hear the sobs in the next room, and couldn't close her own eyes until Tia finally cried herself out and fell into a fitful sleep.

Penelope smiled at her computer screen. She'd seen the email, then. Penelope knew that the instant Tia read it she'd picked up her phone and tried calling Dylan, only to hear that the number had been disconnected. Oh how she wished she could see the look on the little bitch's face when she read the line informing her that she and Dylan were now a couple. She wondered if she should answer the email, break her heart into a few more pieces, but decided that Dylan wouldn't do that, so she reluctantly let it go. She took out the instructions she'd gotten from Angela and typed in some commands. When 'block sender' came up as an option, she clicked it happily—the next time Tia tried to send an email to Dylan she'd get one of those demon things and she'd know it was over.

Penelope stood up and spun in slow circles around her little living room, smiling broadly to herself. Everything had fallen into place, and the timing couldn't have been more perfect. It was all going her way. She'd started intercepting Dylan's letters to Tia over a week ago, and had her plane ticket tucked safely in the little box she kept under her bed, so she wouldn't be showing up for Christmas. Neither of them would get another letter, and all other forms of communication were blocked. She could officially write the teacher out of Dylan's life and out of her hair. She sat down and closed her eyes, taking deep slow breaths in through her nose and exhaling through her mouth. It was time for her next role; the sympathetic friend who would be there to help Dylan move on with his life after being dumped. He'd be back this afternoon, and he'd find out Tia was done with him, then she could sweep in and pick up the pieces. Their first on screen kiss was scheduled for early next week, and his vulnerability would play right into her hands.

The first thing Dylan did when he got back from the shoot was to boot up his computer, then he picked up his new phone and punched the contact icon for Tia's number. It would be early evening for her, and he couldn't wait to hear her voice—he'd had a really rough few days dealing with the Jessa situation and then being so isolated from everything. It would be really hard to tell her about Jessa—the two girls had become friends over the months they'd spent together and he was sure Tia would be nearly as hurt as he was by her betrayal. He'd leave out the part about Jessa being in love with him, though; she didn't need to hear that. The couch beckoned, and he kicked off his shoes and plopped down with the phone next to his ear. He couldn't wait to catch up with her and find out if she'd gotten her plane ticket yet.

When he heard the message that the number had been disconnected, he didn't panic at first. He went back to his contact list and selected her again, waiting for the series of clicks and beeps that connected them across oceans. The message repeated itself, and he frowned. He scrolled through the contact list again and it appeared at first glance that they were all there—the card from the old phone was supposed to keep them all intact.

Shit, he thought, going over to the table and sitting in front of the computer. He'd have to email her, then, and hopefully she'd be home and checking her mail regularly. He could send his new number that way, and then reprogram hers once she called him—there must have been some sort of error when they made the switch. Of course he didn't have it written down anywhere or memorized; in this electronic age you didn't have to know those things, they were just always at your fingertips.

His computer was taking a long time to boot up. He tapped his fingers on the table impatiently, waiting for the welcome screen to appear. *Come on*, he thought, *can something go my way?* The past couple days had done nothing to ease his mind about how he left things with Jessa; he still had a lot of trouble believing that he could have been so wrong about her, or that she could have betrayed him so maliciously. The more time he had to think about it, the less realistic it seemed. But he couldn't ignore the evidence that stared him right in the face—it all came down to that damn scarf.

He just wanted so badly to hear Tia's voice; she would soothe him and make him feel better. When his computer finally lit up, he pulled up his email, smiling when he saw her name in his inbox. His smile quickly disappeared when he read the words on the screen.

Dylan, I don't know how to tell you this, so I'm just going to come out and say it. We have to end things between us. I had the most amazing time with you, but now that I'm home and back to my old life, I realize that things could never work out between us. I can't give up my career, and I realized that there's no way I can stand to be with someone who's going to be gone from me more than they're with me. It kills me to see other girls flirting with you constantly, and I just can't take it. You're better off being with someone who shares your world and who understands the challenges you face. I can't thank you enough for the summer, but now that it's over, I realize that I need normalcy in my life, and I could never have that with you. Please don't try to contact me. I've changed my number and my email so we can have a clean break. I'll always love your music, and we'll always have Paris...
Tia

"What the FUCK!" Dylan yelled, slapping the table with his open palm hard enough to send a glass crashing to the floor. It wasn't possible—things were going from bad to worse. Tia was breaking up with him? In a fucking *email*? It didn't make a damned bit of sense! The last time they'd spoken things had been fine; he ran through their conversation in his mind, looking for any indication that things were anything but good between them and couldn't come up with anything. They were talking about being together for Christmas, for chrissake, and now suddenly, for no good reason, she didn't want to hear from him ever again?

He refused to accept it, and picked up his phone, punching the key before remembering that it wouldn't connect. What the hell? He couldn't talk to her at all? This couldn't be happening! He fell onto the couch, staring at the phone in his hand. She'd really disconnected her number? Just to keep him from calling her?

His computer screen flashed twice, and a skull and crossbones showed up on his screen just before it went blank. "Not this too," he growled, restarting it and waiting, his leg bouncing up and down and his fingers tapping, until it finally came up. When he opened his email, he saw that all the messages were gone—his inbox was empty. "Bloody fucking hell!" he yelled, clicking on the link to his address book. At least those were still there—thank God—and he selected Tia's address and wrote her.

Dear Tia, What the hell is going on? I just got the most horrible email from you. Please tell me it was some sort of sick joke! I am not done with you, not by a long shot. I'm in love with you, damn it, and that counts for something. Whatever issues you're having are because of the distance right now, and that's not going to last forever. I promised that we'd work out anything that got in our way, and I meant it. I just can't let things go like this.

A lot of shit has gone down here in the past couple days and it's been really rough. I had to change my phone number—I'll explain everything when we talk. WE NEED TO TALK TIA, I know we can work things out! It's only another few weeks until we can see each other again—you should have gotten your ticket already. Please call me as soon as you get this message, and please come—when we're together again things will look different, I promise you. I love you!!! Dylan

He added his new cell number and hit send, then sat down immediately to write her a personal letter, but threw the paper down in disgust when he realized it would take weeks to even reach her. *Damn it!* he thought—there couldn't be a worse time to be halfway around the world. He couldn't call her, she didn't have his new number, and he didn't know if she'd even read his email if she was really serious about ending their relationship. He was hurt, confused, and incredibly pissed off, and he picked the paper up off the floor and poured it all into a letter anyway. He put Paris pictures in the envelope with this one—he wanted to remind her of the first time he'd told her he loved her, and of how happy they were together. He sealed the envelope and put it on the little shelf next to the door. He'd have Angela take it into town and post it for him first thing in the morning. He fumed again over how long it would take to reach her, and she suddenly felt very far away from him, further than she'd felt the whole time he'd been here.

He paced the room, and finally pulled out his guitar and started playing.

When Penelope heard the pounding of angry music drifting in through her open windows, she smiled. Dylan got the message, she figured, and she opened her own email to read his response. It was a bit over the top, she thought, but he'd get over her. She'd make sure of it.

Tia poured everything she felt, everything she was into a letter to Dylan. It just didn't seem possible that after their last conversation, he was done with their relationship. She refused to let it go without a fight—they'd shared too much, loved too much for it to just be over. She hoped and prayed that the ticket would come in the mail—if she could just see him again, just tell him how much she'd missed him and how much she loved him—it would all be alright. She included some pictures she'd taken in Paris from the top of the Eiffel Tower, where'd he'd told her he loved her. She played *Worlds Collide*, the song he'd written for her, over and over on repeat as she wrote; six pages and still going strong. She checked her email, and her heart sank like a stone when she saw the mailer daemon. Dylan had changed his email, too—he really didn't want to hear from her.

Chapter 32

She went through the days on autopilot—she couldn't think of anything but Dylan, and people were noticing the difference in her. She tried not to let it show, but as the days passed without a call or an email or any other communication from him, she grew more and more depressed.

It was at the grocery store when she saw the first tabloid pictures. "Romance Down Under," the cover read, and there was a picture of Dylan and Penelope, him carrying her in his arms, topless no less, from the water at some beach. She stood staring, frozen in place, while the lady behind her prodded her to start unloading her groceries onto the belt. It was nearly impossible to keep from fleeing from the sight; she wanted nothing more than to leave her cart and run from the store, but she couldn't help herself—she picked up the issue and thumbed through the photos, wincing in physical pain as she took in glimpse after glimpse of the two of them together: sitting in lounge chairs sharing a beer, locked in an embrace, sharing an intimate meal at a small table, her entering his trailer while he held open the door. "Hollywood's Hottest New Couple," the byline read, and she felt a sick feeling in the pit of her stomach as she skimmed the article and was bombarded by the pictures. They'd obviously been taken from a distance without the subjects knowing, which made it even harder to stomach. It was all she could do to load her groceries onto the belt, pay for them and pack them. By the time she reached her car she was in tears, tossing things into the back seat, barely able to remain standing. She sat behind the wheel for a few minutes while she caught her breath, unable to trust her driving abilities in the heat of her emotion.

She called Lexi as soon as she got into the house, sobbing by the time she answered the phone. "Oh my God," she breathed. "Did you see the newest issue of Person to Person?"

"Obviously you have," she said, her voice full of sympathy. "I'd hoped you hadn't."

"How could I miss it?" she cried. "It was practically screaming in my face while I was standing in line at the grocery store. Oh fuck, it's going to be like from now on, isn't it?" she whispered. "I'm going to have to look at pictures of the two of them together constantly. I don't know how I can take it! It was all I could do to pay for my food and get the hell out of there!"

"I'm so sorry, honey," Lexi soothed. "I don't know what I can say or do to make it any easier—did you write to him?"

"Of course I did," she cried. "I've been writing every day—but I don't know if he's getting them, or reading them..." she broke down, her voice cracking with the emotion. "I guess I just have to face the facts. I'll never see him again."

"Did you ever get the plane ticket?" Lexi asked.

"No," she replied sadly, "it never came. I haven't gotten a letter from him in over two weeks. I wasn't worried at first because I knew he was shooting some wilderness scenes and wouldn't be near a post office, and it's so hard to know how the mail works from there."

"You could go anyway. You know he's going home for the holidays. You'd have a better chance of confronting him there than you would after he got back to the States. I'll buy your ticket—it'll be my Christmas gift to you."

Tia considered it for a minute, but shook her head. "No, I'm not going to do that. He's through with us, he's made that pretty obvious. Besides, there's no guarantee I would even see him. What am I going to do, look up 'Miller' in the phone book and start knocking on doors? It's an awfully common name, and I don't even know his parents' first names. Aaurg!" she yelled. "I'm alone again. I don't know what to do, Lex, it's too fucking much!"

Lexi was at her house in ten minutes, and she immediately put her arms around Tia and held her while she cried. "How about the two of us get away for a week over the holidays?" she suggested. "We could go sit on a beach somewhere in the Caribbean, drink pina coladas and shamelessly flirt with cabana boys, get massages on the beach..."

"Oh damn it, the holidays!" Tia whined. "When I told my parents I was going to Australia, they booked a cruise. I don't even have a place to spend Christmas now!"

"Of course you do—you'll spend it with us!" Lexi said immediately. "You know you're one of the family. My parents would love to have you."

"Son of a bitch!" Tia bellowed. "I'm sure I'll take you up on that, but right now, I don't know how I can celebrate anything. I'd be horrible company on the beach, too, and it wouldn't be fun for either of us. Maybe spring break, OK? I might be more human by then."

"OK, spring break in the Bahamas, then," Lexi suggested.

"Lex," she said sadly, "I need to keep this break-up a secret until after Christmas, OK?"

"Why?" she asked, flabergasted.

"My parents are so excited about their trip, and if I tell them I'm not going to Australia; that Dylan and I broke up--" her voice cracked as she said it, "they'll cancel their trip. Or worse, insist that I go with them. Either way, I don't want them to know just yet. And for God's sake, please don't say anything to Jace—the last thing I need is for him to start bugging me."

Lexi looked at the ground. "About that," she said slowly.

"Oh shit," she moaned, "please don't tell me he already knows!"

"I didn't tell him, but Ryan was there when you called, and I'm sure he heard. He might have mentioned something to him, I can't be sure."

"Shiiit," Tia groaned. "Please intervene, would you? I don't want to deal with him."

"I will, don't worry," she said, but she definitely sounded worried.

The flowers arrived at school three days later, a huge bouquet of tropical colors. Lilly called her down to the office while her kids were in art class.

"Looks like someone's thinking of you today," she said slyly, pointing at the bouquet. "These were just delivered for you."

Dylan! Tia thought, pulling off the plastic to get at the card. They were so much like the flowers he'd gotten her when they'd said goodbye the first time; *pretty and unique, just like you*, he'd said. She pulled the card out of the envelope and read the message, her face falling. "How about a fresh start?... Jace" the card read.

All Tia's hopes came crashing down. "When hell freezes over," Tia whispered under her breath, tossing the card in the recycle bin. She completely deflated, and was close to tears.

Lilly looked at her with concern. "Now that doesn't look like the face of someone who just got beautiful flowers from her boyfriend," she said. "What's wrong?"

Tia looked up at her friend, unable to hide her pain. "Dylan and I broke up, Lilly," she admitted. "These aren't from him, but I was hoping they were."

"What? When did that happen? Why didn't you tell me?"

"A couple weeks ago," she sighed. "I haven't said anything to anyone yet really. I don't want it to be true, and I keep hoping that we'll work things out somehow. Plus, my parents have planned a trip for Christmas, and I don't want them to feel obligated to..."

"Australia," Lilly said sadly. "You were supposed to go and meet him there." She pulled Tia into a hug. "Oh honey, I'm so very sorry. But he's not worth a lick if he doesn't know what a good thing he's got in you."

"He's already got someone else now, actually," she said. "Someone he works with." The tabloid pictures ran through her mind again. She'd seen five other covers on several different magazines before she'd started ordering her groceries online and having them delivered.

"No wonder you've been in such a funk lately," she said, rubbing slow circles over Tia's back. "I just thought you were fighting that bug that's been going around." She pulled back and took Tia by the shoulders. "So what're you doing for Christmas, then? Marcus and I would love to have you join us."

"That's sweet Lilly, thanks, but I think I'll probably be going to Lexi's."

"Well, the invitation's open if you need it," she said, "and you know I'm always here for you if you want to talk. You know I love bashing men, especially over a bottle of Merlot."

Tia glanced up with longing at the picture of Dylan that still held its place of honor on Lilly's bulletin board. "I'll let you know," she said, walking out of the office.

"Wait, don't forget your flowers!" Lilly called to her.

"You keep them," she said, her voice flat and emotionless. "I don't want them."

Chapter 33

Penelope checked out the photos Angela had taken with her telephoto lens. "I like this one, this one, and this one," she said pointing to the images. "Go ahead and submit them."

"Got it," she said, agreeing with Penelope's choices. Most of them had been taken during filming so the relationship was purely fabricated, but since they were both pretty good actors, they looked natural, like they were a real couple. Plus, by the time Steve got done with them, they'd all be in different locations that looked nothing like the set.

Penelope had letters now, dozens of them. Angela now delivered them straight to her, and she'd been instructed to destroy the ones that came for Dylan. She was much more interested in the letters Dylan sent anyway—she was able to erase Tia's name and insert her own, adding them to her collection of times she and Dylan hadn't yet shared, but would soon enough. Her photo album was full, and she'd moved on to a second scrap book. The letters were coming so frequently now that she hadn't had time to keep up—her little shoe box was nearly full and she needed to find some time to get to them; put them in their proper places. It was only a matter of time now until Dylan turned to her for the comfort that he so desperately needed—the touch that only a woman could give. She left him alone the first week; let him wallow in the fact that his precious schoolteacher had dumped him. He was moody and irritable and she did her best to get him to confide in her, but he said nothing about the break up. She was also disappointed that he kept writing her—sometimes two letters in the same day—and that he didn't take down a single picture of her. She let it go for a few more days, but when she saw him sitting in a chair in front of his trailer the next Friday morning, staring blankly into the empty field that bordered their makeshift accommodations, she poured him a mug of coffee and went out to see him.

"Good morning!" she chirped, balancing the steaming mugs.

He jumped in his seat—she'd obviously startled him from his deep thoughts.

"Sorry, I didn't mean to scare you," she giggled. "I saw you sitting out here without coffee and figured you might like a cup."

"Thanks," he said absent mindedly, taking the coffee and cradling it in his hands without drinking it.

"What's up?" she asked casually. "You look like you got up on the wrong side of the bed this morning."

"I didn't sleep at all," he said.

"Dylan, is something wrong?" The concern in her voice was just enough to sound both innocent and genuine. "You know, it's been pretty hard not to notice that something's been going on with you the past couple weeks. I'm your friend, remember? You can talk to me about anything."

"It'll be fine," he said, still hoping he'd hear from Tia and not volunteering any further information. He'd sent at least a dozen emails and written two more letters last night. There was still a chance she'd respond, and until then, he wasn't giving Penelope anything that she could misconstrue.

Penelope was disappointed that he didn't share the news with her, but didn't let it show. She went up behind him and wrapped her arms around his neck from behind and whispered in his ear, "Guess which scene we need to practice?"

Shit, he thought. Tomorrow they'd do their first romantic scene and have their first on- screen kiss. Dylan had figured he'd get through it by thinking about Tia, but now, thinking about her broke his heart. He'd have to get through it somehow, but right now, the last thing he wanted to do was pretend to be romantic with Penelope Valentine. He didn't know if he could pretend anything, actually—a deep depression was taking hold of him and he felt powerless to fight it.

"Can we do it a bit later?" he said. "I was thinking about running into town this morning, picking up a few things and dropping off some mail." He could check to see if he'd gotten any letters from Tia then too, and get away from this place for a little bit.

"Actually," Penelope said, thinking fast, "I've got some stuff going on this afternoon and then we have the evening shoot...and Angela is going into town anyway. Just make a list and she can get whatever you need. Sorry, but I think we're going to have to run the scene now."

"Fine, whatever," he said absently, going into the trailer and coming out with a pad, a pen, and two envelopes. He scribbled a list, and handed the stack to Penelope.

"I'll just go get my script, and drop these to Angie. I'll be right back!"

She exhaled with relief that Dylan hadn't insisted on going to the post office—her plan depended on the two of them not having any contact. Angela had told her that Tia's letters were still coming too—

why wouldn't either of them just give it up? She'd have to keep a closer eye on that in the future, she realized—if just one letter got through, everything would come crashing down. She slipped the envelopes under a magazine on her coffee table to read later—she could hardly wait. The letters he wrote these days were dripping with love and sentiment, and she loved imagining they were all about her. Soon enough, he'd be saying those things to her, and her stomach did little back flips at the thought. She grabbed her script, dropped the shopping list at Angela's, and grew giddy with anticipation at the thought of her and Dylan's first big make-out scene. She hoped they'd have to practice it over and over before it was perfect.

She was more than a little disappointed when they got to the kiss and Dylan backed off. They had run the lines, professing love for each other in hushed tones. It was the easiest role she'd ever played; she didn't need to act anymore when she told Dylan that she'd been in love with him for longer than she could remember and couldn't believe they'd wasted so much time not being together. When she leaned in for the kiss, though, Dylan pulled back and put his hands on her shoulders, stopping her forward momentum. "Um, the scene's not over yet," she said seductively.

"It is for now," Dylan said, turning away. "I think that was great, we'll nail it in one take tomorrow."

"But the kiss..."

"Is for when the cameras are rolling," he finished. "I don't need to practice that; I'm fairly well accomplished, trust me."

"But we don't know what it's like to kiss each other," she said. "We need to work on the chemistry."

"There isn't any chemistry, Penelope. It's acting—pretend and make-believe. It just has to look good on camera, and it will."

Penelope was incredibly disappointed, but couldn't let it show too much. She wanted their first kiss to be perfect, not in front of the entire crew, and certainly not in one take. She'd have to blunder a line or two, or giggle or something, to make sure they needed to run that scene over and over again. "Of course it will!" she said as she ground her teeth behind her smile. "Hey," she added, changing the subject, "are you hungry? I made my aunt's casserole again last night and it should be out of the oven in," she looked at her watch, "eight minutes. Interested?"

"No thanks, I'm not hungry," he said, turning and walking into his trailer and shutting the door. She heard the strum of his guitar, sad slow notes drifting out the window and headed back to her own trailer. This day hadn't gone as she'd planned it at all.

Three more weeks passed, each of the players surviving in their own private hell. For Tia, it involved going through the motions at work, hiding her feelings, and trying to appear cheerful on the outside when her insides felt raw and shredded. She'd had a fair amount of practice when she'd first lost Nick, but this was different—Nick had been taken from her, but Dylan had made the choice to remove himself from her life. None of it felt right to her, and no matter how hard she tried to convince herself that it was over, she couldn't help holding out at least a shred of hope that he'd come to his senses and come back to her—regardless of the evidence staring her in the face constantly, she couldn't make herself believe he would chose Penelope to spend his life with.

She'd taken off the Eiffel Tower necklace and placed it in her jewelry box, but people at work noticed and asked why she wasn't wearing it so she had to put it back on to keep up the façade. It pained her whenever she caught sight of it in the mirror and she'd remember what Dylan had said as he put it around her neck that night in Paris. It was supposed to help her remember that no matter how far apart they were, she was always close to his heart.

She refused to go into any store or even the gas station for fear of being confronted with another picture of Dylan and Penelope smiling or embracing on the cover of a magazine. But no matter how she tried, she couldn't escape it. She was in the dentist's office when she saw the headline that read, 'Engaged?' above a picture of the two of them, their foreheads touching, looking deeply into each other's eyes. She'd had to leave and reschedule the appointment.

The television was quickly becoming a source for reminders, as well. There were so many tabloid TV shows, commercials for tabloid TV shows, entertainment news during regular broadcasts—but as bad as it made her feel, she couldn't help but stare whenever Dylan's image was projected on the screen. She wanted to hate him for what he did to her, and the hurt and anger were still close to unbearable, but there was still that little part of her that just couldn't make sense of it—she still had too much trouble believing that Dylan would just dump her without an explanation—it just wasn't the kind of person he was. As the weeks went by however, and she turned her calendar over to December, staring sadly at the little hearts and smiley faces she'd drawn all around the words *'Dylan in Australia!'* over the bottom half of the page that would be her Christmas break, her hopes faded into fog and drifted away, and she realized that she was going to have to completely rethink her New Year's resolutions. She was going to have to decide to go on with her life without Dylan.

Penelope was incredibly frustrated by Dylan's lack of interest. She was running out of time—her goal was to be in his bed before Christmas, and to have him ask her to join him in Australia for the holidays. Obviously, Tia wasn't going to be showing up, she smiled.

Penelope didn't speak to her family at all; her mother was a demanding bitch who always wanted something from her, and her father hadn't been part of her life until she started acting, showing up suddenly and wanting to be a daddy again. Yeah, right. Her older sister was so jealous of her younger sibling's success that she refused to speak to her. She was probably still furious that Penelope had stolen her husband, but she'd given him back, hadn't she? What it meant was that she had no plans for the holiday; no wonderful get together to share old times and hand out presents. She'd told Dylan that she was going to spend the holidays with her favorite aunt, she of the famous French toast casserole, and she hoped that when dear old auntie kicked the bucket, if nothing else, Dylan would take pity on her and invite her to his celebration. That was the last resort; of course, she'd planned to be a couple by then and get a real invitation. But that was only a few weeks away now, and she hadn't made any headway in getting him to make a move on her. She'd given him plenty of opportunity and made it obvious that she was willing, but he was still stuck on that stupid girl. He was still writing her letters nearly every freaking day, hoping that she would give in and respond. Maybe it was time for him to lose her address, as well as all her other contact information. She needed him to get his mind cleared of her once and for all. She'd have to look into that.

It was killing her that he was nothing more than professional with her on the set, too. Their first kissing scene was downright depressing for her—she meant to screw something up so they'd have to reshoot the scene and she could kiss him again, but when his lips touched hers, she just melted. She tried to intensify the kiss, but he gave it exactly what the scene called for and refused to accept her tongue. When the director yelled "cut," he turned and walked away without a word, wiping his lips with the back of his hand where her tongue had touched him. There were still a couple pretty hot scenes coming up before the break though, and the big ones in Bora Bora when they got back. She was already dreaming about that.

She grew increasingly flustered that Dylan hadn't shared the break up with her, too. He had to know that she was aware that the letters had stopped coming, although Angela had confirmed that they were still rolling in regularly. She wanted him to confide in her, to let her know himself that he was available again. It bothered her that he was still wasting time and energy on such a plain and ordinary person—he was a big star and could have anyone he wanted, and he was still writing her, begging her in his letters to just call him; to give him an explanation. He still loved her, he wrote, and he refused to believe that they were over. At least he wasn't writing twice a day anymore, so perhaps he was finally getting ready to move on. She'd have to make sure he had every opportunity to do just that—and soon. It was already December and they had just a little over a week of filming left before they broke for the holidays, and she had every intention of spending them in Australia with Dylan.

Dylan was getting through the days, but barely. He still hadn't heard anything from Tia, and it was eating at him. Angela had arranged a bouquet for him days ago—big tropical flowers like the ones he'd sent after their first goodbye, when things were still uncertain between them. She'd have received it by now, and he thought it might prompt her to call him. Hell, he didn't know if she was even reading his letters.

He just couldn't get it out of his head that everything had been perfect—or at least as perfect as it could be for two people living so far apart—the last time he'd spoken to her. He still couldn't convince himself that Tia would dump him with a two paragraph email and never look back—she had too much compassion for that. The letters she wrote him were never less than three pages long, and the tone of the email just didn't sound like her, which kept nagging at the back of his mind. He'd already decided that he'd find her again when he was through with the movie—he needed to get an explanation from her face to face, one way or another. If she looked him in the eyes and told him she was through with him, he'd walk away; but he couldn't do it just yet.

He had to face the facts though, he supposed. If she didn't want anything more to do him, there was damned little he could do about it from the other side of the globe. He wouldn't be back in the states until February, and he was scheduled in the studio with the band in early March. He'd hoped to write the songs for the new album while he was here, but all he managed to write were mushy love songs for Tia. A few would make the cut, but he needed a lot more variety to bring to the table. The guys had sent him some tracks, but he hadn't had the heart to work on any fun music. He needed to get his head out of his ass and move on, he thought. Tia had made her decision, and apparently, it was final. What kept him hoping, though, was going home. She had to have gotten the ticket before the shit hit the fan; maybe she'd feel guilty enough or lonely enough or something to come and see him after all. That was what he couldn't get out of his head; why he couldn't just move on.

Penelope was driving him crazy, too. It was obvious that she knew something was up—she had to have noticed that there weren't any letters coming in from Tia, and he hadn't spoken to her on the phone in what seemed like forever. She seemed to be pressing things too, trying to make something happen between them that was never going to happen. Even if he'd never met Tia, Penelope Valentine was far from his type. No matter how nice she'd been he still believed that she was out for herself at all costs, and he wouldn't put it past her to use his breakup with Tia to her advantage. She was already pushing the envelope whenever she could, trying to make a lot more of their on-screen scenes than there should be, making suggestive comments, pressing herself against him in ways that were more than friendly. They'd had to film several scenes that were fairly intimate, but the biggest ones were yet to come, especially when their characters traveled to Bora Bora, where their broken romance would take a serious U-turn. He worried a lot about her level of professionalism when it came to being nearly naked with him on the beach.

There was another, smaller love scene that they'd shoot next week, just before they broke for the holiday, and he was already dreading it. Penelope was really trying to up the ante during rehearsals, insisting that they run through the love scenes—that she needed some practice before the real thing. "There's more to filming a love scene than knowing the words, Dylan," she'd said, "we have to know how and when to touch each other, where to change our breathing, which way to turn our bodies—you can't just get on set and wing it."

He hated to admit it, but she was probably right. He needed the practice more than she did—he'd never performed a heavy love scene, and really didn't have a clue what he was doing. Being in character wasn't enough—he had to feel something to make it come across as real, and lately, he hadn't been feeling much of anything. His whole life had become an act, and he was doing a pitiful job just playing himself.

Chapter 34

They were in his trailer running lines when Angela came in. Penelope threw her a hard glance. "We're rehearsing, Angela," she said coldly. "I told you I didn't want to be interrupted."

"I'm sorry," she said, eyes down, "but your sister is trying to get a hold of you. She said it was very urgent, but she keeps getting your voice mail."

Penelope threw her hands up in frustration. "What does that little bitch want?" she spat, pulling out her phone and punching the power button.

"I don't know," Angela said, "she just said that it was extremely important that she talk to you." As scripted, Angela walked out, apologizing again for the interruption.

"She never calls me," she explained to Dylan as she waited for her phone to come on line. "I'm so sorry, I'm sure it'll only take a minute."

"No problem," Dylan said, grabbing a bag of chips from the counter and munching a few as he dropped onto the couch. If she needed privacy, she could walk out, he thought. It was his trailer.

Penelope punched a few buttons on her phone, and waited for the connection to go through. "What?" he heard her say into the phone, without so much as a greeting.

Dylan watched as Penelope's face fell and went pale. Her voice changed to a whisper. "No," she breathed. "She what?... "When?..." I can't believe...and you're just telling me now?" She listened intently for a couple moments as the color rushed back into her face with fury. "I can't believe you would do that!" she screamed. "I know you hate me, but...you bitch!" She stumbled, and Dylan jumped up to catch her fall. She sank into the sofa where he'd been sitting and dropped the phone to the floor. He reached down and picked it up, but hearing no one on the other end, pushed the disconnect button and set the phone on the arm of the couch.

"What is it?" Dylan asked, genuinely concerned. She looked as if she were about to pass out.

Penelope just stared straight ahead, unseeing, and tears began slipping from her eyes. Dylan took her by the shoulders and shook her a bit to get her attention. "Talk to me, Penelope, what's going on?" he demanded.

"It's my aunt," Penelope croaked, "the one who's French toast I've made you? She's... dead! Heart attack...and those bitches already buried her!" She inhaled sharply, and the tears flowed steadily. "She was in the hospital for almost a week, and they didn't even call me to tell me..." She broke down into sobs, and threw herself into Dylan's arms. He held her and let the tears come; he knew the sorrow of loss, and regardless of his feelings for Penelope, he couldn't let her suffer alone.

"I'm so sorry, so sorry," he breathed as he held her. "If there's anything I can do..."

"I just can't believe she's gone!" Penelope gasped. "I just talked to her last week—oh God, it had to be just before it happened—and she was fine! Now she's dead?" She stood up and paced around the room, angry. "They didn't even tell me! I could've called her! What the fuck? I couldn't even send flowers to her funeral! It's not right!" She opened the door and yelled for Angela, who appeared within seconds.

"I need you to check on something for me," she sobbed to Angela, giving her the details. "Find me an obituary—did they really already bury her without even telling me?"

Angela left quickly to verify the obits, and Penelope sank back onto Dylan's couch. "She was the only family I had," she sobbed, leaning into his chest and crying on his shoulder. "The rest of them are horrible, horrible, people who hate me because of my success..."

Dylan put his arm around her shoulders and let her cry it out. "Penelope," he said gently, "I can't believe your own family would really..."

"Yes they would!" she interjected. "You don't know them—they hate me Dylan, they really do!" she sucked in a huge breath and let it out with a shudder. "They'd do it just to spite me;" she said angrily, "to see me suffer." She began sobbing again, and pressed her face into Dylan's chest once more. Angela returned, and her face pretty much told the whole story. Penelope saw it, as well.

"It's true, isn't it?" she whispered.

"I'm afraid so," Angela said, her eyes full of pity. "After I found the obituary I made a few phone calls, and she..." she paused, catching her own breath, "they buried her yesterday morning."

"Oh my God!" Penelope wailed, turning to Dylan. "Can you get me some wine, please?"

Dylan shook his head. "I don't really think that's the best idea..."

She turned to Angela. "Angela, get me some wine, please!" Angela scurried to fulfill her boss's wish, returning just a moment later with a full glass and the rest of the bottle.

"What can I do for you, Penelope?" she asked compassionately. "Please let me help. I know how much you loved her, and how much you must be hurting right now."

"It hurts so much!" she wailed, grabbing another tissue and wiping at her eyes. "Maybe can you stay with me tonight, Angie?" she pleaded. "I just don't think I can be alone."

Angela's eyes widened for a second, then softened. "Of course I will," she said, "just let me go try and reschedule that meeting with that TV exec, and I'll be right back," she said, turning to go.

"Oh no," Penelope whispered. "Is that the one you've been waiting on for weeks? The one it took you so long to get?"

"It's OK Penelope," Angela whispered. "You need me right now—I'll figure something out."

"No way, Angie," she said. "You've worked too hard to get that meeting. You have to go. What time is your appointment?"

"Seven tomorrow morning," she said sadly. "I was going to leave here about five."

"Oh, and you'll need your sleep. You can't spend the night on my love seat and expect to be in shape for a meeting that important. I love that you'd cancel for me, Ang, I really do, but I can't let you do it." She looked at Dylan hopefully, the question clearly written in her eyes.

Shit, he thought. He owed her this much—she'd shared her assistant with him, and tried to be kind... and he knew what it was like to lose someone. No one should go through it alone, and she really didn't have anyone else. "Please, Dylan," she whispered. "I don't think I can be alone tonight."

He compromised. "I'll sit with you until you fall asleep," he said. "That's really all I can do."

"Thank you," she whispered, taking a deep breath and wiping tears from her face.

He gathered his laptop, his guitar, some paper, and some notes from the guys and walked with her back to her trailer. At least he could get some work done, he thought, maybe pen some lyrics while he had some different emotions running through him. Music had always soothed his soul, so maybe he could play a little for Penelope; help her relax and get some sleep. He managed to convince her that wine wasn't going to help, and he put on some water for tea while she went to take a hot shower.

Dylan pulled out his notebook and started scribbling lyrics. The mixed feelings running through him were tugging his thoughts to Tia, once again, and he poured them onto his paper. *The veil hangs over midnight and I'm sitting here alone...Can't see you; touch you; face to face can't even get you on the phone...The moon hangs heavy as my heart blocking stars out from the sky...Alone and dark without you and I can't figure out just why/ You know you are my heart...I feel all torn up and broken whenever we're apart...Can't seem to do the simplest things can't even start/I need you back I need you near There's just this veil of midnight when you're not here...*

He was interrupted by the slam of the shower door. Startled from his thoughts, he turned quickly as she stepped out of the bathroom, completely naked.

"Bloody hell, Penelope," he barked, "put some goddamn clothes on!" He quickly moved to a stool at the counter so that his back was to her.

"I'm sorry if I offended you," she said, "but I always sleep in the nude. I can't stand clothes when I'm trying to sleep. Besides," she added, "I have these great Egyptian cotton sheets that are just wonderful against bare skin—you should feel them."

"I'm not feeling anything," he murmured.

"Oh come on, it's not like it's anything you won't see anyway, I'll be naked all over you when we do that love scene next month."

"Well, it isn't now," he said, keeping his back to her. "Just put something on or at least get into bed and pull up the covers."

"Oh fine," she said, climbing into the bed. Dylan stayed on the stool at the counter and took a pull from his beer, turning the pencil over in his fingers. So much for getting some work done, he thought ruefully.

He could hear Penelope crying softly in the bed behind him, the hitch of her breath shuddering against her sobs, and he was frozen. Going to her wasn't an option, he wasn't about to put himself into a situation that she could misconstrue, but he hated hearing someone in pain. He grabbed his guitar and started strumming a few chords—maybe it would help a little. Mentally, he put himself in his mother's studio and tried to create a mood—something soft and soothing but not sad. He lost himself in the music and didn't hear her come up behind him. She tugged up his shirt in one quick motion and pressed her breasts against his back, his guitar hitting the counter and digging into his ribs. His mind flashed to Tia, all those months ago, trapped by Bud's unwanted advances at *Last Stop*.

"Hold me Dylan, please," she begged close in his ear. "I don't want to be alone right now. Please."

He wanted to push her back, but gritted his teeth and held his ground, speaking firmly and clearly in a low voice. "Get off of me, Penelope, now, and get back in your bed, or I'm going to leave."

She began crying again, but pulled herself away and sat on the bed, wrapping the sheet around her. "Why don't you want me Dylan?" she whined. "Why are you being this way? We're both alone here, and don't think I haven't noticed that you haven't had a phone call or a letter from your little teacher in weeks!"

Dylan stood, and started collecting his things. He definitely didn't need to deal with this shit right now.

Penelope continued, her voice desperate. "We're both adults, we both have needs, and I need someone right now so desperately—I'm all alone in the world right now, Dylan, and you're the only friend I have—why are you turning your back on me?" she choked between sobs.

Dylan turned to face her, trying to keep his face calm. "I thought I made it perfectly clear when I said there wasn't ever going to be anything like that between us. With or without Tia, I'm not interested in a relationship with you, Penelope."

"But you haven't even given us a chance!" she leaned forward, dropping the sheet and exposing her right breast. She quickly pulled the sheet back up, but Dylan wasn't at all sure that dropping it had been an accident. Coming here had been a mistake, obviously, and it was time for him to go. He found it unbelievable that she would try to seduce him at a time like this—when she was mourning the loss of her favorite aunt.

"I'm sorry, but I've got to go. You can call Stan and see if there's someone else who can come stay with you, but it can't be me." He snapped his guitar into its case and tucked his laptop under his arm.

"Wait!" she wailed. "We're friends, right?" her voice was desperate now, pleading, "Please just let me come to Christmas with you, spend some time away from work and just get to know each other better. Now that my aunt's gone, I'll be all alone for the holidays—no one should be alone at Christmas!"

He turned to her with his things in his hands. "No," he said shortly. "Absolutely not—not even an option. Get it out of your head right now." He'd never consider inviting her—the thought of introducing Penelope to his parents made him wince. She began crying harder, begging him to stay, but he slipped out without another word and let the door bang shut against her pleas.

When he got back to his own trailer, Dylan went to his fridge and grabbed a beer, popping the top and taking a long swallow. The day had been exhausting, and he was drained. It was hard enough pretending to be in love with someone on camera, but when that someone kept trying to push things in real life, it became downright aggravating. He'd kept trying to tell himself that Penelope was really changing, that she was really becoming a better person and maybe even a friend, but doubt had continued to nag at the back of his mind. Tonight she'd made it pretty obvious that she still wanted a relationship with him, and that was going to seriously affect the tentative friendship they'd developed. He was looking forward to getting away and getting back home, where at least he'd see his parents and be away from her for a while. There was still the chance that Tia would change her mind and come—she hadn't sent the ticket back, so he assumed she still had it. Just another couple weeks now and he'd know the truth once and for all, and figure out how to get on with his life.

Chapter 35

Dylan finished off his beer staring out the window, and then hopped in the shower to wash the smell of Penelope off him. She wore some overbearing lotion or something, and his body and clothes reeked of it after the way she'd pressed up against him. He let the water run over him until it went cold, thinking about the last time he'd had Tia pressed against him. Fuck, he missed her.

He threw on some lounge pants and a t, grabbed another beer from the fridge and flopped down on the couch, jumping up immediately when he sat on something hard. He reached down between the cushions and pulled up Penelope's cell phone. "Bloody hell," he whispered to himself. It must have fallen between the cushions after Penelope got the call about her aunt and pretty much threw herself at him. He was about to toss it onto the table until morning when he changed his mind. He could just imagine her finding it missing and slinking over to his place to get it. Even with the dead aunt, he wouldn't put it past her to wait until he'd turned in and then try again to get into his bed. She'd certainly been shooting for that earlier in the evening. He picked it up and sighed; might as well bring it over to her and make another quick exit.

It was just dark and the moon hung full and heavy in the sky. This far from town a million stars seemed to twinkle overhead, and he thought maybe he'd take a walk after he delivered the phone and clear his head a little bit. Lights blazed in Penelope's trailer, and he could hear one of his songs playing through the open window with her voice singing along to the lyrics. She sounded happy, he thought, not at all like the woman he'd left less than an hour ago, crying over a dead relative. He knocked hard so she'd hear it over the music, and the door swung open from the rap of his knuckles; it had obviously not latched when he ran out of there earlier.

"Hey Penelope," he called as the door swung open, "you forgot your..."

Dylan froze in place, his hand still raised from the knock, stunned as he took in the scene before him. Penelope sat on her couch, surrounded by piles of papers, pictures, books, magazines and albums. She sat like a stone, her eyes wide like those of a frightened child caught in a forbidden act. Dylan's eyes locked on a picture that had fallen to the floor, a picture of him and Penelope at the top of the Eiffel Tower. Except he'd never been with Penelope to the top of the Eiffel Tower, and there was no way she could have this picture. He shook his head for a moment and blinked his eyes, but the image didn't change. He immediately recognized the sapphire dress that Tia had bought on the Champs Elysee and worn the night he'd first told her he loved her; only it was now Penelope's smiling face that swam above it. His eyes darted quickly across the table and the couch and he saw other pictures; London, Munich, Glasgow, Rome—all containing his own smiling image coupled with Penelope's. It wasn't possible, and it took a minute for his brain to absorb what he was seeing.

Penelope suddenly regained her power of movement and immediately began scooping the objects into a box. "Oh, hey Dylan," she said nervously. "Ummm, I'm really busy, can you come back later?" her voice shook with emotion and her face burned red.

Dylan leaned over and picked up the photograph that lay at his feet. He could see the cut marks of the scissors and feel the change in thickness where another photo had been laid underneath and glued. Tia's face had been cut out, replaced by Penelope's likeness.

"What the hell!" he growled, "how the hell did you get this, and why the fuck did you cut Tia out and put yourself in?"

Penelope just stared with glazed eyes, and continued shoving things into the box.

"Answer me, damn it!"

She scrambled for an answer, but she was clearly flustered. "Don't be mad," she squeaked. "I had some copies of your pictures made—it...it helped me get into my role with you as a couple," she continued haltingly. "I..."

"I never gave you these pictures," he yelled. "How the hell did you get them?" His eyes fell then on a pile of magazines, his picture all over the cover, with Penelope by his side. He sorted through the pile, reading headlines like, "Romance Down Under," and "Hollywood's Hot New Couple," and "Engaged?" Anger boiled up in him like an erupting volcano, colors exploding behind his eyes, and he threw a handful of them across the room, and then grabbed some more.

"What the fuck are these?" he hissed through gritted teeth, shaking them in her face, barely able to believe what he was seeing. "We never posed for these! How the hell did the tabloids get pictures of us together like this—*kissing*?" Then it hit him. "Bloody hell!—these are from filming!" he raged. "None of this is real!" In the back of his mind it dawned on him that Tia had seen them too, probably every time she went to the grocery store. He felt sick to his stomach as he checked the dates on the magazines and saw that they went back months.

Penelope's mouth opened and her jaw moved up and down, but only a few whimpers escaped from deep in her throat. She was still trying desperately to sweep the contents from the table into a box, but she was so flustered that she sent papers flying to the floor. Dylan reached over and picked up an envelope that was addressed to Tia in his handwriting. Bewildered and fuming he thrust out his hands, demanding she hand him the box. "Give it over," he said slowly and deliberately. "Now."

She clutched the box to her chest and yelled, "Get out! Get out of here right now!"

"I'm not going anywhere. Give me the fucking box!" He reached over and grabbed it from her hands, spilling its contents again over her lap, the floor, the table, the couch. She rose up to gather them again, desperately, but he put his hand on her shoulder and pushed her back onto the couch. All her resistance seemed to drain from her then, and her entire body slumped as silent tears began to spill down her cheeks. Dylan picked up a letter from the table, and his heart sank as anger once again threatened to erupt in his blood. He read the greeting, *Dearest Penelope*, her name written over a little white strip that covered the original recipient, and thought he'd explode. It was a letter he'd written to Tia almost a month ago, *the original letter,* and as he read the words he realized Tia'd never seen and looked around at the extensive collection that lay spread around him and at his feet, he knew. Penelope curled into fetal position and sobbed as Dylan picked up letter after letter, picture after picture. His senses overloaded and more colors exploded behind his eyes as he tried to keep from shaking her.

"What did you do!?" he bellowed. "What the *fuck* did you do?"

"Please, let me explain," she pleaded.

"How can you explain this?" he asked incredulously, his voice full of rage. "You stole my letters, Tia's letters, my pictures—my life!" He howled like an animal in pain, and shook his head to gain some control of his temper and try to make sense of what he was seeing. Something else caught his eye and he picked it up off the floor, turning it over in his hand. It was a first class ticket from Chicago to Melbourne, and he sucked in a breath with a hiss and held it for a moment before speaking. "You cold hearted bitch," he said, ice in his voice. "She never even got this! She thinks *I* dumped *her*!" He put his hands on his head, pushed hard against his temples and tried to think, but at that moment the whole world seemed to be swirling around in his brain as the enormity and implications of the situation took shape in his mind.

"Dylan," she pleaded desperately, sliding to the floor onto her knees between the couch and the coffee table. "Just listen, please! I did it for us! It never would have worked out with her, and you know it! She doesn't deserve you! You and I are so good together—we're a perfect match—but we just needed some time to get to know each other, and we couldn't as long as she was in the way...You would have hurt her eventually—she can't understand you the way I can! She can't love you the way that I do!" She reached out for him and he stepped away, repulsed.

"You don't know the first thing about love, Penelope, and you sure as hell don't know the first thing about me. You honestly thought that you could just get Tia out of the way and I would love you? I can't even bear to look at you right now—you disgust me," he spat, turning his back on her and pulling more letters out of the box. There were dozens of them, and he felt absolutely sickened.

"Dylan, no—please! I really do love you!"

He turned back toward her. "You stole my fucking life! You pretended to be my friend, pretended to help me out, but all along you were sabotaging my relationship, stealing my letters, and trying to ruin my life! You don't even know what reality is, lady, but you're sure as fuck about to find out!"

He pulled her phone from his pants pocket and she reached for it, but he turned his back on her again, punched some buttons and put it to his ear. "Stan?" he said into the mouthpiece. "It's Dylan. I need you to come to Penelope's trailer immediately. It's an absolute emergency." He pushed the 'end' button and stared at the sobbing woman on the floor.

"Please don't," she said begging. "Please don't give up on us yet."

Dylan exploded. "What are you not understanding here? There is no 'us'!! There never has been an 'us'!! There never will be an 'us'!" He began gathering up his life—feeling a stabbing pain in his heart each time he added another of Tia's letters to the pile—all the words she'd never seen. He imagined the pain she felt thinking he'd abandoned her; he knew it all too well.

They heard the sound of the golf cart approaching and the director appeared at the door, a panicked look on his face. "What's going on?" he asked from the doorway. "Is Penelope alright?" Then he stepped inside and saw the mountain of papers and photos strewn across the floor and Penelope gasping for breath between huge, racking sobs. "What the hell?" he asked, looking at Dylan.

He addressed Stan loudly, so Penelope could hear every word. "I need you to call the police, Stan. Right now." he told the director. "I want her arrested."

"What are you talking about? What's going on?"

"This woman has been stealing my mail," he said, handing a stack of letters and photos to Stan, who looked at them wide-eyed. "She's written her name on the letters I wrote to my girlfriend, cut herself into my photos, sent pictures from our shoots to the tabloids to make it look like we were a couple, and God knows what else." His mind began moving at hyper speed as more pieces of the puzzle fell into place within his mind. The cell phone incident, the computer crash, the change of assistants...and suddenly he knew that she couldn't have done it alone.

Stan looked at Penelope, bewildered. "Did you really do this?" Penelope just looked up at him, her face wet with tears and wracked with pain. "What in the hell were you thinking?"

Dylan continued as Penelope choked and wiped her tear and snot streaked face on the sleeve of her shirt. "I am telling you right here and now that I refuse to do another scene with this woman. I will not act with her, and have every intention of getting a restraining order so that she can't even come within sight of me. And, I intend to prosecute her to the fullest extent of the law."

"But we only have another month of filming," he said, "we leave for break in a week---can't you..." but the look in Dylan's eyes was solid and steadfast.

"Not one more scene," he said, "and not one more word to her until I see her in court." He looked at Penelope. "Don't let her leave or have a phone, don't let her touch anything, and call the police immediately. She didn't do this alone, and I have some serious questions for her assistant." He turned and stalked out the door, slamming it on Penelope's wailing.

It was just a few steps to Angela's trailer, but she had her music cranked up and didn't hear the commotion he'd just left. His music, he noticed again; could it be more ironic? He rapped sharply on her door, and she cranked down the volume before swinging it open. "Hey Dylan," she said lightly. "Was your music too loud for you?" she smiled at her own joke until she saw the look in his eyes. Her smile vanished, and a concerned look crossed her face. "What's wrong?" she asked.

Dylan pushed past her and entered her trailer. He'd been in it a dozen times or more, but now he looked around with suspicion. "I just came from Penelope's little freak show," he said, shaking a fistful of letters and pictures under her nose. "I know you were part of it."

Angela backed herself against the wall, put her hand to her heart, and whispered, "Oh shit."

"Oh shit? Oh shit!" Dylan yelled. "You have no idea what kind of shit you're in, missy, but I'm sure the cops'll explain it all to you when they get here."

"The cops?"

"Mail fraud is a crime, last time I checked," he said. He counted off on his fingers as he ran through his list of charges. "Could I add computer tampering? Changing numbers in my cell phone?" her eyes flashed wide, and he knew his answer. "What about libel? How many other things, Angela? I trusted you—I was never anything but nice to you, and you helped that little bitch ruin my life?" He shook his head, and took a deep breath. "You'd better start talking right now, and tell me all of it, because you and your boss are going down. Hard."

She started to cry, but held herself together a bit better than Penelope had. "She promised me a role in her next movie if I helped her," she said. "She told me that you and the other girl weren't right for each other. I tried to get out of it, I really did, but when I told her that I felt bad about what I was doing, she threatened me..."

"But you kept up the act, didn't you Angela? You should get a fucking Oscar. You played the part perfectly."

"Dylan, I'm sorry!" she exclaimed. "I never wanted to hurt you!"

"What did you think would happen? You knew I loved Tia, you saw how hurt I was, how many letters I was sending to try and get her back, and you delivered her letters to that *bitch*?" Then a thought exploded in his mind, and he gasped. "Wait a minute—oh my God," he said as the thought gained clarity. "Did she write me? Did you give her letters to Penelope too?"

Angela's gaze dropped to the floor, and she ground the palms of her hands into her eyes in a feeble attempt to block out the reality of her situation.

"Angela," he demanded, taking her wrists and forcing her to meet his hard stare. "Did Tia write to me?"

"Yes," she said in barely a whisper.

"Holy shit," he said, pressing his hands to his temples and shaking his head violently. "Holy shit! What did you do with her letters, Angela?"

"I...Penelope told me to burn them," she paused, sucking in deep gulps of air. It was all Dylan could do not to shake her.

"Did you?"

"No," she whimpered. "I couldn't."

"Angela, what did you do with the letters?" he demanded so forcefully she jumped.

"I kept them," she breathed.

"Kept them? Are they here?" He suddenly felt his heart jump when he realized that she hadn't dumped him after all, that he could see her handwriting again, and read her words.

Angela nodded and went into her bedroom, coming out with a shoe box. She handed the box to Dylan, sank onto her couch and stared blankly at the wall. Dylan sat in a chair and began pulling out letter after letter addressed to him in Tia's neat teacher script, some sealed on the back with little stickers. A whiff of her scent wafted out of the box, and he breathed it deep. He tore open one of the letters and felt his heart leap when he read the greeting, *Dylan, my love*, and the first line, *I'm missing you terribly today, and can't concentrate on anything but how badly I want to hold you*. He held the treasure in his hand; more precious than gold; but he knew he had to get the story out of Angela before Penelope had any chance to get to her and before the cops started asking her questions. He brushed the letter against his lips and placed it back in the box, clutching it possessively in his lap, and turned back to Angela. "Tell me everything," he said simply, and he sat, shocked, for nearly an hour as she told him the whole scheme, her role, and Penelope's plans for their imagined future. She paused only once to glance wide-eyed at the window when the rolling red lights of the police car came to a stop outside.

Dylan had to find her right away. After spending hours with the police, he sat awake all night reading her letters, and they broke his heart to pieces. Angela had kept them in order, so the first few were full of happy news, expressions of love, hellos from Lexi and Sean. She'd even written about the night Bo had taken her to dinner when he was passing through town, and he almost smiled when he read that Bo had asked her to run off with him and forget about the "Little Strummer Boy." As he got further through the stack, however, the tone of her letters changed. He could see by the dates on the letters that they were sent right about the time his own life came tumbling down. They were full of confusion and pain, and she was begging him to call her, just call her and explain, and she said she still loved him and that she didn't understand why he would dump her with an email, without a reason, and his heart broke. When he read the letter that asked how he could be with Penelope, he thought he would scream. *You've been all over the tabloids*, she wrote, *and the hardest part is knowing that because of who I am and who you are, I'll never even be able to get close to you again*. A tear fell from his eye as he absorbed the pain in the words, then he put it down, feeling sick to his stomach. She thinks I caused her that pain, he thought, and I can't even explain to her why.

The next morning, Dylan met with Stan and explained that he was leaving. "To hell with the contract," he told him. "This is my life we're talking about." They worked out a compromise—Dylan would film the rest of the necessary scenes using a double for Penelope that morning, and then he'd release Dylan from the rest of the contract. He had enough footage, he said, to complete the movie if they could use doubles for the other love scenes. They could even cut Bora Bora out completely and film the scene here with a few rewrites, which would save the production company a ton of money anyway. They'd done enough to cover the basic storyline and he thought they could fill in the rest. Dylan shook Stan's hand, thanked him profusely, and flew back to the trailer to start packing his bags.

Chapter 36

He had a lot of things he needed to fix because of that woman—she'd done a hell of a lot of damage to his life. The first thing he did when he left Stan's office in the morning was to pull Jessa's phone out of the drawer in the kitchen—he hadn't touched it since the day he took it from her and the battery was dead, so he plugged it in and powered it up, standing over the counter and scrolling through her contacts. He tried "Mom," and got an answer on the second ring.

"Hello?" the familiar voice chirped, and Dylan sighed with relief that he'd found her.

"Jessa," he said, overwhelmed with the emotion of hearing her voice. He'd been so unfair to her; hadn't even given her a chance to explain, and he didn't know if he deserved her forgiveness.

"Dylan?" she asked, her voice full of confusion.

"Oh Jessa, I'm so sorry. I never should have doubted you for a second. Penelope…"

"Of course it was her," she said. "It's about damn time you came to your senses."

"Jessa, I don't know where to start. She's ruined everything."

"Tell me what she did, Dylan. It's been driving me crazy not knowing."

He started at the beginning—with his own stupidity and lack of faith—telling her how Angela had hired an actress that looked like Jessa to wear the same scarf and hand out his private phone number at the airport. "When the girl on the phone described you to a tee, I just lost my head," he told her. "Angela was there, telling me how you'd said I'd be sorry…I still shouldn't have doubted you though, but I did, and now I really am sorry. Can you ever forgive me?"

"Tell me the rest," she demanded. "and I'll think about it. You were a complete ass, you know—I never once gave you a reason to doubt me, but you never even gave me a chance to explain."

"I know," he whispered. "Believe me, I'm kicking myself for that too." There was no doubting the sincerity in his voice, and Jessa's heart nearly broke at the sadness she heard there.

"What else, Dylan?" she asked, the rough edges in her voice softening. "I need to know."

He told her the whole story breathlessly, his anger simmering in every word. She listened and didn't interrupt, taking it in but having a hard time believing anyone could be so cruel and selfish.

She waited until he finished the story before exploding. "Are you fucking kidding me?" she screamed so loud that Dylan had to hold the phone away from his ear. "I can't believe that anyone could do something so horrible! And Angela was in on it too? I don't even know what to say!"

"I can't even begin to tell you how pissed off I was last night—I'm still absolutely livid," he growled. "It was all I could do not to wring her neck—both their necks, actually. I spent most of my evening dealing with the police—giving statements, and then stayed up all night reading Tia's letters. It just killed me reading about how much pain she's in," he whispered. "She's not going to get away with this, I promise you."

"I'll have a little something to say about that too, you can bet on it. She's going to pay!"

"She may have ruined my life," Dylan said sadly. "Damn straight she's going to pay."

"Holy shit Dylan, poor Tia! She doesn't know any of it does she? What are you going to do?"

"Oh God, Jessa, I have to go find her. They changed her phone number and her email address, and this isn't something I can say in a letter that's going to take weeks to get to her—it has to be face to face, and it has to be now. I need to get back to the States as soon as possible—today, if I can. I've got a few hours of work to do this morning, but I've already started packing and I…"

"I'll get right on it," she interrupted. "Just do what you need to do there, and I'll handle everything."

"Does that mean you forgive me?" he said with a huge sigh of relief.

"Of course I do Dylan. I knew it wasn't you—it had to be her doing—but you had to figure it out for yourself, and I'm so glad you finally did. But I'm still seriously pissed that you doubted me, and for that, *you're* going to have to pay," she added with a smirk.

"Have you found another job?" he asked hopefully.

"I haven't even looked, actually, I've been on kind of a holiday; catching up with my family and all that. Why," she added coyly, "are you looking for an assistant?"

"I am in the market," he said smiling. "If you'll come back, it'll be with full pay for the time you've been off, and I swear I'll never doubt you again."

"That's a deal!" she exclaimed, then her voice softened. "I'll be happy making my first order of new business helping you and Tia get back together again. This had to destroy her, and she doesn't have a clue. Give me your new number, and I'll start right now, and call you as soon as I have something."

"You're an angel, Jessa, do you know that? I swear I'll make it up to you!"

"You already have."

He gave her the number and ran out of the trailer, jumped in a golf cart, and rushed over to the little studio. So many emotions coursed through his veins that he knew, beyond a doubt, that he'd give a stellar performance.

Dylan threw the last of his things into his suitcase and looked around the little trailer he'd called home for the past few months. The last thing he grabbed was the picture that still sat on the little shelf above the couch—the picture of him and Tia in Paris. "I'm on my way, baby," he said to her image before he tucked it in his carry on and went outside to pace, waiting for Jessa's call.

It was forty five minutes before his phone rang, and he answered on the first ring. "What have you got?"

"It's not great, but none of them really are," she said. "There's a flight that leaves at 7:30 tonight, with a twelve hour layover in San Francisco that'll get you there at a little after five tomorrow morning, Chicago time. Friday morning, that is. It's the best there is—most of the other available flights have two stops, and are even longer. It's twenty-eight hours of travel time not counting airport waits before and after, Dyl."

"I'll take it," he said, looking at his watch. It was nearly 3:00, and it was a little over an hour drive to the airport—that would get him there just about the time he needed to be if he left in the next twenty minutes or so. He'd have to find a ride, fast. "Thanks so much—at least now I know it's only hours before I can see her again."

"That flight's going to be a bitch, though," Jessa said.

"God knows I've slept on planes before." He was about to click off, but remembered a crucial detail. "Bloody hell—I get there Friday morning, you said?"

"Yup. Bright and early."

"Shit. I have Tia's home address, but she'll be at work by the time I get through customs, get my luggage, and get a ride. I have to see her right away. I know she works at a school, obviously, but I don't know which one. Could you…"

"Consider it done. I'll find out and arrange for a limo to meet you at O'Hare. I'll call you back in a few minutes once I have the flight all booked, and again when I have Tia's info, just so you know. If you don't hear from me on that before you fly out, buzz me from San Fran, and I'll fill you in. Oh, one more thing," she added. "There are showers in the lounge at San Fran, so bring a change of clothes. You can't show up to see her all grungy after more than a full day of traveling."

She thought of everything, he thought, and he was so lucky to have her back. "I love you!" Dylan yelled into the phone, elated.

"I know you do, Dylan," she smiled, happy to have her life back. "Now get the hell out of there, will you? You've got a plane to catch!"

Dylan clicked off the line and called Gary, his guitar prodigy from the editing department. They'd become friends, and had played together a fair amount over the time they'd been here. "Gary, it's Dylan," he said hurriedly. "I need a favor—can you sign out one of the staff cars and take me to the airport? Like, right now?"

"Hell yeah, dude—I can do that. I can be there in, like, ten minutes. Does that work?"

"It's perfect," Dylan answered, shoving the phone in his pocket and running in to grab his bags.

***

Lilly was busy at her desk and didn't notice the limo pull up in front of the school or the man who got out of it until he was standing inside her office. When she looked up, her heart nearly stopped.

"Hi," he said quickly. "Ah, I desperately need to see one of your teachers; is class in session yet?"

"Oh. My. God," Lilly whispered as she recognized him, feeling the heat rush to her face and putting both palms down on her desk to steady herself. "You're…" but she couldn't quite get the words out.

Dylan saw the photo he'd signed, all those months ago, tacked to the bulletin board beside the woman's chair and reached back into his memory for a name. "You must be…Lilly, right?" he asked, remembering. "Tia told me a lot about you." He put out his hand and she giggled nervously before taking it.

"You're…" she stammered again.

"Dylan Miller," he said. "Nice to meet you, Lilly."

"Wait a minute," Lilly said, shaking her head. "You're *Tia's* Dylan?" He nodded. "I should have known!"

He smiled then, and Lilly thought she might faint. "She didn't tell anyone about me, did she?" he asked rhetorically.

"She told us plenty about you," she said, "but not that you were...well, you!"

"I should have guessed. But Lilly?"

"Yes?" she answered, still unable to catch her breath.

"I've been traveling for thirty five hours and came here straight from the airport. It's really urgent that I see Tia. Can you arrange that for me? Please?"

Lilly shook her head, trying to get back her composure. "Now just a minute," she scolded, hands on her hips. "She was in love with you, you know, and what you did hurt her so much. So before I do anything, I'm gonna ask you one time—and you be straight with me, hear?" Dylan raised his eyebrows, willing her to continue. "Are you going to hurt her again? Cause she's a prize, that girl, and I won't watch her go through that again." She folded her arms across her chest protectively, and Dylan liked her immediately.

"That's not my intention at all, and it's what I really need to speak to her about," he said, trying to hold on to his patience. "I know she's a prize, and I have so much to explain to her—I really can't wait another minute."

"So it's good news you're bringin' her, then?"

"God I hope so," he breathed. "Please Lilly?"

The tone of his voice and the look on his face convinced her completely. "Well, they're in a staff meeting right now, but if you follow me, I'll see if I can interrupt. It isn't every day a celebrity like you visits our school, so I think maybe the boss'll make an exception."

"Thank you," he said, relieved, as he followed her down the hall. His heart was thumping nervously and he was having a hard time finding his breath. He was just steps away from seeing her again, and every cell in his body ached to go to her, to wrap his arms around her. He knew, though, that he'd have to explain things first if he even stood a chance of holding her again. An audience was fine with him too—by tomorrow the whole world would know what Penelope had done and that suited him just fine.

Lilly stopped at a door and poked her head in. "I'm sorry to interrupt," she said excitedly, "but there's someone here to see one of our teachers, and I know that if I didn't bring him in to meet all of you I wouldn't live to see the end of the day." She looked to Ned, the principal, for his OK.

"That's fine Lilly," he said. "Our speaker is stuck in traffic and has to reschedule, so I was going to call it short anyway."

Lilly's eyes were positively blazing, and everyone watched the door. "Now you all stay in your seats, you hear? The man's got something to say, and I don't want you all jumpin' up to greet him before he's had a chance to say it. Got it?"

They looked at her like she'd lost her mind, but they shrugged. When she held open the door and Dylan stepped in, the air was nearly sucked from the room with the collective gasp, then the voices started in unison, "Oh my gosh! You're...I can't believe it...What the..."

Tia sat glued to her seat, frozen in place. For months she'd been hoping to see him again, and now he was standing just a few feet away from her. Her breath caught and her heart instantly started hammering in her chest. Part of her wanted desperately to go to him, to wrap her arms around him, but another part wanted to beat him within an inch of his life. He'd hurt her so badly, and until she knew why he was here, she would maintain her dignity. At least she still had a little bit of that left.

Dylan's eyes swept the room until they met Tia's, on the left side of the long table around which the fifteen or so staff members sat. She was the only one not making a sound. His heart nearly melted at the sight of her, but he knew she wouldn't accept his embrace. He could only hope that she would after she heard what he had to say.

"What are you doing here, Dylan?" she asked finally, softly.

For a moment he was struck speechless, unable to take his eyes off her, lost in the timbre of her voice. Immediately, all eyes turned to her and the rest of the women at the table were suddenly all talking at once... "Wait a minute, *this* is *your* Dylan? The one you went to Europe with? You were dating Dylan Miller all this time and you didn't *tell* anyone? You were in love with Dylan Miller??" The questions were being fired at her from all directions, but her eyes never left his. There was so much emotion tangled in them, he thought, that they were impossible to read.

"Oh God, Tia," he said, breathless. "There's so much I need to say to you, but just seeing you, I don't know where to start." His breath caught again when he saw her unconsciously raise her hand to her throat where the Eiffel Tower glittered on her neck. *She still wears it*, he thought hopefully, *she still remembers*.

"I didn't think you had anything else to say to me," she said. "Or so you told me in your email."

"Oh, I have a lot to tell you, believe me, the first being that I never sent you an email. Not the one you think I did, anyway." Her eyebrows rose, and he continued. "I'm sure I don't have a lot of time before you have to start work, so all I ask is that you hear me out."

Tia motioned with her hand, shrugging, telling him to go ahead with his story. He took a deep breath and started at the beginning.

"I never dumped you, Tia, and I'm guessing—bloody hell I'm hoping—you never dumped me." She looked at him with confusion in her eyes, but didn't answer. "I got an email too. From you, supposedly, telling me that you were done with me, that you couldn't stand how different our lives were..."

"I never sent you an email like that!" she exclaimed.

"And I never knew you got one like that, supposedly from me," he continued. "It was Penelope," he said. "She hatched a huge elaborate scheme to get you out of the picture, and it worked."

"I don't understand," she said, her mind racing.

"The other day, I walked into her trailer, to return her phone," he said, "and I found out the truth. Some of it, at least. The police are still working on the details."

"Whoa, the police?" she asked, sitting more upright in her seat.

"Penelope's going to be arrested as soon as she sets foot back in the States, and I'm going to make sure she pays for everything she's done," he announced.

Tia's head was swimming. She was still trying to get past him saying he never sent the horrible email, and that he got a similar one from her. "What are you talking about, Dylan?"

"Mail fraud, computer hacking, libel, for starters," he said. "She set us up. I walked in and she had pictures and letters spread out all over her place, pictures and letters I'd written to you that were never sent. She cut your face out of the pictures and put herself in. She erased your name on the letters and wrote in her own. It was some sick fantasy that she was trying to make come true, and she needed you out of the picture so she could get what she wanted."

"But I saw the pictures in the tabloids..." Tia said, but as soon as the words were out of her mouth, she remembered what Dylan had told her in Paris, on the day he'd laid out the complications they'd face as a couple... *They try to link me with other celebrities, fabricate relationships—there has to be a whole different level of trust between us...* A spark of hope flickered at the back of her mind.

"All fake. Most of those shots were taken by her assistant while we were filming the movie. We look like a couple because we were acting at the time. I didn't know that she was selling them to the tabloids—hell; I didn't even know she was taking them. No one did. She's going to be in trouble with the studio for that, too."

"Wait a second. I can't believe Jessa would let this happen. She'd see right through her!"

"Jessa was her first victim," Dylan said sadly. "Penelope's assistant, Angela, hired someone who looked just like Jessa to pass out my private mobile number at the airport—that's what started the whole thing. She even had the nerve to take Jessa away on a girls' weekend first, and talked her into buying a really unique scarf, then bought an identical one for the actress to wear to make it look like Jessa was the one who betrayed me..."

"Oh no, poor Jessa!" Tia said.

"I know—it was terrible. I fixed it with her yesterday," he said quickly, "but at the time I fell for it and I fired her on the spot—and Angela became my new assistant. She was working for Penelope the whole time of course. I had to change my phone number, and Penelope, pretending to help me deal with the catastrophe, changed your number in my phone so I couldn't get in touch with you. Then they sabotaged my computer while I was out in the wilderness, sent the emails and changed the addresses, intercepted our letters—they cut off all our communication. Apparently, they thought that if I believed you'd dumped me, I'd just fall for her. She ruined our lives, Tia. She stole us from each other, and I don't even know the whole extent of it yet. She took months away from us."

"How could she do that?" Tia asked, shaking her head. "How could anyone be so cruel?"

"I don't know how to answer that, because I can't even begin to figure it out myself," he answered. "It may be a long time before we know the whole truth, but Person to Person is running my story—it'll be on the newsstands tomorrow."

"But you never talk to the tabloids!" Tia exclaimed.

"I had no choice—it was the only outlet to get it out there quickly. Plus, it's the way she manipulated the whole fabricated relationship, so they had to save face too. I worked on it on the plane ride over. They agreed to let me tell my own story, and my lawyers approved the copy before it went to print. I got a restraining order against Penelope, refused to work with her for even one more scene...the last few days have been hell, Tia. I had to finish up filming what I needed to, and they have to piece the story together without our big love scenes—I refused to do them. Once I found out what she'd done...once I found out you didn't dump me...I couldn't even look at her again—all I could do was find you, to tell you..."

"Tell me what, Dylan?" she asked softly, hopefully, her heart drumming in her chest and every nerve in her body tingling in anticipation.

He reached into his bag and pulled out a stack of papers tied with a red bow. "These are copies of all the letters I wrote to you, Tia. The police kept all the originals as evidence, but I insisted they give me copies. I had to give them to you." He handed them over the table and they were passed down until Tia held the large bundle in her hands. There were dozens of them, and her eyes filled with tears. On the top of the stack was a first class ticket to Australia. Her heart nearly melted as she looked back up at him with real hope in her eyes.

"Oh Tia," he breathed. "No matter what, I never stopped trying, never stopped thinking about you, never stopped wishing that you'd call me." He paused, and looked deeply into her eyes. "I never stopped loving you Tia, not for a second. Please tell me that you'll..." But he never got to finish the sentence, because she had leaped from her chair and into his arms and finally he was holding her, touching her, smelling her, kissing her...

"Oh Dylan, I never stopped loving you either," she whispered frantically into his ear as she held him close. "I couldn't ever stop loving you. Oh God, I've missed you so much..." Tears of joy spilled from her eyes as she pulled him closer, breathing in his scent, kissing him, and feeling his arms wrapped tightly around her.

The burst of applause from the room was almost as deafening as a concert venue, but neither of them heard it. There was only the whispered love, the frantic kisses, and the desperate need for contact between them.

Finally, Tia turned and looked to her coworkers, her friends, and said, "Well, you've obviously figured it out already, but now I can finally introduce you to the man I love," she said, her smile taking over her face and tears still spilling down her cheeks. This is my Dylan," she whispered, smiling up at him and snuggling closer. He leaned down and kissed her again, full on the mouth, before looking up and saying, "It's, ah, nice to meet all of you." The applause and whistles continued, and then they were all rushing up to shake Dylan's hand and to hug them both. It was near chaos until the principal held up his hand and called for order. When they were finally quiet, he spoke.

"You know Tia," he said with a wink, "I don't think you're looking very well, and I think maybe you need to take the day off. I can have an aide cover your room until a sub can get here. Are you OK with that?"

She looked at him, then at Dylan. "More than OK with that," she replied. "I can honestly say that I'm feeling a bit feverish," and she wrapped her arms around him again, amazed at how comfortable, how right he felt even after such a long time away and the pain they'd both been through.

"Actually," Dylan said, "I'm booked here for the weekend, but once this story breaks, it's going to be crazy. I'm scheduled to do the whole talk show circuit early next week, and I'm not waiting another minute to go public with us. Any chance you can get a few days off? I really want you to be with me." He looked hopefully at the principal.

"You haven't used your personal days yet," he said. "I'll take care of it for you—it's probably better that you aren't here when this story breaks—it's going to bring a lot of attention to our little school, I'll bet."

Dylan nodded. "You'll definitely want to keep the doors locked, and probably get the cops out here for at least the first few days," he said. "The paparazzi will be out in force, I'm afraid."

He looked at Tia. "Call me on Tuesday. I'll talk to the superintendent and see about getting you more time. It's only a week until Christmas break; by the time we get back in January, hopefully things will have died down." Then, he addressed the rest of his staff. "This school isn't a newsroom, either. I trust that all of you will keep this to yourselves until Tia decides how she wants to handle things. We certainly don't need the media making an early appearance. Any questions will be deferred to me, OK?"

Everyone nodded their agreement.

Dylan looked at Tia. "You'll still come for Christmas, right?"

She laughed, and Dylan thought he'd never heard a more beautiful sound. "Wouldn't miss it," she smiled, snuggling against him. "Not for anything."

The bell rang then, signaling the start of another school day. The other teachers had to head back to their classrooms, stopping to hug the couple once more on the way out. Dylan and Tia stood in the teacher's lounge, listening to the pounding of children's feet and the sounds of their voices. They waited until the start of day bell rang, and then slipped out the side door and into the limo.

"God, I've missed you so much!" he said between tender kisses. "I was so scared I'd lost you!"

"I'm so glad you came back for me," she breathed. "I missed you terribly—oh Dylan, it just feels so good to hold you again!"

"I've got a room in the city," he said, kissing her again.

"My house is closer," she breathed, running her fingers through his hair and pressing herself against him. God, he felt so good.

"Even better," he whispered. They had the weekend together before they went public, and he was looking very forward to making up for lost time. He pulled her in tighter and pressed his lips to hers. He was going to spend the rest of his life making it up to her, he figured, and he couldn't wait to get started.

ABOUT THE AUTHOR

Kim DeSalvo holds a master's degree in education and works as an elementary school teacher. She lives in the Chicago area with her husband and two hairy mutts. She is an avid reader, an environmentalist, and a music lover. Travel is one of her passions, and she enjoys bringing the places she's visited to life in her writing.

Incidental Happenstance is the first novel she's published, but not the first she's written—and it's definitely not the last.

This book is a work of fiction. Any resemblance of characters to actual people is complete happenstance, except for those of you who know who you are. Although the majority of the places in the book are real, the author has taken liberties; especially in the descriptions of luxury hotel suites, as they don't fit into her vacation budget.